# THE MASTER OF DRAGONARD HILL

# THE MASTER OF DRAGONARD HILL

*A Novel by*

RUPERT GILCHRIST

The
Leisure
Circle

# Contents

*Prologue*

# A BACKGROUND OF FIRE

*Dragonard Plantation*, 1791
St. Kitts, The Leeward Islands, WEST INDIES

Naomi lingered in the centre garden of the greathouse this morning, sitting at the breakfast table and studying the breeding list which had been sent up to her from the slave quarters.

The breeding list told Naomi what black wenches were pregnant and what negroes had planted the seed in those women.

Naomi herself was black; she had full lips and a slight flare to her nostrils.

But—unlike the slaves of Dragonard—Naomi was a free black. She was a white man's mistress. She lived in the greathouse with an Englishman called Richard Abdee and, among her many privileges, Naomi had a room hung with silken gowns and a European *toilette* consisting of creams, oils, and powders . . . and a secret lotion for taming the natural kinkiness of her hair, turning it into a flowing mane of loose curls, transforming her from a common negress into an exotic *femme de salon*.

This morning, though, Naomi's hair spread carelessly around her prune-coloured face as she studied the breeding list. Her long red fingernails toyed with a piece of almond bread on a Limoges plate as she read the names of the pregnant negresses.

Suddenly, Naomi dropped the bread morsel. She jerked up her head and snatched for a crystal bell setting on the round table and, quickly beating it in the air, she shrilled, 'Nero! Nero!'

Waiting for the servant to answer her call, Naomi looked back to an entry on the list—*Seena. Cookhouse wench.* The *X* that

9

meant pregnant. But there was no name for the sire.

She rang the bell again.

The servant, Nero, finally appeared between the swags of gold brocade hanging in the doorway of the centre garden.

Nero was a handsome young negro with broad shoulders, a flat stomach and well-muscled legs. Although he wore his livery of white breeches and white cotton shirt with an air propriety, he was unable to keep his God-given huskiness from bulging beneath the thinness of these constricting clothes. Nero was like a child given the physique of a man.

Leaning on one arm of her chair, Naomi held the list of names toward Nero and spoke to him as she spoke to all the blacks on Dragonard—as her inferiors. 'How many Seenas we got here, boy?'

Nero wrinkled the tobacco-coloured skin of his broad forehead and blinked at his slim mistress. He scratched his skullcap of woolly black hair and asked, 'How many *whats*, Miss Naomi?'

'Seenas!' Naomi repeated louder. 'It says here that Seena is pregnant. But yesterday I saw the only Seena I know and she don't look knocked-up to me.'

Nero shrugged disinterestedly. He was a house servant and the details of the slave quarters had little to do with him. He only knew that there was an old black woman in the slave quarters who was in charge of birthing. He answered in his usual drawl, 'If Grandma Goat puts it down there, Miss Naomi, then it must be so.'

Naomi studied her houseboy. Nero had worked for her before she had moved here. He had been with Naomi in a brothel that she had owned at the south end of this island. She spoke to him honestly. 'Boy, it don't say on this list who's responsible for this sucker that Seena's supposed to be having. If it's Manroot's git, why don't it say so here?'

Nero hesitated at the implication of Naomi's question. It was true that the black overseer, Manroot, had been allowed to marry Seena. Nero remembered that Manroot and Seena had gone through the crude ceremony called 'jumping-the-pole'.

But he also remembered hearing rumours that Seena was pregnant by another man.

Dipping his head, Nero answered softly, 'Like I say, Miss Naomi, I don't really knows about these breeding things of Grandma Goat's.'

Naomi impatiently sat on the edge of the gilt chair and demanded, 'Talk, Nero. You know more than you're telling me about this. Is Seena pregnant or not?'

Nero tried again, 'If Grandma Goat . . .'

Springing from the chair, the wide marabou sleeves of her dressing-gown trailing behind her, Naomi screamed, 'Damn Grandma Goat! I don't care what that old nigger woman says. Let her run that stud farm for Abdee. I want to know whose baby Seena is having.'

Nero still hesitated. He had heard the plantation gossip about Seena spending nights with Abdee but he did not want to be the one to break this news to his mistress. Nero still could not comprehend the kind of affair that Naomi was having with her Englishman. He only knew that she was his lover and that they were happy together.

Naomi read Nero's eyes and, narrowing her own, she said, 'Abdee's been fooling around with that Seena, hasn't he?'

She had guessed the facts immediatedly. Of course. But as it was often difficult for Nero to be loyal to both this black woman who owned him and the white man who owned Dragonard, he tried to hedge his predicament by saying, 'Some things here I just don't understand, Miss Naomi.'

Naomi said snidely, 'You don't *have* to understand, boy. Abdee and me have the understanding. It's between us. About our screwing. He might be white but he's nigger at heart. He's all nigger excepting the fact he don't go in for marrying anymore. He just lets his *black* niggers do that now.'

Nero moved uncomfortably from one foot to the other. 'Yes, Miss Naomi. I knows that. I knows that Seena went through the marrying ceremony with Manroot.'

Naomi slapped the table. 'Exactly! With Manroot. And Abdee made Manroot his overseer. Manroot is good, too. But if one thing would kill Manroot—or turn him mean—it would be if some man starts screwing his woman. Even Abdee himself.'

Nero asked guardedly, 'Miss Naomi thinks Manroot causes troubles for somebody if that happens?'

Naomi blurted, ' "Miss Naomi" don't want nobody causing trouble here over nothing. There's too much nigger troubles boiling in these islands already. Boy, niggers are starting to think about themselves. They're putting the torch to crops. They're burning houses. They're killing masters. But this nigger—' Naomi said, thumbing her chest, '—this nigger is living in one of those big houses with one of those masters and I don't want no niggers driving me out. Do you understand that, boy? I don't want no flames licking at my little ass!'

Nero looked in horror at Naomi. 'You think Manroot do troubles like that at Dragonard, Miss Naomi?'

Naomi relaxed, confessing, 'I don't know what that big son-of-a-bitch will do if he gets mad. He worships Abdee. Abdee is one of the few white planters who thinks about niggers. Helps niggers. But if Abdee is helping himself to some of that Seena pussy—' She tensed again.

'Who you going to ask about that, Miss Naomi?'

'Ask? Ask what?' She stared blankly at him.

'Who you going to ask if Master Abdee is helping himself to . . .'

Naomi shook her head. 'I ain't going to ask nobody, boy. *You* are! You are going to trot your ass down to Grandma Goat's right now and find out what you can about Seena having this baby.'

Nero stood staring at her. Naomi had been his mistress for many years and he would do anything for her. Nevertheless, he still had to admit to himself that Naomi was a busy nigger, busy protecting everything that she owned and busy wanting to get more. So, rather than dare question her further, Nero nodded his consent.

Before Nero left to run the errand for Naomi, he bent over the table to begin gathering the breakfast dishes.

Naomi asked sharply, 'Why you picking up these dishes, black boy? We got girls to do that!'

Continuing to pull the plates and crystal tumblers across the damask cloth toward him, Nero answered truthfully, 'It don't hurts me none, Miss Naomi. I'm here so I can do this job and then I goes down to Grandma Goat's for you.'

Naomi flared at him, 'The trouble with you, boy, is that you're too God-damned good! You're too God-damned kind! You've got to be selfish to keep your place in this world. You've got to be mean! If you're a nigger like me and you are, black boy, you've got to be double mean. And double selfish. That's the only way a nigger's going to survive.'

Nero listened quietly to Naomi's harangue as he calmly proceeded to stack the plates on the edge of the round table. The harsh words which Naomi was saying to him were true to a certain extent—true for some blacks. But Nero hoped for the day to come when black people did not have to talk this way. He was waiting for the day when black people could all be the good people he knew that they were in their hearts.

When Nero had finished piling the dishes, he looked at Naomi, who was still standing next to him by the table. He said softly, 'I sends somebody in to fetch these, Miss Naomi, and then I go down to Grandma Goat's to finds out about that Seena wench.'

Putting her hand on Nero's strong forearm, Naomi said softly, 'Boy?'

'Yes, Miss Naomi?'

Her red lips began to lift into a smile. 'Boy, do you go with wenches? Or do you—are boys your *specialité*?'

Grinning widely, Nero nodded at the birthing sheet on the table. He said, 'You keep reading that list, Miss Naomi, and you comes to "Pinkie".: That's me who knocked-up Pinkie, Miss Naomi. I'm doing my part for Dragonard, too.'

Turning, Nero walked from the centre garden.

Naomi watched him leave, looking at the taper of his broad back and the tight chew of his round buttocks. She had owned Nero for eight years and had never sampled him once. She thought about all the pretty black boys in the world to try and how she still had not got her fill of her white man.

13

She wondered what Nero would look like when she got ready for him.

The morning air outside was hot, thick with the heavy perfume from the oleanders growing in profusion at the back of the greathouse and, as Nero walked down the back steps to expedite Naomi's demand, he sniffed the rich fragrance and listened to the voices drifting up the grassy slope from the slave quarters.

Nero liked being at Dragonard. He loved the fresh air, free from the stench of the town. He also had grown to appreciate the nearness of the soil, the activity in the fields, the busyness in the slave quarters, the whole world here that was detached from the rest of the island.

St. Kitts was a sixty-five-square-mile island of rich volcanic loam which the colonials had found was ideal for growing sugar cane. The white people on St. Kitts were outnumbered now ten to one by the blacks. The white islanders were mostly English and it was they who had changed the island's name from St. Christopher to simply 'St. Kitts'.

St. Kitts had a bloody history. The English and the French had been fighting for dominance here well over three hundred years. But now that the French were having a revolution in their homeland, the English were certain that they could stay in power on this fish-shaped speck of land located in the Leeward Islands of the West Indies.

Like the island of St. Kitts, this plantation at the north end of the island also had a past of French ownership. But that was in the days before it was flourishing as well as it was now, prior to the time that Richard Abdee had come to be master of this plantation, long-ago when Naomi still owned her brothel at the south end of St. Kitts and Nero worked for her there.

Looking back at those old days at the brothel in Basseterre, it only seemed natural to Nero that Richard Abdee should have found his way to *Chez Naomi*. It was in that busy house on

14

Barracks Lane that Abdee had discovered a soul-mate and a friend in Naomi. After all, there was not much difference between a whore like Naomi and a whip-master like Abdee, was there? They had both sold themselves for money.

Whip-master was the job that Abdee had done when he had first come to St. Kitts, a slave-master for the Government. In fact, it was from that job of whipping that Abdee had got the name for his plantation. Dragonard. The 'Dragonard' had been the title for the man who flogged the slaves in the main square—The Circus—of Basseterre. The word 'Dragonard' had come from the name of the splayed-tip whip which the original French mercenaries had used on the blacks, the whip that reputedly had the bite of a dragon's tongue. But the English Government had long since abandoned that post of discipline in Basseterre—the Dragonard—and it was only Abdee who kept the name alive here on this plantation which used to be called *Petit Jour*.

These memories about St. Kitts and the plantation slipped from Nero's mind now as he saw the bulky shape of Sugar Loaf standing on the edge of the vegetable garden.

Sugar Loaf was the cook at Dragonard and, in the two years that Nero had worked in the greathouse with her, he had never seen the ebullient black woman without her enormous white-folded turban bobbing on her head and the two silver star earrings dangling from her fat brown lobes. Sugar Loaf and Nero had come to be good friends.

Standing now with her chubby brown hands anchored on her wide hips, Sugar Loaf called to Nero, 'Boy, you looking for work to do?'

'I'm doing work,' Nero answered cheerily. 'I'm running an errand for Miss Naomi.'

At the mention of the name, Sugar Loaf pushed her flat nose to the air. The towering folds of her turban shook like the stiff petals of an enormous white gardenia. She said, 'Miss Naomi! Ha!'

Nero called to her, 'When you going to be friends with Miss Naomi?'

Sugar Loaf held her head at a proud angle, answering, 'Miss Naomi, she a free nigger. How's I ever going to be friends with a fine lady like your Miss Naomi?'

Nero smiled. 'You just don't like niggers putting on airs, do you, Sugar Loaf?'

Folding her arms, Sugar Loaf shouted, 'I just don't like niggers, boy. Niggers is lazy. Now you gets on your errand or comes here and sees what you can do about this garden patch. Look at these weeds! Just look at these weeds! I asks you, is the cook meant to weeds the garden patch, too?'

Nero could see that the garden did not need weeding. But he knew that Sugar Loaf liked to complain. Griping and complaining, she always said, that was what kept her young.

Waving good-bye to his fat friend, Nero continued to saunter down the hill from the greathouse.

Now walking with a happy lilt, Nero began to feel warm. He was not only warmed by the sun but also by the wonderful feeling of living in a home with black people he knew, in a place where there were vegetables growing in the garden, regular meals to devour every morning, noon, and night, and people working the earth.

Nero heard many black people saying bad things about being owned by white people but, judging from what he saw at Dragonard, Nero thought that living like this was the same as living in an all black community which supported itself. Dragonard, it seemed to Nero, was like a village that had no visible dependency on the outside world. Dragonard made its own laws and, as far as Nero knew, the black people here benefited from most of them.

Nero slowed his gait at the bottom of the grassy hill when he saw three black men sitting in the shade of the wash-house. He recognized two of the men as Shorty and Puck, the two painters whose job it was to keep the outbuildings of Dragonard whitewashed and sparkling clean.

Now both Shorty and Puck lounged on the steps of the wash-house with their wooden buckets setting at their bare feet. They were talking to a stranger. He was a negro dressed smartly in tight white breeches, a white shirt, and a wide-brimmed Panama hat. He must be a town nigger, Nero thought at first glance, a free black man.

The coal-faced stranger turned his head toward the hill and, shading his eyes against the sun, he called to Nero, 'Morning, Nero! How you like living up here?'

Nero stopped and looked quizzically at the black stranger in the Panama hat. Then, recognizing the tribal marks slashed into his black cheeks, he gasped, 'Calabar!'

This slim man named Calabar called back to Nero, 'You only know me from those nights down at Naomi's whorehouse. But I used to live on this place myself. I used to ride down from here when I came to Naomi's . . . now, what name did Naomi call her special parties? Her—what she call them—her *soirees*?'

Nero stood dumbstruck, staring at Calabar. His mind went back to *Chez Naomi*, to the candle-lit basement where Naomi had held those masked gatherings where white people could pay money to watch other people performing strange acts. And remembering why Naomi had hired Calabar to perform at her entertainments in the cellar, Nero's eyes went directly to the crotch of Calabar's tight breeches.

Raising both hands from between his legs, Calabar bragged, 'Still got my old pecker there, boy. Still got it. But like me, my old pecker is free to poke where it likes.'

Nero said coldly, 'If you and your pecker so free now, Calabar, why you poking it back here?' He was also remembering what a trouble-maker that Calabar had been.

'I come to look around, boy. And I sees a lot of things changed around here since Mistress Honore gave me my freedom papers. But you didn't know Mistress Honore, did you, boy? Mistress Honore was my mistress here. But Abdee came along and married her and then kicked her white ass off the place. He didn't even take no mercy on her being pregnant. Pregnant by him.' Calabar laughed.

Nero stared at Calabar. He knew for certain that he was up to some kind of trouble.

Calabar did not take long to begin. 'That man Abdee, he's

17

not all he seems to be, you know, boy. No white people's what they seems to be. I comes now from an island called Santo Domingo and I knows. I sees white people there doing terrible things to us black people. But I also sees, boy, what us black people do for ourselves . . . if we tries.'

Nero remembered Naomi telling him about negroes rebelling and burning houses. He asked, 'You comes here to make trouble, Calabar?'

Calabar smiled at Nero. 'Miss Naomi, she used to pay me to make trouble, pretty boy.'

Nero knew enough about those facts to argue with Calabar. 'But that was just showing-off in her cellar. That was just games. Spanking white ladies and poking little girls with your big pecker. That was just doing games for white people to see whiles they're drinking French wines!'

Calabar bragged, 'I made some trouble for Abdee once, too, boy. I made some big trouble for Abdee right up there in that fine white house on that hill behind you. You ask your master about that trouble sometimes, boy. Or you go find some of those Fanti niggers and see what they have to say about Abdee and me and some slaver called Captain Geoff Shanks.'

As Calabar chuckled now Nero suddenly saw that all of his white teeth had been filed to sharp points. Nero remembered Calabar having tribal marks and a poker-sized prick but he did not recall his teeth being as pointed as a shark's.

He asked Calabar, 'What you come back here to do? You trying to turn our people against Master Abdee, Calabar?'

Still chuckling, Calabar shook his head. 'Friend! Friend! I thought a couple years of life here might makes you grow up to be a man. But you still gots those stars in your eyes, boy. You've still got big hopes shining in those soft eyes of yours.'

Then, suddenly, Calabar changed the subject. He asked Nero brightly, 'How's Manroot? I hears Manroot's overseer here now. That makes him thinks Abdee is a real good master, I bet. Being overseer keeps Manroot busy, too, I bet. Probably too tired at night to notice—'

Calabar paused, turning to his two companions on the steps

beside him and asked, 'What's the name of Manroot's woman? They call her—what they calls her—Seena?'

Nero's mind suddenly became confused with facts and obligations. He knew that Calabar had somehow discovered the secret about Abdee knocking-up Seena and, realizing that, Nero remembered the errand on which Naomi had sent him.

But the visit down to Grandma Goat's shack would just have to wait. Nero had to go quickly back up the hill to tell Naomi who had come back into their lives. Calabar had always meant trouble.

It was night now, the end of the hot day, and a change of light had come over the island. As the daylight hours at Dragonard had the fierceness of the sun to show the rises and dips of its tropical terrain, at night, it was the moon, the glowing phosphorescent moon which illumined the fields and the lush creeping foliage of the surrounding jungles.

The greathouse sat high and proud in this stark blanket of moonlight, its white walls reflecting the glow like a mirrored Kashmiri box, the double surround of windows spilling their own contribution of light out onto the circular driveway in front of the house and over the bulky border of oleanders on the other three sides.

Unlike the blaze of the day time hours, the slave-quarters in the valley behind the greathouse lay silent in the moonrays. Down there it had become the routine of the negroes to go to bed at the sound of the nine o'clock bell and, by midnight, they were fast asleep, only four hours away from the morning bell for another work day. This early-to-retire, early-to-work routine was all part of the discipline which Richard Abdee had imposed on the plantation since he had become master here.

Despite his rigorous schedules for the slaves, Abdee allowed laxity in the rules when it suited himself: Tonight in the tackroom adjoining the stables, he was accompanied by a nubile young negress. It was Seena. She had slithered off the straw pallet next to her sleeping husband and crept outside their hut to join Abdee in this meeting place.

The tackroom smelled sweetly of leather from the saddles and harnessing, the only light in here came from a tallow candle setting on a wooden keg. Its soft yellow glow caught the moist gleam of two naked people, two moving bodies of contrasting colours—the satiny black arms and legs of the young negress curled around the rigid body of Richard Abdee.

The hard muscles of Abdee's back now glided under his tight skin as his legs stretched rigidly from the floor and his shoulders rose above Seena's head. He was bringing the girl to a pitch. She never reached an excitement like this with her husband.

Abdee was different from Seena's husband in many ways. Abdee was a man of force and, during the work hours of the day, he commanded the respect of all his black people as he rode his yellow stallion through the *plats* of sugar cane. It was an honour for a slave to be even greeted in the fields or the boiling-house by Abdee. His public acknowledgement of a negro was like a father bestowing a special treat on a child.

It was an even greater privilege for a negress to be chosen as Abdee's bed wench for a night, a week, or for however long he wanted her. As Abdee shared his house with a freed negress—Naomi—he laid with his other wenches in the stables, in the mills, here in the tackroom, or just on the dirt of the open fields.

Seena had been Abdee's wench for nearly three months now, the longest time for any black girl on Dragonard to•have the white master, and she guarded these meetings as a cherished gift. Seena was not seventeen years old yet but she had learned quickly that a woman, even a slave, could accumulate certain riches in life by winning the favours of an important man. So, apart from owning Seena, Abdee was her beneficiary and she did not want to lose him . . . and the extra bolts of cotton, the gold sovereigns, the rations of salt, the pork which came with her status of being the master's wench.

But Seena's infatuation with Abdee had recently grown from seeing only his prestigious value. She had advanced from being merely covetous of worldly goods. She had developed an appetite for this sullen man with the light skin. Seena knew that Abdee was older than she was. He was thirty-five-years old, an age which, to her, seemed ancient. But Abdee's body had the same firmness as a young black buck's. His yellow hair was long and silky to fondle like the fringe on a rich shawl. And when Abdee straddled Seena, plunging deeper and deeper inside her, she felt the same pain as she had first felt from the size of her African husband. But another difference between Abdee and her husband was that Abdee knew how to make that pain turn into pleasure. He knew how to work the pain until it became a thrill for Seena and, in these three months of being with him, she found herself waiting for that hurt.

Seena lay now on the blanket in the tackroom, propping herself on one of her coffee-brown arms and gently smoothing back the blond hair from Abdee's deeply bronzed face. If Seena only saw the colour of Abdee's face, hands, and forearms, she would say that he could have a drop of negro blood in him. But now as he lay naked in front of her on the floor, Seena saw the fine ivory cast of his light body and he looked white. Undeniably white.

Abdee's forehead was strong; his brilliant blue eyes set deep in his brow. He had a lean, chiselled face and the slimness of his body belied the strength and muscle which he possessed. Abdee was over six feet in height but the fine proportions of his body gave him the air of being not so large a man. There was no bulk or unnecessary girth to Richard Abdee. His quiet and aloof manner also added to his enigmatic presence.

His words to Seena now were clipped. He said, 'This is the last time you'll come here.'

Seena pulled her hand quickly away from Abdee's face and her eyes widened as she looked down at him to hear more.

Resting his head on his hands clasped behind his neck, Abdee stared up at the row of saddles hanging from the rafters above him and continued, 'You're down on the list for having a baby.'

In her usual hoarse voice, Seena quickly denied, 'I ain't

having no baby, Master Sir. Who tells you that? Who tells you that lie?'

Abdee calmly ordered, 'Don't argue.' He was not thinking about children now. He was thinking about harvesting and shipping the crop to England. He had worked hard to get Dragonard and he wanted to build it larger. He was thinking of a small island off the coast of St. Kitts which he could transform into a depot for shipping sugar from all these islands.

Seena anxiously asked, 'Grandma Goat tells you that, don't she? Grandma Goat says I misses my bleeding and she says she sees that sign, ain't she? Well, she lies to you, Master Sir. She lies to you.'

'From now on, Seena, you stay with Manroot at night.'

Seena blurted before she realized what she was confessing, 'But my baby can't come from Manroot, Master Sir. We sleeps together for two years now and he ain't takes in me yet! Manroot wants a sucker but his seed ain't no good, Master Sir. His seed ain't no good.'

Abdee knew the sad fact that Manroot was sterile. Abdee also knew that his overseer desperately wanted his own family. But he said coldly to Seena, 'Well, you're going to have a baby now. You're down on the list.' It was not Abdee's place to worry about any further complications among the slaves.

Seena sat up on her bare haunches now, her pendulous brown breasts hanging forward. 'I *ain't* going to have no baby, Master Sir! I ain't!'

Impatiently, Abdee ordered, 'Bring me my clothes, girl. Then you get the hell out of here.'

Seena had been with Abdee long enough to know this clipped tone in his voice. But realizing that she was going to lose not only the privileges of being the master's wench but also the new sensations she had learned from him, Seena sunk to the floor next to Abdee's warm body. Gently, she tried to snuggle close to him. Reaching her open mouth up to the pit of Abdee's arm, she began to lick the silky growth of his hair, tongueing the salty perspiration of his arm pits like a brown cat licking cream from a shallow saucer.

Abdee failed to respond to such personal endearments.

Next, Seena reached her left hand down to his naked groin and began to fondle him, to squeeze that lifeless bulk of masculinity which only minutes before had caused a flood in her body. But that part of her master, too, told Seena that she was no longer wanted for these secret midnight meetings. On previous nights, when she had fondled Abdee as they lay spent like this on the floor—or in the fields—she had always been able to achieve some response from him. But now her agile brown fingers awakened nothing. Abdee was dead to her. He was gone. And Seena knew that she would be going, too, that she was meant to return to her hut to live an uneventful life with Manroot. To have nothing but the devotion of her husband.


The maleness of Richard Abdee, his private faculty which had prodded Seena into mature womanhood, was the subject of discussion in the music room of the greathouse tonight.

But Naomi was different from Seena. She had had professional experience in her bordello and could respond quite coldly to Abdee's uniqueness. She said now to her unexpected visitor, 'Abdee is hung just as hefty as you are, Calabar. In fact, Abdee is the only man—white man or nigger—whose pecker is as big as yours. Abdee's pecker is crowned as good as yours, too, Calabar, and maybe that's the reason you're so jealous of him!'

Calabar said, 'I ain't never had no jealousy for white men. That's why you and me are different, Naomi. You try to be like the whities. You try to live like whities. You try to talk like them. Dresses like them. You move in here and even try to be mistress. Naomi, in this big white house, you're forgetting you're a nigger.'

Calabar had only been here with Naomi for a few minutes and, judging by the way that he had surveyed the music room when he had unexpectedly entered through the French doors,

Naomi had immediately known that the story which Nero had told her was true—Calabar had come back to Dragonard to make trouble.

Rather than let Calabar know that he had unnerved her by suddenly appearing in front of her like an ugly apparition from the night, Naomi had pointed calmly to the settee across from where she was sitting, and had said that he could sit there—that is, if he did not have any horse manure on his boots!

When Calabar had ambled across the carpet in front of her, Naomi lifted the long rope of pearls from the low cut bodice of her red gown and languidly began to swing the beads as she waited for him to settle himself. She was relieved that Abdee was not here in the house. Naomi had hoped she could get rid of Calabar as quickly—and quietly—as possible before Abdee returned.

But now when Calabar was openly accusing her of copying the lives of white people, Naomi's temper flared. 'I could have the flesh stripped off your back for talking to me like that!'

Smiling at her, Calabar said, 'You even talk like a white bitch.'

Naomi shouted, 'I could whip you myself!'

It was Calabar whose eyes twinkled now. 'With the dragon's tongue . . . Madame Dragonard?'

Naomi glared at Calabar. She knew now that he was going to dredge up every fact from the past. Holding her dark eyes on him, she asked, 'Why did you come snooping back here? You got your freedom, what else do you expect to get here?'

Looking at the vaulted ceiling of the music room, Calabar said nonchalantly, 'I comes back to help my people.'

Naomi scoffed at such an absurd idea. 'Since when you've become so good, Calabar? You've come back here to get even with Abdee. I know you hate him. He knows it, too. But why? Abdee's never done anything to you. Shit, boy! It was his wife who *freed* you!'

Calabar smiled. 'Yes, Mistress Honore did free me . . . when she was running away from him.'

'What's that got to do with you, you stupid ape? She went

back to France two years ago! Were you expecting to help her, too?'

Calabar continued smugly, 'Mistress Honore left this island with Abdee's child in her belly. She took her maid and the maid's yellow kid with her, too. That kid was another one of Abdee's gits. Or didn't you know that he went around giving suckers to every black wench in sight?'

'I know all about Abdee and his gits.'

Calabar's tribal marks spread as he grinned. 'Then tell me about Abdee and Seena.'

Naomi asked cautiously, 'What do you know about Seena? You haven't been here one day yet and you're saying you know something about Seena. How do you even know there's a wench here called Seena?'

'Remember, I know Manroot. And I know about the marriages taking place here now. Seena is married to Manroot and, what I remembers, Manroot is a big Fanti chieftain. He thinks mighty high of promises like marriage.'

'Calabar, if you've come here to stir trouble for these people, I'll skin you alive, myself. I'm a Fanti, too, don't forget, and I know all about skinning. Oh, yes, Calabar! Don't you think that I haven't noticed what you did to those teeth of yours. Don't you think I didn't see that the first thing you stuck your ugly face in my French windows there. But, look at these, you son-of-a-black-bitch,' Naomi warned, holding her long fingernails toward him. 'Look how sharp these are!'

'You a *hougan* now, Naomi?' he asked calmly.

'I'm a woman!' she shouted, springing to the edge of her settee. 'And I'm protecting what's here. These people are leading a good life on Dragonard. The best life these niggers can look for now. Shit, some of us niggers were sold off by our own brothers. But life's getting good here at Dragonard. For the Fantis. For the Mundingoes. For the Ashanti. Life's a hell of a lot better at Dragonard than some had in Africa! So think about *that*!'

'Things can always get better, Naomi. With a little outside push.'

'A push? From you?' Naomi sprawled back on the settee and laughed at him.

'I see what's happening on the other islands, Naomi, and I see what niggers can get if they try hard enough.'

'When the time comes for changes to happen here, they'll happen. But you ain't going to push them, Calabar. Not with all the jealousy and hate you have. You'll just make them run for the torches. And these niggers will end up getting whipped and hanged by their necks.'

Slowly uncrossing his legs, Calabar rose to his feet. He said, 'You've got your notions, Naomi. I've got mine.'

Naomi reached again for her pearls as she watched Calabar stalk across the carpet toward the French doors. She was wondering what he really wanted here. She could not believe that he had come back to St. Kitts as a liberator. Calabar was not that heroic. If anything, he was a tyrant himself.

It was on that night that the fire first began to flicker on Dragonard. Many years later, Naomi would wish that she had killed Calabar that night, that she had put a knife between his shoulder blades as he strolled out the French doors of the music room.

It was not until the next morning that Naomi decided to broach the subject of Seena's pregnancy to Abdee himself—and, on introducing it to him, she also planned to break the news of Calabar returning to St. Kitts.

The scene for Naomi's confrontation with Abdee was his bedroom. She slowly opened the door to the stark, high-ceilinged room and crept in while he was still asleep.

Dressed in only her *robe-de-chambre*, a flimsy gown which hung loosely from the shiny contours of her naked body, Naomi tip-toed across the gleaming teak floor until she reached his walnut bed. Dropping her gown to the floor, she slithered onto the bed, the mattress ropes creaking as she moved toward Abdee's naked body. She softly whispered, 'You're so warm.'

Abdee put his hand on top of Naomi's arm as she wrapped it around his bare chest and, pulling her toward him, he asked sleepily, 'What are you doing up so early?'

Gliding her forefinger down the soft yellow hairs which ran over his firm stomach, Naomi reached his morning erection and said, 'Look what else is up.' She circled the large crest of the standing penis with her forefinger, then lightly ran her middle finger down the firm hint of the arc which became the taut cord to his spreading scrotum.

Abdee moaned pleasurably at Naomi's teasing and, grunting, he rolled over on top of her. It felt good to him to be with a woman he knew.

Naomi's original intent had been to come to Abdee's room to talk seriously to him but, not being totally single-minded about this early morning mission, she gladly welcomed the first overtures of his warm limbs.

Knowing how Naomi would react, Abdee centered the palms of his large hands on the firmness of her breasts and waited for her arms to fold around him. Also, pressing Naomi under him like this always made Abdee long for the warmth which he still called 'the dark mysteries of Africa'.

By whatever rhythm Abdee chose to glide into his perceptive lover, he knew that she would follow him. He knew that Naomi's hips could keep tempo with his own rapid drives. Or, if Abdee felt in a slow and languid mood, she would intuitively control herself to suit that occasion, too.

But their love making was not always so gentle. There were those nights—or days—that domination stormed inside Abdee and he felt compelled to subject Naomi, to put her through the most base rigours of obedience, to conquer her by every pendulous swing of his phallus, seeing her respond to the hypnotic effect caused by his insistence of power.

Naomi followed those biddings. But according to an agreement that these two well-matched lovers had made many years ago, Naomi always demanded her share of strength in such a situation, too. In no context did Naomi see herself as a perpetual slave to anybody. Inevitably, it soon became her turn to

27

rise and then it was Naomi the Almighty who ascended to a height above Abdee, lifting herself above his shoulders like some majestic and spraddle-legged African goddess demanding her own due. Naomi saw no reason why a woman should be in constant devotion to a phallus. She believed that a man should be made to open his mouth and eat some feminine sweetness, too, even if he had to be slapped into a subservient position. But Naomi only struck Abdee when he struck her.

This morning's act of enjoyment was more gentle than that, a pleasant joining together to re-acquaint themselves. Abdee and Naomi had not made love to each other for three days now and the voluptuous figure which their contrasting bodies created on the large walnut bed was intended mostly for embracing, fondling, brushing of lips, and after their moment of excitement burst simultaneously for both of them, they lay side by side on the crumpled sheets.

Naomi's black curls now spread across Abdee's strong biceps and her smooth legs clamped one of his firm thighs.

Toying with her verbena-scented ringlets, Abdee asked softly, 'What did you really come in here for?'

Naomi knew that she did not have to be crafty with Abdee. He knew her ways as well as she understood him. She answered directly, 'I'm worried about trouble.'

'What kind of trouble,' he asked unconcerned.

Naomi hesitated, not knowing exactly where to start now. Making love with Abdee always softened her plans.

He asked, 'Does it have to do with . . .' Then he paused to think of the wench's name.

Naomi helped him. 'Seena?'

Rubbing his matted hair, Abdee asked wryly, 'How do you always remember who they are?'

'They don't all look the same to me.'

Abdee laughed. He enjoyed this rapport with Naomi. Contentedly, he began, 'Well, you don't have to worry about Seena. I told her to stay home from now on.'

'She's pregnant.'

'Ummm. I saw that, too. But, hell, why not? Manroot just

28

might like that. He's not getting much results himself, you know. Two years now and he and Seena still have nothing to show for themselves. The rest of the Fantis almost doubled.'

Naomi did not want to go into Manroot's problem nor Abdee's attitude toward fertility on Dragonard. This was not the time. A more complicated problem had arisen. She said bluntly, 'Calabar is back here.'

Abdee lay dead still. When he finally spoke, his voice sounded coarse from sleep. 'Calabar? That's one black face I'll never forget. Calabar is probably one of the ugliest men I've ever seen.'

'Well, he's back. And I think he's come here to cause trouble.'

Abdee quickly discredited the idea. 'What can he do?'

Gaining excitement, Naomi explained, 'He's just come from Santo Domingo and he's full of ideas for black rebellions.'

'I don't think he'll have any luck here. My people are living better than most whites on this island.'

Naomi persisted, 'He's already heard about Seena.'

'Being pregnant?'

Naomi nodded.

'Shit! Word does travel fast around this place, doesn't it? But what's Calabar going to do about that? Try to make trouble out of it with Manroot?' Abdee was remembering the old friction between Calabar and Manroot. Their tribal differences. Abdee knew that if Calabar did tell Manroot anything, it would be in such a way as to detract from his beliefs.

Naomi said, 'Calabar says whites take advantage of the blacks.'

Laughing, Abdee asked, 'What other exciting news has he brought from the outside world?'

Playfully jabbing Abdee in the ribs, Naomi said, 'It's serious. He's got some kind of grudge against you. Or—' She hesitated now, still not liking to mention one particular name to Abdee. Her voice became cautious as she said, '—or maybe it's really a grudge he has about Honore.'

'All these old names!' Abdee laughed, pulling Naomi toward

him until their naked stomachs pressed against one another again.

Laying together now on the wide bed, their eyes looked over each other's shoulder, both staring in the opposite direction, their minds working separately.

Abdee was thinking about Dragonard. How Dragonard was his whole life. How nothing meant more to him. Not wife, an heir, family.

And as Abdee was contemplating the freedom which he had built for himself on Dragonard, Naomi also thought about her independence, her progress, the territory and years which she had covered since the time she had been owned as a slave.

Then, as Abdee and Naomi entertained their separate thoughts, their warm bodies drew closer together until, suddenly, a loud shouting rose down below the bedroom window.

Abdee and Naomi heard the call, 'Master! Master Abdee Sir! Master!'

It was the beginning of the troubles.

Naomi insisted on getting dressed and going with Abdee. They left the greathouse by the back door where Nero joined them. Solemnly, the trio trudged down the grassy slope toward the slave quarters.

Down by the wash-house, the sound from the early morning workers drifted toward them from the nearby sugar *plats*, an unrehearsed dirge for the sad spectacle which Naomi, Richard Abdee, and Nero saw—the corpse of an enormous black man swung from the grey branches of a dead oak tree.

It was Manroot. His lifeless body creaked back and forth, back and forth.

Manroot looked even larger dead than he had alive. He looked even more like a roughly hewn piece of African sculpture. His shaved black head slumped stiffly from the hemp rope by which he had hanged himself. His giant hands extended uselessly at his sides.

30

Seena knelt in the dirt below Manroot, clenching his bare feet against her face. She was wailing that she had killed him. She screamed that her greed had killed her husband.

Abdee did not interrupt. He quietly studied the sight of the hanging negro giant and his wife crying at his feet.

Had Manroot done this act so that his soul would be freed from his body? So his soul could travel back to Africa? Had Manroot lived long enough in slavery? Or had it been his inability to plant children in his wife that had made him take his own life? Or his wife's unfaithfulness to him? And the jeers of an old enemy?

Abdee did not try to answer any questions. He stared soberly at the spectacle of his devoted overseer whilst Naomi clung tightly to his arm, whispering, 'This is Calabar's dirty work. This is Calabar's dirty work. He told Manroot about you and Seena.'

Nero stood silently behind Abdee and Naomi. If blames were to be laid, he believed that Manroot had been killed by Calabar. Miss Naomi was speaking the truth now to Abdee. Calabar had come back to Dragonard to make trouble.

Closing his eyes, the young houseboy, Nero, lowered his head and thought about God. He thought about the one God of the white people and all the Gods of Africa. He prayed to them all that the two years of peace that he had seen the blacks enjoying on Dragonard would continue. He prayed that Calabar would not ruin the life here for all of them.

Young Nero thought about the future. He knew that the white man's number for this year was 1791. He also knew that in nine year's time there would be a big and wonderful event. The world would be seeing a new century. A new beginning. And, so, young Nero wondered, would that special year—1800—also be a new beginning for the black people, too?

Here at the scene of Manroot's suicide, the young Nero stood behind Naomi and Richard Abdee and he prayed for peace for all people—for black and white people alike. He hoped that they could live peacefully together in this world by the year 1800. That in nine years' time there would be no masters, no

31

slaves. Only free people. Good people. People who loved their work.

And in his prayers, Nero asked that this senseless death of Manroot would not start the blaze that Calabar had talked about, the fire that Miss Naomi feared, the flames of a black revolution that could destroy Dragonard Plantation.

*Book One*

# THE MARK OF THE STAR

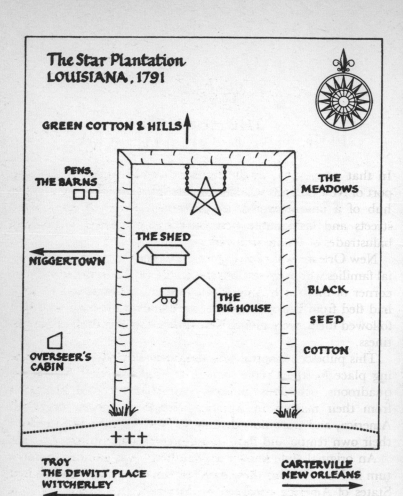

The Star Plantation
LOUISIANA, 1791

GREEN COTTON & HILLS

PENS,
THE BARNS

THE
MEADOWS

THE SHED

NIGGERTOWN

BLACK

SEED

THE
BIG HOUSE

COTTON

OVERSEER'S
CABIN

TROY
THE DEWITT PLACE
WITCHERLEY

CARTERVILLE
NEW ORLEANS

🐴 STABLES
.......... PUBLIC ROAD
+++ CEMETERY

*Chapter One*

# THE AUCTION

In that year, 1791, in the territory known as Louisiana, the port of New Orleans was showing its first signs of becoming the hub of a unique world, a young city proud of its cobbled streets and fashionable new buildings decorated with deep balustrades of ornate ironwork.

New Orleans was evolving into a mecca for the proud colonial families who were settling this fertile region in the south-east corner of the North American continent. The aristocrats who had fled from Europe, and the ambitious tradesmen who had followed them, were giving New Orleans its first dash of haughtiness.

This pubescent capital was also being singled-out as a meeting place for the Creole society, the light-skinned Africans—quadroons, octoroons, mustees—who had received liberation from their masters in America, the West Indies, or South America, and were now drifting to New Orleans to introduce their own tempo and flare into the emerging culture.

An original style known as 'Southern' was gaining momentum in New Orleans these days. In this year, 1791, the United States of America consisted of thirteen states which lay in a cluster to the north of Louisiana, settled along the eastern seaboard like a nest of young birds hatched fifteen years ago by the Declaration of Independence. But this rich lower region of the North American continent had an individual flair which separated it both from the standards of the North and the consciousness of Europe. Although formally controlled by Spain, and showing a heavy French flavour in its architecture and mannerisms, New Orleans still insisted on its own rules for growth in the wilderness.

The Southern feeling was especially felt when the mainstay of the Louisiana economy, the planters, travelled long distances from their rice, sugar, and tobacco plantations to do business here. It was in the New Orleans markets that their crops were sold and dispatched to mills and outlets across the Atlantic.

The planters also visited New Orleans for the slave auctions. Slave labour was in growing demand now in this young country. The cotton crop especially devoured all the black people that arrived in slavers from Africa, the Caribbean, and Brazil.

An assortment of slave halls and yards were sprouting around the city, establishments ranging from run-down shacks which sold 'Niggers & Mules' to great maze-like pens through which passed as many as seven thousand black people a year.

One of the most trustworthy slave houses in New Orleans at this time was Lynn and Craddock, a brick building nestled among the stylish Creole houses on Rampart Street. The management at Lynn and Craddock advertised their prestigious event as a *vendue* . . .

> *Messrs. Lynn and Craddock have the honour of*
> *cordially inviting you to a quality* vendue
> *presenting only the most prime stock of*
> *both male and female negro slaves to be seen*
> *in the American or West Indian markets.*

At Lynn and Craddock, the price for a negro began at five hundred dollars. This price was high but the negroes sold there were of a superior quality, falling mostly into the category which the planters called the 'fancies'.

Another accepted fact at Lynn and Craddock was that no white lady could be admitted to the salesrooms. This unwritten law also extended to the inspection night of the slaves which was held on the eve of the auction—an event which often attracted a larger crowd than the auction itself.

Lynn and Craddock held their inspection after the supper hour. Tonight, when Albert Selby arrived in the lantern-lit yard behind the building on Rampart Street, he saw a crowd of men already milling through the shadowy aisles laying between the slave pens.

Albert Selby owned the plantation called The Star. Although he was prosperous from raising black-seed cotton, Selby was not expensively dressed. A trip to New Orleans did not impress Albert Selby. He was not wearing a beaver or a tall silk hat, nor one of the tricorns still being sported in these parts. Albert Selby was a 'straw man', as he called it, preferring a hat for its coolness and shade.

Although it was dark now, and no need for a shade hat, Albert Selby wore his. Tonight was hot and sticky and made Selby's bones feel lazy. He was not an old man but in New Orleans—especially at a fancy slave auction—he felt out of place and older than his fifty-six years. He longed to be back home.

Selby's hair was white, hanging long and silky from under his straw hat. His face was weathered and wrinkled from years of outdoor work, and his only splash of vanity was a Van Dyke goatee which he dyed a deep henna red.

Hoping to avoid the auctioneer's representative standing near the gate, Selby moved in the direction of the crowd. It was not until he reached the first pen that he breathed more easily. He did not want to hear a spiel of salesmanship. Albert Selby knew exactly what kind of black he had to buy.

In the kerosene lighting, Selby looked around him and saw a small group of children huddled together inside the single-rail pen to his right. These were the saplings. As Lynn and Craddock dealt mostly in adult blacks—fancies—there were never more than a dozen children to be seen here. And, tonight, no prospective buyers stood in front of this pen.

In the opposite pen were the black women being sold with their babies. The lanterns hanging from the rafters here illumined a small bank of shiny black flesh crouched against the inside wall. A small baby cried in the moving shadows and the stench of sour milk fouled the odour of straw. Selby moved on. He did not need any women with children.

The next two stalls held the labourers. In keeping with Lynn and Craddock's tradition of selling mostly fancy black people, these labourers were not mere field hands. They consisted of grooms, cobblers, cooks, all the specialized labourers needed on a plantation.

The crowd of onlookers grew thicker here and, as Selby tried to walk through, his way was blocked by a group of men surrounding a black woman. She was in her early twenties. Her hair was plaited into intricate designs on her skull. She revolved slowly inside the circle of men, turning as they inspected her body. When a gruff voice ordered her to stop, she stood patiently as hands began to pour over her nakedness. Behind this group, a second negress held open her wide mouth as a prospective white buyer examined her teeth as if she were a horse. Behind her, another man studied the pink soles of a black woman's feet, pulling now at each toe.

Across the aisle by the males' pen, a black man bent forward and gripped his ankles as a planter knelt on the floor behind him, using both hands to hold open the negro's buttocks. The planter was examining the negro for haemorrhoids. He cursed when Selby accidently jostled him on the way past and returned to inspecting the slave.

The crowd grew more and more dense as Selby progressed. The smell of cigars mingled with the musky odour of the negroes' bodies. Selby paused now in front of another negro male being examined by a swarthy looking man—a Spaniard. A blank expression covered the negro's flat face as the Spaniard stood in front of him and weighed the size of his penis, bouncing the bulky softness up and down in the palm of his hand as if he were estimating its poundage. He squeezed with the other hand to gauge the contents of the scrotum.

Temporarily engrossed, Selby watched as the Spaniard nodded for the negro to turn so that he could examine his back. There were whip marks on it. After touching the long wails cut into the negro's skin, the Spaniard told him to face him again

38

and he re-examined the weight of the slave's genitalia, deciding if it justified the disfigurement of his back.

Selby stifled an urge to warn the Spaniard about a marked negro, to tell him that whip cuts usually meant that a slave was troublesome or prone to running away from his master. But as an auctioneer's representative stood next to the Spaniard, urging him to peel back the negro's foreskin, Selby did not linger here. The representative obviously knew what his customer wanted.

Finally reaching the end of the wide aisle, Selby suddenly saw a change in both the buyers and the slaves. These were the true fancies here and the white men mostly stood studying them, drawing one another's attention to the particulars of the females in one pen, the males across the way.

Moving toward the females, Selby edged into an opening at the end of the railing and looked toward the wide pen.

These black people showed less fear of the white people. They stood with assurance, knowing that they were going to sell for a high price, confident of their worth. Only the exceptional stock was at this end of the aisle. They even laughed and visited among themselves. A few women wore their hair long like white ladies and they sat combing it, oblivious to the staring eyes.

Spotting a mulatto woman, Selby beckoned her to come out of the darkness.

As the mulatto began to slink across the straw toward the railing, she lowered her hands to lift the loose cotton shift over her shoulders.

Selby shook his head. He did not want her to strip off her clothes. He said, 'Just a few questions.'

Reluctant to let the shift fall back into place, she said, 'Yes, Master Sir.' She stood running her hands down the loose dress, accentuating the full curves of her body. She knew why most white men bought fancy slaves.

Appraising the woman in this lighting, and seeing her brazenness, Selby shook his head. 'No. Not you.' He looked past her to see what else was available in the pen.

The mulatto woman asked, 'What Master Sir wanting?'

Selby ignored the question. Her directness angered him but he knew that fancies were often impudent. They were known to speak out of turn. He pitied the people who bought them.

As the mulatto woman lingered in front of Selby, he kept looking past her, wishing that he could be more dictatorial with slaves. He could handle his own people back home but, then, he did not have any head-proud fancies on The Star. He dreaded now that he might have to take one home.

Suddenly a hand grabbed Selby's shoulder and a voice boomed, 'Albert Selby! What's a fogey like you buying a hot piece like her for? That wench there will lay you in your grave!'

Selby turned and saw a familiar face. It was one of his wife's second cousins. Selby could always tell his in-laws by the freckles on their faces.

After an exchange of greetings with his distant relative, Selby explained that he and his son had come to New Orleans to buy a slave. Selby proceeded to confess that he was having a difficult time in finding what he wanted. His wife had sent him to Lynn and Craddock to find a suitable companion for their daughter.

The cousin laughed. 'This wench here ain't going to do for that. She's too much of a hell cat. I'll tell you what. Come instead and have a drink with me!'

Selby pulled at his red goatee, saying, 'Can't rightly say yes to that. My boy's waiting back at the hotel.'

The cousin was astounded. 'Why ain't your boy here with you?'

'He's just seventeen,' Selby said.

'That's what I figured. And that's just the age boys really enjoys this.'

Selby bristled. 'If I ain't enjoying this, I don't expect my boy to. We don't go around fingering our folks on The Star.'

Near them, a group of white men broke out in a raucous laugh. A black woman struggled to get away from them. An auctioneer's representative hurried forward with a riding crop and a crack was then heard. The white men applauded.

Turning back to Selby, the cousin said, 'Maybe we can meet after the auction tomorrow.'

Selby suspected that his in-law wanted to borrow money. Or to endear himself to the owner of The Star. He answered, 'I'd like nothing better but I've got to work on getting a wench. You know how riled-up Rachel can get.'

After a few more words, Selby and his cousin said their good-byes and Selby was left by himself again.

Glad to have rid himself of his wife's cousin, he looked around at the crowd. It was approaching midnight but more men were crowding down the wide aisle. The cigar smoke grew thicker now and Selby's eyes were beginning to burn. He decided that he had had enough of this for one night. He would put his trust in finding something tomorrow. It would be easier to see the blacks without all this crowding.

Bracing himself, Selby bumped his way down toward the gate.

Finally emerging from the thick of the crowd, Selby stood by the pen which held the mothers and children. Taking off his straw hat, he fanned his face.

'Master Sir?' a voice called behind him.

Selby looked.

A young boy stood inside the railing. He was light-skinned and his head was shaved. He looked old enough to be sold in the saplings pen. He called to Selby, 'You want to see my Ma, Master Sir?'

Selby put on his hat.

The boy continued eagerly, 'My Ma's good, Master Sir. You buy my Ma and you get *three* of us. Look—' The young boy flexed his arm to show Selby his muscle.

Selby moved to go.

Turning quickly around, the boy showed his round buttocks to Selby and, smiling over his shoulder, he rubbed them.

This disgusted Selby.

Facing Sebly again, the boy pleaded, 'If you don't like me, Master Sir, just fingers my Ma!'

Selby continued toward the gate. He did not like buggering. Nor did he like boys who pimped for their mothers.

41

The next day, Selby dutifully went to the auction sale.

With him came his seventeen-year-old son, Roland Selby, who also was not too excited by being here in the stifling, crowded room.

Roland said, 'This is all a waste of time, Pa. We're not going to find nothing for Ma here.'

Selby was of a similar opinion. He had seen nothing so far in this mahogany-panelled hall except white people putting on airs and negroes who were bred and trained to live in a house far more sophisticated than they would find at The Star. But to keep his son from abandoning him, Selby said, 'Your Ma will have both our hides, Ro, if we come home without something for Melly.'

Roland did not have time to worry about a companion for his little sister. He had to get away from here to keep a secret appointment. He said to his father, 'Why don't you stay, Pa. No need us both choking on this air. I'd stay and let you go if I knew niggers as well as you do, Pa. But I don't. Why don't I just mosey around town and look at the sights.'

Young Roland's diplomacy usually worked on his father. Albert Selby had become a father late in life and he doted on his two children. Five-year-old Melissa got away with more than Roland. But Roland was old enough to know how to lie to his father.

Seeing that his words were working on his father, Roland said, 'Pa, I do think I'll get sick if I stay cooped up in here one minute more. I do feel a bilious attack coming on.'

The trick worked. Selby always gave in to his son. He said, 'I guess it won't hurt none you leaving me. But don't stray far. I don't want you getting lost. And be back at the hotel by six o'clock, you hear? I want to eat and get to bed early. We got to get a bright start home tomorrow if we find a wench or not.'

Roland dutifully promised his father that he would meet him back at the Hotel LaSalle by six o'clock. And pushing through the crowd of men, he soon disappeared.

It was only moments after Roland's departure that Selby

saw the first wench who approached the requirements which his wife had given him.

Even from where Selby was standing, he could see that the negress being displayed next to the podium was not overly fancy. She was not a slut wench but neither was she a rough field hand. She was not too lean, nor was she too fat. Her face was sober too, which pleased Selby, as he knew his wife would not be content with a loud and jolly negress around the house.

But two things about the woman bothered Selby. One was her age. She looked to be in the troublesome neighbourhood of thirty. That would not please his wife. Thirty was too old for a child's companion.

The second problem was that the wench was holding a small child in her arms. She was being sold with . . .

The group of men shifted in front of Selby and now he could see that the wench was not being sold with one child—as he had thought—but with two children! Selby saw to his horror that the older child was the same boy who had tried to get him to finger his mother last night. He began to have doubts now about the wench.

But the light-skinned boy looked harmless as he stood silently next to his mother. Being displayed on the podium, he looked hopelessly vulnerable. Selby had a fleeting thought how piccaninnies like him would probably do anything for a home, even solicit for his mother. Selby was softening.

The more that he listened to the auctioneer's rapid speech about the wench's qualifications, the more excited he became again about the wench as a companion for Melissa.

Her name was Ta-Ta. The auctioneer said that she had been brought to Louisiana by a French noble lady from the Caribbean island of St. Kitts. The auctioneer reminded his audience that the lucky gentleman who bought her would also get two piccaninnies in the price. The auctioneer pointed at the light-skinned boy standing next to the woman and the child she held in her arms. The smaller child clung to the wench's neck and the older boy stood like a small soldier at his mother's side. Selby was having second thoughts about him, too.

43

The sale then began as the auctioneer called for the basic price of five hundred dollars.

A silence greeted his call. The planters here today did not want sober-faced dams with their own children. No offers came from the floor.

The auctioneer called for five hundred dollars again.

Selby lifted his straw hat from his head and, waving it in the air, he called, 'Two hundred and fifty dollars!'

Chuckles greeted Selby's offer. Some voices told him that he had bid too high.

The auctioneer was of a different opinion. He called to Selby from his podium under a fan-shaped window, 'I can't let this wench go for less than five hundred dollars, Mister Selby. She's been trained by a noble lady as a boudoir maid. She's fluent in both English and French. And look—' the auctioneer said, reaching to take the smaller child from the negress's hand, '—look, this is only one of the two suckers you get!'

But the negress called Ta-Ta would not release the child from her arms. The auctioneer grabbed harder for the child but Ta-Ta pulled away from him. The child hugged tighter to her neck, clinging to her like a frightened animal, burying his face into her neck.

The auctioneer reached next to the older boy and said, 'Look! This sapling here is old enough to be sold by himself. But I'm offering you all three of these fine West Indian blacks for five hundred dollars! Make it four-fifty, Gentlemen, and all three are yours!'

'Three hundred,' Selby called.

'Make it another hundred, Mister Selby, and you take them back to The Star today.'

Having entered into the spirit of the auction, Selby stayed at three hundred dollars. He knew that there were more expensive negroes to come in the sale and that the auctioneer was anxious to move on to them.

With a loud bang, the auctioneer's gavel closed the sale, agreeing that Albert Selby of The Star Plantation had purchased one negress from St. Kitts called Ta-Ta, along

44

with two half-caste boys, also from that island in the Caribbean.

Selby moved forward to sign the papers.


Roland Selby was like his father. He also found New Orleans damp and sticky, the air not being cool and light to breathe like it was back home. Although it was not raining, a wetness permeated Roland's clothes. There was even a dampness to the colourful walls of the houses he passed now as he hurried along the narrow streets. Roland thought that New Orleans was like a city made out of boiled sweets and licorice and it was all getting too sticky in this humidity.

But more concerned about where he was going than the climate of this city, Roland congratulated himself for getting away from his father. Roland liked his father. He had more respect for him than he had for his mother. She was always so impatient with everybody. Roland could not understand how his father could have lived all these years with her.

The whole idea of families—how families acted, thought, and treated one another—confused Roland Selby anyway. That was why he had had to lie to his father to get away from the auction sale. Slaves and cotton and planting had little interest for him—not since he had met Sarah Witcherley. But as Sarah *was* a Witcherley, Roland had no one to tell but her about his plans for a new life. Their new life.

The feud between the Selbys and the Witcherleys bewildered Roland. He did not know why the two neighbouring families were fighting. He had no idea how long that war had been waged. But he knew that the Selbys were not the only ones to bear a grudge. If Sarah's father discovered that his daughter was secretly meeting a member of the Selby family, the Lord only knew what he would do to poor Sarah. Fearing what would happen to himself, too, Roland had made certain that he conducted this whole affair with Sarah Witcherley in secret.

Stopping now in front of a low doorway, Roland saw a shiny brass plaque announcing: *Dr. Eustace Creed*. This was where

Sarah had told him to meet her today. Dr. Creed was a cousin on her mother's side of the family. He had no way of knowing that Roland was not welcomed by Sarah's parents.

Roland clanked the iron knocker and waited until a fat negress opened the apple-green door. She was short and plump, with skin the reddish-brown colour of cinnamon. She held the door open with one arm and blocked Roland's entry with the other.

Roland said politely, 'I want to see Miss Sarah Witcherley.'

Studying his clothes, the pug-faced negress asked, 'She expecting you . . . Master Sir?'

Roland knew that his good suit had made an impression on this grisly servant for her to ask him even that much. He knew that a negress like this guarded her masters—and mistresses—from all outsiders.

'Yes,' Roland answered, taking his grandfather's gold watch from the pocket of his white waistcoat. And, in a fleeting moment, he imagined how his grandfather must be turning in the family cemetery knowing that a timepiece of his was marking the hour for a Selby to keep an appointment with a Witcherley.

The black woman left and briefly returned to the door. Gruffly telling Roland to follow her, she led him down a dark hallway and into a small parlour. Roland had not time to study the effects in this small reception room because, there, just inside the door, stood Sarah.

It seemed hours to him before the black maid shut the door but, as soon as it clicked in the lock, Roland pulled Sarah into his arms.

Sarah Witcherley was only six months younger than Roland Selby. She had the same yellow-red hair as his and the same delicate complexion, but without the freckles. As she buried her face into the shoulder of Roland's suit, she did not say a word, just holding her arms around his waist.

Roland stood tall and calm, slowly petting the back of Sarah's soft hair, feeling her thin frame trembling against his body. There was no doubt in his mind now. He was going to

46

marry her. The Selbys be damned! The Witcherleys be damned, too! Roland knew now for a fact that he would elope with Sarah as soon as possible. In fact, if he did not marry Sarah soon, he might not be able to restrain himself any longer. If his passion for her continued like this, he would certainly make more trouble for her—and himself—than he would if he left her unmarried. He did not want his natural urges to lead him to being lynched and leave Sarah alone to become an object of scorn for the rest of her life.

Since meeting Sarah, Roland had grown tired of getting his physical satisfaction from the black wenches on The Star. His Pa had given him his first girl to sample when he was fourteen. But Roland now wanted more than that. He liked the sensation that the black girls gave him but since he had first seen Sarah at a garden fair one year ago, he found that his mind was always on her. When he went to take her soft breasts in his hands and found instead the full bosoms of a black wench, he lost interest in any sexual acts. Even the musky smell of a black girl irritated him lately. Roland was willing to risk even his life to have the real thing. He knew he loved Sarah.

Reaching down to her, he pulled up her dimpled chin and said, 'Sarah, for the one hundreth time, let's get married.'

Her green eyes showed fear.

'Don't you want to?' he asked.

Roland knew the answer by the pounding he felt from her heart. But he had to step back from her to hide the reaction she had caused in his pants.

'The last thing I want is to hurt you, Ro,' Sarah said, dipping her head.

'You'll never hurt me.'

'I could be the cause.'

Roland knew that she meant her family. He said, 'We're going to run away from all that.'

'But my Daddy. He's coming back to fetch me tonight.'

Laughing, Roland hugged her tightly to him, saying, 'Oh, my Sarah! My Sarah! As much as I want to run away with you now, we have to wait. But not for long, honey. See, I've got a plan.'

47

'What plan?' Sarah asked cautiously.

'You just go back home with your Daddy tonight, Sarah. And I'll go home with Pa. But don't worry. I'll get word to you.'

'You can't come to Witcherley!' she said.

Roland assured her, 'No, I won't come to Witcherley. I have a plan that will take us far, far away. We'll leave Witcherley and The Star and all their foolish, old problems for ever!'

Then, hugging her tightly, Roland longed for the time when they truly could be together. He had always heard that a man was not supposed to feel this way about a white lady. That a man was supposed to respect white ladies. He was only supposed to want to lay with white ladies to have heirs. But the idea of being with Sarah to have children excited him like nothing else in the world. Even the idea of going to bed with Sarah and *not* having a family filled him with passion, too. But Roland told himself that Sarah was a lady—a fine white lady—and he must not use her like he used the wenches back home at The Star.

He left, assuring her that his plan would be a success.

## Chapter Two

# A NEW HOME

The experience of staying in a hotel filled with planters on a spree had been a gruelling ordeal for Albert Selby. It was with great relief on the following morning that he sat beside Roland in the wagon, bumping along homewards with the parties and noise of New Orleans already six hours behind them.

Selby's thoughts were now on his wife as the rough board wagon rattled over the rutty road. He and Roland were well into the deep country of Louisiana, away from the smooth roads which led south to the Bayou regions. Selby was wondering if he had made a mistake at the auction sale.

The negress called Ta-Ta was sitting quietly behind Selby, huddled in one corner of the wagon bed. She had not struggled when he had taken her from Lynn and Craddock's. She had climbed peacefully into the wagon, still holding the smaller of the two boys in her arms and let the older child fend for himself.

Selby had not yet examined the small child. But the bigger one, the boy with the yellow skin, had stepped forward and announced with his shoulders proudly thrown back that his name was Monkey. He would have probably said more if Ta-Ta had not grabbed him by one of his ears and then slapped him with the flat of her hand. The boy made no further references to anything, not even about Selby fingering his mother.

Selby wondered if Monkey really was Ta-Ta's child. Slave wenches usually had no particular maternal bonds to their children but Ta-Ta acted as if she hated the yellow boy. He was like an unwanted puppy to her.

There was no doubt to Selby about a connection between

49

Ta-Ta and the younger child. He had seen enough cross-bred suckers to know that the younger boy had a strong dose of white blood in his veins. His hair was not coarse like Monkey's head of black wool. The younger piccaninnie had straight black hair. Selby doubted if he had Indian blood in him, though. His hair was fine and silky like human hair. But Selby had seen little more of the child than his hair because Ta-Ta still held him tightly in her arms.

As Selby bumped along in the wagon now, he scratched nervously at his red Van Dyke beard and realized that he had not heard as much as a word from Ta-Ta. Breaking the monotony of the creaking wagon wheels, he nodded at the three blacks huddled behind him and asked Roland, 'You get a word out of her yet?'

Roland held the reins from the team of white mules and stared blankly ahead of him at the road. His mind was on Sarah Witcherley.

'Ro! I asked you a question!'

Roland suddenly snapped out of his trance. 'Sorry, Pa. I was just thinking—just thinking about . . . about getting home.'

Selby grunted. 'Pretty bad sleep last night myself. Be glad to be back in my own bed, too. Never did like hotels. Too much noise.'

Roland agreed quickly that neither had he enjoyed last night's sleep, adding for conviction, 'And that ham we had for breakfast this morning, Pa! Did you see how the rind was burned? Storky would throw out ham like that. Throw it right out the back door before serving it up to us.'

Selby went further to defend their black -cook. 'Storky wouldn't burn bacon in the first place. Storky never blacked up a piece of ham since we had her. But it was those salt rising biscuits this morning that gagged me.'

Then quickly looking over his shoulder at the three slaves in the bed of the wagon, Selby lowered his voice to ask again, 'Did you get any word out of her, Ro?'

Still consumed with Sarah Witcherley, thinking that any reference to a female had to do with her, Roland looked at his father with shock. What did he mean? Was he talking about Sarah Witcherley?

Selby saw that his son still had not understood him. He shouted impatiently, 'That Frenchie nigger I bought? Did you talk to her yet?'

Roland's face suddenly relaxed. 'Why, no, Pa! Ain't you?'

Selby shook his head and muttered, 'Might as well try now.'

Turning around on the high seat of the moving wagon, Selby called to Ta-Ta crouched on the splintery boards of the bed, 'You there! You know about raising young ladies?'

Ta-Ta looked up at him with round eyes. She did not answer. She stared back at Selby like a brown owl.

Selby barked louder, 'You supposed to talk two different languages, you! Let's hear one of them!'

Holding Selby's stare, Ta-Ta opened her wide lips to speak. The child still clung to her neck.

Selby asked impatiently, 'What you call that runt you're gripping to your titties there? He looks big enough to shift for himself.'

The reference to the child obliterated any sign of speaking from Ta-Ta's face. She lowered her head again, clenching the child.

Filled with disgust, more disgusted with himself for buying a wench that he had not even questioned rather than with her for not answering him, Selby turned around in his seat. He said to Roland, 'Your Ma is really going to hit the roof over this one. If I was half a man, I'd leave right now and head west. Fighting redskins would be a tea party compared to what's waiting for me when I get home.'

Again, Roland did not hear his father. His mind had returned to the girl he loved and to his plan on how he was going to escape with her. But unlike his father's words about fleeing west, Roland's plan was real.

With only the rattle of the board wagon and the steady pace of the white mules, the small party continued north from New Orleans. Eating as they travelled, swallowing what they could from the luncheon hamper that the hotel had packed for them, and throwing the rest over their shoulders for the yellow boy to scramble for, Albert and Roland Selby passed under spreading oaks, tunnelled through the thickly growing acacias, and left behind the last meadows of the coastal country.

The orange sun was hovering over a line of distant cypress pines when a second wagon rattled up the road behind him. The wagon thundered closer and, as it recklessly passed them in a cloud of dust, the driver pulled his hat over his face. Selby thought that he recognized the driver as a red-necked farmer called Jack Grouse. He mentioned to Roland that it was queer for Grouse to be in such a hurry for a change. Roland did not answer. Selby also wondered why Grouse had tried to hide his face. Roland still showed no interest in the incident. They continued at their own trodding pace.

Finally, they reached the first familiar looking fork in the road, the trace leading left to Carterville. Two hours would see them back at The Star.

The sun was setting now and Albert Selby finally saw the double row of leafy oaks which lined the long approach to the house. It was the most welcoming sight in the world for him, the old trees looking like enormous dark bolls of cotton, silhouetted against the purple sky of this late hour, and the windows of the three-storied house twinkling at the end of the drive.

Before travelling down the tree-lined avenue, the wagon passed under the weather-worn gates to the right of the main road. Like Selby himself, this entrance to The Star was crude, weather-worn, unpresuming at its first impression. Two tall wooden poles rose on each side of the road with a cross-beam running between them. From the beam hung a rickety wooden star. It had been constructed many years ago by five slats of wood, each slat being three feet long and joined by wooden pegs because there had been no nails with which the carpenter could build in those early days. Now, decades later, the wooden star was slightly askew, having hung from the cross-beam through torrential rains, destructive winds, blistering heat-waves and two freak snow blizzards. Despite its age and condition, though, this ensignia of The Star Plantation was Albert Selby's most cherished treasure. As always, when he passed under his hanging star, he doffed his hat in thanksgiving—thankful to be home. It was the closest that he ever came to a prayer.

When Selby put his straw hat back on his head, he began to look around the driveway to see what had changed during his absence.

Roland drove the mules down the darkening avenue of oaks and Selby sat drinking in the familiar aroma which wafted through the evening light.

Selby suddenly sat upright. Looking around him in the leafy shadows, he asked Roland, 'Hear that? Hear that screech?'

Quickly pulling the reins, Roland called the mule team to a halt. Listening, he also heard a disturbance, a screaming followed by a cracking noise. It sounded like the crack of a whip.

Frowning, Selby said, 'Tucker? Is that Tucker lashing my niggers again? Damn it, if I catch that Tucker using his whip on my niggers I'll give it to him myself!'

Roland said, 'Tucker don't whip no more, Pa. Not since you gave him strict orders only to punish with the hornet.'

Selby was not convinced about what his overseer would do. He said, 'I never did trust that white trash.' He listened again to hear the noise.

A loud crashing came from the bushes at the right side of the road. It was followed now by the high-pitched voice of a woman.

Roland gasped, 'That's Mama Gomorrah!'

Selby listened to the falsetto sound of the angry voice and, also recognizing it as an old woman's tantrum, he said, 'Blast it, Ro. I think you're right. But what in tarnation is that old biddy doing out here in the bushes at night?'

At that moment a negress jumped from the bushes and ran in front of the mules. She was small and skinny. Her white hair

53

frizzed around her face like a storm-swept cloud. The mules balked at the sudden appearance of the black crone and, as Roland tried to hold them to rein, the negress froze, staring up at Selby in the wagon.

Selby shouted down at her, 'What you doing, old nigger woman, hopping out of the brush like that and scaring my mules?'

Spryly coming toward the wagon, trailing a twelve-foot long leather whip in the dirt, Mama Gomorrah said excitedly, 'I finds them sinners, Master Sir. I finds them sinning right here on your land and I sneaks up on them in the dark and I lets them have it once—' She snapped the whip in the dirt. '—I lets them have it two times—' She snapped the whip again, raising a larger cloud of dust.'—And I lets them have it three times! Four times! Five times! I was just getting to making it five when they jumps up and tries to runs away from me. But I chases them, Master Selby Sir. I chases them and I lets them have the whip for doing the sin.'

Selby sighed a breath of relief that this was the only trouble. Mama Gomorrah was in charge of the black children born on The Star. She lived with them in a long building called The Shed. But, also, according to Mama Gomorrah, an angel had appeared to her when she was only a young wench and the angel had commanded her to whip whomever she found committing the sin of Gomorrah.

Selby knew about Gomorrah, the wicked city in the Bible. Sodom was another city. Selby knew what sin had been named after the Sodomites. But nowhere in his scant knowledge of the Good Book did he know what sin was attributed to the people of Gomorrah. According to Mama Gomorrah, it was a completely different sin from Sodomy. But she never talked about it in detail. She only patrolled The Star at night with her whip to find the people committing it. The one person Selby knew who could offer him an explanation was his wife. She read the Bible daily. But he would rather remain in ignorance about the sin of Gomorrah than to ask Rachel Selby the specifics of a sexual deviation.

Through the years, Selby had learned to humour Mama Gomorrah for what he considered to be her eccentricities and appreciated her for her good qualities. He told her now, 'Old wench, you leave those sinners to the Lord for a spell and follow us up to the house. I've got a chore for you to do.'

Obediently, Mama Gomorrah coiled her whip and walked alongside the wagon as it moved toward the lights flickering at the end of the avenue of oaks. As he rode, Selby reminded her, 'Any punishing done is done by Tucker. You know that.'

Her silence answered that she did know.

Selby continued, 'And, nowadays, any punishment done here is not done with a whip but the hornet.'

Mama Gomorrah looked quickly up at Selby. There was something that she wanted to tell him about Tucker and the hornet. The hornet was the hand-carved instrument shaped like a long, thick butter pat with a series of small holes drilled into it. Each swat of the hornet felt like the sting of a bee. But Mama Gomorrah kept her mouth silent. It was not her place to tell Selby about his overseer. Tucker was a white man and she was a black slave. Selby had to find out for himself about Tucker and the whip and the hornet.

The wagon now creaked to a stop in a patch of light spilling from the house to the driveway. The house was three storeys high and only a bit more inviting than the entry gates of the plantation. Built of wood like a square-shaped fortress, it was painted a fresh coat of stark white. The wide wooden porch and the deep dormer windows on the shingle roof gave the house a look of stature. The thick growth of bougainvillea added a necessary softness to its bulky proportions.

Still sitting on the wagon, Selby called down to Mama Gomorrah, 'Old woman, I want you to take these two piccaninnies I got back here and I want you to take them down to The Shed. Give them both a good going over. Scrub and dose them for nits. Pick their hair for lice. Worm them with some of your pine tonic. Burn their clothes and see what clean togs you can find for them.'

Mama Gomorrah nodded, rising to the tips of her calloused

toes to peek over the side of the wagon at the new wench and the boys.

Jumping down from the wagon, Selby called to Ta-Ta, 'You, there. Shake the dust off yourself and come inside the house with me. I want to see what sense the wife can get out of you.' Already, Selby was dreading the encounter with Rachel Selby.

But when Selby called for Ta-Ta, and when Mama Gomorrah reached into the bed of the wagon to wrench the child from her arms, Ta-Ta pulled herself into the far corner of the splintery bed. She would not budge. She would not release the child from her grip.

Tired from his hard journey, and nervous about any complicated scene with his wife, Selby called impatiently to Mama Gomorrah, 'Better bring me that whip you got there. Let me see if that will pry the wench out of there.'

The threat of a whipping made Ta-Ta speak. But her words were not what Selby had anticipated. Clutching the child tighter in her slim arms, she hissed at Selby in a low voice, 'Whips me! Whips me all you wants! Whips me till I bleeds! But you ain't getting this baby!'

Selby stared at her in disbelief. 'So you do have a tongue.'

Behind them at that moment, a woman's stern voice demanded, 'What's all this commotion out here? What's all this racket you're causing, Albert Selby? Why you getting home so late? And who's that black wench you got in the wagon? What are those piccaninnies doing here? What is all this? What *is* all this?'

These questions all came sharp and fast from Rachel Selby as she stood, arms crossed, in the doorway of the house. She was a hard-faced woman who had the drawn cheeks of a spinster. Her hair was salt and peppered, pulled severely back from her face and tied into a mean knot at the nape of her neck. The only thing generous about Rachel Selby's face was her eyebrows, which were thick and black as a man's, hanging ragged down over the pale hollows which held her tiny brown eyes. She wore a black knit shawl around the narrow shoulders of a faded cotton dress—also black—which was only decorated by a narrow band of black lace encircling both her slim wrists. The flash of a plain gold wedding band on her boney finger looked inconsistent with the rest of her sober apparel.

Doffing his hat, Selby said respectfully, 'Good evening, Mrs. Selby.'

'Humph!' Rachel answered, marching briskly across the porch and stiffly descending the six wooden steps to the dirt driveway. She walked directly to the wagon and, peering in at Ta-Ta, she asked, 'Where'd you get her? What's she doing here?'

Selby hesitated.

Looking from Ta-Ta, down to the child in her arms, and then to Monkey sitting brazenly on the wagon's edge, Rachel Selby demanded, 'And these two dirty piccaninnies? Whose are they? What are you bringing home two dirty little piccaninnies for, Albert Selby?'

The only words that Selby could think to say were, 'Where's Melissa?'

'Where do you think? In bed!' Rachel snapped and looked at Roland still sitting on the wagon. She asked him, 'Why did you let your father do this, boy?'

Roland answered, 'This is what we went for, Ma. This is the maid you wanted for Little Sister.'

Hesitating for a moment, Rachel walked around the wagon and said flatly, 'I didn't send you for no worthless wench, Albert Selby. I sent you to fetch a companion for your five-year-old daughter.' Looking directly at Ta-Ta, Rachel continued, 'And this one can't be a child's companion in a coon's age. Unless her years go backwards! She's old enough to be Melissa's grandmother ... God rest Bathsheba Fairweather Roland for being compared to a worthless nigger.' Rachel continued to glare hatefully at Ta-Ta, who returned the malicious look.

Leaving her piercing eyes on Ta-Ta, Rachel said, 'I hope the Lord Almighty forgives you for buying and selling niggers, Albert Selby.'

Old Selby sputtered, 'Buying and selling? I didn't "sell" no niggers to get these three. And what did you do if you didn't send me to New Orleans to buy a companion for Melly? You said nothing we had on The Star was fitting enough for her.'

Rachel turned on her husband. 'A companion for an innocent child is one thing. But you know full well what the Book says about slavery. Slavery is the tool of Satan!'

Selby's mind was swimming with confusion now. He and his wife owned five hundred negro slaves. Rachel had inherited three hundred and fifty negroes from her family alone, never letting Selby forget that they were her property, passed on to her from her forefathers, the Peregrine Rolands. But, now, in her extemporaneous interpretation of Scriptures, she was finding something else to blame on him. Slavery.

Young Roland tried to be optimistic. He said brightly, 'She can speak Frenchie-talk, Ma!'

Rachel glared at her son for speaking out of place and, turning to her husband, she asked, 'You want a daughter of yours to talk rubbish like a Frenchman, Mister Selby? Do you plan to send her up the Ohio with all the whores of Babylon?'

Selby sputtered, 'But alot of fine white ladies are speaking the French language these days. It's getting to be right fashionable.'

'Hussies! All of them! Hussies! How dare you spit in the face of the Lord, old man. How dare you spit in the Lord's holy face when he was good enough to give you a fine child so late in your life!'

Selby tried, 'Rachel, please—'

But there was no coaxing or cajoling Rachel out of her black mood. She was determined to go to the extremes now. 'I suppose when you were buying up these slaves with my money— money you made from my land, the soil of the Peregrine Rolands—you also forgot what the Scriptures said about selling people like cattle. I suppose you forgot, too, about the misuse of hard-earned money. Money from the land you got from my people. Money you came easy to. Money from the Peregrine Rolands.'

Selby dared not remind his wife that it was his money which had paid off the mortgages on this place, mortgages put on it by none other than three generations of drinking, gambling, womanizing Rolands.

Rachel continued, 'I suppose you forgot, too, about Our Lord Jesus Christ driving the money lenders from the temple and then dying on the cross so there would be fair change for all of us!'

Finally, Selby had taken as much as he could. He was too tired now to argue with this unreasonable woman who altered Scriptures to suit her whims. He did not want to argue. He wanted to get away from her. He wanted to go to sleep. He was tired. Turning to Mama Gomorrah, he said softly, 'Take them all down to The Shed. The wench, too. I'll come see them in the morning.'

Rachel shrieked from behind him, 'Not if you're struck dead in your sleep for sacrileging the Lord's Day, you won't!'

Selby was stunned. 'The Lord's Day? But today is Thursday, Rachel. Not Sunday. It ain't the Lord's day today *or* tomorrow!'

Rachel turned toward the house and, holding the long skirt of her black dress in her fingers, she rigidly climbed the steps. She called without turning her head, 'Every day is the Lord's day, Mister Selby. And every day is your day of judgement. So be warned.'

Then she disappeared into the house, slamming the tall door with such force that the tinted panes rattled in both doors which formed the double entrance to The Star.

At that same hour of the night, two black men stood hidden in the brush alongside the public road which led from The Star to the small town of Troy. The two black men wore leg irons and their hands were manacled. One negro offered his shoulder as support to the shorter man, the second negro holding his stomach in sickness.

59

The white farmer who had passed Selby earlier on the Carterville road, Jack Grouse, sat in his wagon talking to a burly man standing on the ground. Their faces were half-lit by the light from a lantern resting on the wagon.

Jack Grouse asked anxiously, 'You sure your boss ain't suspicious about this, Tucker?'

'Suspicious about what?' asked the barrel-chested man called Chad Tucker. 'Selby's got so damned many niggers here he don't even know how many there are on The Star.'

'But I sees Selby on the way here tonight. I sees him and his kid bringing home more niggers.'

Chad Tucker slowly shook his head in bewilderment. His black hair was cropped short and his square chin was dark with blue stubble. A growth of wiry black hair sprung from the open V of his shirt and his thick arms were gnarled with muscle. Tucker was the man who actively ran the plantation. He was the overseer of The Star but even he did not know about Selby buying more slaves. Selby had told him that he was going to New Orleans for three days but that was all.

Tucker now said to Grouse, 'It just shows how plumb crazy that Selby is getting. Buying more niggers and he don't have no proper count of the ones he already owns.'

Nodding at the two negroes in the dark bushes, Grouse asked, 'What if them niggers go shooting off their mouths where they're from?'

'You got yourself a whip at home?'

Grouse nodded.

Tucker gruffed, 'Then use it on them.'

'Whipping might be too late if they talk.'

Tucker asked, 'Did the last one cause you trouble with yapping?'

Grouse shook his head. 'Not yet. You trained her too good before.'

'That's part of the overseer's job. Training niggers to hold their peace.' Tucker slapped the rolled coil of the whip in his hand and continued in a harsher voice, 'Listen, Grouse. You ain't doing me no favour by buying these two bucks. I thought

I was helping you out by selling you a couple more niggers at cheap prices.'

'And you're sure Selby don't keep no count of his niggers?'

'Why you getting so fidgeting about Selby? He's rich. It don't hurt a rich man like Selby to lose a couple of niggers now and then.'

Jack Grouse sat nervously on his wagon. 'I sure could use me two good field niggers.'

Nodding toward the bushes, Tucker said, 'Well, if you want them, there they are. Providing you brought the money with you tonight.'

'I got the money. I got seventy-five dollars right here in my pocket for you.'

'And another seventy-five to come in six months.'

Jack Grouse moved to step down from the wagon. 'I guess I should take me a look at them now.'

Blocking him from stepping down from the wagon, Tucker said, 'Look at them? What in hell you expecting, Grouse? A bill of sales on top of it, too?'

Grouse began, 'You can't expect a man to buy—'

Tucker threw out his chest. 'What for you talking about expecting? Here I come in the middle of the night to do you a favour. I get out of bed. Leave my wife. Leave my home. Even risk my job here. And for what? Just to do you a favour.'

Grouse shamefully lowered his head.

'The fact is, Grouse, it pains me to see a hard-working man like you with no niggers to help him. And then I sees a rich son-of-a-bitch like Selby who has so many niggers he can't even count them. So what do I do? I stick out my fool neck to help you. And then you want to go inspecting niggers!' Tucker shook his head in distaste.

Grouse mumbled, 'I just wanting to be careful.'

Tucker said disgustedly, 'I can't make sense out of you dirt farmers sometimes. I help you buy niggers on the cheap and then you expect to go fingering them in the bargain, too. You get a few niggers to your name and suddenly you think you're a big shot planter.'

Wiping his nose on the sleeve of his shirt, Grouse said, 'That Purvina you sold me. She been right ailing lately.'

Tucker exploded. 'What's that got to do with me? You probably don't let her out of your shack enough. Most likely you ain't giving her enough greens. You got to let a house nigger have a little time outside in the pasture, you know. Just like you lets a cow out of a barn.'

'Can't let a big mouthed nigger go traipsing all over the place, can I? What if somebody sees her?'

'Who's going to see anything over at your place? Not even a God-damned hound dog strays over that far. Now make up your mind, Grouse. You buying these two quality niggers I brought here tonight or ain't you?'

Scratching his head under the greasy brim of his hat, Grouse said, 'See no reason why not, I guess. Like you say . . .' He dug in his pocket for the money.

Grabbing the payment from Grouse's boney hand, Tucker counted the money and stuck it into his pocket. Then turning to beckon the two blacks waiting in the bushes, he called, 'Come on. Get the lead out of your ass-holes.' He unfurled the whip over his head with a crack.

The two negroes slowly moved from the brush, the chains dragging in the dirt as they clanked toward the wagon. The sick negro still leant on the other.

Seeing that the one negro was not walking correctly, Grouse said, 'Hey! Just a minute! What the hell's the matter with that short one? He don't look too good to me.'

'Good? What do you mean, good? These here are prime niggers.' Tucker quickly snapped his whip at the heels of the lagging negro. He said, 'He just needs a little waking-up, that's all. They've been sleeping. It's the middle of the night, ain't it, when most folks are sleeping?'

'You sure you ain't selling me no ailing niggers, Tucker?'

Quickly pushing both negroes into the bed of the wagon, Tucker said, 'For the money you're paying, Grouse, you can use these two for hog food and you'd still come out ahead of the deal.'

The two negroes were now loaded in the back of the wagon and Tucker did not have to worry about Grouse discovering that one of them was sick. Coming around to the front of the wagon, he said, 'You just do likes I says, Grouse. You gives them their greens and lets that Purvina gets some fresh air now and then. You won't have no troubles with none of them. Like I said before, though, these niggers are your responsibility now. I can't be held responsible for how you treats your niggers.'

Reaching for the reins, Grouse said, 'Just so you ain't selling me no ailing niggers, Tucker. You selling Selby's niggers out from under his nose is one thing. But selling a man sick niggers . . .' Grouse shook his head.

Tucker assured him, 'You got nothing to worry about, Grouse. You just keep your head and you've got nothing to worry about no more. You got a nigger helping your missus in the house. You got two niggers now to do your work in the field. Why, Mister Grouse, to my mind, you're sitting on top of the God-damned world. Just be sures you give your niggers a taste of the whip now and then to keep them working. Feed them their greens. Air them. And then there's only one more thing I want to remind you of, Grouse.'

'What's that?'

'One more thing besides the extra seventy-five dollars you owes me.'

Grouse waited.

'Like I told you, these niggers are yours now. I don't want to hear about them again. I want to forget you have these two niggers understand? As far as Chad Tucker knows, these two niggers runned away from The Star by themselves.' Grinning up at Grouse, Tucker said, 'You know what I'm saying.'

'I know,' Grouse was anxious to leave.

Tucker also was anxious to cut this meeting short. Lightening his tone, he said, 'And remember, Mister Grouse, if you hears of some interested party like yourself, some trustworthy farmers who needs an extra nigger or two, you just lets me know. I ain't in no position to offer much but every now and then I sees where I can spare a nigger or two from The Star. I just might be persuaded to part with a few more.'

'I'll let you know,' Grouse said, moving the wagon.

'You just do that, Mister Grouse. Come time for you to pay me my next seventy-five dollars, you just lets Chad Tucker know about any trusting party like yourself who wants to buy him some cheap niggers.'

Jack Grouse nodded and, switching his dappled horse, he hurriedly began to drive the wagon up the dark road.

'Slow! Slow!' Tucker called in the night. 'You got to learn how to drive niggers, friend! Niggers ain't used to riding like white people are. You drive niggers wrong and they get sick. I don't want you driving them wrong and then cuss me because one of them is sick when you get him home.'

Turning then from the road, Tucker disappeared grinning into the bushes.

Albert Selby went to his bed that night feeling depressed. Under his gruff facade, he was a self-effacing man. He told himself now that if he had been more careful at the auction, he could have found the kind of servant that his wife had wanted, someone younger and more suitable than Ta-Ta.

Selby always spent the nights alone in his bedroom. The only two times in his life that he had shared a bed with his wife (their wedding night not being one of the occasions) were the two instances when Rachel had announced to him that it was time to give the Lord a child.

As many Southern ladies felt the same distaste for sex as Rachel Selby did, it was a custom for their husbands to have a negress to satisfy their sexual urges. But it was even too dangerous for Selby to have a bed wench at The Star. He had to find his satisfaction away from home.

Tonight, however, Selby was prepared to spend another miserable night alone. But he was more sad than usual because he had not seen his daughter. Melissa had already gone to bed when Selby arrived home and his wife had forbad him even to peek into the young girl's room.

Two hours had passed and, regardless of his exhaustion from the journey, Selby still was wide awake. Lying on his feather mattress, he was feeling old and alone when, suddenly, he heard a soft rapping on his door. He feared that it was Rachel coming to abuse him about something that he might have done wrong. Then he heard a voice whisper anxiously, 'Master Selby, Sir! Master Selby!'

It was one of the servants.

Selby did not chance bidding the servant to enter but, hopping out of bed, he hurried across the plank floor of his bedroom in his nightshirt and cautiously opened the door.

Seeing Mama Gomorrah standing in the dark hallway, he quickly looked up and down the hallway to make certain that Rachel was nowhere in sight, and beckoned the old negress into his room.

Albert Selby received his second surprise tonight. Mama Gomorrah led a young child into the room behind her. It was the younger of the two boys whom Selby had bought at the auction.

Setting the child on a straight back chair in the corner, Mama Gomorrah turned to Selby to tell him about her discovery.

Mama Gomorrah tugged at her earrings, the two small silver stars that dangled inside her wild mass of white hair, and began to explain how this child was not a black boy at all. He was a human, a white baby, and she had discovered this because of her silver star earrings.

Ta-Ta had come from the Caribbean island of St. Kitts. Her mistress had been a French lady. Ta-Ta spoke both English and French. The only contradiction between fact and what the auctioneer had promised was that one of the children was not of African ancestry, was not a slave.

The yellow-skinned boy had not been lying. His name was

Monkey. He was the negro of the pair. But the other child was a white baby. He was the son of a French woman. And Ta-Ta had only relinquished him from her arms when Mama Gomorrah had insisted that no human baby could spend the night in the slave quarters. She had to take him up to the big house.

Albert Selby began asking Mama Gomorrah precautionary questions. How was he to know that Ta-Ta was not being cunning? What proof did he have that this was not a clever ploy of Ta-Ta's to get her child out of slavery and raised as a white person? Many half-breeds passed easily for white people. Selby also reminded Mama Gomorrah that it had been obvious that the smaller boy was Ta-Ta's favourite. She could quite easily be lying to help him.

Reaching into her shapeless white dress, Mama Gomorrah produced a rolled piece of parchment from between her sagging bosoms. Selby studied the document in the low light from a lamp and saw that it was a birth certificate. It was signed by the captain of a French ship named the *Therese*. The document was dated two years earlier. There was no doubt about its authenticity.

Mama Gomorrah jigged now with excitement to continue telling Selby the story which had been sparked off by her pair of old silver earbobs.

Ta-Ta had known another negress who wore the same kind of silver stars on her ears. She was a negress who had been sold to a plantation on St. Kitts many years ago. She was a black woman noted for her cooking. She was called Sugar Loaf.

Selby nodded. He had sold a fat wench called Sugar Loaf to the West Indies. He did not usually sell his slaves but he did remember a Frenchman who had offered him a phenomenonally high price for a negress who could cook. The Frenchman had wanted an American negress who was not as familiar with voodoo as the West Indian negroes. The Frenchman had feared that, through the cooking, the negroes on his plantation would try to poison him. And one of the most important things that Selby remembered about that cook called Sugar Loaf, apart from her delicious meals, was that she had been sired at The Star in the days that the slaves' ears were still pierced. Sugar Loaf had been one of the last slaves here to receive the silver ear-marks. The man who had bought her was certainly French, too. His name was . . . Selby could not remember his name. He would not be able to find it in his books, either, because he had never been good at keeping records. But he did remember that it had been a Frenchman from the West Indies who had bought Sugar Loaf.

Selby listened to Mama Gomorrah and learned that Ta-Ta's French mistress had been named Honore Jubiot. The name meant nothing to him. Mama Gomorrah continued by saying that Ta-Ta had told her that Honore Jubiot had later married an Englishman. The Englishman's name was Richard Abdee but, according to Ta-Ta's story, Honore had been unable to live with her new husband. He was too evil. So, she gathered what valuables she could carry from the plantation and fled from St. Kitts two years ago. She had been pregnant at the time.

Honore Jubiot—or Abdee—set sail in 1789 in a French frigate for France but, as it was the height of the Revolution, the captain changed his course to the coast of East Florida in the hopes of joining a convoy of stronger ships.

The *Therese* was still at sea when the first pains of labour struck Honore and, after a day and two nights of agony, she gave birth to a son. He was named Pierre, the son of Richard Abdee of Dragonard Plantation, St. Kitts.

The captain of the *Therese* had been kind to Madame Abdee and her entourage and, on landing in East Florida, he had established them in the home of an American captain whom he trusted. They would have been happy there, living in the captain's home, paying for their lodging by occasionally selling a piece of *faience* taken by Honore from Dragonard.

But Honore had never recovered from her pregnancy. Before the next month had passed, she was overtaken by consumption and soon buried in the marshy ground of East Florida. Ta-Ta was left alone with two children, one who was hers and the other, the son of Honore and Richard Abdee.

Apart from the two children, Ta-Ta had also found herself burdened with the trunksful of treasures which Honore had managed to salvage from her home. Before then, Ta-Ta had borne no responsibility larger than counting how many strokes to brush her mistress's hair. Now she had to be resourceful. She had to begin by hiding as much of the Dragonard treasures that she could. Embarking on a long series of midnight forays into the swamps, Ta-Ta had carried bundles over her back—bags filled with silver and gold and precious stones—and buried them in a secret place to the north of the captain's house.

On the last night of these surreptitious journeys, Ta-Ta had taken the yellow-skinned boy, Monkey, with her to help carry a heavy trunk. Rather than leave the baby alone in the house, she had wrapped him in a shawl and hung him from her back. She had successfully buried that last trunk of treasure and begun to make her way back to the house with the two boys when she was seized.

Mama Gomorrah told Selby that Ta-Ta had not been able to continue too clearly past that point of her story. Ta-Ta was still suffering from the shock of the six men attacking her, a gang of slave-traders who had spotted her and the two boys in the swamp that night.

The most degrading acts of indecency had been taken with Ta-Ta. The slave-traders alternated in raping her and probing into her with blunt wooden objects. This brutality had lasted not only for that one night in the swamps, but all through the next day in the coastal village of Crabstone and the following night in a wayside tavern. Still keeping Ta-Ta as the object of their perversion, they finally spirited her and the two boys away from East Florida and took her in bondage to Louisiana.

Mama Gomorrah had not been able to pry the details of the sexual depravities from Ta-Ta. She was still trying to ease the pain of them in her mind. But Ta-Ta had told Mama Gomorrah that the slave-traders finally sold her to a woman evangelist who, in turn, sold Ta-Ta and the boys to Lynn and Craddock in New Orleans.

Selby listened patiently to the story, often having to stop Mama Gomorrah to make her wipe the saliva from her chin and speak more clearly. When she had finished, Selby sat looking at the birth certificate and then to the child who still sat on the straight-back chair in the corner, his small head drooping with fatigue. Selby said in a low voice, 'You are to tell no one about this. Understand? You are to keep quiet, old woman.'

Mama Gomorrah nodded vigorously. 'Yes, Master Selby Sir. I tells no one.'

Looking back at the slumped body of the boy, Selby continued, 'You did right by bringing him to me.'

'No human baby is meant to live with us niggers, Master Selby, Sir.'

Selby shook his head, studying the tired boy. Such an arrangement would not be right.

'But whats we do with him now, Master Sir?'

'Pierre. That means Peter,' Selby said as if thinking aloud.

Mama Gomorrah crouched on the floor in front of Selby waiting for him to explain his plans. The light from the lamp flickered on her sharp face and made her white hair shine like dewy cotton.

Selby said, 'He will stay here in the house.'

'But what about—' Mama Gomorrah nodded toward Rachel Selby's room.

Selby answered, 'Nobody has much choice. This boy stays here in the house with us.' Looking at Mama Gomorrah, he said, 'But not a word of this to anyone, you understand? Not even to Mrs. Selby. Let me explain this to her my way. You keep your big mouth shut, do you understand?'

She nodded.

'In the meantime, we'll move that Ta-Ta wench up here to the house, too. Storky can find work here for her. And you find some place for that yellow sprout.'

'He's no trouble, Master Selby, Sir. He's nigger to the gut.'

Selby nodded, then let his eyes wander back to the boy sitting on the chair, studying his delicate limbs, how his dark hair fell down to his smooth forehead, his long eye-lashes

69

fanned in sleep over his olive-coloured skin.

Selby asked, 'Did you wash him like I said?'

Mama Gomorrah nodded again. 'Wormed him and everything, Master Sir. But seeing he's white, I ain't got no clothes proper to give him.'

'Clothes are no problem. We can make clothes. The problem now—' Selby hesitated. '—the problem now is where he's going to sleep. I know. You get one of my dress shirts from that chest over there. One of those linen shirts. Put him in one of them. Roll up the sleeves so it fits. Rip them off if you have to. Just something to give him to sleep in for tonight.'

Looking around the large bedroom, Mama Gomorrah saw only one bed. 'Sleeps where, Master Selby Sir?'

Selby walked to the child and, gently reaching to him, he said, 'You don't look too big, little fellow. I bet you don't kick neither. How would you like to share my bed for a night?'

The child moved on the chair. Blinking sleepily up at Selby, he saw a face that was not going to harm him. He reached toward Selby with open hands.

Before Mama Gomorrah left the bedroom, Selby told her one more thing. He told her to remove her silver earrings and never to wear them again. He gave her no reason for doing this but this sternness made her obey. They were to be buried with Ta-Ta's story.

After she had gone, Selby and Peter settled into the same bed. Peter's head sank into the soft pillow and he immediately fell into a deep sleep.

An hour passed and a soft flame still glowed on the bedside table. Selby remained awake. He had forgotten about the fatigue that he had felt earlier. He kept nesting pillows around Peter's small head, tucking the sheet under his chin when he threw it off in a bad dream, brushing the long silky hair from the boy's forehead when it threatened to cover his face.

Selby was happy now.

Chad Tucker had come back to his house and lay now with

his wife in the small lean-to attached to their cabin as a bedroom. He was still excited about selling two negroes to Jack Grouse, and laughing about one of them being sick.

But Claudia Tucker did not share her husband's good mood. Not even the money from the sale made her happy. The moonlight shone through the rag hanging over the small window of the lean-to and lit a pouting expression on her chubby face. She said, 'You go get yourself caught, Chad Tucker, and then what'll I do for a man?'

'I won't get caught. We just keep that log book here in the cabin with us and nobody knows how many niggers are here.'

Claudia twitched her snub nose. 'You be careful.'

Turning over on his side, making the corn-cob mattress crunch as he moved, Tucker said, 'I feel real warm inside knowing you worry about me like that, honey.'

Claudia lay motionless beside him. Her pencil-thin eyebrows slanted as she said, 'I just don't know what I'd do if Selby finds out and sics the law onto you.'

Tucker did not hear what she said. He was thinking again about selling negroes from The Star. He whistled. 'Seventy-five dollars! And another seventy-five in six months' time. And maybe even more if I find me some new buyers.'

Claudia sat bolt upright in bed and, pulling one of the arms of her night-gown back over her shoulder, she said, 'You are just selling all the niggers right off this place, aren't you? You are just selling all the niggers and pretty soon there's not going to be a good buck left in sight. If you're so set on selling niggers, why don't you sell off a few of those black bitches?'

'Aw, honey,' Chad said, pulling her back down beside him. 'Are you still upset I sold that Cal buck tonight?'

Claudia said sharply, 'We had us good times with that Cal buck!'

'But Cal was getting sick, Claudie. Matter of fact, I thought he wasn't going to make it up to the road tonight. He was getting awful sick.' Snuggling his hairy body around Claudia's softness, he said, 'Don't worry. We'll get us a new buck.'

In a weak voice, she said, 'But that Cal buck, he sure was

71

hung big. I doubt if we can ever find us a buck hung as big as that Cal was.'

'Hung big, Claudie, but the rest of him ain't too special.'

'Hung real big,' she insisted.

'Don't worry. We'll get us a new one.'

'Hung as big as that Cal?'

'Hung bigger.'

'And not a lot of stinky old black skin hanging off the end of his pecker like lots of niggers have?'

Tucker agreed, 'Not a lot of black skin. In fact, honey, if there is any skin, I'll hack it right off. Hack it right off with the butcher knife just to make you happy.'

Turning toward her husband, Claudia asked, 'And you'll teach him how to use the hornet. I don't like to be a pig and have everything myself. I loves you, Chad.'

'Teach him anything your little heart desires,' he said, letting his big hand find its way into the neck of her night-gown. He began to fondle her nipples and then pinched them until they were hard. He reached his other hand up the long skirt of the night-gown until he found the warmth between her plump legs. As he joined his fingers together into a large clump and began to move them in and out of the warmth, he teased, 'Feel that new buck poking into your pretty? Feeling him coming to you already?'

'Feeling you in my pretty, Chad. Feeling you there and—' She paused to think.'—feeling you poking around in my pretty and I'm ready to take our new buck in my mouth. I'm opening my mouth wide right now and—'

The moonlight showed Claudia lying with her legs spread apart and her head resting on the pillow with her mouth open. The night-gown was bunched around her waist.

Chad lay on his side facing her. The hair on his broad shoulders and back glistened in the soft light like fur. As he kept moving his clenched fist in and out of her legs, he moved his other hand from her breasts and grabbed for his bull-like penis. He moved that hand back and forth now, too, causing his scrotum to slap against his hirsute thigh as he joined Claudia in her idea about a new black man. 'That's the way, honey. You open your mouth big and wide for our new buck. Go on . . . maybe you won't be able to take the new prick because it's so big.'

Claudia began to breathe through her open mouth. 'His big nuts are resting on my chin now, Chad. I feel them there.'

'That's right. His nuts are pressing down on your pretty little chin while you're taking him in your mouth and I'm on top of you humping away. Feel me humping you hard?'

'I feels you humping me, Chad. You're humping me and I'm sucking that new black pecker and his nuts are pressing against my chin and—'

Chad Tucker now began driving his hips as he lay beside his wife and, protruding his wide buttocks, he said, 'And that new buck's got the hornet in his other hand, ain't he, honey? Just like Cal used to do with the hornet.'

'Just like Cal,' she said. 'Me sucking him and him paddling you with the hornet while you're driving your fat dick into me. Drive your fat dick into me, Chad. Drive your fat dick into me.'

Together, Chad and Claudia Tucker lay like this in the dark of the lean-to built onto their cabin as a bedroom, sharing a vision of the negro who was to replace the slave sold tonight to Jack Grouse.

## Chapter Three

# THE STING OF THE HORNET

The next morning, when Rachel Selby heard that one of the children which her husband had brought home from New Orleans was a white boy, she said, 'Then send him right back where he belongs!'

Albert and Rachel Selby were sitting alone at their breakfast in the dining room. Roland had gone to Troy for liniment and Melissa was dragging Peter around the house like a doll.

Selby answered his wife, 'I'm afraid we can't send the boy away, Rachel. We don't know where he belongs.'

Ladling a spoonful of creamy mush into her mouth, swallowing it as if it were poisonous, then daintily dabbing her pale lips with a stiffly starched napkin, she said, 'Then how do you know he's not just one of those light skinned piccaninnies? What makes you so sure he's—white?' She grabbed for her cup of coffee.

'There are papers,' Selby said with a taint of smugness. 'There are legal papers.'

'Papers? Then, let's see those papers.'

Selby looked down the length of the table at his wife. He said, forcing himself to be firm, 'Rachel, I told you there are papers. I also told you the boy is white. Are you saying now that your knowledge of niggers is better than mine? If you are saying that, then there is no reason for me to go out to the fields anymore. I'll stay here in the house and you can take charge of the fieldhands and the crops and the running of this place.' He knew what he had said was not all true. He seldom went to the fields anymore and he had long ago lost interest in the actual running of The Star. But he did know that Rachel was terrified of the world outdoors and would rather die than to deal with the fieldhands. She was frightened of negro males.

She argued stubbornly, 'If that child is as white as you claim he is, why would a decent parent abandon him? Unless his parents aren't decent and he's—' She forced herself to continue. 'Unless they were not even—' Her black eyes glared from under her ragged brows. '—not even joined in wedlock!'

'Could be, Rachel. Could be. I've heard of such things happening to white folks.'

'Well, what does that make him?'

'Are you condemning a child? A human-being not even grown yet, Rachel?'

She snapped, 'Then what do you have to say about *her*? That wench you brought home for your daughter's companion?'

Selby answered calmly, 'That Ta-Ta wench solves the problem about who takes care of the boy, doesn't she? The child will be no extra burden on you and can't truthfully say that we don't have room enough in the house for her, too.'

Rachel threw down her napkin on the table. 'You go all the way to New Orleans to find a companion for your daughter and then come back home with a slopper for somebody else's . . . illegitimate child! Albert Selby, I've never heard the likes of it.'

Selby nodded his head toward the sound of Melissa playing with Peter in the adjoining parlour. He said, 'Doesn't that mean anything to you? Just listen to little Melly laughing. I haven't heard her—'

Stopping, Selby looked at the two children as they came through the tassled curtains hanging from the arch separating two rooms. Melissa was leading Peter. He was already her new playmate and friend.

Melissa Selby had fair hair like her brother but it hung in natural curls to the shoulders of her pink gingham dress. Her cheeks were round and rosy from the country air. She had stocky legs and plump arms. Not a fat girl, though, she was healthy from the good food coming from the kitchen of The Star.

Even Peter looked healthy this morning. His dark hair was parted on one side, having been neatly combed across his forehead earlier by Selby himself. He wore a plain pair of short white pants and one of Melissa's shirts. On his pudgey feet he wore only a pair of the girl's silk hose rolled down to his ankles.

Also, Melissa had tied a silk ribbon around his neck. It was one of her hair ribbons and from it was suspended a small silver star, one of a pair of the bobs long ago put into the slaves' ears.

'Look, Papa,' she called, running to her father's chair. 'Look what I gave Peter.'

From the other end of the table, Rachel snapped, 'Bring that here, Melissa. Take it off that ribbon right now and bring it to me. Your great-grandfather made those stars.'

Melissa obediently took the small star from the ribbon and gave it to her mother.

Lifting Peter in his arms, Selby beckoned Melissa to come to him, too. He said, 'Wasn't that kind of you, Melly. You're getting to be a real little lady to be so sharing.'

Melissa looked up at her father and said, 'He's my dolly you brought me from your trip, isn't he, Papa?'

Shaking his head, Selby said, 'No, Melly. I think he's a little more than a dolly.'

'Is he a new brother for me?' she asked, looking at the child sitting on her father's lap.

From the other end of the table, Rachel's voice shrilled, 'Albert Selby, this is going too far!'

Selby looked at Peter toying with the blue ribbon around his neck and slobbering onto his shirt as he studied the crease where the star had been. Selby said, 'Melly is only asking questions that she'll be able to answer for herself soon enough, Rachel.' He was intent on leaving matters stand like that for the moment.

Earlier this morning, when Selby had been combing Peter's hair in the big house, preparing him to have breakfast at the

76

family table, Mama Gomorrah was sending Monkey off to the Overseer's shack.

Chad Tucker's wife, Claudia, had been complaining lately to Mama Gomorrah that she did not have a slave to fetch and carry for her, someone who could be the choreboy in their two-room cabin.

Mama Gomorrah knew that white people like the Tuckers were more severe with black people than the planters who actually owned them. The negroes themselves constantly looked for an opportunity to make life difficult for those people they called 'white trash' and Mama Gomorrah's revenge for the Tuckers was to send Monkey to them as a choreboy. He impressed her as being sly.

Claudia Tucker was sitting alone at the table when Monk appeared in the doorway of the cabin. Since her marriage to Tucker six years ago, Claudia had let all signs of curl disappear from her brown hair, wearing it now in a greasy imitation of Mrs. Selby's coiffure, pulled back from her forehead and knotted at the nape of her neck. Whereas Chad Tucker looked young for his thirty-one years, Claudia Tucker appeared older than her twenty-seven. She resented living in the shadow of the Selbys. She hated not having money and, when she did have it, she had no place to go and buy things. Her husband just buried it in the ground.

Claudia Tucker was thinking about the one brightness in her life—a new virile buck to share with her husband—when she suddenly saw the yellow-skinned boy looking through the door at her. She asked, 'What you gawking at?'

Monkey forced a smile. 'That old woman sent me to slop for you.'

'Where's your respect, nigger boy? Ain't you been taught to address decent white folk?'

Lowering his head, he said, 'Yes, Mam.'

'Yes, Miss Tucker, Mam,' she corrected him. 'You call me Miss Tucker, Mam and you call my husband Master Tucker, Sir, understand?'

Monkey nodded.

'What they call you?'

'Monkey . . . Miss Tucker, Mam.'

She grunted. 'I ain't having no monkies around my house. If I let you stay here you're going to be called . . .' She held her head at an angle and thought. 'I'll call you Monk.'

'Yes, Miss Tucker, Mam.'

'I suppose we got to give you a place to sleep here, too,' Claudia said, straightening the skirt of her dress.

Monk shrugged his shoulders. 'I don't know, Miss Tucker, Mam.'

'That's our bedroom there,' she said, nodding to a pair of blue panels hanging over a doorway. Pointing toward the opposite corner, she said, 'You sleep there, back of the cookstove.'

He nodded.

'But what we talking about sleeping for when there's work for you to do. When Master Tucker comes home tonight, I want this dump looking sparkling for him, you understand?' She appraised the dirt floor, the mended furniture, the leaves of withered cabbage lying on the table, the heaps of dirty dishes and greasy pots. This represented many days' accumulation of filth and Claudia had been sitting in the kitchen before Monkey arrived, wondering where she should start. Now that she had a choreboy, though, the cleaning task was solved.

She began, 'Go gather some cookwood and start a fire in the stove. Heaten up some water to wash all them dishes and pots and junk. They go over there on that shelf and if you break one single God-damned thing you get switched on that little black ass of yours, understand, brat? Next, you take that slop bucket there—'

Claudia continued finding work for Monkey to do as the day progressed. She did not speak to him except for giving him more orders. She did not care about him except how he was going to make life easier for her.

All through the day, Monkey—or Monk as he was called now—obediently answered, 'Yes, Miss Tucker, Mam.' 'No, Miss Tucker, Mam.' 'Rightaway, Miss Tucker, Mam.'

Chad Tucker returned to the cabin that evening and assessed

Monk with a quick look. He asked Claudia,' 'Has he given you any sass?'

Claudia said, 'If he did, I'd clout him on that bald head of his, wouldn't I?'

Tucker grunted his approval and slumped down to the table.

They ate their supper of pork and clabber, talking in low voices as Monk stood against the wall behind the cookstove. Claudia quizzed her husband if he had found a replacement for Cal. Tucker asked her if the log-book with the slaves' names in it was safe here with the boy in the house now. He wanted to know if Monk was going to be an intrusion in their life. She longed for some news of another companion for their bed.

After supper, Chad and Claudia Tucker retired from the table and went into the improvised bedroom. Monk was left behind to pick up the pork rinds which the Tuckers had dropped to the floor during their meal.

This was Monk's first chance to eat today. But as he was crawling under the table, chewing what meat he could find on the fat, he heard a giggle come through the faded blue cotton panels and he heard Claudia complain, 'But my arm gets tired holding it!'

Stopping, Monk perked his ears to hear more. He was mature for his age and Claudia's soft voice awakened an adult curiosity in him. All day she had been bossing him and now he heard her speaking softly for the first time. She whined, 'I can't do it, Honey. I just can't.'

'Go on. Try a little,' Tucker coaxed in a deep-throated voice.

Monk knew about sex. He remembered what the slave traders had done to his mother, although Ta-Ta to him was just another black woman. But he had enjoyed watching the burly white men when they had seduced her. Monk wanted to be burly and strong like the slave-traders when he grew older.

Craving to know what Tucker was trying to get Claudia to

79

do, Monk crawled along the dirt floor to peek under the ragged hem on the uneven blue panels.

He was surprised to see such pale whiteness of Claudia's bare thighs. But as he focused more clearly on the bed, he was further surprised to see how fat her thighs were, fat and squashed under the bulk of Chad Tucker like bread dough. Tucker was lying on top of his wife—both of them naked—and, also for the first time, Monk saw a man with hairy legs. The muscles in Tucker's body were strong and they became hard now as he pressed rhythmically on top of his wife. Simultaneously, he was trying to get her to reach her arm around him. She was holding a three-foot-long board in her hand. It was drilled with holes and Tucker was trying to get her to hit him with it on his hirsute buttocks.

Rearing back his groin, Tucker held his furry buttocks in the air, saying, 'You got to use that hornet if you want to feel the sting!'

Claudia whined that the thick paddle was too heavy to hold with one hand. She said that she was feeling enough of him inside her without exciting him to get bigger and thicker. She said he was deep enough inside her. She really wanted a new negro buck.

But Tucker impatiently repeated, 'You won't get any of the sting! We got to get the sting. Try me with the sting, honey, the sting!'

Watching their curious performance with growing fascination, and feeling himself expanding inside his own osnaburgh trousers, young Monk passed under the curtains and slowly approached their bed.

The Tuckers were involved in their predicament and did not notice Monk's nearness to them. But when the hornet was suddenly removed from Claudia's pudgy hand, she looked to see who had taken it. She turned her head and not only saw Monk standing next to the bed but also that he had dropped his pants to the floor and was now exhibiting a masculine proportion that surpassed that of her husband, an excitement the size of an extraordinarily developed adult.

80

Claudia gasped. 'Nigger? What you doing in here with that prick? You're supposed to be out there with that dishpan!'

But when Chad looked at the young intruder, he saw that Monk had not come into the bedroom with any ordinary curiosity. Tucker realized that the boy was already caught up in the mood of the occasion. That, without any invitation, he was already one of them.

While they were still looking at him with astonishment, Monk had agilely taken the hornet from Claudia's hand and was now beginning to rub its smoothly planed surface against the hirsute skin of Tucker's naked buttocks.

Chad looked down at his wife and shrugged. Already, he was wiggling his bare buttocks against the gentle revolves of the wooden paddle, as if he were teasing it into further action.

Claudia Tucker, in turn, relented and reached for Monk's premature maleness. Grasping it in her hand, she began to squeeze the black skin, gripping the swollen oiliness as she simultaneously resumed pumping her hips again.

As Chad Tucker resumed his rhythmic drives into his wife, his buttocks began to slap against the paddle which Monk still held against his rising movements. But as Chad's thrusts drove harder and harder into Claudia, Monk began to move the paddle downwards. He began to bring the paddle—the hornet—against Tucker's buttocks in harder and harder strokes, causing his skin to become a bright red, the colour even showing through the thick mat of curly black hair covering his buttocks.

Soon, Monk was using both of his hands to wield the hornet, slaming Tucker's posterior with the paddle as he drove deeper into his wife. He was giving her what he called his 'sting'.

Both the Tuckers were a stream of perspiration by the time that Chad Tucker started to shout, 'Getting it? Getting it?' He arched his wide shoulders as his wife tore at his skin with her crooked fingers. They were reaching their crest of excitement as Monk steadily increased the forces of the slaps from the perforated paddle.

But it was not until Monk sensed that Chad Tucker was at his highest point—was shouting the loudest—that he let go with the hardest slap of all, the slap that he had to use both hands on the paddle to deliver. With the contact of that hard blow against Tucker's red buttocks, Tucker drove deep into his wife, giving a loud shout that shook the small cabin and Claudia screamed at the top of her lungs, 'Stop!'

Then, as Chad and Claudia Tucker both collapsed together in a silent heap on their corn cob mattress, Monk drew himself closely up to their cohesion of white flesh. Claudia barely had the energy now to turn and look at the sight of Monk's stiff maleness bobbing above her husband's shoulder, near her own face. She moved to brush Monk away from them.

Chad Tucker objected. 'Go on. Take him.' He turned, eyeing the excitement close to his own face. 'He's about ready to pop anyway.'

Claudia Tucker reluctantly brushèd the hair back from her sweaty forehead and, leaning forward, she opened her mouth to take the flow of white warmth from her new choreboy. And as Monk burst over her lips, Tucker watched the explosion and marvelled, 'That's a load. That's a real load.' Then looking to his wife's working cheeks, he coached, 'Take the pudding, honey. Take the pudding.'

Afterwards, Claudia said briskly to her husband, 'If you think he's going to take the place of that Cal buck, you're crazy! I ain't pestering with no kid! I want a MAN nigger!'

Tucker ignored his wife's complaint, ordering Monk to go back to the kitchen and start washing the supper dishes. He said, 'If you steps out of line, brat, I'll use that hornet on *you*!'

Monk answered, 'Yes, Master Tucker, Sir.'

## Chapter Four

# NIGGERTOWN

The slave quarters of The Star were called Niggertown. They had been built by Peregrine Roland at a site one mile from the big house to keep away the musky stench of the Africans.

Niggertown consisted of two long rows of run-down cabins built from the logs cut from the surrounding land. A second and shorter row of houses set back from the main dwellings. These were the original slave hovels built on The Star and were still in use almost a hundred years later.

The Star was a thickly wooded plantation. A virgin pine forest still surrounded Niggertown, a small community of steep-roofed shacks, a dusty main road, and an abundance of yellow dogs nosing for scraps.

Chad Tucker and his wife lived between Niggertown and the big house.

The only other dwelling on The Star was the building called The Shed which acted as a nursery for the children born by the slaves.

Although The Star had not set out to be a breeding plantation, or thought of itself as one now, it was inevitable that children would be born here and all infants were taken away from their mothers two weeks after birth to prevent any maternal affections developing.

Mama Gomorrah was in charge of The Shed and under her tutelage the children of The Star learned to hoe, weed and, in general, to be useful until they could be put to work in the fields, the looming houses, the barns or the pens.

Work such as looming, carding, spinning took place in an

old barn near the livestock pens. These set back from The Shed. Mostly female slaves were sent to The Barn to learn their vocations on The Star, but both young girls and boys learned about cotton—how to 'drop' the plants into the ground and to tend the rows.

Mama Gomorrah always looked for a job which she felt suited a child. She did not know how right she had been in sending Monk to the Overseer's cabin.

The Tuckers had now accepted Monk as one of themselves.

In the big house, Peter was easily fitting into the schedule of family life on The Star.

It was Ta-Ta who was failing to find a niche for herself.

But Albert and Rachel Selby had more serious problems now than to worry about Ta-Ta—Roland Selby had run away from home.

Roland had given no hint that he was going to leave The Star. His mother and father had not suspected that he was unhappy at home. One morning, he did not come down to breakfast—two weeks after he had returned from New Orleans with his father.

Both Albert and Rachel Selby feared that Roland might have gone out for an early morning ride and had hurt himself in an accident. They knew, too, that Roland liked to go looking at a nearby freak of the countryside called Walley Caverns. He often sat on the rocky rim of the chasm to think.

In his worst moment of despair, Albert Selby remembered Ta-Ta's story of being seized by slave traders. But he seriously doubted that red-headed Roland could be sold as a negro.

It was not until Selby began combing the countryside that he stopped at the cabin of an older settler and finally learned the true reason for Roland's mysterious disappearance from The Star.

The old settler, Hiram Bodean, told Selby that the Witcherley family was also looking for a runaway. He said that the Witcherleys were looking for a girl.

Drawing on his clay pipe, Hiram Bodean creaked back and forth in his cherry-wood rocker on the porch of his house and said, 'Seems a queer coincidence, don't it? Two runaways in one week. A Witcherley girl and a Selby boy. Both in secret.'

Selby knew then that his son had not had an accident, had not been thrown from his horse or been seized by gypsy traders.

Much worse had happened. Roland Selby had betrayed his family by eloping with a Witcherley girl.

Albert Selby loved his son but he hoped that he would never see him again.

And Roland did not return to The Star.

This was painful for Selby. But he was glad to be spared what he might do to Roland if they were to meet again.

Rachel Selby crossed her son's name from the family Bible and, when Melissa asked for her brother, the subject was quickly changed. Rachel Selby even went as far as to draw Melissa's attention to Peter rather than let her pursue a conversation about the Selby who had eloped with a Witcherley.

But soon Melissa stopped asking for Roland, contented to play with Peter who was closer to her own age.

Peter became more popular with Selby, too. As the boy grew older, he was able to go riding with Selby, sitting in front of him on the saddle.

Selby liked to explain to Peter about the plantation. He taught the growing boy about the cotton plants—the black-seed, long staple cotton that was found on the lower fields of The Star. Selby also explained about the other kind of cotton, the green seed plants which had been difficult to clean until recently. Selby told Peter that a Yankee named Eli Whitney had invented a machine which could clean the green cotton—a cotton gin—and that if it proved to work satisfactory, The Star would grow very rich. Green cotton flourished in the back fields of The Star.

Peter was only a child but a good student. He listened intently as Selby spoke and waited until he had finished before asking any questions. Selby knew that he was going to be a level-headed person.

Peter's body also began to improve. His arms and legs strengthened and the fresh air had given his olive-coloured skin a sheen. His straight black hair was glossy and his eyes, a bright cornflower blue.

When Peter was six-years-old, it was obvious that he was going to be a slim but good-looking boy and Selby felt proud that he had made the decision to keep the child.

Unlike Roland, Peter did not call Selby 'Pa'. He called him 'Father'. The propriety of the title seemed to alleviate the fact to Selby that he had no blood ties with the boy. Peter learned to address Rachel Selby as 'Mrs. Selby', but always more warmly than she ever spoke to him.

There was only one trait in young Peter which Selby did not appreciate. But he had nobody to blame for it but himself as it was in their rides around the plantation that Selby had first allowed him to play with a leather riding crop.

Peter loved to hear the whistle of the riding crop as he slashed it through the air. At first, his happy laugh warmed Selby, a laughter that tumbled out of Peter's mouth as he swung the crop back and forth. But later Selby became worried when Peter hit the black children with the crop, running into a group of children who were pulling weeds around the house and chasing them in all directions.

Castigating Peter as gently as possible for playing so roughly with the crop, Selby warned him that they did not whip people here on The Star. Selby tried to teach Peter that it was not right to hurt the negroes that way, telling him that if he hurt negroes then they could not work. It was bad.

Childishly protesting that he was only playing a game, Peter did not sulk for long and, when he started swinging the crop again, it was against a gardenia bush. The bush was more fun to whip than the children. The bush sprang back at Peter and did not run away. Peter soon forgot about whipping negro children.

One afternoon in his sixth year, Peter was playing contentedly in the back yard of the big house with the riding crop, slapping it into the ground and watching the dust rise in clouds.

Suddenly, Ta-Ta appeared from what seemed to be nowhere and she snatched the crop from his hand and shrilled, 'Dragonard! No! No! No! No!'

Surprised to see Ta-Ta outside the house, Peter looked up at her face and his cornflower-blue eyes widened with fear.

Ta-Ta was relentless with him, shaking him by his small shoulders and scolding, 'Not like your father. No! No! No! No!'

Peter had barely spoken to Ta-Ta in the last four years. He and Melissa had often sneaked up to the top of the house and tried to peek at Ta-Ta in her attic room. When they saw her sitting in a rocking chair, they would run laughing down the stairs. Ta-Ta seldom came down to the main part of the house anymore and Peter thought that she was a witch.

Confused by her words now, as well as not knowing how or why she had come down here to the yard, Peter broke from her grasp and ran for the only father he knew—Albert Selby —the man who took him riding and taught him about The Star.

'See that?' Chad Tucker asked Monk.

Tucker and Monk had been walking on a wooded path which cut behind the big house and seen Ta-Ta snatching the riding crop from Peter.

Monk kicked at a wood chip as he strolled alongside Tucker. Walking with his hands tucked inside the waist string of his baggy white pants, he still smirked at the spectacle of Peter and Ta-Ta. To Monk, Peter and Ta-Ta were just a white boy and an old wench. The last four years had made Monk part of the Tucker's life. He had not seen much of the big house but, from what he had seen, he knew that he was happier living with the Tuckers in their shack.

Everything about the big house and Albert Selby angered Chad Tucker, though. He was still irritated about the idea of growing green cotton on The Star. It not only meant more work for him but Selby was talking about organizing a special gang of workers for planting green cotton. Tucker feared that such an action might mean an exact count of the slaves. In the last four years, Tucker had secretly sold twenty-three black people from The Star. Monk had been helping him lately in these late night sales, too.

Chad Tucker contaminated The Star; his presence here brought an evilness to this land like a hurricane carried havoc and destruction.

He was always quick to belittle Selby and his household when he could. He now said to Monk on the path, 'That old nigger wench was drunk as a coot.'

'What's she drunk from?'

'Whiskey. Selby gives it to her. I know.'

Keeping his eyes to the path, Monk asked, 'Why's the niggers at the big house allowed to drink whiskey but down in Niggertown they gets in trouble if they even sniffs a jug of corn?'

'Because niggers up here are supposed to be special,' Tucker sarcastically explained. 'These are house niggers!' He spit.

'What's me then?'

'You're kind of a special house nigger yourself, boy. You're special because you were assigned to me.' Tucker strutted now with his own importance. He boasted, 'And when I gets through teaching you about whipping and selling niggers, boy, you'll be the most special nigger on this whole God-damned plantation.'

Monk was fourteen years old now and, although he was not as tall as Chad Tucker, he was much bigger than the other black boys his own age on The Star. Monk's broad shoulders were already capped with muscle and his biceps were round with strength from the four year's work that he had been doing with Tucker.

A life outdoors had given Monk's skin the glossy colour of amber. His coarse hair was still closely cropped against his skull, leaving a straight black line above his almond-shaped eyes and prominent cheekbones. Monk was developing the brutish perfections of a fine physique. He also was becoming an ambitious young man. He wanted to make something out of himself and he suspected that Chad Tucker could help him to do it.

Monk said to Tucker now, 'Guess I am pretty special if I gets to go selling niggers with you at night, Master Tucker, Sir.'

'Shhh!' Tucker said, looking around him at the afternoon shadows in the forest. 'I told you not to mention that, you crazy bastard. If old man Selby even hears I got me a little business on the side he'll turn me into the law.'

Looking cautiously around him, Monk said, 'I didn't mean no harm, Master Selby, Sir.'

'I know you didn't, boy. But you got to be careful all the time.'

The two men continued walking quietly until Tucker asked, 'What would you like to do tonight? We got us those two bucks spotted—' he looked carefully around him now in the woods. 'We got those bucks, Priam and Toby, almost ready to sell to George Gresham. Do you want us to go scare them alittle more? Or would you rather we go down to Niggertown and get us some poontang for sharing?'

The idea of finding some 'poontang', a lusty young black girl, excited Monk now. But he knew that if he chose to go to Niggertown after a girl tonight, Chad Tucker would insist on joining him. Lately, as Monk had been finding his way around the plantation, he was discovering that he had a better time with a female without Tucker being there, too. Laying alone with a wench seemed to be more natural to Monk. He was losing interest in the threesomes that he had with Chad and Claudia Tucker in their shack. And going 'poontanging' with Tucker was not different than what they did with Claudia— Chad Tucker always selfishly insisted on riding the woman while Monk had to wait to take the wench when Tucker had finished with her, or, sometimes, Monk just had to let his excitement explode in the girl's mouth while Tucker was sprawled in the place where Monk wanted to be. Also, the prospect of using the perforated paddle on Tucker's bare buttocks as he was lying astride a girl filled Monk with little excitement. He knew, too, that Tucker was wanting more than the hornet from him now. Although Tucker had not come right out and asked Monk for it as of yet, he knew by Tucker's constant references to the size of Monk's masculinity, and how Tucker had been squeezing his hirsute buttocks lately when Monk was paddling him, that he wanted Monk to do something that disgusted him, an act between two men that had nothing to do with true manhood.

But Monk also knew that he had little freedom in what he did on The Star. He realized that, as long as he kept Chad Tucker happy, humouring his selfish whims, his own life would be easy. Monk did not want to be sent to work for long hours in the fields, or given one of the menial jobs in the stables or the storehouses. The Tuckers were Monk's protectors on The Star and, to get what he wanted, he had to play dumb to Tucker's perverse insinuations and hope that he could find a wench for himself when the Tuckers were not closely observing him.

Trying to sound excited now by Tucker's two suggestions, Monk answered, 'I think we should go scare Priam and Toby some more. I think I gots a lot to learn from you about whipping . . . Master Tucker, Sir.'

Tucker beamed under the praise from the young boy. Whether he realized it or not, he had allowed himself to become more friendly with a negro than he would openly admit. 'I'll teach you all I can. But the next thing we have to do is try and get you a nice pair of leather boots. Just like mine,' he said, looking down at his own shiny black boots which stopped just short of the round caps of his knees.

The idea of getting boots instantly appealed to Monk. To have a pair of boots—even shoes—would move him one more notch up above the other slaves. He said, 'I sure would like my own boots, Master Tucker, Sir.'

Tucker continued loftily, 'Breaking in slaves, a man needs himself a good pair of boots. Boots are as important to a man as his whip.'

Monk knew that Tucker liked to talk about whipping almost as much as he actually liked doing it. The subject excited him like sex.

Tucker continued to explain his own peculiar ideas of discipline to Monk as they walked between the banks of ferns spilling onto the path. 'See, boy, first of all, you get your slave to go and fetch the whip for you. And then when he brings the whip to you—bringing it to you in his mouth like a no-good dog—you take it from him and make him *kiss* it. That's right. You make your slave kiss it. Kiss the whip right on the handle where you'll be holding it when you're whipping the dirty bastard. Then, you make your slave get right down on the dirt and kiss the toes of your beautiful boots. And if your boots are just a little bit dusty, or has some muck on them, you make your slave clean your boots for you before you give him the privilege of feeling the sting of your whip.'

Tucker spoke now as if he were in a spell. 'Yeah, boy, leather boots are as important to a master as a whip when he's breaking in a slave. You bet. That's what makes a man feel like a real master—a pair of boots and his whip. Not a—' He laughed scornfully. '—not some damned *hornet* like old Selby says to use on a slave.'

'Where you learns so much about being a master, Mister Tucker, Sir?' Monk asked earnestly.

Tucker laughed softly as he rubbed his hand over the blueish shadow of a beard showing on his cleft chin. 'It just comes naturally, boy. It just comes naturally to you if you're man enough.'

Monk laughed, too. 'I sure sees you treating those niggers like you man enough.'

The role of playing teacher appealed to Tucker. He bragged, 'You hears them niggers calling me their "master" don't you, boy?'

Monk nodded, remembering how Tucker mistreated the black people in Niggertown. They had no choice but to call Tucker whatever title he told them to call him. They were frightened of the consequences.

Tucker continued, 'Course, old man Selby, he would split a gut if he knew who those niggers call the real master on this place. But none of those niggers will go telling Selby about it because they know what they'd get from me if they did. They'll get whipped and then sold!'

'Those niggers won't tell on you, Mister Tucker, Sir. They do only whats you tells them to do. You can makes them say or do anything you wants and they do it withouts telling Selby.'

Planting his arm warmly around Monk's naked shoulder again, Tucker walked along, saying, 'I learned a lot about mastering from my Daddy. My Daddy wasn't what hi-faluting people like your Selbys would call a respectable citizen. My Daddy first came to this country instead of going to prison back home in England. The judges back in England gave my Daddy a choice of going to jail for killing a man over there or to come here to work in America!'

'Some choice!' Monk scoffed.

Chad Tucker grinned in agreement. 'And it was my Daddy who told me, "Son, what you make of yourself in life is what you make people call you. If you let a man get away with calling you shit, then shit is what you're going to be for the rest of your days." Yes, it was my very own Daddy who first taught me to be called master. People who ain't master is shit, he says, and they gets to be treated that way.'

Monk sobered. 'Being black, course, I ain't got no Daddy to teach me such things.'

Tucker looked quickly at Monk and, before he realized what he was saying, he blurted, 'What the hell? You got me!'

Monk nodded. 'Sure, Mister Tucker, Sir. Mighty grateful for you, too. But I'm still black.'

After thinking momentarily, Tucker said, 'Who knows, boy? You might have a Daddy almost as good as my Daddy was. No saying you don't have any black blood in you. I can't say you ain't a nigger. But by the yellow colour of your skin, you're not hundred percent nigger. You must have *some* human blood in you. So, who knows? you might have a Daddy who gives you that light colouring. You know you wouldn't be the first one!'

The idea of having a father delighted Monk. He walked taller now, proud that he might have a father somewhere in the world, a person he did not even know existed. But the idea of having a mother did not enter Monk's mind. Who cared about the woman who had birthed him? He did not know where his mother was nor did he want to know. He only thought about men and manhood because that's what he wanted to be—a man!

Soon, as Monk and Chad Tucker came out of the woods at the crest of the knoll, they saw Claudia Tucker waiting for them in the doorway of their small shack nestled among the Chinaberry trees in a dirt basin. She idly kicked at the chickens pecking around her feet in the doorway as she examined a sore on the knuckle of her left hand.

Tucker stopped and, staring wistfully down at the dilapidated cabin, he dropped his arm from Monk's shoulder and said, 'Lucky to have me a good woman like my Claudie, I am. A man needs himself a good woman, too, a woman who's willing to give him every day of her life. Just like my Claudie.' Then, moving his bottom lip under his front teeth, he tightened his mouth to shrill a whistle at her as he began lumbering down the slope to the cabin.

Looking up at the sharp sound of the whistle, Claudia stood by the door and began to wave at the two men.

Following closely behind Tucker, Monk's heart beat fast as he wondered what Chad would do if he knew that his treasured Claudie lately had been trying to entice him alone into the woods at night. He wondered if Chad Tucker suspected that Claudie—like Monk—was also getting tired of being three in a bed. That she was trying to tempt Monk into pleasuring her without Tucker taking part in the arrangement. That she was trying to get Monk to bed with her when Tucker was not in the cabin.

Standing in the doorway, Claudie called, 'Got something cool for my two workers to drink, I do!'

93

'Want something more than a cool drink,' Tucker answered as he thumped passed Claudia into the shack, squeezing one of her pendulous breasts as he went in front of her.

Claudia's eyes momentarily followed her husband into the cabin and, then, looking at Monk following closely behind him, she arched herself so he could pinch her, too.

But Monk knew that he could not take such liberties with a white woman, even if that white woman and her husband did include him in their marital arrangements. Being a slave, Monk still had to address Tucker with proper respect and he certainly could not go around pinching a white woman, even if that white woman seemed to want such liberties taken with her.

As Monk passed in front of Claudia, she reached out her pudgey arm and quickly squeezed him in the bulging crotch of his pants, following her obscene gesture with a surreptitious wink and a whisper, 'Big, black prick!'

Monk was the most potent negro buck that Claudia Tucker had ever known.


Ta-Ta sat in her attic room these days and saw the world below her. She saw the distant furrows of the upper fields and the black people picking their way down the rows of cotton in the lower fields. She saw the roofs of Niggertown and saw the treetops of the forest.

In the far distance, Ta-Ta saw the public road which led to Troy and, at night, she often saw lanterns moving by the road in the dark and she could see the lights in Tucker's cabin.

From Ta-Ta's attic room high in the big house, she could also see the yard directly below her. She had watched Peter slowly becoming part of the Selby family. Ta-Ta often thought that she was watching him forgetting who he really was. She had to act as his guardian angel when she saw him becoming friends with a whip like his father. The Dragonard.

Ta-Ta's memories of Dragonard were too strong to forget.

94

They often became so intense for her that she had to scream them out of her head.

The rum helped to ease her pain of remembering too much. When she had first come to this attic room, there had been a demijohn of rum in one corner. It belonged to her new master, Albert Selby. Now, every three days, he left a bottle of rum outside the door for her. Albert Selby never troubled her by talking so she knew he was a good man.

Cradling the rum between her legs, Ta-Ta sat in her rocking chair and stared at the world beneath her. But instead of seeing pine trees and cotton fields and wagon trains moving slowly to the cotton gin in Troy, some days she saw rolling sugar fields and the drooping fronds of palmetto trees and flocks of kisk-idees flying across a blue sky with sea-swept clouds. She saw the island of St. Kitts.

Ta-Ta had found a box of wax crayons setting on the stairs and, taking them into her room, she had set about to draw the good things on her wall. She drew her mistress's bed. She made a rough outline of the mirror and dressing table. She had used a yellow crayon to colour her mistress's long hair.

Every morning now, Ta-Ta stood behind the picture of her mistress on the wall and pretended to be brushing her hair just as she used to do. Her mistress was Honore Jubiot. Somedays, Ta-Ta would fasten an opal necklace around her mistress's slim neck.

Ta-Ta's crude drawings covered more and more space on the walls of her room at The Star. When her memories became fierce, she drew outlines of the men who had stolen her from East Florida and then she punished them for doing it. She beat the walls which had the pictures of the men who had hurt her.

The memory of their masculinity was stuck in Ta-Ta's mind and she drew phalluses between the men's legs and then she slashed those monstrous things with a red crayon—blood.

Ta-Ta had many good and many bad things to live with now and they all surrounded her on the walls. The dressing mirror. A hymnal. The opal necklace. The packing trunks. A baby with the name Pierre. Her mistress dying. The phallus. Ropes that coiled like snakes. The whip that bit like a dragon's tongue. Dragonard. She had drawn them all on the walls in the attic room at The Star.

# Chapter Five

## TRAPS

The manor houses of the American South were worlds within themselves, domains set off from the activity in the other parts of the plantation. They often existed in total ignorance of what the slaves and hired white help did in their own private hours.

The social exchanges between the families of the big houses flourished mostly at church gatherings, picnics, and barbecues, all entertainments organized exclusively for the planters.

Apart from those meetings, another occasion on which the Southern families assembled was for what they called a 'crush' or a ball. When the houses were large enough, the guests would be invited to stay overnight, or even for the entire weekend.

But when the houses were small, or the owners did not like entertaining on such a grand scale, then those socials were really not more than what could be honestly termed as a 'supper'.

Rachel Selby, steeped in her strict religious heritage, saw fit to open the doors of The Star for a supper but nothing larger. The idea of entertaining guests overnight in her house was unthinkable. She had known of white men performing lewd acts at night, respectable hosts even offering negro girls as bed wenches to the male visitors for the duration of their stay, and she certainly was not going to have any activities like that festering under her roof. A supper would have to suffice for her husband's friends.

Being a teetotaller, Rachel Selby denied her supper guests alcohol. Whenever gentlemen came to The Star, it was Selby who saw that there was a plentiful supply of corn whiskey stashed outside in the stables, waiting for them when they felt like a walk in the evening air. But, ostensibly, the Selbys served a non-alcoholic punch at their parties, a pink and often overly sweet beverage called 'strawberry shrub' made from a recipe which Rachel Selby had inherited from her august forebearers.

Regardless of how many opportunities that Rachel had to ruin the gaiety of a supper at The Star, the neighbouring planters accepted the invitations out of their fondness for Albert Selby.

There was only one man who refused to come to The Star's supper. He was Judge Tom Antrobus, Selby's oldest friend and confident, as well as his legal advisor. Judge Antrobus had an innate distrust for anybody who was a descendant of Peregrine Roland and always preferred to meet Selby away from The Star. He hated that land.

Five days before the night of the supper at The Star, the rooms had been chosen for entertaining and the work had begun on them. Double coats of Beardsmore wax was applied to the mahogany flooring. The two chandeliers lowered and polished. The Oriental carpets taken outside to be beaten and left to breathe in the shade of the elms, safeguarding the rich burgundy, yellow, and blue dyes against bleeding in the direct heat of the sun.

The portieres in the parlours were held back from the tall windows by black children while negresses balanced themselves on tall ladders as they shined the large panes of rippled glass.

The three best services of dishes—a set of pale blue Sèvres, one of yellow-and-green Doulton, and full service of white Federal—were all carefully arranged on the long walnut dining table to be counted, then carried into the kitchen where they were washed and dried, and finally brought back into the dining-room and set on the sideboard in neat piles of twelve for serving.

While the activities progressed at a feverish pitch in the dining-room and the two adjoining parlours, preparations moved at a similar pace in the kitchen.

The Star's head cook was a tall, proud Ashanti woman who,

because of her height and lofty attitude, had long-ago been named Storky. So great was her importance at The Star that the other negroes all called her 'Miss Storky'.

It was with Storky that Rachel carefully went over the menu for supper, being reassured by the calm-mannered cook that some of the dishes had been started and the ingredients for the rest were all at hand in the larder or the spring-house.

The supper guests would be able to choose from large platters of honey-cured ham, cinnamon pork, fried chickens, roast turkeys, plus a variety of roasted, stewed, and hickory-dried beef. There would be sweet yams and molasses-beans, three varieties of fresh greens, a large crystal compote of seasonal fruit and, apart from the five kinds of bread, Storky would oversee the baking of four different cakes, date and walnut loaves, ginger cookies, as well as mixing a double batch of raisin pudding and making raspberry blancmange. The condiments, including the apple-and-date chutney, were also the products of Storky's busy kitchen.

In addition to her usual kitchen helper, Storky was given the authority to send to Niggertown for any extra women or men she needed to assist her both in the preparation of the supper and the actual serving of the small feast, as well as the extra cleaners for the house.

The big house had two parlours on the first-floor which were swept and polished as thoroughly as any room on the ground floor for the supper. One was a modest sized sitting-room painted blue in which the ladies could gather in privacy. The second was an adjoining parlour where Melissa would lie and talk to the ladies.

Melissa was ten-years-old now, too young to attend a supper. But a couch was to be made-up in that second upstairs parlour where Melissa could receive family friends. She would be covered by a patchwork quilt—it was a *Star of the Night* pattern, a design passed onto her by her grandmother on her mother's side—which Melissa had pieced together with her own hands.

The biggest problem of this year's supper was what to do with Peter. Like Melissa, he was not old enough to be included in the actual party and, as he was not an heir of the Selby family, Rachel saw no reason why he should be included at all.

Albert Selby respected his wife's wishes that Peter should not have an active part in the evening. But, as the event was still five days away, Selby set himself the task of thinking of a way in which Peter should not be banished completely from the supper at The Star.

As preparations for the supper progressed in the big house, Claudia Tucker was making plans of her own in the overseer's cabin.

Claudia had decided that the time had come for her to be alone in bed with Monk. In her eleven years of being married to Chad Tucker, Claudia had never been to bed with another man—without Tucker being in bed with them, too—and she decided that now was the time to do it.

Chad Tucker had gone to the upper fields this morning to supervise the new hoeing for green cotton. Claudia was alone in the cabin now with Monk.

Sorting through the tin plates stacked on the shelf, Claudia suddenly threw them all to the dirt floor in a loud clatter.

Monk looked up with surprise from the axe head he was soaking in a bucket of water.

'A pig wouldn't eat off these plates,' Claudia screamed, kicking at the pile with her bare foot. 'They've got gobs of food stuck all over them. Gobs and gobs. And it's disgusting for a white lady to eat off them.'

Monk continued to look at Claudia in bewilderment. Since he had been accompanying Tucker around the plantation, he had not been doing his house chores. Although Monk had not been told explicitly that his role had changed in the Tuckers' household, he had understood that it had. Claudia had been doing the cooking and washing and cleaning and slopping the pigs.

Coming to stand over Monk, Claudia put her hands on her

hips and asked, 'What do you think you're trying to get away with?'

Monk blinked.

'Don't try to be all sexy with me, nigger. Just because you're young and sexy, don't mean I'm just going to let you get out of your work around here, cause I'm not!'

Looking at the plates spread on the floor, Monk said, 'Master Tucker don't tells me—'

Pulling back her bare foot to kick him, Claudia said, 'Don't give me none of that "Master Tucker" shit, nigger. I'm the mistress of this house. Don't you forget that.'

Monk had not seen Claudia in a bad mood like this for a very long time. He felt helpless. He did not know what had caused it. He had seen Claudia herself wash the plates this morning after breakfast.

'And stop looking up my skirt to see my pretty.'

Monk's mouth fell open.

Planting both of her bare feet on the floor in front of him, Claudia shrilled, 'Okay, nigger. If you want to see my pretty then look at it.' She lifted her skirt. 'Go ahead, look!'

Slowly, leaning back from her, Monk said slowly, 'I'm sorry, Mistress Claudia Mam. I'm sorry if you think I means trouble. I don't means no trouble with you, Miss Claudia Mam.'

'Don't lie to me. Say it! Say you want to screw that pretty little thing there.' She pulled her dress over her head now and threw it to a corner.

Monk tried not to look at her flabby body. He tried to focus on her angry face. He shook his head, protesting, 'No, Miss Claudia Mam. You don't hears me right. I don't says nothing at all likes that.'

'You don't have to say it. I sees it in your eyes, nigger. I sees in your eyes how you want me.'

Monk looked quickly over his shoulder. He did not want Chad Tucker to catch them like this. Tucker might misunderstand.

Standing over him, Claudia said, 'Are you going to screw me or not?'

Looking up from the floor at her face—framed by her pendulous white breasts—Monk began to understand what she was doing. She was threatening him.

'Nigger?' she said, arching one of her pencil thin eyebrows.

He nodded.

'Nigger, I'm a white woman.'

He nodded again.

'And anything I say is gospel truth, nigger. Understand that much?'

He nodded.

'If I say you want to screw me, you want to screw me.'

He did not nod in agreement to that.

'And if I runs out of here yelling and screaming that you ripped off my dress and tried to rape me, you'd get your balls chopped off. Just like that!' She snapped her fingers, then continued maliciously, 'I'm a white lady, nigger, and what I say is true. Other white folks believe *me*. Not niggers. I'm a white lady. I'm white.'

Monk murmured, 'Yes, Miss Claudia, Mam.'

Claudia continued in a softer voice, 'Now, I want you to get off that God-damned floor and I want you to drop down your pants and—' Looking quickly around the cabin, she said, '—and I want you to stand up on that chair over there by the table.'

Monk hesitated.

'Get up.'

Monk slowly rose to his feet and his hands fumbled to untie the rope around his waist. His pants then fell to the floor in a white heap.

Walking quickly around him, Claudia slammed the cabin door and said, 'Now what did I tell you to do, nigger?'

'To get on that chair.'

'Right. So hop to it.'

Monk hurried and took one of the wooden chairs from under the plank table. Climbing up onto the seat, he watched Claudia as she slowly walked toward him, her breasts swinging from side to side.

She studied his naked body and said, 'I thought we'd go to bed but I think now I likes it this way. Yes, being I has to teach you, boy, I think I likes it this way for the time-beings.'

Standing in front of the chair, she reached to take Monk's maleness in her hands. Holding it, she said, 'So you're the pecker that wants to go pushing into my pretty, are you?' She was looking at it as she spoke.

Monk stood quietly above her. He did not know if he was meant to answer her question. Claudia had never talked to his penis before. Nor had her husband.

Moving her face closer to Monk's crotch, she asked, 'Are you? Are you the prick that's after Claudie's little wet pretty? Are you?'

Monk was a healthy young man and he could not control himself from becoming hard with her fondlings.

Smirking as she watched the penis grow in size, Claudia said, 'I thought so. I thought you were after little Claudie's wet patch. But just to teach you a lesson—'

She quickly lifted Monk's penis and, opening her mouth wide, she lunged for his scrotum. Holding up his penis in one hand, using the other to stuff his soft brown sac into her mouth, Claudia buried her mouth into his crotch. When she had secured his entire scrotum in her mouth, she slowly tightened her lips.

Monk felt Claudia's teeth clamp around the roots of his testicles. His penis wagged in hardness across Claudia's face but he could still see the evilness in her eyes. They were open and staring up at him.

Suddenly releasing him, Claudia pulled back her head and, wiping her mouth on her bare arm, she said, 'See how easy it'd be to nut you, boy.'

He nodded. His phallus was like a rod jutting out from his well-muscled body but he still felt the sensation of her biting teeth.

She continued, 'And niggers get nutted if a white lady like me says they tried to rape them.' Cupping both hands under her breasts and arching her back at Monk, she added, 'And if

103

you *don't* lay me, boy, don't think I won't say that.'

She suddenly turned and, with one quick swipe of her arm, she swept everything from the table. 'We ain't got all day till that son-of-a-bitch gets home. So let's get going.'

Monk stood on the chair, looking at the bare table top.

'And I want you to give me that pecker like you mean what you're doing.' She climbed onto the board top.

Stepping from the chair to the table, Monk forced himself to say, 'I means it, Miss Tucker, Mam.'

Claudia Tucker had him trapped.


By the night of the supper at the big house, Rachel Selby had finally agreed to a place for Peter in the evening's arrangement. She had consented that the six-year-old child could sit at the top of the stairs and look down at the guests for one hour. But not a minute longer.

Long before the first guests arrived, Peter had dressed himself in his white cotton nightshirt and came to his place.

Looking through the bannister, he saw Storky bustling across the entry hall, her stiffly starched apron crackling as she made last minute touches—carrying blue bowls of flowers, rushing to replace a beeswax candle which had fallen from a pewter wall sconce, flourishing a feather duster to catch a spot that had been missed on the wainscotting, and shouting orders the entire time to the other black servants.

On the landing below Peter, Rachel swished past the wooden bannister and called to Melissa, 'Settle yourself on that couch, young lady. Stop fretting with those curls. Your hair is frightful enough the way it is.'

Peter envied Melissa for having this opportunity to meet the guests, even if they would just be the women. He hoped that he would be allowed to attend a supper when he was older.

His heart began to beat when he heard the clatter of wooden wheels on the driveway. He next heard Rachel calling, 'Mister Selby! Mister Selby! I see those Greysons out front. You're the one who wanted them here so go greet them yourself.'

Selby appeared on the landing below Peter. It was the first time that Peter had seen him looking so distinguished, dressed in a black frock coat with a full cut to its skirt and polished high boots glistening over his white breeches. His goatee was freshly painted a deep red and his long, silky hair was glistening white.

Seeing Peter, Selby poked his head out into the well and called, 'Hey, Sonny! Don't fall asleep up there.' The prospect of company always put Selby in a good mood.

Rachel snapped behind him, 'Who are you talking to?'

'Just Sonny,' Selby answered, winding his gold pocket watch.

There was the rustle of skirts and Rachel demanded, 'Is that child creeping down here already? I told you he should be locked in his bedroom.'

Selby assured her, 'Don't fret, Rachel. Don't fret. Everything is under control.' Then, tucking his watch and fob into his waistcoat, he pulled it down into position over his white breeches and began to stroll slowly down the stairs to receive his first guests.

For the next hour, Peter held onto the bannister, listening to the carriages and wagons clatter to a stop in front of the house and watched people arriving through the double doors. He saw the tops of everybody's heads, their hair partings, the lack-lustre patches of the men's toupees, the aerial view of the women's fat chignons imprisoned in their hair nets. He strained his ears to catch snippets of their conversations but he heard only the echoes of merry greetings and the swishing of silk skirts.

Peter soon forgot about going to bed. He leaned through the bannister now to see a plump woman wearing a tall white wig which cascaded curls down over her shoulders.

Suddenly, he heard a muttering behind him.

Turning, Peter saw Ta-Ta standing on the landing. She was dressed in the same ragged white Mother Hubbard that she had been wearing on the afternoon when Peter had last seen her in the yard.

Ta-Ta did not acknowledge Peter huddled in front of her on the top step. She stood frowning down at the guests in the entry hall. She did not approve of what she was seeing. Ta-Ta's face was drawn and stoney brown. But she was haughty.

Wanting to escape from her, Peter quickly scooted down to the next step. He hated her for being here.

Continuing to ignore Peter, Ta-Ta pulled the skirt of her Mother Hubbard around her legs and sank to the step that Peter had vacated, as if he had done it for her.

Peter saw that he was caught. He could not move farther down the steps because Rachel Selby might see him and then send him to bed. If he jumped to his feet and dashed past Ta-Ta, she might grab at him again.

Soon, Ta-Ta began to speak, muttering words to herself that Peter could not understand. He tried to ignore her until— suddenly—he felt a sharp dig between his shoulder blades.

Ta-Ta had poked him with her toe.

Looking over his shoulder, he frowned at her and turned back to look at the activity below.

Ta-Ta jabbed her toe into his back again, muttering this time to him.

Peter remained motionless on the edge of his step, wondering what he should do. He was upset that she had come and ruined this for him. But he also was frightened of her.

Ta-Ta's toe dug into Peter's back a third time and she whispered, 'Master Peter?'

How did she know his name?

Ta-Ta's whisper became louder. 'Master Peter?'

Peter turned rigidly to look at her.

Gripping her skinny arms around her knees, Ta-Ta leaned forward and rasped, 'Promises me on your Mama's grave?'

Peter stared at her. His 'Mama'? He did not have a 'Mama'. He just had a man whom he called 'Father'.

Reaching to her thick lips, Ta-Ta pinched them between her forefinger and thumb to mime an oath of silence. Then, shaking her frizzy head, she whispered, 'No, no, no! Not a Dragonard.'

106

Dragonard. Peter had heard Ta-Ta say that word before. She had said that same funny-sounding word to him in the yard two weeks ago. Dragonard. He had forgotten it.

Pinching her lips again, Ta-Ta kept shaking her head. She was trying to tell him something.

But what did she mean? His 'Mama'? Dragonard? To keep his lips pinched together? Closed? Peter could not understand what she meant. He could not understand anything she was doing or muttering. She reeked of sweetness, too. Peter whiffed a strong odour coming from her body.

A voice then called to them from the landing below.

Peter turned and saw Rachel Selby standing at the foot of the steps. She called, 'Boy, it's time for you to go to bed. And you, you crazy black woman, what are you hoping to find out here?'

Both Peter and Ta-Ta sat motionless now.

Rachel looked more harassed than usual tonight. Although she was dressed in a delicate lace shawl and a new black bombazine dress with a glittering bib of black jet beads, she did not seem to be having a good time. She looked tired.

She shrilled louder at Peter and Ta-Ta, 'There's enough intrusion in this house tonight without having you two! Go away. Go to bed. Both of you!'

Puzzled by her hysterical attitude, Peter turned to look at Ta-Ta.

But Ta-Ta had disappeared. All the doors on the top landing were shut. There was no sign of Ta-Ta anyplace. She had gone back to her room.

Rachel Selby called impatiently, 'Why are you dawdling, boy? Go to bed.'

Peter reluctantly rose to his feet. This was not what he had thought a big party was going to be like at all.

Leaving the noise, the songs, and the laughter of the party below, Peter went sadly to his bedroom.

The noise from the party in the big house tonight did not carry through the woods to Niggertown. The guests came and went in their carriages and wagons but the negroes still slept.

Niggertown was silent now, lit by a high moon. There was no movement on the dirt road running between the two main rows of steep-roofed cabins. Even the yellow dogs were sleeping.

The only activity was at the rear of the six cabins which set away from the rest. These were the oldest and most dilapidated slave quarters on The Star and a black man named Priam lived in the smallest of the six cabins with a woman who had bore him eight children. The black woman was called Betsy and was soon due to have the ninth child of Priam's.

A second man named Toby shared the cabin with Betsy and Priam. Toby had been promised a young wench from Mama Gomorrah when she sent down the next batch of saplings from The Shed next spring.

Tonight, Priam and Betsy lay sleeping together on a pallet on the dirt floor and Toby lay by himself near the door.

Toby was the first to hear the commotion outside the cabin. He rose to see what was happening when the door to the cabin suddenly opened and moonlight poured onto the floor.

Chad Tucker barged into the cabin and, behind him, Monk followed with a whip coiled in his hands. Priam, Betsy and Toby had had them here at the cabin before.

'Nigger!' Tucker bellowed. 'Talk so I know where you are.' The darkness was filled with his coarse laughing.

Monk stood next to Tucker and whispered, 'Toby's back here. That must be Priam there with his wench.' Monk was still cautious about betraying the slaves.

Covering Betsy with his arm, Priam said, 'This wench about to have a sucker, Master Tucker, Sir.'

'It ain't her I come to see,' Tucker answered as he moved toward Priam. Kicking his naked body with his boot, he said, 'I come to see if you need some freshening up.'

'No, Master Tucker Sir. My back ain't healing good, Master Sir.'

'How's your mouth doing? Have you been blabbing around about being sold?'

'No, Master Tucker, Sir. I ain't saying nothing.'

Snatching the whip from Monk's hand, Tucker said, 'You know you're coming with me up to the public road tomorrow night, don't you? You and that Toby buck are both coming with me.'

Putting his arm around Betsy, Priam pleaded, 'This wench might be having her baby tomorrow, Master Sir!'

The whip cracked in the darkness and Tucker boomed, 'Don't sass me, nigger shit!'

'I ain't sassing—'

The whip snapped a second time. This time it struck Betsy. Tucker said, 'There you go doing it again.'

Seeing that the whip had snagged across Betsy's bare side, Priam forgot about Tucker's temper and jumped to protect her.

Casting the whip behind him, Tucker brought it down on Priam's back one, two, then three times. Priam writhed with pain, holding tighter onto Betsy. Her pregnant stomach began to heave.

Priam did not speak now. Toby did not speak. They waited for Tucker and Monk to shut the door of the cabin.

As soon as Tucker had gone, Priam examined Betsy and looked at the wound gashed by the whip. He pleaded with her to speak to him.

Betsy only moaned and tossed her head in agony. The shock of the whip was bringing her baby.

Toby nervously watched Priam as he clutched Betsy. He said, 'Let's me runs get Mama Gomorrah.'

Priam grabbed Toby's shoulder and shook his head. He whispered, 'No. She asks us questions. No, Toby.'

Toby pleaded, 'But your Betsy's birthing!'

Priam stared down at Betsy's face wet with perspiration. He said, 'If we talks about Tucker and this . . .' He stopped and shook his head. 'No, Toby, we can't talks. We can just brings the baby ourselves.'

'You and me birth the baby?' Toby gasped.

'It's the only way without talking. Without showing these marks. Without us all dying.'

'Priam, you crazy.'

'Betsy and her baby and me are all crazy to live, Toby. That's how we crazy. We tells and Tucker comes kills us.'

Toby nervously scratched his head. 'I ain't birthed no babies.'

'Me neither. But—'

Then Priam hurried in the darkness of the cabin to find—first—a small piece of wood for Betsy to bite when the pain became worse.

Chad Tucker and Monk walked along in the moonlight. Tucker recoiled his whip and, stuffing the butt into his belt, he asked Monk, 'You enjoys that boy?'

Monk murmured, 'Yes, Master Tucker, Sir.'

'What's you so quiet about the last couple of days for, boy?'

Shaking his head, Monk answered soberly, 'Nothing, Master Tucker, Sir.'

The sight in the cabin moments ago had reminded Monk how cruel Tucker could be. He was worried what he would do to him if Claudia told about them laying on the table top three days ago. Monk did not know what craziness that Claudia would do next. Tucker terrorized the black people in Niggertown but it was Claudia who was filling Monk's life with fear.

Tucker said, 'Let's go home and give Claudie her good time now.'

Monk looked at him in horror.

Studying the round whiteness of the moon, Tucker said, 'You ain't seeming so hot tonight, boy. What's the matter? You getting tired of my missus?'

Monk's heart quickened. He said immediately, 'No, Master Tucker, Sir. I ain't getting tired of nothing. I just do like you says.'

'That's a good boy,' Tucker said, putting his arm around Monk's broad shoulder. 'What you need to perk you up is some *real* excitement. And tomorrow night you'll get it. Tomorrow night we sell those niggers to George Gresham.'

'Yes, Master Tucker, Sir,' Monk said, thinking how exciting those slave-selling trips used to be. But now his life had been suddenly ruined by Claudia Tucker. He was worried about tonight, tomorrow, the next day. He was beginning to feel just like any other slave on The Star—living daily in fear. Claudia Tucker could have him castrated.

## Chapter Six

# THE DEWITT PLACE

'Drunkards! Whores!'

Rachel Selby's shouts baffled her husband the following morning. Apart from smacking of improprieties, her words today were specifically more rude than the usual accusations which she levelled against people.

It was noon now. Melissa and Peter had gone outside to play and the servants were busily putting the house back into order.

Rachel still had not emerged from her bedroom. She was refusing to unlock her door, answering any enquiries about her health by shouting that she did not want to breathe the air in a house which had been contaminated by drunkards and whores.

Drunkards? Whores? Selby sat alone at the dining-room table, sipping his third cup of milky coffee after lunch and tried to recall the events of the previous night. To the best of his knowledge, every last guest had bent over backwards to respect Rachel's obsession of abstaining from liquor. There certainly had been no drunkards at the supper.

As for the matter of 'whores', Selby could not pinpoint a single incident in which a lady might have misconducted herself in front of his wife. Rachel had composed the guest list herself, inviting only middle-aged, married couples who indulged in conversations about home, family, and planting. And if the talk had ventured from those three subjects, it only went as far as politics, the impending war of France with Spain and its implications on Louisiana and the American states.

Sitting with one elbow propped on the table, Selby rested his head on his hand, idly drawing straight lines into the damask table cloth with his coffee spoon and wondering if his wife had taken some new kind of turn.

Selby sat suddenly upright. Had Rachel smelled alcohol on one of the men who had gone out to the barn for a quick drink of corn whiskey? That could be the explanation for her calling people 'drunkards'.

But whores? What would have been the cause of that slander against the good women who had come escorted last night by their husbands? Selby would swear on a mountain of Bibles that those women, one and all, were clean-living, church-going souls who led a good and happy . . .

Happy. Happiness. That was the key, he feared. Rachel might have snapped under the strain of the misery which she had created for herself. She could have finally broken down with the realization that other females in the world were Christian, clean-living, and still happy. Whatever the reasons were, though, something in Rachel's mind had put her into this state of mental frustration. He had never seen her quite so unbalanced, so . . . crazy.

Selby sat slumped over his coffee cup, weighing the possible causes of his wife's advanced case of misanthropy when he suddenly heard a noise. Looking up, he saw the young house-maid named Biddy burst through the archway into the dining-room, holding her white apron to her face. Selby sat erect on his chair, staring at the young negress as she ran sobbing hysterically toward the kitchen door.

'Biddy!' he called out to her. He knew that Biddy was a foolish, screeching girl but he had never seen her in such a state.

Not stopping to answer Selby, Biddy raced toward the kitchen door.

The door pushed forward from the other side and Storky barged into the dining-room, almost knocking Biddy to the floor.

Biddy dropped her apron in surprise and wailed, 'Oh, Miss Storky!'

Storky was dressed in a long white smock covered by a starched, floor-length pinafore apron. With a white handkerchief tied around her horse-like face, she looked at Biddy and then glanced over at Selby sitting at the table.

Selby nodded toward the archway through which Biddy had just come and then to the spot where she stood with Storky. He shrugged.

Suspiciously narrowing her eyes, Storky grabbed Biddy by both shoulders and, shaking her back and forth, she demanded, 'What do you mean by this? Bawling all over the house likes this? Tell me the meaning of this, wench.'

Biddy squirmed, holding her skinny black arms over both her face and the array of pigtails which covered her head.

Slapping away Biddy's hands, Storky shouted angrily, 'Don't you try to hide yourself from me, wench. Don't you try to hide yourself from Miss Storky.'

Biddy screamed in her falsetto voice, 'I ain't been pestered, Miss Storky. Honest, Miss Storky. I ain't been doing what Miss Selby says I been doing. I ain't been pestered.'

Hearing the mention of his wife's name, Selby rose from his chair and, striding over to the door, he asked Biddy, 'What did Mrs. Selby say to you, girl?'

Biddy began hysterically, 'Oh, Master Selby, Sir. Miss Selby, she says I lets white men grabs in my skirts and I lets white men take liberties with me and I—'

Storky slapped Biddy's mouth. 'Shame on you! Shame on you telling lies about white folk, you nigger wench. Shame on you.'

Biddy looked at Selby to protest, but seeing Storky pulling back her arm to slap her again, she grapped her apron and ran screeching into the kitchen.

As soon as Biddy had disappeared, Storky looked at Selby and said, 'You can whips me if you wants, Master Selby, Sir, for stopping her. But that girl sures was lying.' Storky was now a picture of her usual propriety.

Selby asked, 'Have you been up to Mrs. Selby's room today, Storky? Have you heard anything?'

Lowering her head, Storky answered, 'The excitement from the supper has made us all a little tired, Master Selby, Sir.'

Selby appreciated Storky's diplomacy. He said softly, 'I hope you're right, Storky.'

Lifting her head, she said, 'If Miss Selby does have something in her mind about wenches and white folk, Master Selby, Sir, it ain't to do with that Biddy girl. Biddy needs what Miss Selby is saying, all right, but Biddy is scared of men. Biddy always been that way.'

Selby nodded. He knew that fact about Biddy.

As Storky turned to go into the kitchen, she added, 'Biddy's not a special wench, Master Selby, Sir. Lots of nigger girls around The Star looks skinny like that Biddy wench. Maybe Miss Selby sees somebody she *thinks* is Biddy.'

Selby nodded again. 'Probably.'

Hesitating in the doorway, Storky asked, 'Is that all for now, Master Selby, Sir?'

'Yes, that's all, Storky.' Selby said, then added as an after thought, 'Oh, Storky. If anybody asks where I am this afternoon, just say I had to go see Judge Antrobus.'

'Yes, Master Selby, Sir,' Storky answered. 'Does that mean you're not home for supper?' She knew Selby's schedule whenever he went to see Judge Antrobus. He always came home late.

Selby answered, 'That's right, Storky. If any one asks, tell them where I've gone.'

'To see Judge Antrobus.'

Selby nodded. He had to get out of this house.


Rachel sat quivering now on the edge of her bed. She had heard Biddy go screaming down the stairs and finally the house was quiet again.

Rachel believed that Biddy *was* a sinful girl. She further

believed that all the black wenches on The Star were sinful. She could tell that by their rolling eyes. They were looking for sin.

Biddy had almost driven Rachel to despair by pounding on the bedroom door this morning and asking her if she wanted to eat.

Having tolerated as much of Biddy's noise as she possibly could, Rachel had screamed through the door and told Biddy exactly what she thought about her. Biddy was a sinful black slut.

Rachel was alone again.

The thought of going outside the bedroom repulsed Rachel. Seeing the remnants of last night's party would only remind her about the women who had been there, the women whom she had thought were her friends.

Rachel had never realized until last night how stupid other women were. They hung on their husbands arms as if the men were chivalrous knights. Did they not know that those same men spent nights with black sluts exactly like Biddy? That all men were evil?

Rachel asked herself now if there was anything in the world more evil than a male.

She answered herself—'Niggers!'

Standing up, she went to the oval mirror hanging over her dressing table and looked at her reflection. As she stared at her face, one hand found its way to her breasts. She rubbed at the breast, trying to flatten it, to brush it away from her body.

Turning sideways, she looked at the silhouette of her slim body in the mirror.

She had a small waist and her breasts still had a definite curve to them. Never before had she realized that she must be quite tempting to a black man. She had heard a story last night about a Savannah lady being raped by a black man.

Stopping, Rachel considered the story. Had that story about rape been the cause for her sudden change of mood last night? Had thinking about that story also made her unhappy today?

Throwing up her head, she thought, yes, of course it was the reason. She had reason to be frightened of black men. A white woman was completely helpless with a black man and here at The Star she was surrounded by the ravenous brutes. If a Savannah woman had been raped in the middle of town by a black man, what chance did she have here in escaping the same fate?

Sinking down to the edge of the bed, Rachel tried to imagine what it would feel like if a black man would rape her. She remembered the weight of her husband's body on the night that she had conceived Melissa. He had been so heavy and she remembered being embarrassed by the words he had spoken to her. He had said them with whiskey on his breath.

Rachel put the words out of her mind. Men spoke foolishness, she thought now. She hated men and the women who tolerated them were stupid. Whores, they were whores! Only whores slept with men reaking of alcohol. Drunkards and whores!

Standing up from the bed again, Rachel went back to the mirror. Looking at herself, she saw a tear rolling from the corner of her eye.

Why am I crying? she asked herself.

Am I lonely?

She sniffed. No, she was not lonely. She was frightened and she thought that she had every reason to be frightened, too. A lady had been raped right in the middle of Savannah and here she was totally vulnerable on a plantation full of negroes.

Rachel Selby hated this life on a plantation. She hated its negroes. She hated The Star.


Judge Tom Antrobus lived at Fairfield, five miles northwest from the Star. But that was not the direction in which Albert Selby set out on his bay mare this afternoon when he cantered onto the dusty public road from his property.

Having tipped his straw hat by habit at the rickety wooden star hanging from the crossbeams of the front gate, Selby squared the wide brimmed hat back onto his forehead and, turning right, he rode southwest on the road that led to Troy.

A few clouds streaked the blue sky today; at two o'clock, the sun burned hot and Selby was glad that he was not taking the road all the way to its terminus at Troy. He was thankful for having escaped from Rachel, too. Selby was finding that as he grew older, he tried to ignore the difficulties that might arise in his life—an argument in the house or a crisis on The Star.

Selby had whole-heartedly enjoyed himself at the party last night. He had received old friends, some of whom he had not seen for many months, others for years. But there was one person who had been missing from the gathering. Although respecting the fact that Judge Antrobus adamantly refused to step foot on The Star, or any other property that had a connection with the Roland family, Selby did like to talk to his old friend. But, in a curious way, Selby was always pleased that the Judge refused to come to his home; by having to leave The Star to see him, Selby was able to accomplish two or three other things on the same visit. And, today, Selby was glad that he had to leave home to see the Judge. He needed this escape.

The large, shadey groves of elm trees on either side of the Troy road passed quickly now as Selby galloped faster, hurrying toward the established rendezvous with his friend, anxiously looking forward to the restful surrounding that always awaited him at their usual meeting place. It had become Selby's habit to visit Judge Antrobus at the Dewitt Place, the secluded cottage on the road to Troy that was owned by two sisters, Charlotte and Roxanne Dewitt.

More than a few males in this neighbourhood, married men as well as single, had reason to pay a call at the Dewitt Place. Although it was an accepted fact in the South that many white gentlemen took sexual liberties with the black wenches on their plantations, not every white man enjoyed such freedoms. Rachel Selby was not the only strict woman in these parts. Other wives and mothers also kept a constant watch over their husband's and son's activities. Thus, it was those upright, God-fearing females like Rachel Selby who unwittingly had created a local demand for the Dewitt sisters.

Prostitution would be the last profession in the world which someone would assign to two ladies who looked and lived like the Dewitt Sisters. Charlotte was in her mid-sixties and Roxanne confessed to being fifty-seven years old. They both dressed in conservative frocks, simple cottons sprigged with violets or pastel dimities decorated with nothing more ornate than a cameo broach or a modest string of heirloom pearls. The older sister, Charlotte, had let her hair go completely white, wearing it in a neat plaited coronet on top of her head. Roxanne's hair was still a youthful chestnut brown, pulled into an unassuming roll over each ear. The ladies were generally thought to be two spinsters living on a modest family inheritance. No one but their faithful following knew that their livelihood came instead from the immoral earnings of young white females.

The young ladies who worked at the Dewitt Place always came from faraway places, mostly from the states to the north, and never stayed in the Louisiana Territory longer than four months. As the Dewitts were not considered to be, nor thought of themselves, as madams of a bordello, neither did their short-term visitors fit naturally into the category of whores. The Dewitts' girls were drafted from the ranks of proper young ladies who needed extra cash at a critical moment, sophisticated adventuresses who were temporarily down on their luck, or merely pretty girls who wanted to snatch a sample of life before they committed themselves to the rigours of married life back home. There was no room in the Dewitt household for common women of the street.

Apart from enjoying the obvious physical attractions offered by the smooth-skinned young ladies who came to stay at the Dewitt cottage, the regular customers at the establishment often congregated there to discuss local politics, the seasonal condition of cotton and tobacco, social events in the community. A small corps of males used the Dewitt Place as a gentlemen's club. And the club was exclusive, a place run strictly for gentlemen because the Dewitts carefully screened all the men before they allowed them onto their place. The two business-minded spinsters did not want to risk exposure and be driven from a neighbourhood where they had discreetly but profitably existed now for more than fifteen years.

Reaching the thick blind of tall cypress trees which blocked the Dewitt land from passersby, Selby reined his mare and listened for the sounds of a rider or a farm wagon coming from around the far bend of the road. But all was silent. He heard only the music of a creek tinkling alongside the road.

Hopping from his horse, Selby opened the gate and led the mare onto the Dewitt land. As he always felt a special comfort when he passed under the wooden standard of The Star, Selby felt a particular kind of warmth, too, when he came through these gates at the Dewitt Place. Apart from admiring the two ladies' ingenuity for guarding their true identity in the community, he praised them for having chosen a house so well protected from the scrutiny of the public eye. He felt safe here.

Astride his horse once again, Selby trotted up the poplar lined drive, already feeling revived from his problems at The Star. He fanned his face with his straw hat as he came in view of a small, double-storied white house setting at the end of the drive. With iron fretwork crowning its steep roof, the Dewitt house looked prim and guiltless of sin.

Selby saw no horses tied to the post near the wide gallery which surrounded the house on three sides but he realized that that was no sign to tell whether or not other men were here today. The Dewitts always had their visitors' horses taken around to the stables at the back of the house. That was one of the jobs done by George the negro groom.

George was one more enigma of the Dewitt Place. He was the same age as Selby, if not older, but appeared to be a much younger man. With the stamina of a bull, he often joined in the activities of the bedrooms. George had a fine mahogany-brown body and enjoyed exhibiting it to the guests. George often performed vigorously with the young girls in front of paying customers.

But George's role at the Dewitt Place included more than

being both groom and show man. He was also the long-term lover of Roxanne, the younger Dewitt sister. So unspeakable was a union between a white woman and a black man in these parts, though, most of the visitors here did not know of the relationship. Selby was one of the few who did.

Hitching his horse to the front rail, Selby still did not see George and guessed that he was engaged in one of the bedrooms. Sauntering across the gallery, Selby tapped lightly on the door and then saw the white plaited crown of the older Dewitt sister through the frosted panes of the door. He listened as she unfastened the bolt on the door.

Charlotte Dewitt wore a buttercup-yellow dress today. She fondly embraced Selby as he entered, holding both cheeks to him to be kissed before leading him into the parlour through a pair of tassled green draperies.

Three men were already seated in the parlour, a small room covered with primrose wallpaper and furnished with couches and chairs upholstered in floral prints. One guest was Judge Antrobus, a portly man with ginger sideburns. Charlotte Dewitt introduced the other two guests as Antony Taylor and Monsieur Romaine. Taylor was a banker from Carterville and Romaine had come from the island of St. Thomas, travelling to New York. After giving Selby a whiskey and replenishing the other drinks, Charlotte fluttered from the room to prepare a room for Taylor.

The conversation among the gentlemen in the parlour was stilted. The only two who had come here to talk were Selby and Antrobus but they were not going to speak in front of strangers. The topic of conversation began at the popular subject of Eli Whitney and his struggle to keep the patent on his cotton gin and progressed to opinions on slavery. Monsieur Romain said that the West Indian islands were becoming rife with slave rebellion. He warned that the American markets would soon be glutted with mutinous slaves from the Caribbean. He cautioned the others not to buy them.

Charlotte returned and, clasping her dainty hands in front of her waist, she asked both Taylor and Romaine to follow her.

She had finally made arrangements for both of them.

Selby and Judge Antrobus were left alone.

Antrobus began in his usual gruff voice, 'Losing any more niggers at The Star, Selby?'

Relaxing, Selby shook his head, 'Things have quieted down for a while. But I still can't figure out where they ran. Nobody else seems to be having the problem.' He did not seem to be too concerned.

'What does Tucker have to say? Anything?' Judge Antrobus never visited The Star but, as he was Selby's legal advisor, he knew everything that Selby knew about the plantation and often felt more concern than Selby did for its future. He despised the family who had settled The Star but recognized its crop potential, especially now that green cotton and the cotton gin were widening the market.

'Tucker can't figure it out either.'

Judge Antrobus sneered. 'Tucker. There's a scoundrel if I ever saw one. When are you going to get you a new man?'

'You can't find a white man who's willing to work thesedays. But if Ro had stayed on—' Selby stopped. The ease of the Dewitt Place had made Selby forget that he had promised himself that he would never mention his son's name again. He quickly changed the subject to something bright. He asked, 'Anything new here?'

A leer spread between Judge Antrobus's red sideburns and, looking quickly at the archway, he said, 'Something *very* new. Do you remember that Faye Willows girl?'

Selby thought back to the faces and names he had seen and heard here at the Dewitt Place. Resting his head on the back of the couch, he thought aloud, 'Faye Willows. Faye Willows.'

Judge Antrobus helped. 'The filly you decided against. Because of your—' Antrobus patted his chest. '—ticker.'

Pulling on his goatee, Selby smiled and confessed, 'That includes about most of them here.' Selby knew his heart would not sustain any vigorous love-making with a young lady.

'Faye Willows,' Antrobus prompted.' The one who wore out everybody except good old George.'

'The red head!'

Judge Antrobus nodded. 'And knockers out to here.'

Selby smiled. He remembered Faye Willows all right.

Judge Antrobus whispered, 'Well, there's one here like that now.'

'No wonder I didn't see George,' Selby said smiling, remembering a scene about George and the original Faye Willows.

During the days of Faye Willows, George always had met Selby in front of the Dewitt house with the words, 'Good thing you ain't riding a stallion today, Master Selby, Sir. That Miss Willows is taking on every blasted thing that's got him a dong!'

George was right. And, although Selby followed his better judgement by never going with Faye Willows, he had seen enough of her to satisfy himself.

It was five years ago that Selby had sat on the floor of a bedroom—beside two merchants from Troy—and watched Faye Willows making her reputation. She was performing not only with George the groom but also with a strapping young sailor with a headful of tight yellow curls.

The sailor had come to the Dewitt Place with a letter of introduction from an uncle in New Orleans. He had brought with him a three month's store of sexual starvation, which proved to be hardly ample for Faye Willows.

It had never been clear to Selby whether the creamy-complexioned girl was innately desirous of sex or whether she responded to the sight of having identical male organs in each hand, one George's, one the sailor's, and both like rods of steel but in opposite colours. She liked to look and observe what was happening to her, it seemed, as much as she enjoyed the sensations.

Faye Willows groaned theatrically as the sailor began plunging eagerly into her. She cleverly screamed and swooned to make the beefy youth feel more magnificent than he actually was. She cajoled him toward the full steam of his excitement.

And as much as the sailor tried not to explode, Faye Willows employed her warm vacuum to release his pent-up excitement and drain every last drop which he had been hoarding at sea.

She then switched her attention to George. Tongueing the ebony version of the sailor's large phallus, she moistened this black counterpart until it glistened with her saliva. Next, she rubbed her enormous white breasts against it like a cat snuggling along the length of a thick black tree. Miss Willows virtually purred with contentment, enjoying the closeness of such a monumental specie of manhood next to her naked body, gasping when George reached his huge black hands down for her white breasts, beginning to kneed her large strawberry-pink nipples with his working black fingers.

Unlike the youthful sailor, George was not so easily flattered by Miss Willow's reactions to him being inside her. He had been praised before, and often more honestly. When she howled and panted, both cursing and adulating his prowess, calling attention to how he was stirring her furry patch with his stone-like phallus, George only grinned at his audience, expanding his black chest like a gorilla.

George took great pride in his fitness. Whenever he performed in front of the white customers here, there was always a smile on his face.

Now, as the three men squatted on the floor watching his lean hips moving back and forth, back and forth against Miss Willow, George grinned shamelessly.

Selby had marvelled not so much at the voraciousness of the white girl as he had praised the physical condition of George. George's chest looked like a plate of Roman armour, the hairs that had turned white with age resembled small metal shavings. He still had all of his teeth, too, a glistening white line which spread wide in his mouth as he continued rhythmically into the girl.

As George was still going, the sailor lay collapsed on the bed, sprawling face down on the mattress, spent by the rigours of Faye Willows. The sailor's only reaction to her now was a groan as she reached for the downy crack in his buttocks and, as George kept pummelling her with his phallus, she poked a moistened finger into the sailor's rosebud anus.

But Faye Willows did not have such an easy time with George. Although not brutal, George worked the girl until she finally gasped, 'I surrender! I surrender!'

George stared at her with large eyes. His masculinity was still half-held by her wet femininity. He asked, 'Surrender? This ain't no war, Miss Willows, Mam! We don't have no wars here!'

Selby and the other two men on the floor applauded George's truthful words.

At the Dewitt Place there were no battles, no altercations, no differences, not about race, creed, or colour.


'Did you and the judge have a good talk?' Charlotte Dewitt asked Selby.

Charlotte and Selby were sitting side-by-side in an ornate brass bed in a bedroom upstairs called The Rose Room. Charlotte had come back to the parlour to tell Judge Antrobus that his new girl was ready. Then she and Selby had adjourned upstairs together, removed their clothes, and climbed into bed.

With two white pillows propping up his back, Selby lay in the light turned golden as it poured through the closed window blinds. He answered, 'We had our usual gab.' He did not want to tell Charlotte about their memories of Faye Willows. He cherished his relationship with Charlotte too much to talk to her about such matters.

Charlotte said, 'I haven't had time lately to chat to you about hardly anything, Albert. How's little Peter? Is he well?'

'Peter's a fine boy. I couldn't be more proud of Peter than if he were—my own.'

'And Melissa? She must be thrilled having someone like Peter.'

'Melly is doing just fine,' he said, squeezing her hand.

'That's good,' Charlotte said, pulling the quilt over her narrow shoulders. She knew that she did not have to ask Selby any more questions than those. Melissa and Peter were his two favourite subjects. She knew he loved them even more than The Star. She knew that all of his negroes could run away and, as long as Selby had Melissa and Peter, he would be happy.

Now, all that Charlotte had to do was to make him feel good in his body.

Continuing to slide down under the quilt, Charlotte reached to take Selby's maleness in her hands. She fondled him until he was hard enough to put in her mouth. She was too old to want an orgasm herself but she enjoyed—loved—bringing pleasure to a man who had been so thoughtful to her over the years. The Rose Room was Charlotte Dewitt's and Albert Selby's private world, a retreat of pleasure where she curled on the mattress between his legs and kept the glow of masculinity alive in his body.

Chad Tucker waited until dark that night before he and Monk set out with the manacles and leg irons for the dark shadows of Niggertown. They were going to take the next two men—Priam and Toby—to sell to the small farmer, George Gresham.

Before entering Priam's dilapidated cabin, Tucker paused outside the plank door and, looking up at the sky, he said to Monk, 'We got us a good moon tonight, boy. We should be able to get through the brush without getting ourselves too tangled.' Tucker was in his usual boisterous mood.

This was not Monk's first venture of selling slaves with Tucker. But he was nervous. He always feared that some night they would get caught, that something might go wrong with Tucker's plan.

As Monk stood on the threshhold of the old cabin—holding the iron shackles in his hands—Tucker burst in through the door.

The sudden bellow of Tucker's voice brought Monk into the cabin.

The stub of a candle made a small glow against the far wall of the cabin tonight. Monk saw Tucker there pulling Priam up from the dirt floor by a bare arm. In the far corner, Toby knelt next to Betsy's body. Monk saw that she was lying under a blanket.

Tucker yelled to Monk as he struggled with Priam, 'Bring me a pair of irons, boy. Quick!'

Monk dropped the equipment to the floor with a clank and moved toward Tucker with a pair of manacles.

Priam defiantly tried to free himself from Tucker's grasp, screaming, 'I ain't leaving my woman. I ain't leaving my woman.'

Tucker brought his arm down hard against Priam's head and he fell to the floor. Standing over him, Tucker pulled his whip from his belt and sneered at him, 'Make a noise like that again, nigger, and I'll kill you.'

Next, turning to Toby—still cowering by Betsy's body— Tucker ordered, 'Get your black ass over here.'

Toby hesitated, looking at Tucker and then glancing down at Betsy lying under the blanket.

Moving alongside Tucker, Monk asked, 'Ain't that the wench who's birthing a sucker?'

Tucker studied the woman's motionless body on the dirt floor. He said to Monk, 'Let's see if it is.'

Walking toward the corner, Tucker stuck one boot under the blanket and kicked it from the body.

Bending, Tucker looked at Betsy lying on her side. There was a small brown infant with its mouth fastened onto her breast.

Standing, Tucker used his boot again to turn Betsy onto her back.

As he did this, both of Betsy's arms fell limply to the sides of her naked body and her head hung motionless to one shoulder. The blank stare in her open eyes showed that she was dead.

Bending over her body again, Tucker took the butt of his whip and prodded the infant which had slipped to the crook of Betsy's arm.

The infant remained motionless, too.

Next, Tucker poked the butt of the whip into the infant's mouth and then brought the butt up to his eyes to examine it.

Standing, Tucker muttered, 'Hell.'

Monk cautiously asked, 'What's the matter?'

Wiping the butt of the whip on his breeches, Tucker said, 'She's dead. That sucker's been nursing her titty. But he's getting nothing but—'

Tucker held the butt of the whip to Monk. 'That ain't milk coming from her titty. That's . . . *blood*.'

Monk turned away his head.

Looking back at the dead woman and baby, Tucker murmured, 'The blood must of choked the kid. A fine mess. Both of them are dead now.'

Monk grabbed Tucker's arm and whispered, 'We better get out of here. Somebody's going to find out.'

'Get out? Run? Run away from two dead niggers?' Tucker shook off Monk's hand in disgust.

Monk begged, 'What if somebody finds out?'

'Boy, I have an agreement to sell George Gresham two prime bucks tonight. I'll be damned if I don't.'

'What about—' Monk looked at the naked body of Betsy and the dead baby lying together on the dirt floor.

Tucker pointed his whip at Toby and ordered, 'You there. Toss her and that kid in the blanket. We'll take them part of the way with us.'

As Tucker was talking to Toby, Priam moved behind him. He was going to attack Tucker.

But, quickly spinning around, Tucker lashed his whip at Priam, striking him across the face.

Priam fell back to the floor. His face was gashed with blood.

Tucker turned back to Monk. 'Come on, boy. Get this Priam nigger in irons first. He's a little jittery, it seems. Then we'll shackle the other bastard. You can come back here tomorrow and mop away any signs we leave behind.'

Monk's fingers moved nervously as he worked to slide the pins into Priam's leg irons. Tucker held his boot on Priam's throat as Monk locked manacles on his wrists.

The second negro, Toby, was frightened and easier to shackle than Priam. And, as Tucker stuck the pins into his leg irons, he told Monk to pull the four corners of the blanket over the two dead bodies and tie them securely into a knot.

Next, quickly surveying the cabin before they left, Tucker told Monk, 'You don't have to do much here tomorrow, boy. Just make it looks like they run. The whole bunch of these damned niggers were runners. I'll report it tomorrow night to Selby.'

Turning to Priam then, Tucker said, 'Grab your wench, nigger, and pull. We'll cart her as far as the pothole. There's one over near the road.'

Tucker led the way from the cabin, jerking Toby by the arm.

Outside, he complained, 'Shit. I thought tonight was going to be easy. We had a full moon and everything. But what do I get saddled with? Two dead niggers. And one with a bleeding face. We'll have to wipe up that, too, so Gresham don't see it rightaway.'

He shoved Toby ahead of him into the night.

Monk followed behind Priam.

Priam moved with difficulty in the dark. Apart from still bleeding from his face, he had to pull the blanket which held the dead bodies of his Betsy and their child. And he did this in leg irons.

The four men continued toward the pothole. There, they would drop the bodies where they would never be discovered on The Star.

*Book Two*

## LIGHT OF DAY

*Chapter Seven*

# NEW WISHES, OLD DREAMS

Winter had come again to Louisiana and, on this gloomy New Year's Eve, the land was shrouded by a starless sky, and a dampness permeated the bones of the people who comprised the vital life force of The Star.

The men and women of Niggertown huddled around the fires in the middle of their dirt-floored shacks. The fires were small and smudgey, built from wet fuel which smouldered more than it blazed, filling the shacks with smoke. The people's eyes watered and, when they coughed, their black bodies convulsed with disease planted deep in their lungs.

Like a cruel beast, the cold winters of America stalked the negroes' bodies. The biting winds sapped the stamina from their hearty frames. And even those young negroes who had been born in this country felt their vitality slipping when the first leaves began to fall from the trees in autumn. But with all the difficulties that the Bantu, the Ashanti, the Mundingoe, and the Hausa had in adjusting to the erratic climate of Louisiana, the drudgeries of plantation work had to continue and they clung desperately to the hope that the warm days of summer would return. Yet, in December, the sun seemed as faraway as the freedom which they had also once enjoyed in Africa.

A short distance through the woods from Niggertown, Mama Gomorrah had bedded down the small children for the night on the deep wooden shelves built along three walls of The Shed. The wizened old woman herself crouched in front of a stone fireplace, her whip curled next to her on the floor like a tamed python, and the light from the flames shone like fairy lights in her wild, white mass of hair. She was busy tonight sorting through a pile of old tow clothing, deciding which garments were warm enough for the children to wear for the remainder of the winter and which pieces should be cut and resewn into clothes to accommodate their growing limbs. When springtime came, the older children would move from The Shed to shacks in Niggertown and take on the full responsibilities of adult slaves. They would need adequate pants and smocks not only for the new labours that they would be doing but also to cover their ripening bodies.

A young black boy named Posey knelt near Mama Gomorrah in front of the stone hearth tonight. By some quirk of nature, normal boyhood was by-passing Posey. His face was too pretty and his mannerisms were effeminate. But this soft-manned boy had a precocious eye for recognizing beauty and he had got his name—Posey—by gathering wild flowers, bringing them back to The Shed or taking them to the big house.

At this late hour, Posey concentrated on the flowers which he had collected last summer and autumn from the fields and the gardens on The Star. Having tied their stalks together into bunches of twelve, Posey had hung his flowers to dry on a high rafter in The Shed. Now, as his small, slim fingers picked delicately through the fragile collection, he put the flowers into separate piles—the asters, the daisies, the cornflowers, the dahlias. Next, he redivided them by colour. Also, apart from harvesting flowers to dry, Posey had gathered stalks of wheat, ears of corn, even jimson and fireweed, which now all looked crisp and golden and red, perfect ingredients for an arrangement in some tall vase on a mantle in the big house.

But there were people tonight on The Star who were not as industrious as Mama Gomorrah, or so thoughtful as Posey. They were the three people who, among other duties, were directly responsible for the slaves, to see that they had fire wood, that it was dry, and that they did not catch diseases. But Chad Tucker, his wife, Claudia, and the yellow-skinned boy who had been sent long-ago to help them, Monk, wilfully shirked their responsibilities at The Star. Tonight, the three of them were curled together on the same bed in the Tuckers' cabin. Their six legs were interlocked on the mattress, lying limp like the legs of a dozing animal, a curious dog which possessed one pair of hirsute legs, one pair of smooth white legs, and one pair of legs which were the rich colour of amber. And as they slept now under the influence of corn whiskey, Chad, Claudia, and Monk were oblivious to the fact that their own stove had burned dead and that the air around them had become cold. The corn husk mattress rustled when one of them moved, but, they remained asleep, their thoughts far away in their separate dreams of power.

In wintertime, the path between the overseer's cabin and the big house was buried deep in dried leaves, and the bare limbs of the trees formed grotesque shapes against the dark sky. As the wind continued to howl, the trees creaked and the fallen leaves churned into thicker layers across the barren landscape. This New Year's Eve did not appear to be a momentous occasion.

The moon glowed in a dim blotch behind the thick clouds; the big house stood alone and solid, ugly without its decoration of bougainvillea and hedgerows at the end of the driveway. All the lights in the dormer windows and the upper floor of the house were black at this late hour. In the attic, Ta-Ta lay curled under a grey woollen quilt on her narrow cot. A draft from the rattling window made her shiver but the rum she had drunk still warmed her soul. And, as she lay like a prisoner in this garret room, her mind travelled to the faraway hills and the soft yellow fields of the plantation in the West Indies where she had been happy and young and owned a green dress with a scalloped skirt. She dreamed of Petit Jour and the woman who had been her beloved mistress, Honore Jubiot—a primitive image of her chalked onto the wall next to Ta-Ta's cot.

On the floor below Ta-Ta, Rachel Selby tossed feverishly on her large walnut bed. Her drab hair was twisted into a single plait, which looked like a dead worm that had crawled out of her brain and now was lying lifeless, limp on the crisp white linen of her bed pillows. Suddenly, jerking her head in her sleep, Rachel would mutter a rude word or an improper phrase. Having less control of her mind in the passing years, she was unable to repress the stream of foul words which—without warning—would spring from her mouth. And worse, she did not think that she was saying anything particularly offensive.

The time was well past eleven o'clock now, almost midnight, and the only sign of light in the big house glowed from the front parlour window, pouring a token of brightness out into this bleak December night.

Inside the parlour, Albert Selby, Melissa, and Peter were all gathered in front of the blazing hearth. Near this happy trio set a wooden bowl of apples, a basket of walnuts, a blue-and-white dish of peppermint candies, and a plate of frosted cakes decorated with raisins and glacé cherries. This colourful array of treats showed that tonight was a very special event for all of them. Not only was it New Year's Eve, but it was the eve of a new century: a few minutes would see the beginning of the year 1800.

As the ornate metal minute hand on the mantle clock slowly crawled past the Roman numerals of eight, nine, ten, ticking away the last of 1799, an excitement mounted in the snug parlour as the three people tried to think of wishes for their new year.

Albert Selby was comfortably seated in his Dorset chair to the left of the fireplace. A dab of Storky's bread pudding still clung to the red hairs of his goatee and, on the bib of his white shirt, was spotted some carrot soup. But nothing could blemish Selby's enjoyment tonight. He thrilled at seeing Melissa looking so happy. He hoped that, with luck, the winter would continue to be good to her. She had avoided catching any colds so far, as well as the flu germ that had been circulating among the girls with whom she was meeting these days to learn numbers and writing.

Melissa Selby was fifteen years old and, in this first bloom of womanhood, she was already a polite and well-mannered young lady. Her complexion was creamy; her nose, small and slightly retrouse, and her hair, long and blonde, which she wore in a bow at the nape of her neck. But apart from her physical attributes, one's attention was first attracted to her warm personality; then, he would notice the developing feminine contours of her body. Melissa was not rushing forward into adulthood. She was too busy learning reading and writing, the lessons which she had been denied earlier when there had been no school marm to visit this remote area. Melissa's ambition now was to do everything possible to help her father. She knew how hopeless he was with his ledgers and, wanting to be his right hand someday, she had chosen this way to start. She was observant enough to see already that Chad Tucker was neglecting his obligation as overseer at The Star. But how long would she have to wait to correct that problem?

Apart from her school learning, Melissa was showing an aptitude with a needle, having graduated from elementary quilt-piecing to the more intricate labours of embroidering and lace making. But most of all, Melissa loved to spend hours in the kitchen. Storky was teaching her how to preserve melon rinds, knead and bake bread, even how to put up apple-and-raisin chutney.

Selby was delighted in Melissa's appreciation of domestic values. Although his daughter showed no interest for life in a parlour, Selby did not care. And as Rachel seldom ventured downstairs from her sickroom these days, there was less and less interference into the lives of these three people.

As for Peter, Selby could hardly believe that the boy was now a year older than Monk had been when Selby had first brought the two boys and Ta-Ta from New Orleans ten years ago. Since then, Peter had learned quickly, falling easily into the pattern of life here at The Star. Now reaching Selby's ear in height, Peter promised to be a tall and slim man. Selby knew that the boy's body would be wide in the shoulders, too, and that he would have a slim waist. Although it was still too early to tell what final appearances that Peter's face would eventually take, Selby knew that he would be handsome.

Peter's skin was dark, his hair was silky black, and his eyes were as blue as ever. A line of pubescent black down now covered Peter's upper lip, though, and his cheeks were blemished with youthful pimples. But his nose was straight and narrow, his dark eyebrows balanced into two neat lines. And those glowing cornflower blue eyes had a genuine honesty to them.

But Peter's hands did not match his arms yet. They were too large and awkward for his maturing limbs. His feet were also big and often clumsy, not moving fast enough for the strength that was gathering in his long legs. Selby had noticed with further amusement how, lately, that Peter was trying to hide the size of his genitalia, dressing—first—on the left, and—then—on the right, never quite finding a comfortable position for the new bulk of his masculinity. But realizing that Peter would also overcome that discomfort, Selby privately forecasted a fine maturity for the boy. He already felt that Peter would do justice to both him and The Star in whatever capacity he would eventually take here. Selby had put the fact out of his mind that Peter had come to him from a *vendue* table in New Orleans.

At this moment, Melissa was urging Peter to make his wish for the New Year. But she warned him not to say it aloud, because, if he said it, his wish would not come true.

Peter's tongue was as awkward as the rest of his body these days. He asked in the wavery voice that was neither child's nor man's, 'But what if what I want is something that somebody has to know about so I can get it?'

Slapping playfully at him, Melissa said, 'Oh, leave it to *you* to make things difficult!'

Peter turned to look up at Selby sitting in the chair. 'But it's true. How is Father going to know what I want?'

He still called Selby 'Father'.

Covering her ears, Melissa warned, 'Don't say it! Don't say your wish!'

Selby took Peter's side in this argument. 'Yes, Melly. What if Sonny wants something that I've got to know about?'

'Okay, stick together, you two,' Melissa said, spreading the full skirt of her pink candy-striped dress around her on the carpet. 'But I'm not going to tell you *my* wish!'

'Who cares!' Peter grumbled.

Putting his hand on Peter's shoulder, Selby asked, 'Now, what is your wish, Sonny?'

Throwing out his chest and shutting his eyes, Peter said, 'I wish . . . I wish . . . I wish that I could have my very own groom!'

'And so be it,' Selby said. 'And not only shall I buy you your very own groom but I'll let you pick him out yourself. No old, trumped-up, cotton-picker for you, Sonny! In fact, we'll go to New Orleans to choose him. How does that sound?'

Before Peter had time to thank this man whom he had come to call Father, Melissa began waving her hands at the both of them to be quiet. Then, as the mantle clock began to sound bong, bong, bong, Melissa closed her eyes and, crossing two fingers on each hand, she made her wish to herself.

It was now officially the year, 1800.

*Chapter Eight*

# BLACKS FOR SALE

Against the unfavourable odds of winter, the first warmth of spring sun brought life again to the Louisiana countryside. It was a time for clearing away the debris of autumn, to plow the fields for planting corn and cotton, to sow the vegetable gardens, to clear the underbrush from the orchard and mend the split-rail fences: spring was a time to resume old work on The Star and begin new cycles that would see the labours for both summer and autumn.

The people of The Star, the black men and women of Niggertown, slowly shook away their drowsiness of the winter months and, as the spring sun began to thaw their bones, their hopes for life became revitalized. Being companionable by nature, the plantation negroes happily joined together into gangs to clear the fields of stones and bramble bushes, working together more diligently on these demanding chores than they had done in isolation on the less tedious jobs of greyer days. The warm sun unified the people of Niggertown.

Always in the springtime, there was a scramble in Niggertown for the young faces whom Mama Gomorrah sent from The Shed. The veterans of Niggertown pulled and yanked at the maturing boys and girls, examining their smooth bodies, questioning them for details, finding which ones they wanted to work beside them during the day and take under their roof at night. These rough and tumble inspections had nothing to do with parentage. No mothers or fathers looked for their offspring. The springtime scrambles were conducted on the frankest physical level. All family ties had been cut long ago with each umbilical cord.

In the big house, Storky resented the number of people who came to her in the springtime, arriving at the kitchen door to seek her advice. Storky had to answer questions and settle arguments for the people of Niggertown, solving jealousies between the black men who had not been raised to the position of drivers in the field and those who had, or try to explain the intricacies of sexual fidelity to young black girls who were beginning to feel a surging devotion for one man in particular.

Back in Africa, there had been no problems of monogamy. African women learned from an early age that the male could choose as many women as his wealth allowed. But here in Louisiana where there was no system of hierarchy, the black people were confused by the mating examples set by white people and frustrated by the social restrictions imposed upon them by slavery. Storky found herself patiently explaining the bitter facts of a slave's life to strange black people, Africans whom members of her own tribe, the Ashanti, would have killed rather than helped. In the springtime at The Star, Storky became both chieftain and *hougan*, leader and priestess, and all these infringements on her precious time were done at a point when house cleaning was reaching its zenith.

Storky had her own problems of romance, too. When the grey branches of the trees first began to pop with green buds, a brawny negro called Samson would desert the blacksmith shop in favour of hanging around the kitchen door, waiting for Storky to beckon him inside.

But Samson could not abandon his work to visit Storky. She would not allow that because, in the springtime, the blacksmith was needed more than ever on The Star.

Storky made Samson obey two rules if he wanted to be her lover. He must only arrive at the kitchen door when the rest of the plantation was asleep and he had to leave when Storky arose early in the morning to light the fire in the cookstove. No matter how adeptly Samson had pleasured Storky the night before, she would give the big black man a swift kick with her foot if he lay on the floor snoring a moment too long.

This particular morning in the spring of 1800, the sky outside was still dark. Storky knew that she had to cook breakfast and have it on the table extra early today. Master Selby was taking Peter to New Orleans and they would be leaving at sunrise.

Storky had not slept much last night. Samson had been in an overly amorous mood and, without admitting the fact to her hulking lover, Storky had felt a definite desire for him, too, having let herself be persuaded into repeated acts of physical pleasure. When Storky set her mind at ease, and allowed her body to follow in unison, she enjoyed these moments with Samson. Down here in the kitchen, the two large black people could thrash around on the plank flooring all night, making as much noise as they wanted. But despite Samson's towering size, he was quiet and smooth-moving, laying with Storky on the pallet and performing with an athletic facility. This trait of Samson pleased Storky's sense of neatness as much as it thrilled her and, always, when she felt Samson's hardness come pushing deeply into her, she felt as much pride over his dexterity—his sexual manners—as she felt from the delight of its effect.

Samson had been particularly praiseworthy last night. He had brought Storky to an ecstatic climax no less than five times, two of which had nothing to do with his phallus but with the adept tricks which he had done with his serviceable big mouth and knowledgeable fingers. Now, as the plantation blacksmith lay curled on the pallet beside Storky, she lay staring into the darkness above her, planning the morning's work ahead of her. Apart from breakfast, she had to prepare a hamper of food for Selby and young master Peter to take with them in the wagon.

Thinking how Selby was taking Peter to New Orleans to buy a groom, Storky's white teeth glistened in the darkness as she grinned. She doted on the ten-year-old boy as if he were one of her own people. And she could not believe he was old enough to have his own groom.

Storky respected Peter as a white person. But she had learned the secret that Selby had bought him by mistake as a negro slave. Nothing could be kept for long from Storky. On hearing that story, though, Storky felt even closer to Peter. She knew that he had had as little control of his life as a black person had over his own.

To Storky's manner of thinking, Peter possessed the warm heart of a negro. He was not loud and boisterous like so many young white boys whom she had seen at The Star.

Storky reflected on how lucky she had been with white people. Or, at least, with some white people. In her secret thoughts, she hated Rachel Selby but, because of Rachel's sickness, Storky saw very little of her in the kitchen. She only heard Rachel's rantings through the thickness of her bedroom door. Privately, Storky chuckled that a woman so strict and religious as Rachel Selby had been reduced now to muttering indecencies. Storky did not understand the white people's god, but she suspected that this might be that god's way of punishing a woman who had caused so much misery in other people's lives. Such prudishness was as unnatural as the sorry condition from which Rachel now suffered.

Storky's thoughts were suddenly disturbed by the faraway call of a rooster. She bolted to her feet. She had to hurry and made preparations for Selby's trip to New Orleans with young Master Peter.

By five o'clock in the morning, Selby and Peter were seated at the table in the dining-room, eating fried eggs and ham by candlelight. Storky was back in the kitchen busily putting the finishing touches on the hamper she was packing for their journey. She had prepared them fried chicken, thick slices of cold ham, boiled eggs, carrot sticks and a small basket of lemon cakes. She also included a jug of coffee for Selby and a jug of milk for Peter, plus a large jar of water.

Storky was pleased to fix special treats for them but she was sorry to see them leave The Star—even for three days.

Barely two hours had passed since Selby and Peter left— rattling down the driveway in the rough wagon—when Biddy rushed into the kitchen. Melissa and Storky were working side-by-side at the kitchen table. They were rolling pastry to make fresh rhubarb pies.

Waving her small brown hands as if they were on fire, Biddy excitedly exclaimed, 'Miss Melissa! Miss Melissa! Your Mama's asking to see you rightaway in her bedroom, Miss Melissa.'

Reaching for a towel, Melissa quickly wiped the dough from her hands and said to Storky, 'Mama. It's the first time Mama's asked for me in weeks. I better hurry see.'

Behind Melissa's back, Storky narrowed her eyes at Biddy. She was angry at Biddy for bringing this message. Everybody had been trying to keep Melissa as far away as possible from her mother's room. Melissa might be fifteen years old but she was too young to hear the foul words which Rachel Selby often said.

Rushing from the kitchen, Melissa held her skirts as she ran up the first flight of the circular staircase. She was happy that her mother felt well enough this morning to see her. For so long, Rachel had not wanted to see anybody.

Rapping lightly on the mahogany door, Melissa called, 'Mama. It's me. Melly.'

The answer was sharp. 'Come in.'

Two weeks had passed since Melissa had last seen her mother, and entering the room, she was surprised to see how well she was looking this morning. Rachel did not show any of the signs of infirmity that Melissa had expected. Her eyes were sharp. Her hair had been brushed back from her face. And there was even some faint sign of colour in her gaunt cheeks.

Rushing to the side of her mother's bed, Melissa grabbed her cool hand and said, 'Just you and me are in charge now for three whole days at least, Mama. Won't we have fun. Just us.'

Turning her head away from Melissa, Rachel stared at the lace curtains gently flapping on her window and answered sourly, 'They made enough noise leaving.'

Melissa fortunately caught herself in time and did not say why her father and Peter had gone to New Orleans. Selby had warned Melissa not to tell her mother that they were going to buy a groom, another slave for The Star. Melissa said now, 'Peter was so excited that Papa is taking him . . . on this trip. Wasn't that good of Papa to do?'

Rachel laughed bitterly. 'So you think it's good for women-folk to be left alone!'

'But, Mama. We can take care of ourselves. Nothing can happen to us.'

Looking back at Melissa, Rachel mocked, 'Nothing can happen to us, girl? Well, what about all those niggers out there?'

Melissa stared at her mother. Instead of appearing well to her now, Rachel suddenly looked shrivelled and old and cantankerous. Her shaggy eyebrows hung over her piercing eyes like clumps of grey moss. Her mouth was pale and drawn as tightly as a string-purse. The only thing that Melissa could say to her was: 'Storky will take good care of us, Mama.'

'Storky? Ha! She's as black as the rest of them. She would join in with them no-good niggers and help hold us *down*!'

'Hold us . . . down?'

Rachel asked, 'Girl, how old are you?'

'Fifteen, Mama.'

'Has that boy tried to catch you yet? That Peter?'

'Peter? Catch me? We play together, Mama, but—'

'Play! I don't mean play. I mean has he tried to *rape* you?'

'Rape me?' Melissa was stunned. She knew what the word 'rape' meant. The girls at her school spoke about it in whispers. That was what had supposedly happened to a Witcherley woman a long time ago, she had been 'raped'.

Rachel was oblivious of the serious effect which the word had on her young daughter. She continued maliciously, 'Those black men, Melissa? Have they tried to show themselves to you, too? Have they tried to get you to hold what they've got, to take it in your hand?'

Slowly rising from the edge of her mother's bed, Melissa said slowly, 'Mama, I don't know what you mean.'

'Humph! At fifteen, I'm sure you know exactly what I mean. Don't you try to hide anything from me, young lady, by saying that you don't know what I mean. If you tell me that, I'll just

145

think you're trying to hide something from me *and* the Good Lord Almighty.'

'Mama, I'm not trying to hide anything from anyone. I do not know what you're talking about. Now, if you want to say something, please come right out with it, please! Please, Mama, let us be friends. I see so little of you, Mama, and—' Melissa moved to sit on the edge of her mother's bed again, reminding herself that she had been very ill, and probably still was.

Curiously, this confrontation with Melissa seemed to serve as a tonic to Rachel. She readjusted the pillows behind her back and, sitting higher in bed, she said briskly, 'You wonder why I stay in my bedroom, don't you? Well, I'll tell you why. I lock myself up in here so they don't rape me, that's why! So those niggers won't get wild ideas in their heads and try to *rape* me. Yes, white ladies are what those niggers really want, you know. Black men don't like pestering with Storky all the time. They would rather be with us, white womenfolk. You and me. Me! They would rather have me than stinking, black sluts like that Storky. Or Biddy. Oh, ho, ho! I know what that Biddy likes to do! I know what that whiney little black wench—'

Melissa had risen from the bed again in horror. She had been retreating from her mother's side during the diatribe against the blacks. Finally, having listened to as much as she could bear, she interrupted, 'Mama, please! I like Storky! And whatever you say about her, Mama, whatever you believe about Storky, she does not . . . smell! I like Biddy, too! And you can't talk about them like that. You can't.'

Calmly, Rachel accused, 'I suppose you're sweet on those big nigger bucks, too. I suppose you already got started on that nasty business. Oh, ho, ho! I've seen what those niggers' got in their pants. No pants can hide what those niggers have. And, being that we're on that subject, little Miss Nigger Lover, I might as well tell you the whole truth about them now. Those niggers aren't brought from Africa to *work*! They don't have an energetic bone in their bodies. They're lazy and slothful and dirty. But what they do have, what those niggers do have is a big prick! A prick! That's why we white people bring them

146

here. For their pricks. We all want those niggers' big black pricks!'

Melissa's head was spinning. She had not heard talk like this ever before in her life. She had not heard the facts of life so specifically discussed. And wanting to stop it right now, but also wanting to remain respectful of her ailing mother, she glanced around the bedroom, looking for some distraction for her.

Suddenly, her eyes seized upon a pile of letters, announcements, hand bills and petty circulars which had arrived at all houses in the neighbourhood. When such useless messages arrived at The Star, they were usually sent up to Rachel's room to keep her occupied in her infirmity, to amuse her into thinking that she was being useful.

Quickly seizing the pile of papers, Melissa thrust them onto the bed and said to her mother, 'Before we say another word, Mama, you must open your mail to see if someone is coming to call on us today! Oh, wouldn't that be terrible, Mama! Wouldn't that be absolutely awful if, say, if Reverend Briggs came calling today and we had nothing in the house to serve him. No scones or fresh bread or strawberry cakes, or—'

Next, Melissa snatched a silver letter-opener from the bedside table and, holding it to her mother, she said, 'Now, open the letters. And what can I bring you while you're opening your mail, Mama? Would you like some . . . coffee? Or, how does a nice pot of mint tea sound to you?'

Grudgingly examining the first sealed piece of brown paper, Rachel Selby mumbled, 'Tea. But not *mint* tea. Mint colours my urine.' Looking up at Melissa, she coldly explained, 'It makes my piss yellow and stinky.'

Melissa stifled her blush. Hearing her mother talk about toilet habits in such a blatant way was as shocking as having heard her refer to a negro's genitalia.

'Then plain tea it shall be, Mama,' Melissa said meekly, bending to tuck in the blankets before she left the bedroom.

Rachel suddenly shrieked.

Standing upright, Melissa stared at her mother.

Having opened the first announcment, Rachel waved the

brown sheet in the air, shouting, 'So now any trash can buy niggers, can they? Look! Lynn and Craddocks! Look! They used to be restricted to quality folk. They used to be on our side! But now any common muck can buy niggers there!' Dropping her trembling hands to the counterpane, Rachel tossed her head back and forth on the white pillows, wailing, 'Oh, what will I do? What will I do? Niggers everyplace! Every white trash in the Territory having niggers! Niggers all over the place! Niggers raping me! Niggers jumping on me! Niggers grabbing me by the throat! Niggers holding me down on my bed! Niggers biting my breasts! Niggers giving me babies!'

'MAMA! *MAMA!*' Melissa begged, struggling to calm her mother. But as Rachel continued to writhe, screaming on her bed, Melissa left her side and ran from the room. She must get her Mother that pot of tea from the kitchen but it would be a pot of tea strongly laced with laudanum—a drug to sedate her.

By mid-morning on that day, Claudia Tucker was sitting in the doorway of her shack. As Selby had gone to New Orleans, Chad Tucker had abandoned his work and taken Monk cat-fishing with him.

Basking alone now in the spring sunshine, Claudia thought how Monk had changed since he had first come to her as a choreboy. He had been a sassy but bright little sapling. He was quick to learn. Monk had thrown himself into his role both in the Tuckers' bed and in Chad Tucker's private venture of selling slaves to the poor farmers.

But then something had happened to Monk. And Claudia sat now in the sun puzzling what exactly had changed him. Monk no longer seemed to have any life to him. To Claudia, he was turning into just another dreary nigger.

Claudia's secret love-making with Monk had not lasted very long. She had lost interest in him when she had seen how nervous he was of Tucker discovering them. Monk had not tried to be defiant.

Reflecting now, Claudia saw that Monk had been like a colt which she had broken more easily than she had expected. She had broken him, too. Monk's whole spirit had changed, collapsed.

And what this meant to Claudia now was that there was only one man in the world who could keep her happy—that was her husband. Chad indulged her fantasies. Claudia even suspected that he had known that she and Monk had been screwing. But he had not stopped them—Claudia grinned to herself—because Chad knew that she was really the boss of the family.

Chad Tucker was not entirely without any faults himself thesedays,' though, Claudia thought as she sat in the sun. He had sold only one nigger in the last twelve months and not more than twenty in the last eight years. She remembered when he sold all the bucks that he could get his hands on. Even her favourites. But now—

Claudia's thoughts were suddenly disturbed by a young black boy crouching in the yard a short distance away from her.

Looking toward a flock of chickens pecking at the dirt under a chinaberry tree, Claudia saw a young negro child kneeling amongst them. The child looked to be about nine years old and was dressed in a white osnaburgh shift. But Claudia could not tell if the child was a girl or a boy.

She called, 'Hey, nigger?'

The child raised its cropped head.

'Nigger, you a girl or a boy?'

'I'm Posey,' the child called.

Studying the child's smooth brown skin and delicate features, she said, 'That's no answer for a white lady. I'm Miss Tucker, Mam.'

'I'm Posey ... Miss Tucker, Mam,' the child answered, holding up a handful of chicken feathers. 'I'm gathering these for Mama Gomorrah.'

Claudia called, 'What's that old woman wanting my chicken feathers for? She ain't asked me if she could have them.'

'She wants them for magic, Miss Tucker, Mam.'

'Magic!' Claudia let out a breath of disgust. 'Ain't that old critter got better things to do with her time than . . . magic?' Claudia shook her head. She had heard the stories about Mama Gomorrah and voodoo. But she had discredited the rumours. Claudia considered the voodoo stories to be the same kind of foolishness as the stories about the sinners of Gomorrah. Claudia thought that Mama Gomorrah was crazy. Looney.

The child called, 'Mama Gomorrah is the best nigger in this whole world, Miss Tucker, Mam.'

Studying the delicate build of the child's body, Claudia slowly began to get an idea. She had heard tales about fancies—special negroes that sold for very high prices. She wondered if perhaps this child could be sold as a fancy. She could see that the child was not normal.

She called, 'You living at The Shed?'

'I help run the shed, Miss Tucker, Mam.'

A smile covered Claudia's fleshy face and, raising a pencil-thin eyebrow, she warned, 'Better not say that word, nigger kid. Better not say 'run' or somebody might hear you. Lots of niggers like you talk about running and then they get caught and they get whipped.'

Posey stared at her with confusion.

Claudia continued, 'Fact is, I just heard you with my own ears, didn't I, bragging about "running"?'

The child stared at Claudia and then glanced down to his handful of white feathers. The way in which Claudia was twisting his words puzzled him.

'Do you know what would happen to a nigger like you if a white lady like me says she heard you talking about running?' she called.

Studying his handful of feathers, Posey shook his head.

Resettling herself in the doorway, Claudia said, 'Well, you just wouldn't have more chance than cow-shit in a swarm of flies, that's what. Now, if you're going to run anywhere, you better run back to The Shed, nigger. You stole enough feathers from my chickens for one day.' Staring at him, she asked, 'How'd you like some nigger brat to come along and steal *your* feathers?'

Posey finally understood what she was talking about now. He quickly protested, 'I ain't pulled none out, Miss Tucker, Mam. These feathers just lying here.'

'Makes no difference. How'd you like to drop a few feathers and then have some nigger come along and steal them?'

Posey's pug nose wrinkled into a grin. He thought Claudia was making a joke with him. He said, 'I ain't no chicken!'

Claudia mumbled to herself, 'I ain't real sure what you are, nigger. I ain't sure if you're a hen or a rooster.'

Then, watching Posey run effeminately through the bushes, Claudia made a mental note to talk to her husband about the strange-looking child when he got back home this afternoon. Tucker had not sold a piccaninnie before and this would be a perfect time to steal one from The Shed. Selby was away from The Star for three days. And the Tuckers could be in the nigger business again.

The printed handbill from Lynn and Craddock which Rachel Selby had read was true. The New Orleans auction house was opening its doors to a wider audience.

Albert Selby learned this for himself in New Orleans when he saw a large poster attached to a board in the foyer of the Hotel LaSalle. He and Peter had arrived after nightfall and checked in for two consecutive nights.

Fatigued and dusty from the long trip, Selby did not question the other planters whom he saw in the lobby of the hotel, inquiring why the auctioneers had chosen to alter their exclusive policy. Instead, he and Peter went immediately with a negro boy, an arrogant quadroon who was elaborately dressed in green-and-yellow livery, and they followed his swinging hips up three flights of Oriental carpeted stairs to their room. An orchestra played in the lobby of the hotel, its syrupy music clinging to their eyes as they climbed up, up, up the deep-piled steps.

Even in his exhaustion, Peter thought that the Hotel LaSalle

151

must be the grandest building in the world. He stood dazed by the edge of the carved teak railing on the third mezzanine, staring down at the palm-filled lobby below him as the prissy bellboy was unlocking the door to their room with a large brass key. Peter felt as if he were standing on the lofty cliff of some high mountain, gazing down into a mythical valley. The stratas of cigar smoke below him looked like variously coloured clouds. There were literally forests of palm trees on every landing, their wide fronds fanning out beyond the railings. And the orchestra music continued to drift up from the green valley, played by an ensemble of mustard-coated negroes seated on a dais swagged with widths of green-and-brown velvet.

Selby had suspected that—unlike his son, Roland—Peter would be thrilled at seeing a big hotel. Selby had been right. Peter was agog at its splendour. And, for the remainder of the first evening there, Selby planned every detail as a treat for the impressionable, ten-year-old boy. He ordered a zinc tub to be sent to the room, followed by two cisterns of hot water so that Peter could have a bath before they went down to dinner. Next, he showed him how to pull a long green cord to call for a glass of lemonade and have his white suit to be taken away and pressed, all by the same tug.

That night, they ate dinner downstairs at a table on the edge of a sea of chattering diners—the women wearing ostrich feathers in their hair and the men's necks cascading with ruffles—and Selby permitted Peter to order anything he wanted from the enormous white menu, all the entrees elaborately scrolled in red ink—doves cooked in olives and lemon and wine, oysters gently fried in breadcrumbs and filled with rich cream, shrimp Creole, and Gumboes of every description.

The desserts were what enthralled Peter, though, and after gobbling a plateful of a cold sweet called 'Iced Italian Cream', flooded with chocolate sauce and burnt almonds and flanked by fan-shaped wafers, Peter was hardly able to climb the stairs again to his room. Collapsing onto the crisp linen sheets of his bed, his stomach was full from the good food and his mind dancing with the dazzling sights of the Hotel LaSalle.

But the next morning was when the true excitement began.

At eight o'clock, New Orleans was already throbbing with activity. Colourfully dressed negresses waddled down the streets, balancing round baskets of crayfish on their heads, shouting to the louvered windows above them about the stimulating effect which their merchandise would have on a customer's love powers. Black children wearing nothing but the skimpiest of breechclothes swaggered through the morning crowds, bumping the pedestrians with their traysful of glacé cherries, orange rinds, lemon peel, and angelica, these candies sparkling in the sun like an array of Arabian jewels. Old women dressed in black rags crouched on the cobblestones with small paper cones of nuts displayed in front of them on rush matting—pistachios, peanuts, pecans, almonds. Everyone in New Orleans seemed to be selling something—flowers, confections, fresh fruit, seashell necklaces, flasks of perfume—and all the vendors' shrill voices joined in a cacaphony that deafened Peter's ears.

Walking closely to Selby, Peter remembered the advice he had received, to keep his hand on his money pouch as they moved through the jostling crowd of morning traffic. He gawked at an ebony lacquered carriage, a gold-and-red crest painted on its door, as it clattered through the people, spreading them in every direction. He laughed at a cart piled high with wooden cages of cackling hens as it weaved slowly past him. He peered down a side street which was so narrow that clotheslines stretched across it, the laundry gently flapping high above everybody's heads. And, in a dark green doorway, Peter saw a pair of the most beautiful mulatto girls he had ever seen, standing side-by-side, batting their long eye lashes at him, smiling behind the black lace *mantillas* which they held across their mouths with long, carmined fingernails. Selby hurried Peter along.

Finally, reaching a white building with a brass plaque attached to the right side of an arched doorway, Peter saw, 'Lynn and Craddock, Auctioneers'.

He asked, 'Is *this* it, Father?' Compared to the zestful atmosphere of the streets through which he had just come—an amalgamation of French, Spanish, Moroccan, and all the colonies of the Caribbean—this plain white building looked unimposing, even sombre.

Selby had already disappeared through the arched doorway. Peter hurried to catch him.

Beyond the arch, the feeling became more tropical with a fountain splashing in the middle of a cool courtyard. Peter immediately noticed that the men standing in this small court were divided into two distinct groups: there were the roughly dressed farmers on the left side of the fountain and, to the right, stood a collection of finely-dressed men, gentlemen wearing smart cut-away coats and tall, pastel-coloured hats. Peter felt proud when, without hesitation, Selby walked toward the group on the right side of the fountain, nodding at two or three of the haughty men as he passed.

Peter whispered, 'Who are they?'

'Planters,' Selby answered nonchalantly, now leading Peter up a wide, white marble staircase edged on both sides with terra-cotta pots of lush greenery.

Lynn and Craddocks might have been changing their policy by inviting farmers to their *vendue*, but Peter was learning that there still a sharp division in the South between farmers and his own class—like Selby, he was a planter today, too. He even had a white suit.

At the top of the steps, they passed into a large room which had a round window at the far end of it. The temperature was stifling in here and, having just come from the bright sun, Peter could not focus immediately in this vastness—except for seeing a circular shaft of light flooding into the room from the round window, cutting through the clouds of cigar smoke and thick motes of dust. He heard a rumble of voices and, soon, he saw all the buyers gathered in here, a more homogeneous mixture of farmers and planters than had been in the courtyard.

Peter anxiously whispered to Selby, 'Has it started yet?'

Nodding toward the round window, Selby answered, 'Probably. The inspection was last night.'

154

'Inspection?' Peter did not want to miss anything.

Selby explained, 'To look at what you're getting. Examining their legs, teeth, and whatnots, seeing you're not buying a dud.'

Peter looked at Selby. 'Did we miss that?'

Selby shook his head. 'Didn't miss much. A man doesn't have to worry about the calibre of stock in this place. They don't try to cheat a man.' As hard as Selby was trying, he could not eradicate the vision of his last visit here, of the time when Lynn and Craddocks *had* made a mistake and sold him a white boy in an error. Selby had bought Peter in this very same auction hall but, as difficult as it was, he tried to block that memory from his mind. He was telling himself that Peter was his son. Peter was Sonny. Peter was his now.

Anxious to know the complete details of an auction, Peter asked, 'But maybe we should have gone to the inspection last night.'

'Nothing to worry about, Sonny,' Selby insisted, not wanting to go into the specific reason why he had not wanted to bring Peter to an inspection, especially an inspection at Lynn and Craddocks where they specialized in 'fancy' negroes. Such a gathering was no place for Peter or any other young boy, Selby felt. Too many curiosity seekers flocked to the Lynn and Craddock inspections, men who had no intention of coming the next day to buy a negro at all, merely going to the inspection to paw the merchandise. Selby thought than an Inspection here was nothing but a carnival of perverts, attracting men who were more interested in the size of a wench's breasts or the penis on a big buck than they were in their working ability in the fields or a house.

Looking around the smokey sales hall now, Selby said to Peter, 'Stay here while I get us a list.' He moved away from Peter, disappearing into the crowd.

As the auction had already begun, the men in the sales hall stood facing the round window. The sales table set under that window but, from where Peter stood, he could barely see the top of the black silk hat worn by a man standing on a high platform. Peter guessed that he must be the auctioneer and, wanting to see more of him, and the procedures of the sale, he moved forward through the crowd of men.

From his new position, Peter could now see not only the skinny auctioneer but a large, raised platform next to him. He saw three negroes soberly standing on it, two half-naked men and one woman in a long white dress. Their three heads were lowered as the auctioneer held his wooden gavel toward them, talking in a fast voice which Peter could not understand. But he knew that the auctioneer was trying to sell those three people to someone down here on the floor.

But the buyers all around Peter were talking, not listening to what the auctioneer was saying about the three black people. These customers did not seem to be too interested in the auction but more intent on visiting and laughing with their neighbours. Peter could not understand this. He considered the selling —or buying—of people to be a very serious matter. The men around him were treating this as if it were a party.

From what Peter could see of the three negroes for sale, they looked healthy. The two men had fine bodies, their muscles were big and all shiney with oil. They wore nothing but long baggy white pants made from the same rough fabric as the dress which the women wore but all of them looked clean. Peter could not understand why no one was trying to buy them, wanting to take them and give them a home.

Looking at a group of men talking near him, Peter noticed one white gentleman in particular. He was tall, swarthy, and had black sideburns which extended in sharp crescents under his tall white hat. The man also had a tuft of multi-coloured feathers pinned to the hatband. Peter had never seen such a decoration on a man's hat before, Peter moved closer for a better look. It was then that he heard the tall, swarthy man say to his companions, 'Numbers one, two, three, four. Don't touch them. Those niggers are from Dragonard.'

Peter froze at the mention of the word. *Dragonard.*

One of the man's companions asked, 'Dragonard Plantation?'

The swarthy man nodded. 'I hear all the Dragonard stock has been done away with.'

Peter strained his ears to hear more. Dragonard was the word that Ta-Ta had whispered to him.

Selby's voice suddenly called out behind him. 'Sonny. I thought I told you to stay back here!'

Turning, Peter saw Selby pushing his way through the men, waving two sheets of paper at him. 'Here. Take your list.'

Not caring about the list, or worrying about Selby being angry at him for leaving the spot where he had left him, Peter could only think about the word which the swarthy man had said: Dragonard! He had to hear more about the Dragonard slaves. He had to listen about numbers one, two, three, four.

But when Peter turned from Selby to look to where the man had been standing, he saw that he was gone. The swarthy man with the feathers in his hatband had disappeared.

Coming closer to Peter, Selby held out the list and said, 'We're lucky, Sonny. We're just going onto number two now.' As usual, he did never remain angry at Peter.

Taking the list, Peter asked nervously, 'Number two?' Then, looking down to the sheet, he saw only a few words printed next to it. "Two Bucks. One Wench." Looking up at Selby, he asked, 'I thought it was supposed to say who's selling them.'

'Lynn and Craddock are breaking a lot of rules today,' Selby answered under his breath. 'I see, too, they've covered their mahogany walls with tarps! Feared these farmers are going to scratch their initial in them, I guess. But one good thing is that they've stopped serving that blasted sherry. Nobody but women drinks that.' Then, studying the list again, Selby said, 'But don't worry, Sonny. We haven't missed a thing. They always sell the best stock toward the end. They'll never change that. They try to get rid of the bad stuff first. That's why there's no keen interest now.' He nodded at the men conversing around them, showing little interest toward the auctioneer.

Bad stuff? Peter thought. Was Dragonard stock 'bad'. Skimming the list again, he asked Selby, 'But what if we want something that comes up early in the sale?'

Selby corrected Peter. 'Not "we", Sonny. You! What *you* want. You're the one who's doing the choosing today. Not me.

And here,' he said, turning Peter by the shoulders of his new white suit, 'Look around that way. That's where the sale's going on. Up there. Not back here.'

Peter turned to look toward the far end of the hall again but he was really not paying attention to the auctioneer now. His mind was racing with a problem. What should he do? He definitely remembered Ta-Ta saying that word. He distinctly remembered her talking lately about his mother, too. And, now, he thought that if, somehow, that Dragonard was connected to him and the woman who might be his mother, then he could not very well ask Selby to explain . . .

'What's the matter, Sonny? You look peaked. You aren't getting sick, are you?'

Peter shook his head. He mumbled, 'I'm fine.'

'You look a little pale.'

'I'm just trying to . . . decide something.' Peter was thinking about Melissa. He knew she was not his real sister. She had her own mother.

'Well, you don't have to decide too soon. Like I said, all the good stuff comes later.'

'Father—' Peter had to ask Selby just this one question. '—Father, why are these black people bad?' He nodded to the three negroes on the sales table. 'They look fine to me.'

Selby looked quickly around him before saying, 'There's a lot of stories going around here today, Sonny. A lot of mularky stories and a lot of true ones. But I just heard why they're letting in these dirt farmers. See, there's been some rioting down in a place called the West Indies—' Selby stopped, seeing a familiar face in the crowd. He called, 'Joshua Domitt! I'll be damned! Good to see you, Josh! What?' Selby moved to listen to his old friend's question.

By himself again, Peter turned to look one last time for the swarthy stranger. But he was gone. Then, looking at the auctioneer, he saw that lot number three had finally been sold and now the auctioneer was beginning to extol the working competence of the next lot—number four—and the auctioneer was shouting that he certainly expected a larger price than what he had received for the previous lot.

Lot Four consisted of three negroes, all males, two stocky labourers and one tall, handsome man who looked refined enough to work in the house, or, as Peter instantly thought, a groom!

A voice near Peter called snidely to the auctioneer. 'Where these trouble-makers from, mister?'

The auctioneer ignored the question, opening the bidding at two thousand dollars.

A wave of laughter spread across the smoke-filled room at the high price set for these three negroes. The amount would ordinarily be a bargain.

'Seven hundred and fifty is all I'd pay for trouble,' shouted a voice behind Peter.

Trembling now, Peter knew that he had to do something. And he had to do it fast. An inexplicable compulsion made him shout, '*One* thousand dollars!'

The youthful crackle of his voice attracted the eyes of the men standing near him. Peter felt a hot flush rising in his cheeks but, drawing a deep breath, he repeated firmly, 'One thousand dollars.'

It was then that he heard Selby gasp behind him, 'Sonny? What in tarnation are you doing?'

From the platform, the auctioneer called, 'Is that your son, Albert Selby? Does The Star stand behind his bid?'

Peter turned to look at Selby.

With all the eyes in the sales hall upon him, Selby called back. 'Yes, I'm the boy's . . . father. The Star's behind him.'

The auctioneer then began to call one thousand dollars once, one thousand dollars twice ... .

Selby whispered to Peter. 'Sonny, do you know what you're doing?'

Peter answered, 'You said I could pick.' He could not look Selby in the eye.

'But, Sonny, you don't know a damn thing about those West Indian niggers.'

The sharp sound of the gavel closed the sale.

Thus, Peter had bought his first African slaves, the three black men from the Dragonard Plantation in the West Indies.

It was the second day that Selby was away from The Star and Posey sat now by himself in The Shed.

The weather was too warm for a fire this afternoon and the coals of the fieldstone hearth lay in an ashy grey heap.

Crouching on the floor in front of the hearth, Posey examined the chicken feathers he had collected for Mama Gomorrah and which now lay on the edge of the hearth in front of him. He had used berries to dye five of the feathers red and a pot of indigo to colour the other six blue. Mama Gomorrah would use them to make her voodoo pouches.

Hearing a noise behind him, Posey turned to the door to see if it was Mama Gomorrah returning. But instead he saw a man standing in the doorway at the far end of the large room. He knew that the man's name was Chad Tucker.

Rising to his bare feet, Posey smoothed his white smock over his legs and called, 'Mama Gomorrah ain't here, Mister Tucker, Sir.'

Tucker ambled through the door. 'You called Posey?'

Posey nodded, seeing a black man follow Tucker into the The Shed. He knew his name, too. It was Monk.

The Shed was one of the few outbuildings on The Star which had a board floor and, as Tucker's boots made a clomping noise across it, he called to Posey, 'Shuck off that dress you're wearing, Nigger. I want to take a look at you.'

Posey stared at the big white man.

Tucker shouted, 'Ain't you got no ears? I said strip!' As Tucker stood waiting for Posey to obey, he looked around him at the room dimly lit by the daylight pouring through three small windows in a row. He saw the rough-board beds built onto the other walls like three levels of chicken roosts—and called 'roosts' for the piccaninnies—and he also saw a neat line of wooden bowls on a long shelf. Although The Shed was rustic and crude, everything was clean and tidily arranged. Chad Tucker seldom came here as this was Mama Gomorrah's undisputed territory.

Mama Gomorrah was a shrewd woman and, having seen long-ago that Posey would not grow into a normal slave for The Star, she had not taught him the same obedience as she had the other children. She knew that only the passage of time would prepare a misfit like Posey for a role in plantation life.

Posey stared dumbly at Tucker and then looked at the painted feathers lying on the hearth behind him.

Tucker called to Monk, 'You stand there in case the brat tries to make a run for it.' Moving toward Posey, Tucker sneered, 'I'll show him how to strip. Then I'll see for myself what this brat has.'

Lunging forward, Tucker grabbed for the child.

Posey kicked his bare feet and clawed his sharp fingernails at Tucker.

'Brat!' Tucker bellowed louder, then hit the child.

Posey stopped his fight. His brown face tightened to cry.

Tucker now slowly reached for the cotton shift and, raising it, he stared between Posey's legs. He muttered, 'Well, I'll be damned.'

Next, Tucker beckoned Monk to come look over his shoulder at Posey's crotch.

As Monk looked at Posey, Tucker reached his rough hand toward the child's crotch and flicked a small roll of orange skin which hung between Posey's brown legs. His penis was the size of a small screw and he had no testicles.

Flicking the penis again to watch it spring up and down, Tucker laughed louder. 'Hell! You ain't no fancy, nigger. You're nothing but a God-damned freak.' Then, lifting the underdeveloped organ, Tucker inspected the skin behind it. He said, 'Nope. They ain't cut off your balls. You just ain't got none.' He roared with laughter.

Leaning forward, Monk said, 'Let me feel.'

As Monk examined.Posey, too, he also began to laugh.

Tucker said, 'We should've had this worm for fishing.'

Monk ran his finger where there should be testicles.

Watching, Tucker repeated, 'A freak. Nothing but a God-damned freak. Hell, I couldn't get a pig's turd for this freak nigger. Come on, Monk. Let's go back and tell Claudie she better improve her eyesight.'

Laughing, they turned away from Posey and walked to the door of The Shed.

Posey stood in front of the dead fireplace after they had gone. He was bewildered. He wondered what was so laughable about his—he looked down to see his penis. What was wrong with it? Why should they laugh at it? What had they expected to find?

That night, Posey told Mama Gomorrah about the incident with Chad Tucker. She assured the child that he had nothing to worry about and talked instead about the chicken feathers he had gathered and painted for her. She praised him for being so helpful.

Later, when Posey was asleep on the roosts with the other children, Mama Gomorrah squatted on the floor in front of a small fire. Her whip lay on the floor beside her. The light from the fire lit her brooding face.

Mama Gomorrah was thinking now. She first thought about Posey and the feathers which he had gathered for her. They would be useful in making the voodoo pouches which she gave to sick slaves. But she soon forgot about the medicinal pouches and thought about Chad Tucker mistreating Posey that afternoon. Mama Gomorrah was remembering other magic that she knew.

Mama Gomorrah recalled the baston root. The ground of The Star which yielded the deadly baston plant had been salted many years ago and it no longer grew there. But Mama Gomorrah still possessed a small quantity of its powder. The baston root quickened a man's pulse and then killed him. And Mama Gomorrah sat now in the light of the fire and weighed her reasons for giving it to Chad Tucker. Or should she let him continue harming black people until she stopped him another way?

*Chapter Nine*

# 'THE LOUISIANA PURCHASE'

The turn of the new century brought two changes of government to the territory known as Louisiana.

Spain ceded her claims on Louisiana to France in 1801, greatly increasing the French holdings in North America: France now had harbours on the eastern coast of Canada and the port of New Orleans in Louisiana. For commerce, this was a profitable development. Shipsful of furs sailed from the north while cotton, sugar, and tobacco poured across the Atlantic from the south.

But in military terms, the French found themselves in a vulnerable position. France was currently waging a war with Britain and saw that, if she lost on European soil, her North American holdings could be taken as booty.

Also, with the European war, France could not very well afford the expense of protecting such widely-parted colonies in North America.

However, apart from France, England, and Spain, a fourth power was beginning to emerge on the international battlefield—the United States of America.

The American president now was Thomas Jefferson, a leader whom some people hailed as a Renaissance man while less charitable men saw him as a greedy parvenu, a dilettante, and a butcher. But in whatever way that Jefferson was described, he had foresight and was a politician who knew the power of a threat.

Jefferson's cabinet had informed him about France's financial dilemma from the burden of long wars and, considering that fact, Jefferson decided that now was the right time to obtain the Port of New Orleans for America, along with a small packet of land which he wanted in East Florida. If France refused to accept his offer, Jefferson would take the land at the moment when Napoleon was least able to defend it.

In 1803, Thomas Jefferson sent an envoy to France to purchase the property. He had given his envoy permission to pay as high as ten million dollars for it and, if France did not accept the offer, the envoy would tell Napoleon that America would join England in war against France.

Napoleon sent the American envoy back to Washington with the news that he would not only sell New Orleans and the section of East Florida which Jefferson wanted, but he was also willing to sell the entirety of the Louisiana Territory. Napoleon was asking fifteen million dollars, only fifty percent more than Jefferson had been willing to pay for one-fifth the amount of land.

Jefferson pushed a bill quickly through Congress to raise money for Napoleon and, in 1803, paid four cents an acre in the transaction that was to be known as 'The Louisiana Purchase'.

This rich acquisition stretched west from the Mississippi River, from Canada down to the boot of Florida. Immediately, Jefferson dispatched explorers to traverse and chart this latest addition to the United States of America.

The pioneers already established in the southeastern regions of the Louisiana Territory continued life as they had, first under Spain, then France, and, now, the territorial rule of the American states to the north.

There was no visible effect on the Southern commerce, excepting that a Napoleonic embargo was lifted from the Port of New Orleans and cotton was now allowed to be exported once again to England, replenishing the Manchester mills after a two year hiatus.

The Star had not suffered during the embargo, being only in the first stages of growing and shipping green cotton. Eli Whitney's cotton gin was just beginning to change the prosperity of south-eastern America.

It was not until 1808 that Washington politics began to effect life in the South. A bill was passed in 1808 which forbade the further importing of slaves into the Louisiana Territory. The African slaves already in America—and their issue—would have to suffice as a labour force for the growing cotton economy. This was grave news for the South.

But the Southern planters were a resilient people. They saw how they could breed slaves from the negroes which they already owned.

Although averting a present clash, the 1808 bill saw the Abolition movement gathering momentum and the first seeds of a bitter struggle were sown between the North and the South. But as statehood had not yet come to the South, there were more important problems at the moment to contend with on the plantations themselves.

## Chapter Ten

# TROUBLE ISLAND

In the last eight years, Albert Selby had experienced little trouble with his people. There had been sickness and minor accidents on The Star but what ailments that Mama Gomorrah could not treat in Niggertown with her potions and voodoo pouches, Selby had sent for Doctor Whithers—the veterinarian in Troy—to ride up to The Star and cure.

But Chad Tucker would not allow 'Doc' Whithers to look at his wife when she became ill.

Claudia Tucker was stricken with a disease at the end of last year. As Selby saw very little of the Tuckers, he did not know how Mrs. Tucker was recovering.

Selby was aware, though, that something must be done about Tucker himself. Tucker was coming less and less to the big house to make his reports. The cotton gin in Troy sent Selby their reports and so he knew that Tucker was not cheating him on the green cotton crops.

Also, Selby had the consolation these days that his slaves had stopped running away from The Star. Rachel had asked him for an exact count of the slaves. Before Selby had time to comply with her wishes, she made it clear that she only wanted to know the number of potent black men there were living on The Star. Selby immediately dismissed her request. He did not want to indulge her phobia of black men raping her. And The Star passed into yet another year without taking a precise census of its people.

Albert Selby continued to count only his blessings.

\*

Selby felt that he was a lucky man. Contrary to what he had feared eight years ago, Peter's hasty purchase of three slaves at the New Orleans auction sale had not brought trouble to The Star. Nearly a decade had passed now and the people of Niggertown had absorbed the three new negroes as they did the saplings sent to them every spring from The Shed.

But the three new negroes—named Ido, Gosh, and Nero—had always been more glamorous to the other slaves than the young boys and girls raised by Mama Gomorrah. The three new slaves came from a faraway plantation on an island in the West Indies.

Two of those West Indian negroes—Ido and Gosh—could not speak the English patois of Niggertown. They talked a gutteral dialect of the Fanti tribe, an African tongue which no slave on The Star understood. Their verbal contact with the people on The Star came through Nero, the black man whom Peter had bought specifically to be his groom.

Nero spoke English but he was a quiet person, almost sullen. He talked very little about the slaves' past and even less about his own. And Nero seldom ever spoke about the island where they had lived in the West Indies. His only name for it was 'Trouble Island'.

When Peter had originally purchased the three West Indian negroes, he had had very little use for a groom. Peter had been not more than a school boy at the time. His horsemanship had been elementary and Nero only made sporadic visits to the stables of the big house to groom for Peter in his boyhood.

As badly as Peter had wanted to buy those three West Indian slaves, he stayed strangely away from them in the last eight years. It was as if he were afraid of them when he got them back to The Star.

Nero did not take advantage of his situation. He had been bought as a groom and he soon found work for himself in the stable of the big house. He curried Selby's mare as well as handling the new chestnut mare which eventually replaced Peter's pony. Nero gradually became a handyman there, too, repairing the stalls, forking the hay, reshingling the roof, keeping the wagon and two seldom-used buggies in good repair.

Although he looked like a fancy, Nero did not assume superiority over the other black people on The Star. He had slightly-flared nostrils and a broad forehead, capped by a growth of tight black hair. He was by far the most handsome negro male on The Star. But he was also the most humble.

Nero turned forty-years-old in 1808, an age incongrous to his body. He had a physique of a twenty-five-year-old athlete. His stomach was flat and hard; his thighs and calves, well-proportioned. When Nero worked in only his white breeches, they bulged with his masculinity and the muscles glided under the smooth tobacco-coloured skin of his broad shoulders and tapering back.

As Peter grew older, he eventually came to work alongside Nero in the stables. Peter talked as little as Nero himself. Their only moments of camaraderie were when they joked about wenching.

Peter had now passed through his childhood and teenage years on The Star. He had accepted life here at face value. He had been influenced by Albert Selby to think that asking questions meant to poke at beehives with a stick—a man got stung by his own curiosity.

Peter grew to be as secretive as the Selby family. Peter had become a Southerner. And a common trait of the Southerners was to lock-up their private lives from the meddlesome outside world.

Soon, Peter looked as natural working in the stables as Nero. His arms finally matched his big hands and his legs had no trouble controlling his feet. Peter was tall, broad of shoulder and hard-muscled. The sun had enriched his olive complexion to a burnt gold and given a silky lustre to his straight black hair. His eyes were still the brilliant cornflower blue that they had been in his childhood but, now, in the dawn of his twenties, Peter had a strong lantern jaw and a chiselled character to his lean face, a look that was more aristocratic than brutish.

Peter had grown into manhood on The Star but, in many ways, he lived the life of a privileged slave. As Southern slaves

169

often felt inside them that they were not meant to call a white man 'master', Peter likewise often felt that he had no link with the man whom he addressed as 'father'.

That spring of 1808 in Louisiana was one long continuation of wet, grey days. The rain drizzled from morning to night and the roads became deep beds of mire.

The whole landscape of The Star was as oppressing as the dark sky. The branches of the trees hung heavy with beaded raindrops and the grass was matted into soggy green and yellow layers.

These dull, wet days did little to improve Claudia Tucker's disposition. She lay for hours and hours on her damp corn-cob mattress, listening to the steady drumming of the rain against the leaning roof of the bedroom. She despondently thought that she would never recover from her illness.

Claudia's sickness was a mystery to both her and her husband. It had begun with headaches, followed by palpitations of the heart, and then her skin had become clammy with cold sweats. She had first thought that she was pregnant but, as she continued to have her violent periods of menstruation—and when no baby appeared after nine months—she labelled her poor condition as 'woman's ague'.

The worst part of Claudia's malady was that she did not have an appetite for sex. Without it, her life became suddenly empty. She could not read and so she was unable to pass her time with books. And she never had the patience—nor skill—for needlework or quilt-making.

Like a dying man is said to see life pass by his eyes, Claudia Tucker lay in her sick bed and saw a succession of her previous sexual encounters.

They had begun when Claudia was eleven-years-old and molested by a coach driver. She still remembered his foul breath and dirty foreskin. To this day, she still had an aversion to uncircumcised males and what she called 'head cheese'.

She remembered how at thirteen, she had spent a night in a barn with two barrel-chested soldiers and had her first experience of fellatio. She remembered how the soldiers had used her all night. She remembered that one soldier screwed her and the other soldier kept poking his fingers into her ears as he held her head to his crotch. She wondered if that experience had been responsible for her liking only masculine men—men who were domineering. And had awakened domination in herself, too?

Claudia had laid next with a boy her same age and she remembered teaching him how to make a woman reach an orgasm, too, and taunted him for not being able.

Her uncle had been her following lover and he had taught her the one item that the soldiers had overlooked—her uncle had been the first man to put his mouth between her legs and probed the lips of her vagina with his darting tongue.

It was then that Claudia met Chad Tucker and, from then on, all her sexual images included his large penis with its purple, turnip-like head.

The black men whom she had shared with her husband possessed no faces now in her memories—nor did they excite her passions.

Claudia's sickness had somehow stiffled all her sexual desires. She even tried to finger her clitoris, attempting to excite herself sexually in her sick bed as a test of her present capabilities. But she did not even respond to herself.

Chad Tucker still slept alongside her at night. She listened patiently as he dutifully reported what wenches he had laid with on The Star. She even let him squirt his excitement onto her naked thigh as he lay telling the story. But Claudia did not feel as if she were missing anything by not partaking in sex these days.

Monk still slept in the cabin but she did not want him to join her and Chad on the corn-cob mattress. Monk held no interest for her now at all, except as someone who could cook her meals and wait on her when she wanted attention.

After exhausting all her sexual memories, Claudia found herself thinking about God. She suspected that no white person could go to hell and she began to wonder what heaven would look like.

Pondering God and heaven, Claudia saw an image in her mind of The Star's big house. It sat in a field of ripe cotton. But the only problem with that idea was that she pictured God as looking like Albert Selby—long white hair and a henna goatee—and Claudia hated Albert Selby.

One day, Claudia asked her husband to buy her a picture of God when he went to Troy. She wanted it to be in a gold frame. The Tuckers still had the money from selling the slaves and Claudia told her husband to dig it up and spare no expense on the picture.

Chad Tucker had not been able to find a picture of God in the small village of Troy. He had only been able to find an itinerant artist's impression of the Greek god, Poseidon. It depicted a noble man—who was half fish—hovering over the waves. He held a three-pronged spear.

Although the picture was framed in gold, Claudia Tucker was not at all pleased with it. She did not want to spend these raining days, lying on a damp mattress, and stare at a fish man standing in water and holding a pitch fork. The more that she looked at it, the more she thought about the money that her husband had wasted.

But thinking about wasted money, Claudia soon progressed from being obsessed by God and heaven. She thought about the money itself. The money that Tucker had made from selling the slaves from The Star and about more money that they could make. She insisted that he dug it all up again and bring it to her.

Putting the money in a flour sack, Claudia kept it in bed with her. And, as the spring rains continued to pour outside, she sat with a worsted quilt wrapped around her shoulders and counted the money.

She began to think about making more money. She now wanted to be a very rich woman.

Claudia knew that it was too risky for her husband to steal any slaves from The Star at the moment. Peter was becoming too familiar with the black people in Niggertown. So, Claudia spent these wet days wondering how she and her husband could get more money from some other ruse.

There were many simple people in the South. Claudia knew that they could take advantage of those backwoods simpletons. She also knew that her husband possessed a very clever tongue when it came to convincing people to do—and to buy—something. Claudia felt that, between the two of them, they should be able to come-up with some way of making more money.

One afternoon, Claudia struck upon her answer. She remembered a poor dirt-farmer called Tommy Joe Crandall and his wife. The Crandalls had wanted to buy a slave from Tucker but—even if Tucker could steal one from The Star now—the Crandalls could not buy it. They were too poor to buy a whole negro.

But Claudia thought of something which they could afford. She knew that the Crandalls had a small savings and she suddenly realized how she could add it to her flour sack of other money.

Becoming so excited by her brilliant idea, Claudia Tucker hopped out of bed and, clutching the worsted quilt around her, she padded out of the lean-to in her bare feet.

There was still a small fire in the stove and Claudia immediately set about to make the first cup of coffee that she had brewed for herself in months.

Sipping the coffee, and clutching the money bag in her lap, Claudia sat with the quilt wrapped around her and waited for Chad to come back to the cabin. She wanted to tell him how they could get money out of the dumb Crandalls.

The rain stopped that day, too.


The sun began glowing faintly through the clouds but, as the mist cleared away, the sun became bright in the sky.

The weather turned warm. The damage of the long rains

173

was soon dried. And The Star suddenly bloomed, with its people feeling that it was springtime at last.

This particular morning, the rich sound of Nero's voice drifted from inside the front stall of the stables. He was brushing down Peter's mare and singing a West Indian song. It was a song with no words, just a rhythm comprised of humming and warbling rising from deep down inside Nero's throat.

Peter worked across the stable from Nero, examining the legs of a foal, wondering if he could get a trotter from this sprightly black horse. His concentration was suddenly broken by someone calling to him from outside the stable.

Listening, Peter heard, 'Master Peter, Sir? Master Peter?'

Rising reluctantly to his feet, Peter brushed the bits of straw from his white breeches and, picking at the tight nankeen shirt which clung to his chest with perspiration, he strode out from the sweet smell of the stall toward the open doors.

He saw a small black boy coming toward the stables, hurrying across a small field of daisies from the big house. It was Ruben, a small black boy who ran errands for Storky. He was carrying a cloth-covered tray in his hands now.

Peter stood in the doorway and smiled as Ruben stopped a few yards from the stables. Holding the tray rigidly in front of him, Ruben threw back his shaved head and announced in a loud voice, 'Miss Storky, she sends me with this coffee and pecan cookies for you, Master Peter, Sir.'

Peter nodded, 'Thank you, Ruben.' He liked to be particularly warm to the black children of The Star.

'Do you wants to drinks it in the shade, Master Peter, Sir?' Ruben shouted.

'Just a minute,' Peter said, looking over his shoulder. 'How many cups you've got on that tray, Ruben?'

The boy blinked at Peter in astonishment. He answered, 'One cup, Master Peter, Sir.'

Nodding in the direction from where Nero's voice was drifting, Peter said, 'I think we're going to need two, Ruben.'

Ruben listened to the singing and blinked again. He recognized the voice as that of a black man. Ruben was new to the big house and did not know that Peter was more generous than most white people. This was not what he had been raised to expect. He asked with astonishment, 'You wants me to runs back to Miss Storky for a cup for—*him*? Is that whats you wants, Master Peter, Sir?'

Peter nodded. 'Think you could?'

The black boy's face suddenly broke into a wide grin. He said, 'Runs? Heck, Master Peter, I can runs. I can runs faster than a hound dog.'

Walking toward Ruben, Peter bent to take the tray from the boy's arms and said, 'Then let's see you do it. And if you're back here by the time I count to fifty, Ruben, I'll let you have one of these nice fat pecan cookies.'

Ruben's eyes widened at the prospect of getting such a treat. Quickly kneeling on the ground next to Peter, he looked across the field at the big house and said, 'You start counting, Master Peter, Sir, and I starts running.'

Peter began, 'One, two, three . . .'

Ruben was off. His sturdy brown legs carried him across the small field of daisies and Peter stood watching him bound toward the back steps of the big house.

But halfway across the flowering patch, the figure of another negro jumped from the grass. It was Posey.

Peter had completely forgotten about Posey being nearby. He had come to the stables earlier this morning looking for empty liniment bottles. He wanted to use them as vases for the daisies he picked and was planning to take them into the big house for presents. Posey was eighteen-years-old now and, although he was tall and sturdy, he still was effeminate and had made no advances toward manliness.

Now, Posey stood in the daisy patch waving his arms at Ruben. He shouted, 'You keeps off my flowers, nigger brat. You keeps off my flowers.'

Peter laughed as he watched Posey berating Ruben—who did not slow his fast strides.

It was not until Ruben had disappeared around the lilac clump by the back steps of the big house—and Posey had settled down on the ground again with his collection of liniment bottles and pile of flowers—that Peter called to the stable, 'Hey, Nero? Want to grease your throat?'

Nero suddenly appeared in the door. He wore only his white kneelength breeches, his chest streaming with perspiration. Wiping his forehead and running his hand over his wiry hair, he said to Peter, 'Ain't been working hard enough to deserve no big treat, Master Peter.'

But Peter insisted, 'Well, you've got a coffee cup coming so you better get ready to use it.' Usually by coffee time, Nero was already away from the stables, already exercising the mare.

Sliding the curry comb from his wide hand, Nero tugged up his pants and reached for his shirt which was hanging from a wooden peg at the side of the big door.

'You don't have to get dressed for coffee,' Peter protested, but impressed nonetheless that Nero had offered to put on his shirt.

As the two men were taking their first nibbles of Storky's pecan cookies, they heard a loud panting coming across the daisy field. Looking, they saw Ruben dashing toward them. Posey sat upright again, protectively clutching his armful of flowers.

Remembering his bargain with the kitchen boy, Peter resumed counting loudly, '. . . thirty-six, thirty-seven, thirty-eight.'

Ruben slid to a dusty halt in front of the stable at Peter's count of thirty-nine. Holding a blue-and-white cup in one hand and its matching saucer in the other, he looked anxiously at Peter and asked, 'Did I makes it, Master Peter, Sir?'

'You got here by thirty-nine,' Peter answered.

Not knowing his numbers, Ruben asked wide-eyed, 'Is that winnings or losing the cookie, Master Peter, Sir? Thirty . . . nine?'

Holding the plate of cookies to Ruben, Peter assured him, 'That's winning the cookies. Thirty-nine out of fifty is winning the cookies by a long shot, Ruben. Go on, take three! And, here, take a couple more to give Posey over there. I bet he likes cookies, too.'

'Posey just likes flowers!' Ruben said, gnawing into his first cookie with one large tooth.

'But he can't eat flowers. Go on. Take a couple to him. And make sure you give them to him, too. I'll be watching you.'

Ruben departed happily, skipping toward Posey to give him his cookies, too. Then both boys walked toward the big house together.

When Peter and Nero had both finished drinking their first cup of coffee, Peter moved now to fill Nero's cup. But Nero quickly reached to take the white pot from Peter's hand to pour himself.

Refusing to accept Nero's gesture, Peter divided the remaining coffee between them and said, 'You sure must have had some good training, Nero. I've never seen a person—a white man or black—who had so much consideration as you.'

Nero grinned. 'It goes back a long ways, Master Peter.' His voice was not deep when he spoke, but soft and gentle.

Peter asked, 'They taught you good in the West Indies, didn't they?'

'Oh, Master Peter!' Nero laughed. 'It goes back alot farther than the West Indies. When I was no bigger than that Ruben sprout, I was bought off a Portuguese slaver by the Roman Church. That was way down in Brazil. That was years ago, Master Peter.'

'The Roman Church? I didn't know a church owned slaves!'

'They do in Brazil. The priests and those women they call "nuns" in the Roman Church.'

'Papists?' Peter had heard about the Papists. They were mostly Spanish, Portuguese, and French. Selby had told him that New Orleans had been a hot bed of Papists. Also, some of the Witcherley family were supposed to be Papists, too.

'Those are the ones, Master Peter. But I can't complain about them. Not that I complain about white folks. But I've got to admit that those Papists treats their niggers better than the other Portuguese men do in Brazil. Those working down in the mines. Those niggers have it bad. The Portuguese people, they gets real mean.'

Peter vaguely remembered then that Nero had told him—or somebody like Storky who had repeated the story—that he had worked in Brazil. But he had never realized that priests had once been his masters, too. Anxious to know more, Peter asked, 'I can understand what work a slave can do on a plantation, or even down in a mine. But what did you do in a church, Nero?'

Grinning again, Nero said, 'Oh, Master Peter! They finds alot of works for niggers to do everyplace. Especially the strong ones. Even the young ones, like I was at that time. Must have been twelve years old when I was promoted from fetching for the priest—the priest liked his fetchers to be young and, at twelve-years-old, I was getting too old for the padre—and so he sent me to the nuns.'

'Nuns? Those holy women who pray all the time and wear long black veils?' Peter asked, feeling an excitement in himself.

'Some of them had veils, Master Peter. And supposing to pray and not visit with each other. But some of them were daughters of rich folks and lived in the convent for one reason or other and they got to carry on like most women.' Nero paused, smiling. 'I remember, I had one mistress who was hornier than anything I sees later on at Miss Naomi's house . . .'

Then Nero stopped abruptly. Lowering his head, he confessed, 'I keep forgetting when I talk to you, Master Peter. I keep forgetting you are a white man. I could just talk to you till my tongue falls out.'

'Talk to me?' Peter laughed. 'Hell, you hardly say anything, Nero. You never talk to a soul.'

Nero shrugged his bare shoulders. 'You're right, Master Peter. I don't talk as much as I think I do. But then, you ain't much of a talker yourself.'

'You're right,' Peter admitted.

Nero sat staring at his big hands, the fingernails looking like clear spatulas over the pinkness. He said soberly, 'When I was your age, Master Peter, I talked too much. I talked to anybody. But then—' Nero took a deep sigh, '—then something happened to my hopes.'

Peter did not press Nero to explain what his disappointment had been. But knowing that Nero was not troubled by talking lightly about sexual matters, Peter playfully slugged at Nero's strong bicep and said, 'I bet you had yourself some good times in that convent.'

Nero agreed by suddenly cupping the crotch of his breeches with both of his hands.

He began to tell the story.

'There's one woman from Brazil I really remembers, Master Peter. One real low woman. She called herself Sister Honoria. But she was no holy sister. Excusing me for speaking about white ladies, Master Peter, but Sister Honoria was just a plain trashy white wench who had to come to the convent so her family would not marry her to a skinny cousin.

'That Sister Honoria just couldn't get enough of being pestered . . . in both holes. Getting pestered by me and, not bragging, Master Peter, but I always have been pretty big, even back then when I was not much older than that Ruben boy. So, I pesters the sister in the front and she was getting pestered at the same time by another buck almost as big as you yourself in her back hole. Now, that's alot of pecker for any woman to be taking. But that wasn't good enough for her. She had a third person, a woman she had tongueing around her front hole while I was donging the same place. No, it just wasn't sister-like at all. But the funniest thing, a thing that scared me at first when she told me to do it. But, later, I didn't mind when it was time for me to do it—when I was finally to be sold—let me explain.

'The convent decided to sell me because the Mother Superior said I was getting too big in my pants and so Sister Honoria had to give me up as her secret boy. She didn't want to lose my pecker so she made me put wax—you know, melted wax from a candle—around my pecker so she could make another pecker just like mine. You know, a whole wax pecker.

Hard and everything. And that's what I left her using on herself. A wax pecker like mine. And who knows? Maybe she's still using it today . . . if she ain't got so hot that it's melted all up inside her.

'Many times after that I thought I was going to melt myself. The convent sold me to a tin mine there in Brazil and down in that mine it was hot as blazes and I saw niggers who hadn't seen no sunlight in ten, twelve years. You say a nigger ain't white but down in them tin mines they looked grey just like some big old rats. They still got them down there now but I don't suggest you go looking, Master Peter. You'll just get sick to your stomach. If the sight don't get you then the stench will. Living their whole lives down there, they don't get out to do nothing. They eats and shits and everything down in that deep black hole in the world. About the only thing they don't do is pester.

'That's why I got out, because of pestering. From Brazil, I was taken to the island in the West Indies called Montserrat by a man called a 'company holder'. He owned part of that Brazil tin mine and he saw me the day I was being lowered down in the hole by a rope. He had a raging fit, I hears later, and he got me pulled out and taken to where he said I would be more helpful and all. He wanted me to breed with some of his wenches living on his island. He took me to his home in Montserrat.

'On Montserrat, I meets alot of new niggers, especially wenches, but the cleverest nigger I ever did meet anywhere was a skinny little wench called Naomi. She was just dusting tables in the greathouse at that time. Oh, Naomi was as bright as a new brass button. Brighter than she was pretty, too. Naomi was nothing but skin and bones to look at in those days. But that didn't stop a gal like her. Oh, no. Miss Naomi sets her eye on that rich Frenchman who owns us and, seeing that he owned her, Naomi saw that he was the only man who could set her free and, to do that, Naomi saw she had to gets more in his good favours. She sets right out to do that, too, and in no time at all, she was married to him. A nigger wench dusting parlours one day and the next day she was married to a fine white Frenchman. Ugly and old and fat but a fine Frenchman just the same. Now, if that ain't something for a skinny wench to get herself, I don't know what is.

'But that marriage don't last for no time at all, Master Peter. That Frenchie got himself into a bad accident the night of their wedding. I ain't saying it was Naomi's fault. There was no proof or saying that she led him off that balcony that night. But he fell to the sea and he died. And I know . . .

'I shouldn't be laughing at niggers' wicked ways but, oh, Master Peter, that Miss Naomi sure knew how to do things more wicked than anybody else, black woman or white. She got her freedom. She got to be head of her own household then. And so she sells all the niggers she don't likes, which was most of them because Miss Naomi didn't like other niggers one bit, and keeping only a handful—including me—she takes us all with her from Montserrat to another island there called St. Kitts.

'St. Kitts was where Miss Naomi opens up her house. She opens it up in the capital of St. Kitts called Basseterre, on a wharf there called Barracks Lane. And then that was when she really starts making lots of money and making herself look like the prettiest nigger in the whole Caribbean. She forgot all about being skinny. She could buy herself anything she wanted she was making so much money. But she was a worker. She worked even at bossing people around to do things for her. Even bossing around poor trash whites. Providing amusement for the white gentlemen customers who come to her whorehouse there on Barracks Lane.

'There's no other word for it than whorehouse, Master Peter, but it seems a shame to call a place as fine as that a whorehouse. It was more like a showhouse. She had real big shows there. In fact, Miss Naomi had everything right there that a white man could want for. If a white man said he didn't want nothing, then Miss Naomi would tell him why he had to have something. She figured out lots of things. She even figured out that lots of white men on St. Kitts didn't really like owning nigger slaves. She said they felt 'guilty' about owning and mistreating niggers.

'So to keep them white men from feeling too guilty, Miss Naomi helped them. She whipped them just like they whipped their slaves. You know, she punished them for doing what she always called their sins. Oh, those whities there loved that word, sins.

'And not just Miss Naomi whips them white men. She had all kinds of other folks working and whipping for her and getting paid for it by the white men. It was something you'd really have to see to believe. And you know, Master Peter, it might sounds awful and bad to you but, after keeping all this penned up inside me all these years, just talking about it makes me feel like I'm seeing old friends. Alot of old friends I knows and loves and . . .

'Me, I never was much good myself at whipping people. Fact, Miss Naomi always told me I should be alot meaner than I was. She told me I should really learn to hate white folks. But no matter how hard I tries to be mean, Master Peter, I just couldn't find hate in me. I just couldn't do all those things she told me to do.

'I remembers one woman . . . Mistress Arabella Warburton. Yes, that was her name. Mistress Arabella Warburton. And, oh, Master Peter, did she want terrible things done to her. She'd beg for it, too. She'd beg for us black boys to slap her face with our peckers. She'd liked to have her face slapped with a soft pecker more than a hard one because a soft pecker meant that she wasn't exciting enough to a man to make him hard and she liked to be punished and made fun of that way. She like to be pissed on, too. All over her face. She'd beg for it. It sounded awful. Just like some bedpot begging you to fill it. I didn't like it at all, not what that Arabella Warburton wanted. In fact, most days at Miss Naomi's house I wasn't very happy one bit.

'But then when Master Abdee came along, I guess, my life took a turn for the good. I got to go live out in the country then. That's what I like. I like life in the country. I like life here at The Star. And back then, I liked moving with Miss Naomi to Master Abdee's plantation on St. Kitts.

'Master Abdee was an Englishman. An Englishman who came to St. Kitts to whip slaves. But to whip real slaves not white men playing at being slaves to women in a whorehouse. See, the English Government on St. Kitts used to have a special man to whip slaves in the main square of the town. The capital called Basseterre. And that's how Miss Naomi came to meet Master Abdee. He was a horny big white man and found his way to Miss Naomi's house rightaway. Or, maybe, I should say, Naomi found her way to him.

'Miss Naomi was no street-walking whore, Master Peter, but she sure lit out of the house when she heard that Master Abdee was in town. She knew what a heap of good it would do for the name of her whorehouse to have people knowing she had been to bed with the new Dragonard.

'Dragonard. That was the name of the British whipper. He was called the Dragonard. The word comes from the name of the special whip he used. Because the tip of it was split just like the tongue of a dragon is supposed to be.

'Only for a short time, though, was Abdee the Dragonard on St. Kitts. It made all the English people mad, too, that he took the job because Abdee was a real proper Englishman just like the other planters there. But he had taken a job that only some white trash person should be working at. And he did it for the same reason he did other things, I suppose. He did it for no reason at all. Master Abdee just did things. That's why he and Miss Naomi hit it off so good, I guess. Miss Naomi always said to me, "Nero, that Abdee is the only white nigger I ever did see". But it wasn't as if she and Abdee was in real love with each other. Like snugging sweethearts. They just got on like good friends. They made love but they didn't hold on tight to each other like most folks. They were different from other lovers. I remember even before Abdee moved Miss Naomi into his house, he didn't come down to see her in Basseterre for months and months sometimes. That was when he got married to a French woman.

'But marrying a French woman didn't change things much for Abdee. Except that he was rich then. And got himself that sugar plantation. It was first called Petit Jour. That was the name of the plantation before the Frenchwoman married Master Abdee. Petit Jour. It means twilight in French talk, they say. Petit Jour. That's a pretty name but Abdee changed it to Dragonard and Dragonard got itself a real bad name toward the last.

'Abdee named the plantation Dragonard after his whipping job. The Dragonard. But that made English folks even hate him more. They tried to forget they did such bad things. But Abdee didn't forget. He didn't care. He just went on as he pleased. Planting. Buying more niggers. And getting all the wenches pregnant. Including Honore.

'Mistress Honore was the name of Abdee's wife, the French woman, Master Peter. Course, nobody on the plantation ever saw the baby that Abdee planted in her because Abdee got too mean for her to live with him so she left. Off Mistress Honore set with her maid, leaving Abdee and Dragonard and everything.

'I don't recall right now the name of Honore's maid because that was all before my time. But there was always some talk about the maid and Mistress Honore in the kitchen at Dragonard. They had sailed off for France quite a few years before the troubles came to Dragonard.

'Those troubles, Master Peter, those troubles are what ruined everything for everybody. Abdee is gone now. Miss Naomi is gone. All the niggers are killed or sold or run away. Everybody is gone and dead. Killed on Trouble Island. And St. Kitts got to be Trouble Island because of the nastiest nigger I ever knew. That's why I only calls it Trouble Island now, Master Peter. A freed nigger called Calabar made it that way. Not a white man, Master Peter, but a black one of my kind and I'm even ashamed to say that . . .

'Ta-Ta! That was the name of Mistress Honore's maid. I remembers now. Ta-Ta. She went to France with Honore on the ship long before . . .'

'Is something wrong, Master Peter?

'Master Peter, if I said something wrong, I hope that God strikes me dead. You're the last person I wants to do anything wrong to, Master Peter. We're friends. I only talks to you like this because we're friends . . .

'Master Peter! Please sit back down, Master Peter. I don't know what I told you wrong but you ain't looking too good, Master Peter.

'Master Peter, come back here!'

Peter did not turn around. He left Nero in front of the stables and kept walking toward the big house. His first reaction to the story had been anger and that anger was mounting now.

The front veranda of the big house was empty as Peter strode quickly around the spreading clumps of azalea bushes and passed up the front steps with two neat leaps of his long legs. He stormed by the wooden porch swings, hanging motionless from their hemp ropes, and jerked open one of the double doors. He did not know exactly what he was going to say to Selby when he found him but he knew that he had to find out about Dragonard and Ta-Ta and himself.

Inside the house, the atmosphere was as calm and as cool as the veranda, a gentle breeze moving across the entry hall, a late morning exchange of air between the parlours on either side.

At the foot of the winding staircase, Peter spied a single liniment bottle filled with wild daisies setting on the bannister post. He knew that Posey was somewhere about the house. Then, listening, he heard a commotion upstairs. Straining his ears to hear more closely, Peter gradually became aware of Selby's voice talking over the distressed wailing of women.

Being of a single mind, Peter began to run up the winding staircase, his black boots taking three steps at a time now. He was going to confront Selby immediately.

A louder wave of moans hit him at the top of the stairs and, looking to where the noise was coming—from the open door to Rachel's bedroom—Peter suddenly stopped, listening to the disturbance in this otherwise calm house.

He began to hear the high-pitched voice of Posey insisting, 'I didn't mean no harm, Master Selby, Sir. I didn't mean no harm.'

Selby's smooth voice consoled, 'Nobody's saying you did, Posey. Nobody's saying you did.'

But Posey's wavering voice continued. 'I was just bringing little vases of white flowers to her room, Master Selby, Sir. I was just bring her little vases of sweet, white flowers!'

As Peter now moved silently toward the open door of the bedroom, he saw Storky standing with her arm around Posey's shoulder. Peter saw that she was trying to comfort the fraught black boy, and, next, Peter saw that the maroon-coloured carpet in this bedroom was strewn with daisies and the upset liniment bottles.

What is this? Peter wondered. Did Posey drop his box of bottles on the carpet? Is that what this fracas is all about?

Moving cautiously toward the doorway, Peter then saw Selby standing near the large, carved walnut bed.

Standing with his back to Peter, Selby looked down over the stooped body of Melissa, who knelt on the floor in front of her mother's bed.

Peter was sober now. He knew that this was no everyday event. For one thing, he did not hear Rachel Selby's shrill voice screaming at these people for intruding into her room.

Posey's wailing continued to cut through the oppressive atmosphere of the bedroom. 'I didn't do nothing, Master Selby, Sir. I just brings her some flowers! But she thinks I mean big trouble and she grabs for that knife there and she starts screaming at me!' Throwing back his shaved head, Posey grabbed at his big ears and shrieked, 'I wish it was me she stabbed. Why didn't she stab me? Why didn't Miss Rachel stab me?'

Standing helplessly in the doorway, Peter did not know what to do now. Suddenly, his own problems seemed to be nothing. The occurrence here had been horrible. He could plainly see

Rachel's body lying half-on the floor, Melissa cradling her mother's head in her lap. Rachel's white night gown was splattered and streaked with deep red stains of blood. Near her limp body rested the horn-handled letter opener. Its silver blade was also stained with blood.

Posey continued to lament, 'Poor Miss Rachel! Why didn't Miss Rachel stab me! Stab me! Stab me!'

Storky finally saw Peter lingering in the doorway behind her and she leant toward Selby to whisper.

Turning from Melissa, Selby soberly asked Peter, 'Sonny, could you ride for Doc Whithers? Rachel has had a bad accident?'

Peter heard his voice say, 'Accident?'

Selby nodded. 'Yes, it was an accident. She thought Posey here had come in to rape her. It looks to us like poor Rachel . . . killed herself rather than have such a thing—' Selby's eyes were empty as he shook his head at the ridiculousness of the idea. Then, he turned away from Peter, looking down to Melissa holding the slim body.

Peter solemnly walked from the bedroom and down the stairs, feeling as if Nero's story of Dragonard had been pushed from his mind.

Behind him, Posey continued to scream, bemoaning the fact that he had been spared death.

To Peter, it was as if he had not yet been meant to know the truth about himself and Dragonard. He felt that The Star was trying to keep him from asking questions, was still holding him back from prodding the beehive with a pole.

The Star had its own problems.

Rachel Selby was dead.

## Chapter Eleven

# FAREWELL, MISS RACHEL

No accusations were made against Posey. His story was accepted as truth—Rachel Selby had believed that he had burst into her bedroom with the intentions of raping her and, rather than suffer such a degradation from a negro, she had stabbed her breasts with the silver letter-opener.

Selby knew how unrealistically that his wife had been acting lately.

Melissa confessed in a sober tone that her mother had had a long and unnatural obsession with the subject of black men and their sexual interference with her.

But Storky's words on the subject closed the discussion of Posey's involvement in the matter. She said, 'The poor boy thinks that yellow worm dangling between his legs is just there to pee with. I wouldn't doubt that that's all it can do, too. And he probably has to squat on a log like a woman to do it, too. Rape?' Storky shook her head, saying, 'No, you'd have to rape him.'

Storky had also seen that it was unsafe to leave Posey alone. His mind was too unsettled now. And, as Mama Gomorrah was too busy to comfort him in The Shed, Storky assigned Biddy to be a companion to Posey, to distract him from his grief with her unending supply of silly chatter.

Peter came back from Troy with Doc Whithers but it was too late. Rachel was already covered with a black pall. Storky took Peter aside, though, and asked him in whispers if he could approach Nero about the matter of Posey sleeping in the stables for a few nights.

Peter put his own problems at the back of his mind to honour Storky's well-intended wishes, to do his part for her and Posey and The Star.

Walking solemnly to the stables, Peter explained the situation to Nero.

Nero listened quietly and agreed to give Posey a place to sleep not only for tonight and tomorrow night, but for as long as was necessary.

Then, as if the matter of Posey were settled, Nero asked Peter, 'How you feeling yourself now, Master Peter? Can you tell me what I said wrong?'

Peter respected Nero's intelligence enough not to play dumb to the question. But rather than explain the reasons for his reaction to Nero's story this morning, Peter patted him on the shoulder, saying, 'We're friends, Nero. But I can't talk . . . I just can't talk yet.'

As of now, Peter still had not approached Selby for some truths.

But such a confrontation was impossible at the moment. There was the problem of burying Rachel Selby.

The funeral took place two days later. The crowd of mourners stretched from the veranda of the big house, down the driveway, and out beyond the wooden star hanging from the front gates.

Rachel Selby represented the last of the direct line of Peregrine Rolands to live on this land and all the aunts and uncles and cousins—as well as the second, third, and fourth cousins—came to The Star for her burial.

As the simple pine coffin slowly passed down the driveway, carried on the shoulders of six neighbour men (Rachel had long-ago stipulated that she did not want 'niggers' to carry her out of this world), the mourners stared at Albert Selby walking in the dust behind the coffin. He held his daughter's hand in the crook of his arm, keeping his eyes to the ground.

Slowly placing one foot in front of the other, Selby grasped his straw hat in his hand. A band of black crepe hung from the hat's wide brim.

Selby wanted to cry but he could not. He felt pity for the waste of a life. He regretted that a human being could have lived on this beautiful, bountiful land and had not once seen its true value. Rachel Selby should have never lived in the South, Selby felt. She should have never led a plantation life. It had been both a waste of this land and a waste of her life. Selby wanted to cry for that.

Slowly, he led his twenty-four-year-old daughter, Melissa.

Melissa was crying for the things that she and her mother had not done together, the silly but important pastimes which a girl loves to share with her mother, and which Rachel and Melissa had not done. Melissa cried for the other things that her mother had missed in life, too, such as love.

Dressed in a long black muslin dress, and wearing a black veil over her head, Melissa moved as reverently as her father.

The only adornment which decorated Melissa's mourning outfit was a golden band hanging from a black cord around her neck. It was her mother's wedding ring.

Albert Selby had taken the ring off Rachel's cold hand and, giving it to Melissa, he had explained that he felt that Rachel would probably be happier to enter Heaven as a single woman. Selby had said to Melissa, 'It's not that we're robbing or deserting your mama, Melly. I just don't think she'd want the angels to know she was ever a plain, ordinary woman.'

Selby had seen no reason why the house servants should have to stand outside the gates with the field hands. He had given them permission to gather on the grass in front of the big house and follow the coffin down past the relatives and neighbours.

The only two members of the house staff who were missing today—apart from Ta-Ta, who never came out of the attic anymore—were Posey and Biddy. Storky had sent them to the meadow with a picnic hamper. Again, her Ashanti intuition had proven correct. Posey and Biddy were already becoming fast friends, bonded by their mutual childishness.

When the coffin reached the gates of The Star, the neighbours and relatives began to leave their positions inside the fence and follow the house-servants. The white people dismissed this breach in protocol as the senile mistake of the widower and they quietly walked behind the negroes.

The field hands joined the procession at the public road, beginning to sing a dirge as they swelled the ranks of mourners. Whites and blacks all moved slowly now across the public road, inching toward the family cemetery which lay deep in the shady woods. The coffin bobbed above the people's heads, resting on the shoulders of the six pall-bearers.

Inside the picket fence of the cemetery, Reverend Gabriel Stark from Troy stood holding his Bible. He waited for the people to file into rows around the outside of the low picket fence before he began his reading. Today was the last day of Reverend Stark in these parts. He was leaving. There would be no preacher here now. Rachel Selby had died just in time.

Albert Selby stood with Melissa inside the picket fence at the foot of the fresh grave. Their hands were clasped together. The singing had stopped, and the bustling of the women's skirts, the whispering, the fluttering of Panama hats began to subside.

Selby suddenly broke the silence. He called in an uneven voice, 'Reverend Stark?'

The hawk-nosed preacher looked up from his Bible. He was surprised at the intrusion.

Whispers rose among the mourners outside the picket fence.

Selby bravely continued, 'Reverend Stark, you and everybody here knows that Mrs. Selby and me lost us a son way back. No use hiding that fact from the Lord—or neighbours.'

A ripple of nervous laughter spread outside the fence. The Roland cousins and aunts and uncles fidgeted.

Selby continued, 'So, standing here now with just my daughter, Melly, makes me feel kind of lonely and . . .'

Selby paused. He looked to the left side of the fence.

Chad and Claudia Tucker stood alongside Peter outside the fence and, as Selby looked in their direction, they began to stiffen, blushing as if at last they were going to be exposed publicly for selling slaves from The Star.

Selby continued, 'So, I hope it don't offend no one today if I call somebody to me and Melly now. Somebody who's been eating at our table and sleeping under our roof for a good many years.'

He called to Peter, 'Sonny? Will you come join Melly and me in here?'

Peter did not hesitate. He stretched one long leg over the low fence and soberly went to Selby's side.

Outside the fence, the faces of the white mourners were either a study of approval or a picture of hatred and envy. The neighbours warmed at Selby's thoughtfulness. Many had not seen what a fine, handsome young man that Peter had become. But the Roland relatives cringed at the possible threat of an outsider inheriting The Star.

Nero stood beyond the picket fence with the black people. And, as his chest expanded with affection for Peter, he prayed for the first time since long-ago at Dragonard. But now Nero prayed for Peter. And he hoped that what he had told Peter had not been too heavy to bear—whatever it meant to him.

But Nero was beginning to suspect what his story had revealed to Peter.


That night, the Tuckers lorded their attendance at Rachel Selby's funeral over the farmer and his wife who had come to their cabin on business.

Chad and Claudia Tucker sat together on one side of the wooden table and faced Tommy Joe and Mary Crandall. The Tuckers were pretending that this visit was a social call.

Claudia appeared to be fully recovered from her illness. She even looked complacent in the candlelight, sitting with her plump hands folded in front of her on the table. Beneath her chair rested a squat cream churn. Inside was hidden the flour sack of slave money.

Chad Tucker was doing the talking to the Crandalls now.

He said, 'Course you realize, Tommy Joe, only the biggest planters were invited to the burying today. And, of course, Claudie here and myself. The rest was nothing but niggers.'

Tommy Joe and Mary Crandall both sat rigidly in their chairs.

Tucker proceeded to list the important people he had mixed with this afternoon at the funeral. He reeled off the names, 'The Breslins, Bill Trunkey. Elijah and Penelope Norton. The Pughs.'

But Tommy Joe Crandall was not listening. He was wondering if he had done the right thing by bringing his wife here to the Tuckers' cabin tonight.

Mary Crandall was worried, too. The Crandalls were poor farmers and Tucker had told Tommy Joe Crandall how to save money. Or was it how to protect Mary's future? She did not remember the details now. Her mind was in a muddle. She was very frightened.

But Chad Tucker had explained everything precisely beforehand to Crandall. He had repeated the story exactly as Claudia had explained it to him.

Crandall needed a negro to help him on his farm but he could not afford to buy one. Nor could he afford to hire a white man to work. Claudia's plan had been presented to Crandall as a consideration for both his and his wife's welfare.

Repeating Claudia's brainstorm, Tucker had told Crandall that he could rent a negro for one night. Crandall could rent a negro from Tucker to mate with his wife—they could birth their own slave.

The idea was repellent to Crandall. The thought of a black man laying with his wife was abhorrent.

But Tucker flooded Crandall with reasons to do it. He told Crandall how poor he was. He pointed out how expensive that slaves had become now that they could no longer be brought into Louisiana. He reminded Crandall that he was sterile and had no hope of raising sons to work his farm when he got older. He asked Crandall what would happen to his wife if he died? Who would provide for her if she was left in the world by herself?

Crandall had told Tucker that he would have to talk it over with his wife.

Tonight, the Crandalls had come to the Tuckers' cabin with the decision to proceed. Mary Crandall would lay with a black man. They also had brought their savings of seventeen dollars with them. They would pay the remaining three dollars to Tucker by the end of the year.

Interrupting Tucker's candle light chat now, Claudia reached across the table to pat Mary Crandall's quivering hand. She said, 'I think you choosed a real smart thing to do Mrs. Crandall—mind if I call you Mary?'

Mary Crandall shook her head and then nervously looked over her shoulder at Monk sitting silently on the dirt floor behind them.

Claudia quickly whispered, 'Oh, that ain't the nigger you're getting. That one's our fetch and carry boy.'

Tucker picked up Claudia's words. 'Monk there? Oh, no. When you start talking about Monk you gets into a higher bracket. Course, Tommy Joe, if you're willing to spring for another twenty dollars—making it a round forty—there's no reason why Monk shouldn't have a go at your missus. He's real prime stock, that one. Real prime. But he'll cost you.'

Crandall's voice was faint but firm. 'We goes ahead with the original deal, Tucker.'

Shrugging, Tucker said, 'You're paying.'

Claudia brightly said, 'If we hadn't been at the funeral today, I'd baked us a peach cake or something to nibble on now. But I just didn't have me no time at all today. Not with all the excitement at the big house . . . and me still getting over my woman's ague.' She coughed.

Tucker said, 'You wouldn't have believed the fine crowd there, Tommy Joe. I'm telling you that . . .'

A knock on the door suddenly disturbed Tucker. He looked at Monk sitting on the floor and said, 'That must be Porkchop. Let him in, boy. Then you go take yourself a walk. Leave us white folk alone.'

Monk slowly rose from the floor.

Mary Crandall grabbed in desperation for her husband.

But Tommy Joe took her frail hand and put it back in her lap. Looking at Tucker, he asked, 'You said you got a bed they can use, didn't you?'

Claudia piped up, 'Course we got us a bed. And I'm real pleased to have Mary use it. But you got to excuse me having no sheet on it. Being up at the funeral and all today, I just ain't had me no time to do no fixing here or nothing.' Looking across the table at Mary Crandall, she asked, 'A girl like you understands that, Mary honey, don't you?'

Mary Crandall did not hear the question. Listening to the footsteps on the dirt floor behind her, she was holding her eyes shut and biting her lip.

The black man called Porkchop was in the cabin and Monk had departed.

Turning in his chair, Tommy Joe Crandall looked at the negro who would be laying his wife.

Porkchop was older than Monk. But he was also a taller man, bigger and rougher, a more chiselled looking specimen of manhood than Monk. His deep-black face was brooding and a straight line of tightly-curled hair set low over his forehead. He had deep set eyes and an aquiline nose. Although it was night, Porkchop wore no shirt. His shoulders were broad and heavily capped; his stomach muscles formed tight lines into the top of his pants. Standing on the dirt floor of the cabin in bare feet, Porkchop waited with his huge arms hanging at his side.

Rising, Tucker said, 'Porkchop here is one hell of a good stud. I know you can count on his spunk taking in your missus, Tommy Joe.' Looking at Porkchop, Tucker asked him, 'How many gits you sewed so far, nigger?'

'Thirty-two that I knows of, Master Tucker, Sir,' Porkchop answered directly.

'Well, I want you to make that thirty-three, boy,' Tucker said to him and, then pointing at the ragged blue curtains hanging between the big room and the lean-to, he ordered, 'Go in there and strip down. Mrs. Crandall will be in in a minute.'

Porkchop walked soberly across the dirt floor toward the curtains.

Still trembling at the thought of having to lay with a black man, Mary Crandall reached for her husband.

But Tommy Joe ignored his wife's panic. He put his hand under her arm and, lifting her from the chair, he slowly guided her toward the curtains.

Standing in front of the curtains with her, Tommy Joe called into the darkness, 'Nigger man, you ready in there?'

A deep voice answered, 'Yes, Master Sir.'

Tommy Joe murmured to his wife, 'You don't have to undress till you get in there.'

Then, Tommy Joe reached into his coat pocket and, removing a wad of yellow cloth, he handed it to his wife and said, 'This here is goose fat. Make him grease himself up good for you. He's going to be big.'

'He's big all right,' Tucker called from the table. 'Fact is, Tommy Joe, why don't you go along in yourself and inspect him. Make sure everything is up to your satisfaction. To see for yourself how good he's hung so you don't think I'm cheating you on a thing.'

Mary Crandall looked at her husband with terror. She shook her head. She did not want him to go with her. But she did pull her husband's ear down to her mouth and she whispered to him. Then, grabbing the wad of goose fat from his hand, she quickly disappeared into the bedroom.

After Mary Crandall had gone, Tommy Joe turned to the table and said, 'Women folks sure can be strange animals, sometimes.'

The Tuckers waited for his reason.

Sitting down on his chair, Tommy Joe explained, 'You know what my Mary just told me? Mary just told me that she's worried now that a nigger's pestering her, she ain't going to be no real lady.'

Chad Tucker tried to smile with sympathy. But Claudia quickly glanced under her chair at the cream churn holding the money. That was her only concern.

Then, the three of them sat at the table and waited. The first sound from the bedroom was the rustling of the corn-cob mattress and, next, the sharp gasps of Mary Crandall, which grew louder until Tommy Joe finally spoke.

He asked, 'These niggers take very long?'

Tucker said, 'Niggers take all night sometimes. But I told Porkchop earlier today to make this one snappy.'

Wiping the perspiration from his forehead, Tommy Joe Crandall said, 'That's good.'

Soon, when there was a lull, Tucker called to the bedroom, 'Porkchop? You finished in there?'

There was still no sound from the bedroom.

Tommy Joe moved to stand. 'Yep. Sounds like it's over. Can't be—'

The rustling noise suddenly resumed beyond the blue curtains. But this time it was accompanied by voices—indiscernible whispers.

Tommy Joe called cautiously, 'Mary? You fine in there?'

Porkchop answered the call, 'She's fine, Master Sir.'

Tommy Joe blurted, 'I'm talking to my wife, nigger!'

'She's real fine, Master Sir,' Porkchop assured him.

Then Mary Crandall called weakly, 'Tommy Joe—'

'You fine, Mary?' He was ready to jump from his chair to help her.

She answered, 'Fine, Tommy Joe. I'm just—just—' Then her voice suddenly broke off as she gasped and, next, the sound of her loud breathing filled the cabin.

The bed began to creak rhythmically again and the gasping grew louder.

Soon, Porkchop's low voice began to say the word 'yeah' in a deep, regulated tempo. And Mary Crandall's voice joined his—a swoon, a groaning of adulation.

Claudia Tucker sat at the table with her arms folded. She was drumming the fingers of one hand against her shawl. She wanted the Crandalls to hurry and leave so that she could count her money.

Chad Tucker was smiling. He had not suspected that this evening would go so well.

But Tommy Joe Crandall sat at the table in a state of nerves. He feared that his wife was enjoying this ordeal. She usually considered sex to be loathesome. But he could tell by her heavy breathing and the sound of the two voices together and the noise from their naked bodies slapping against one another that she was enjoying the act as much as the black man. And in his mind, Tommy Joe saw Porkchop's muscular stomach arched over his wife's pale body, visualizing how her legs were spread in abandonment, losing herself for probably the first time in her life.

Tucker reached across the table and, patting Tommy Joe on the shoulder, he said, 'Relax, Tommy Joe. Relax. Just think about the fine worker you'll be getting in nine month's time. You can raise it just like you want. Just think about that.'

Tommy Joe nodded soberly.


Monk stood outside the cabin in the night.

He could hear through the thin walls of the lean-to that Porkchop was still pestering Mrs. Crandall. He also could tell that she was enjoying herself. No woman who was being raped cried out with such pleasure.

But Monk was glad that he was not in Porkchop's place. He had had his taste of white women. Claudia Tucker had given Monk his fill of white women for the rest of his life. He hoped that Claudia would never recover from her so-called 'ague'.

Monk could not understand white women. One minute, they could not get enough of a black man. Then, the next minute, they threatened to castrate him.

Were black men a threat to white women? Was that why they treated them so badly?

Or were white women really ashamed to admit that they wanted black men for lovers?

Monk did not care now what any white people wanted. He

was tired of being ordered around by the Tuckers. He wanted to be with black people. To have a black woman for himself.

A loud gasp suddenly came from inside the lean-to behind him. Turning, Monk glanced through the rag half-hanging on the window and, by the bright light of the moon, he saw Porkchop's naked body standing next to the bed. He was gripping Mary Crandall around the bare waist and easing her up and down on his phallus. Mary Crandall clung onto Porkchop's neck as he held her in mid-air. She was squeezing against his driving hips, trying to achieve the maximum sensations from his rapidly moving body.

Smiling disdainfully, Monk turned away from the window. The sight both amused and sickened him. He laughed at the way in which the white woman no longer showed any signs of fright. She was completely giving herself to Porkchop. She probably had never had such a thrilling experience before in her life. But Monk was repelled when he thought how he himself had satisfied Claudia Tucker in such a way—only to be threatened later with castration.

Looking up at the sky, Monk wondered if he ever could escape from this tyranny.

*Chapter Twelve*

# THE PATRIMONY OF DRAGONARD

On the next few days following the funeral, Melissa noticed that Peter was acting strangely, avoiding contact with both her and her father; even when Storky or Nero tried to talk to him, Peter shrugged his shoulders and walked away.

Melissa finally confronted Peter on the third day after the funeral. She approached him when she saw him sitting in the parlour, staring at his feet. She asked, 'What's wrong, Peter? Was it that big of a shock?'

He looked at her, his bright blue eyes glaring out from under the fringe of black hair which had tumbled over his forehead. He snapped, 'What do you mean?'

'About Mother!' Melissa answered with equal spark. After the funeral, Melissa had quickly gathered her wits about her again and now was back into a schedule of work.

Although Melissa spent little time applying creams to her face or curling her hair with hot irons, she had a natural comeliness that fed on fresh country air, good sleep, and hard work. At twenty-four years of age, Melissa's hair had become more sandy than it had been when she was fifteen but she still wore it tied at the nape of her neck in a ribbon. She had the common sense to make the bow smaller than in her girlhood, though, and she dressed plainly now to suit her chores around the house.

Melissa had learned to work in the kitchen beside Storky and, not to be pressured by the bossy Ashanti-woman, Melissa had developed a mettle of her own, a single-mindedness not usually found in young Southern ladies, even in this territorial wilderness.

But Melissa was not dogmatic and over-bearing around the house like her mother had been. She was just firm when she had to be, and now seeing Peter in such a feckless state, she decided that this was one of the moments to take things in hand. Sitting down beside him on the sofa, she said, 'Peter, please! If there's anything you want to talk about, let's talk!'

Looking away from her, he said, 'No! If I talk, I want to talk to your father.'

'Then talk to him. He's only in there!' she said, pointing toward the closed door of Selby's study.

'I will. I will. Don't worry.'

But having had enough of his peevishness, Melissa gathered the skirt of her black muslin dress, saying, 'Well, you better talk while you can. You know how much time Father has to spend now with Judge Antrobus straightening out Mother's papers.' Rising from the sofa, she walked quickly to the door of her father's study and, rapping sharply, she called, 'Father! Peter wants to talk to you.'

Selby called from behind the closed door. 'Send him in. Send him in.'

Melissa opened the door and, turning to Peter, she said, 'And don't come out till you're smiling.'

He glared at her from the sofa.

But Melissa was determined. As she walked away from the open door, she said, 'It can't be all that bad.' Then she disappeared.

Peter now had no choice. Slowly rising to his feet, he ran his fingers through his crumpled hair, quickly trying to decide now how he was going to break the subject of Dragonard to Selby.

Slowly, with his head bent, Peter entered the study.


Selby was seated at his rolltop desk against the far wall and, pointing to the chair next to him without looking up, he said, 'Come in and let's hear what you have to say, Sonny.'

Closing the door, Peter shuffled over to stand beside Selby's desk.

Fumbling with papers, still not turning to look at Peter, Selby asked flippantly, 'Tired of sitting, Sonny?'

Peter blurted, 'I'm tired of living a lie!'

'Then sit down and tell me about it.' Selby showed no alarm.

Peter shouted, 'Maybe you better tell *me* about it. Maybe you better tell me how I got here. Maybe you better tell me exactly who Ta-Ta is. Is it true that my real mother left her house in St. Kitts because my real father drove her away? Is it true my real name is Abdee? I've been hearing things that seem to have some kind of connection to me! And I've been wondering if somebody's keeping something from me! What don't I know? *What don't I know?*' His face was red with anger.

Selby's swivel chair creaked as he turned to look at Peter. His voice remained calm as he said, 'Sonny, I think you better take a load off your feet and tell me exactly what you've heard.'

'I'm not your son.'

Selby rubbed his henna-red goatee, saying, 'You probably won't believe it, but that's the only thing in life I really regret.'

His honesty was lost on Peter. 'Then, damn it, whose son am I?'

'Sit down. Please.'

Reluctantly, Peter sank to the horsehair covered chair by the side of the desk, still glaring at Selby.

'In a situation like this,' Selby drawled, 'I don't know who should start first. You or me?'

Peter said angrily, 'I'm sure you know more than me.'

'Maybe. Maybe not. Tell me, when did you first catch whiff of all this?'

'Last week. Nero told me.'

'Your groom.' It was not a question.

Peter nodded.

'Is that where he's from? Your father's place on St. Kitts? Not some place called . . .' Selby hesitated, thinking for the name. 'Trouble Island?'

Peter sat on the edge of the chair. 'Then Richard Abdee *is* my father?'

'Hold on. Hold on, boy. Have patience and remember some of those manners I taught you. Now, I asked you, is that where Nero is from, and, if so, is that why you broke a gut buying him at that auction sale?'

Peter nodded. 'It's more involved.'

'But that auction was a good many years ago, Sonny. How did you know then? And, if you did know all this way back then, why did you wait until now for this explosion? Lord Almighty, boy, you bought Nero a good, six, eight, ten years ago!'

Shaking his head, Peter said, 'I didn't know much then. I didn't know much at all. Just bits and pieces I picked up from Ta-Ta. A few idiotic mumblings. Things she whispered to me or that I overheard.'

Selby was surprised. He had not suspected any of that. He asked, 'Ta-Ta?'

Peter nodded again.

Continuing to stare at him, Selby shook his head in disbelief. 'Ta-Ta? Old Ta-Ta told you? When she was in her cups, I bet. I should have thought of that. But she always seemed too . . . soused!' He laughed at the idea of her talking to Peter.

'Oh, don't worry. She didn't tell me too much. But if you knew that she knew then why didn't you tell me yourself? Why did you let her go around spooking me?'

Ignoring that question, Selby began, 'I bought Ta-Ta and two little piccaninnies a long, long time back. It seems like a century ago now. And I remember the night I brought them home here. Rachel was fit to be tied. She had sent me to town to buy a companion for little Melly. She could have just about slit my throat when I brought home that Ta-Ta.' Selby chuckled now, remembering the altercation of that distant night. His sunburnt face remained creased with amusement as he continued, 'Later that same night, after I had gone to bed upstairs, I heard a little knock on my door. Lo and behold, who should it be but Mama Gomorrah! She had the littlest tyke trailing behind her, just like some little lost puppy dog, he was. A funny, big-eyed little runt, and she brought him into my room and she said to me, "Master Selby, Sir, this here child's no piccaninnie! This one's a human baby!"' Then, looking at Peter, Selby said, 'That little runt was you, Sonny.'

Peter ignored the theatrics of his arrival at The Star and shouted at Selby, 'You bought me at an auction?'

Nonplussed, Selby answered, 'Same place you bought Nero.'

'But how could you?'

'The same way you bought Nero. And two other slaves. With money, that's how!'

'But—'

'But, what, Sonny? You were being sold as a nigger, weren't you? You were up there on the auction table. You were dark and had enough dirt on you to look like a nigger. You were holding onto that Ta-Ta's black tittie like she was your own black Ma.'

'My mother is dead!'

'How was I to know that? I didn't find that out till I got you home. It all came out from Ta-Ta herself. She spilled it all to Mama Gomorrah, who came up here straightway with the facts.' Selby laughed again, remembering that night.

'What's so funny?' Peter asked.

'How you looked. How big and blue your little eyes were. How you looked when we dressed you for bed. We couldn't leave you down in The Shed and you didn't have any clothes up here, so I cut off the sleeves from one of my best linen shirts for you to sleep in. You slept with me that first night. And you slept like a bear, too, all night, and you almost ate us out of house-and-home the next morning.'

Peter was holding his head now, trying to choke back the tears. Selby's memories were finally reaching him. He gasped, 'But, how? Why? *Why?*'

'I'm afraid I can't give you more of answer than that, Sonny. I couldn't have thrown a little tyke out into the night, could I? I couldn't very well take you back to Lynn and Craddocks, demanding my money back, could I? Well, I suppose I could have, but what would have happened to you then? Boy, you had—nobody!'

Peter was speechless.

'Mama Gomorrah got Ta-Ta to part with your birth certifi-. cation and I've got it locked away for you to see when you want to. You can have it now, I guess. On it, you can see the name of your mother. Your father. The ship you were born on. Sonny, your mother was a fine, brave lady called Honore. She gave birth to you on a French ship and landed down in East Florida way. Now, as far as your father is—'

In renewed fury, Peter interrupted Selby with an explosion of facts. 'My father drove my mother away. He took her home. He took her money. My father took everything he could get his greedy hands on and I'm glad the damned slaves killed him.'

Selby was wide-eyed now. 'He did all that?'

'Yes! And I damn him for it.'

'Well, Sonny, if you go on damning and blaming people, you might as well put a few curses on France, too. If it hadn't been for French troubles, your Mama would have taken you there to live. That had been her intentions. That's where she was headed when the French revolution took place over there. Why they had to stop at East Florida.'

Peter shouted, 'But that's just nothing but "if"! What I'm saying is fact! My father drove my mother away and I'm glad they killed him.'

'Now, Sonny, that's no way for you to talk about your Daddy.' Selby paused, looking at Peter, 'You say he's really dead?'

Peter nodded. 'Nero told me he was killed in a slave rebellion on ... Dragonard. He was killed. Killed along with Naomi.'

'Naomi? Now who's that?' Selby asked, behind in the facts now.

'His nigger whore!'

'Tch. Tch. Tch. You *did* find out a lot from that Nero, didn't you? Maybe I should have a talk with him, too.' Studying the papers on his rolltop desk, Selby said, 'I suppose he told you about Monkey then.'

Peter wrinkled his brow. 'Monkey?'

'Or Monk, as he's called now. Chad Tucker's boy.'

'What about him?'

'He's your Daddy's git.'

'Monk? That bully who runs around with Tucker? The one we think is whipping the people? That bully is my . . . brother?'

'Well, I wouldn't really call Monk your brother. You know how feelings are about coloured blood. But, Ta-Ta, she mothered him, sired by your Daddy.'

Still reeling, Peter said, 'Monk and I are . . . half-brothers?'

'You maybe see why I've been holding this back from you, Sonny. There are lots of complications here. I wanted you to be ready.'

'Ready?' Peter asked.

'To face facts.'

'Well, I'm facing them now, aren't I? When they're thrown in my face, I have to face them!'

Selby generously offered, 'Maybe you'd like to go up to the attic and have that talk with Ta-Ta. If she's not too soused, maybe you can learn a little more. If that's what you want.'

'I'll do that when I'm good and ready. If I'm ever *that* ready!'

There was a silence, a short pause before Selby spoke. 'You said you first learned about this last week.'

Peter nodded.

'Before Rachel died?' Selby asked.

'The day it happened,' Peter mumbled.

'And you didn't come to me before now?'

Peter shook his head.

Reaching toward Peter's shoulder, Selby patted him, saying, 'Thank you, Sonny. I appreciate you holding it inside you for a while longer. You're a fine boy. A mighty fine boy. No. I take that back. You're a man. And no matter who your father is or was, Sonny, he'd be proud of you, too. Mighty proud.'

Peter grabbed for Selby's hand, and holding it, his body began to quake as he cried.

'Here, here,' Selby consoled and, although he had not shed a tear for his wife's death, his eyes were filling with moisture.

Selby knew that Peter was a long distance away from him now. He had lost 'Sonny' momentarily.

As the evening clouds began to turn violet, the sun burning out its red flames beyond the dark hills of The Star, Peter still roamed aimlessly over the footpaths which pierced the shadowy woods.

Peter stumbled along, aimlessly kicking at stones, stomping through ferns, slapping at the branches on elderberry bushes. He kept going and going.

Having run in tears from the big house more than an hour ago, Peter still could not return to face it. The cool evening breeze had dried his eyes but his soul was still confused and his brain still raced.

He stood staring now at the bulky outline of The Shed in an open field in front of him. There were no children in sight, only a faint light shining inside two glass windows. And looking at this converted storehouse, Peter realized that he could have been raised in there as a slave child instead of a white boy in the big house. The complications of such a fate, of the unpredictable balance in which his life had hung now frightened him and he continued to run.

Crossing an open ridge now, his thoughts went to Selby, to the story that Selby had told him about Mama Gomorrah bringing him to the big house, how Selby had dressed him in his linen shirt and had taken him into his own bed.

Seated on a rock, Peter stared up into the star dotted sky, realizing what consideration he had received from Selby and what trouble that Selby must have had with his wife about taking an orphan into their house.

Rachel Selby had been a cantankerous old woman, Peter thought now. She had never showed him one bit of warmth. He always had had to call her 'Mrs. Selby'.

But Melissa. Thinking about Melissa, Peter remembered how he had grown up with her, their special friendship, how she had never once begrudged him a place in the family.

Peter then thought about how uncivil that he had been to her earlier today in the parlour. She had only been trying to help him, to urge him to talk to Selby. If it had not been for Melissa, Peter still might not know all these truths. Melissa had made it possible for Selby to help him.

To help him. Help. But that was what everybody at The Star had ever done for him. Help him. Excepting Rachel Selby, everyone had done nothing but to help Peter, help Peter, help Peter. His anger flared now and he thought of being put into that position of needing charity. He did not know if he was angry at himself for needing it, at Selby for giving it, or at his father for making all this necessary, this turmoil and frustration and hate.

His father. Richard Abdee. An Englishman called Richard Abdee.

Without realizing it, Peter had begun walking again and, by now, he had reached Niggertown. Looking at the long rows of cabins, he saw how run down and sordid they looked even in the moonlight. He wondered what the plantation in St. Kitts had looked like. What was Dragonard like? And what had it been like when his mother owned it, in the days of Petit Jour? Twilight.

Peter remembered Nero's description of his father, that Richard Abdee had been handsome but a selfish man. That he had been horny, too, had screwed everything in sight.

His father, Richard Abdee. Peter said the name aloud: 'Richard Abdee.'

The man who had flogged slaves in a public square for a living.

'Dragonard.' He repeated it. 'Dragonard.'


Peter stayed in the night. And, nearby in the overseer's cabin, Chad and Claudia Tucker wondered if they heard somebody moving in the bushes around the cabin.

Claudia was worried about a stranger breaking into the cabin and stealing her flour sack of money.

Chad said, 'Let me bury it again.'

Claudia quickly shot her eyes at Monk sitting dumbly on the floor by the stove. She did not even want Monk to know that she had the money in the cabin now.

Looking to see that Monk was not watching, Chad Tucker mimed the act of digging a hole with a shovel—why not bury the money in the ground?

Claudia peevishly shook her head. She was not going to let the flour sack out of her grasp.

After listening again to the stillness of the night, Claudia called sharply to Monk, 'Boy? Wake up there!'

Monk slowly raised his shaved head. He had not been sleeping. He was just in the usual stupour that he had been in lately.

Claudia ordered, 'Go look outside and see who's snooping around the yard.'

Monk looked at Chad Tucker.

'Do what she says,' Chad gruffed. 'Have a good look, too. Just don't stick your head out the door and say "nobody, Master Sir." Have a real look.'

Claudia and Chad Tucker both waited for Monk to leave before continuing their discussion about burying the money.

The sack of money was slowly becoming an obsession to them.


Peter lay on his back on a mossy patch near a tinkling stream, staring up at the stars and wondering what the skies looked like in St. Kitts at night. He was thinking of sugar crops and the harvests and food. What did people eat in the Caribbean?

Suddenly hearing a noise come from the bushes, he sat up and called into the night, 'Who's there?'

No one answered.

He called louder, 'Who's there?'

Then, as Peter looked in the direction of the noise, he saw a dark figure emerge from the bushes, the curving silhouette of a female dressed in a short white smock. It was a wench from Niggertown.

'What are you doing out at night?' Peter called sharply at the black girl.

Coming closer to him, she said, 'Cooling down.'

'It's not hot tonight. And, besides, you're supposed to be inside at this time.' He did not like reminding the black people about what they could and could not do but, at this moment, he wanted to be alone.

Persistent, the girl said, 'It sure seems warm to me, Master Peter, Sir.'

Like a stranger, he asked, 'How do you know who I am?'

When the black girl did not answer him, he asked, 'What do they call you?'

'Lilly, Master Peter, Sir. I sees you around alot.' Standing beside him now, she asked, 'Can I sits, Master Peter, Sir?'

'Suit yourself.'

Slowly sinking to the ground beside him, she said, 'It's mossy here, ain't it? Nice and soft and mossy but kind of damp, too, ain't it, Master Peter, Sir.'

'I thought you said you were warm,' Peter said, turning to look more closely at her now. She sat so close to him that he could see each small twist of the tiny plaits that covered her head like a series of thick lines of indigo ink. Her eyes were large and heavily lashed. Her cheekbones were high and the moistness of her full lips shone in the dark. The skin on her long neck looked satin soft to Peter and, by the way in which she had pulled the white smock up above her knees, he could see that her legs were well-shaped and textured with the same, fine skin.

As if knowing that she was attractive to him, she boldly reached for his forearm, and beginning to stroke him with her hand, she said, 'Why don't you just leans back, Master Peter, and keeps enjoying the night.'

Peter was caught between desires. He wanted his privacy yet

he felt a growing excitement for this girl. He asked, 'Lay back? I thought you said it was wet?'

'Here,' she said, quickly kneeling and pulling the white smock over her head. Laying it on the moss for him like a blanket, she said, 'Lays on that, Master Peter, Sir.'

Peter sat staring at her, looking in disbelief how she was kneeling—entirely naked—next to him on the ground.

Lilly rested her hands on the full curve of her hips and arched her back at him so that he could see the tautness of her breasts. He saw how her chocolate brown nipples spread into a lighter smoothness.

'Go on,' she coaxed, 'lay back, Master Peter.'

Obediently, Peter sank back onto the girl's smock. Then lying with his hands behind his neck, he watched as she scrambled to sit facing forwards on his legs. She held the heel of one boot in both hands between her knees and called, 'Put your other foot on me and push!'

In no time at all, Lilly had pulled off both of his boots, his socks, lowered his trousers, his small clothes and had gently unbuttoned his shirt. And, still not letting him lift himself from the ground, she crouched over his midsection and reached down with both hands to grasp his phallus. Indirectly, she had prepared that, too.

Peter felt more than excitement and warmth in the girl. He was receiving a security from her, from this unexpected meeting on tonight of all nights. His sexual proclivities in the past had been modest, true, but tonight he felt in a special need for this closeness. He had only lain with black girls before but this girl was giving him a sensation that he had never felt before, a complete abandonment of the body. Or did that feeling only come from within himself, his mood tonight?

Slowing her rhythmic hips, she asked, 'You about ready to pop, ain't you, Master Peter?'

'Why?' He had never before heard a wench ask such a direct question.

'I just knows,' she said, as she eased herself down onto Peter's hardness and, holding him inside, she lay on her side and said,

'Roll on top of me now. You holds it longer that way.'

Without questioning her, Peter obeyed, continuing his deep thrusts into her.

She said, 'Drives in nice and slow and deep and it's good for us both.'

But, regardless of her coaching, Peter felt his excitement increase and, when he felt an explosion building inside him, he quickly pulled out of the girl, letting himself spill all over her stomach.

Raising herself on her elbows, Lilly gasped, 'Why you do that?'

'But you might have a baby.' His statement was true, he knew, that being his practise from the past. But, tonight of all nights, he was particularly conscious of the fact of insemination. He was already thinking of his father, of Monk, of white men and their black wenches.

Lilly lay back down on her smock and started to laugh at Peter. Her laugh was loud and piercing, sounding like a mockery to him.

Next, as she reached to a bush near her head and, ripping off a handful of leaves, she began to wipe the thick, white puddle from her bare stomach and said, 'Well, that's okay, Master Peter. But we tries again and you stays inside me. I have your sucker if it happens. But we tries again because Master Peter, you hung like a nigger. Yes, you the first white nigger I ever sees!'

Peter froze. He had heard those words before. A 'white nigger'. Those were the words that Nero had told him in his story, the phrasing of a black woman talking about his father. The woman called Naomi had said that about Richard Abdee, that he was a 'white nigger'.

So that was what it meant. To be a 'white nigger' meant to have large endowments. Peter asked himself, are distinctions between men really that base?

Pulling his shirt over his naked body, Peter told Lilly to go. He ordered her to pick up her dress from the ground and leave him alone.

Then, standing with his back to her, he shook the last few drops of seed from the head of his penis, his only patrimony of Dragonard.

Monk had not found anyone lurking in the yard around the Tuckers' cabin. But when he had looked farther—as Tucker had told him to do—he saw Peter and Lilly.

Monk still stood in the bushes and held his hand over the hard bulge in his pants. He had been watching Peter and Lilly making love on the ground.

He had heard Lilly jeering at Peter for pulling out of her before he shot. His eyes had followed Lilly as she covered her body with the shift and then he had seen Peter shaking the thick white tears from his penis.

The sight of Lilly's firm body had aroused Monk. He had become erect watching her giving pleasure to Peter. It was different than when he had watched Mary Crandall and Porkchop. Lilly excited Monk but he fought the urge to explode with his hand.

Monk had never made love with Lilly but he had seen her in Niggertown. He wanted to lay her more than any other wench but he did not want her this way, he did not want to shoot his excitement by watching her twisting and squeezing with a white man.

Monk hated Peter for having the one girl on The Star that he truly wanted. Monk hated Peter for not giving Lilly his come. Monk felt that thick white come was the highest praise that a man could give a woman. By denying a woman that load was to humiliate her.

Peter was a damned fool, Monk thought.

But, most of all, Monk hated himself. He had let himself lose his spirit and ambition.

Why could he not have this girl? Did he need Tucker's permission to screw with Lilly?

Standing in the bushes, Monk began to see a new life for

himself. Monk had been broken. The Tuckers had broken him. But now Monk saw that he must fight and cheat and lie to get what he wanted on The Star. And one of those things he wanted was Lilly.

*Book Three*

# METEOR

## Chapter Thirteen

# THE SCAVENGER'S DAUGHTER

Six weeks had passed since Rachel Selby's funeral. In those six weeks, Albert Selby had continued to visit the Dewitt Place. He thought that it would be hypocritical of him to stay away from his true friends.

Charlotte Dewitt had approached Selby in those six weeks about a very curious matter. She trusted her friendship with Albert Selby even to talk to him about 'the Scavenger's Daughter'.

Making it clear that she did not want it for the Dewitt Place, Charlotte asked, 'Am I right in thinking that you have a "Scavenger's Daughter" on The Star?'

Albert Selby and Charlotte Dewitt were sitting side-by-side on the edge of the bed in the Rose Room. Selby was preparing to leave for home. It took him a moment to realize what she meant by 'the Scavenger's Daughter'.

He suddenly said, 'The torture machine. That thing that looks like a big iron sugar-tongs.'

Charlotte shrugged her thin shoulders, continuing to repin the coronet of braids around her head. 'I don't know what it looks like. I just know that it's called "the Scavenger's Daughter".'

'That's what some men call it. But I call it the sugar-tongs. That's what it looks like to me. Sugar-tongs. But big enough to clamp a man in it.'

'You have one on The Star?'

'There used to be one there. It belonged to that old cuss, Peregrine Roland. He bought it from England when he first started keeping slaves here. He used it for punishing them. I remember it has "Liverpool" stamped on it. That's where they made them.'

'Would you be willing to part with it?'

'Now, what would a little lady like you want with a thing like that?'

'Don't misunderstand. It's not for me, Albert. But there's a certain man nearabouts who doesn't want to approach you personally to buy it.'

'Why the hell not?'

She shrugged again. 'I supposed for the simple reason he's not—' She searched for the correct words. '—he's only a farmer.'

'A farmer? Does he come here?'

'Oh, no, no, no. He's not one of our guests. Mercy, no. But I promise you, Albert, he approached me most discreetly and gentleman-like. And he asked if I would put the proposition to you. He said he's willing to pay as high as fifty dollars for it.

'Fifty dollars? For that old rusty thing? Who is this farmer?'

'Don't press me, Albert. Please. That was one of his stipulations. But he assured me that, if you do find out someday who he is, you'll understand his reason for wanting it.'

Selby sat on the edge of the bed, shaking his head. 'The Scavenger's Daughter. I plumb forgot about it being on The Star. Sure, I'll sell it to him. And I'll tell you what, Charlotte. You can keep any money you get for it. Buy yourself a fancy new dress.

'Albert, no!' she protested.

'I insist. Or I won't sell it.'

Charlotte Dewitt finally agreed to accept the money for a new dress and, the next day, Albert Selby delivered the Scavenger's Daughter to the Dewitt Place.

Selby then more fully explained that the Scavenger's Daughter was the opposite of a rack. It pushed a body together instead of pulling it. A person's legs were pressed up to his stomach, his hands clenched in front of his chest, the head pulled forward by an iron neckband. A body could be pulled tighter and tighter into a ball when pressure was applied. A man's bones could be broken by total compression of the screws. And, as that was happening, blood spurted from his mouth and nostrils, as well as from the ends of his fingers and toes, and his chest also burst.

Standing alone, though, the Scavenger's Daughter looked harmless. It looked as Selby had described it, like a big pair of iron sugar tongs. But with an iron collar for the neck, one grip for the hands and two grips for the ankles at the end of each 'tong'.

The buyer of the Scavenger's Daughter remained anonymous for the moment.

In those last six weeks since Rachel Selby's funeral, Peter had not spent any mornings—or afternoons, or nights—in the stables.

Since he had been sixteen, Peter had taken his wenches to the hayloft there for pestering. But he had not even been doing that lately. He had been avoiding Nero.

This late morning, when Peter was leading his mare out from the stall for an overdue ride, Nero called to him, 'Ain't heard you pestering no wenches at night lately, Master Peter.'

Nero was trying to follow the advice which Albert Selby had given him a few weeks ago. Selby had told Nero the complication of the Dragonard story and he had suggested to Nero that he should try to forget about Peter's connection to it. To act natural with Peter and pretend as if nothing had happened. Nero had said that he was not very good at pretending but promised Selby that he would try. He liked Peter.

'I've been taking it easy.' The clipped tone of Peter's voice did not invite conversation.

But Nero persisted, keeping his voice light and friendly. 'Ain't gone and caught yourself the pox, have you?'

'Wouldn't know what it felt like if I did.'

'Your pecker stings when you piss, that's what!'

The mention of venereal symptoms made Peter alert, not that he had been feeling a stinging sensation when he urinated, but because he had never heard any such diagnosis before. He asked, 'You had the pox, Nero?'

'Not me, Master Peter. But I knows. You must remember me telling you I worked for Mistress Naomi.'

Peter's head dropped. 'Oh, yeah. That.' He turned to go, the horse following behind him without its harnessing.

'Master Peter?' Nero's voice was firm, no fawning voice of a black slave.

Peter stopped and, holding the bridle in his hand, he asked without turning, 'Yes, Nero?' It was an exchange of friends, a cool exchange of words between people who have had a quarrel but, nonetheless, they were still friends.

Nero called, 'They say hair can grow on your hand.'

The remark momentarily caught Peter off guard. But, turning to frown at Nero, he saw that his big brown friend was smiling.

Holding one hand in front of his bare stomach, Nero cupped his fingers and lowered his hand to his crotch, moving it back and forth in slow, long gestures as if he were masturbating.

Immediately understanding what Nero was simulating, Peter's face broke into a grin. Then, suddenly throwing the bridle to the floor with a clatter, Peter shouted, 'God-damn it, Nero! Why are you such a good son-of-a-bitch? Why do I really like you?' Peter stood rubbing his neck, looking at the floor and shaking his head in disbelief.

The attempt to break through Peter's shell had worked. Nero moved toward Peter now and grinned widely, his white teeth sparkling against his tobacco brown face.

Reaching out, Nero happily patted Peter on the shoulder and said, 'They do say that, Master Peter. Hair does grow on a man's hand if he jerks-off too much. And if you ain't been pestering none and you ain't got the pox, then you must have been—' He slowly moved his hand again in front of his tight, gaping breeches.

'Do you want to know something?' Peter asked, staring at

Nero with a twinkle in his eyes. 'Do you really want to know something, Nero?'

'Tell me.'

'I just haven't been feeling in a mood for *anything*!'

Nero became more serious. 'I understands that, Master Peter. You don't have to tell me about those feelings. I went three years without pestering once.'

'Three years?'

Nero nodded. 'Three whole years. Maybe even more.'

'But why?'

Nero's eyes sobered, looking at Peter. 'I had me a big disappointment. A big disappointment over something I'd been hoping for.'

'It must have been awful big.'

'It was. I was a fool-hearted kid, I guess, but when I was about your age, I made myself a secret wish for the future. I wished that—' Nero smiled a lost smile, remembering. 'I wished that by the year one thousand and eight hundred, I wished that by the new century there would be no more slavery for us black people, Master Peter. Oh, it wasn't a wish for revolts. No rising against the whites. It was just a wish—' Nero shrugged, as if he now thought the idea was foolish, '—that people could be equal, have the same chances.'

'And do you know what *I* wished for on the eve of that year?' There was a sharpness to Peter's question.

Nero shook his head.

Peter said to Nero, 'You told me you'd wished for peace for all people, for black people and white people to get on together by the year eighteen-hundred?'

'That's right.'

'Do you know what I wished for, Nero?'

Again, Nero shook his head.

'To buy a groom. To be like the other white boys my age. To own my very own "nigger groom". To get *you*!'

A large puff of breath exploded from Nero's mouth, then he said, 'You'd think we'd learn our lesson about telling each other stories, don't you? You'd think the last time would have

221

taught us not to do much talking together.'

Peter was still involved with his story. 'Do you see what a bastard I am, Nero!'

Nero was sorry now that he had tried to talk to Peter. Trying to calm him, he said, 'You ain't no bastard, Master Peter.'

'No, I don't mean that way. I'm not going back again to that talk we had about my mother and my father and all that crap! I mean, Nero, see how selfish I am. Really am.'

'What's selfish about it? That's how you were raised!'

'Nero? How can you be so understanding all the time?'

Nero dipped his head. 'Years do that to a man, Master Peter. If he's got a heart ticking inside him, years give it that teaching.'

'I guess I don't have a heart then.'

'Master Peter?'

Peter did not answer, he was staring blankly at the floor. He looked despondent. He, too, wished that this subject had not been revived.

But Nero had started, so he wanted to finish. 'You got you a heart, Master Peter, you got such a big heart that sometimes I think you're a black man yourself. Yes, Master Peter, when I see the size of your heart, I'd even say you're a "white nigger"!'

The phrase jolted Peter. He asked snidely, 'Don't you mean when you see the size of my prick? Isn't that how a man is compared to a "nigger"? By how big his prick is?'

Nero's own temper boiled now. 'Master Peter, you're God-damned prick don't mean nothing to me. If I thought so, I'd say so. I've seen you for a long time now and we do our share of talking about wenching and pestering and laughing, but I ain't got no eyes for your prick. I wants you to understand that right now.'

Seeing that Nero had misunderstood him, Peter tried to clarify himself, to calm Nero's temper. 'I don't mean it that way, Nero. I wasn't saying you wanted something not right.'

'There's nothing that's "not right", boy.' Nero had dropped the 'Master Peter' and his face was tight with anger. He was talking to Peter man-to-man now, one human-being to another. He had forgotten about Peter's past, the colour of his skin. Nero was talking about the present as well as a future.

He continued, 'There's nothing that's "not right". There's just things that's right for me and right for you and right for whoever they be. And I think your trouble is you don't know what's right for you. That's your trouble, I think. That's why you're being in this stinking mood now. You're trying to find out what you need. You. Peter. You, that person called Peter Abdee.' Nero was glad that he had finally said the name.

This was the first time that anyone—black or white—had ever called Peter by that name. And even though he had been saying the name over and over in his mind, even aloud when he was alone—Peter Abdee, Peter Abdee  he had never heard another voice utter it, addressing him as 'Peter Abdee!'

Nero said now, 'You're tired of laying with black wenches now, ain't you? You're thinking maybe you cause more trouble? Maybe knock up one of them?' He was very angry now.

Peter stared at him.

'Because in your heart, you think of the trouble pestering black wenches caused in the past. Like your Pa did. You remember your Pa. You never knew him but you think about him.'

Peter still did not respond.

'Well, maybe your Pa did sow a lot of half-breeds. But it happens all the time. And maybe it's going to happen so much that you'll see that the god you call "Lord" has really planned it that way all along. Black people to marry up with white people. But that still don't make it right for you now, does it?'

'What *is* right for me, Nero?' It was a plea, a sudden cry to Nero for help.

'Being yourself. Being happy and doing your work. I've been seeing you doing that all right these days. But you've been working because you're hiding in it. But that ain't right for *you*! And maybe what's really right for you—besides enjoying your work when you do it—is to find you the right woman!'

'Woman?'

'Are you wanting to go back with those wenches up there in the loft?' Nero nodded above them at the thick, ragged fringe of straw.

Peter shook his head.

'You maybe want to try the other thing then? Pestering with the boys? Oh, some of them black boys are as pretty as the wenches. Maybe you'd even want them to do some pestering on you. They say there's a place where they all meet over at the meadow and all pair off, maybe you want to go there!'

Peter's blue eyes dulled with hatred.

'How does a woman sound to you, then? One of your own kind? What about getting yourself a wife? You know inside your heart that you can have your own family. Maybe that's what that nigger heart of yours is really wanting. Mine wanted the same thing once but I couldn't get it. Not on St. Kitts, that God-damned "Trouble Island". But you can have it if you wants.'

'I suppose that's what I need.'

'Need! Hell! Lots of folks "need" things. They don't gets it always. But folks who *want* things do gets it. Is that what you *want?*'

Peter's voice was soft. 'Nero?'

'Yes?' he asked, adding now 'Master Peter.'

'You might hate me for saying this but—'

Nero waited.

'Nero, I'm sorry you didn't get your wish a long time ago. I'm sorry things are like they are between blacks and whites. But, Nero—'

'Yes, Master Peter?'

Looking Nero straight in his vibrant black eyes, Peter confessed, 'I'm glad that I got *my* wish. Because if I didn't get my wish, Nero, if I didn't get my groom, I'd never got you, Nero, and—' He shrugged helplessly. '—who'd be my friend then?'

There was a finality to Nero's quick nod. And strength in his brown hand as he now rested it on Peter's shoulder and said, 'If I ever do get my wish, Master Peter, it's going to be through white men like you. Now, look there at your mare. Shame.

224

She's damned near going to stamp hell out of this floor. Better take her for that run.'

Peter kept his eyes on Nero. He asked, 'Aren't you coming with me? I haven't seen you exercising nothing but your mouth.'

Nero quickly accepted Peter's invitation.

This made them real friends again.

Chad Tucker waited until Peter and Nero rode by on their horses before he came out of the tool shed. He was carrying a shovel.

Looking into the direction of Niggertown, he saw the dust from Peter's and Nero's horse vanish now into the noontime sky.

He motioned to the tool shed and Claudia emerged with a bundle in her arms.

She asked suspiciously, 'Why them two getting so chummy lately?'

'Birds of a feather,' Chad Tucker grumbled. 'One's just as uppity as the other.'

Looking at the direction which they had ridden, Claudia asked, 'Why they going to Niggertown?'

'Snooping,' Tucker said, glancing around him to see that he and his wife were alone. 'That white kid is probably thinking Selby's going to heir him this place. He's sizing it up.'

Claudia muttered, 'He's no kid no more. He's a full grown man. But the way he keeps that hair of his all clean and shiny, you'd think he was a woman.'

'His face is girly, too. Never did trust a man who's got him girly blue eyes like that. Might be big and tall but I bet he's weaker than a preacher with gout.'

'Did he see you?' Claudia asked.

Chad Tucker shook his head. Then, walking toward the trees, he beckoned Claudia to follow him.

Claudia carried the flour sack of money wrapped inside her

worsted quilt. They had finally decided to bury it near their cabin.

Walking briskly behind her husband, Claudia whispered, 'Don't you think maybe we should wait till night comes to do this?'

Stepping carefully so that his boots would not break any dry branches on the ground, Chad Tucker said, 'We'd have Monk snooping around then.'

'You don't think Monk would steal from us, do you?'

Chad Tucker laughed. 'A nigger? Steal? Hell, Monk would snatch a fart if he could get his hands on it.'

Quickly, they continued back in the direction of their cabin to the place where they had decided to bury their riches.

Shortly, Claudia called ahead of her to Chad, 'You think Monk knew we had the money in the house with us.'

Chad kept walking. 'I don't know how much that nigger sees.'

'Well, I got me another plan then,' she said. 'A plan to keep him from knowing we buried it. In case he saw it in the house.'

'Tell me later.'

She said, 'To keep him from knowing we moved the money.'

'TELL ME LATER!'

Chad Tucker liked the money as much as his wife did. But he was slowly becoming annoyed with her single-mindedness over it. She could talk about nothing lately but the money.


Albert Selby kept his money in two banks, one in Troy and the other in Carterville.

Lately, Judge Antrobus had been pressing Selby to make a will. Even Selby's two bankers told him that he must start making some plans.

Albert Selby had a plan, though.

He had been brewing a plot and it finally began to take shape on a particularly happy morning. Today was made fresh and vibrant by Melissa coming downstairs to breakfast in a bright blue dress, the colour of a robin's egg. She wore a lemon yellow sash around her waist and her sandy hair was tied back by a striped ribbon. It was her first day to be out of the dreary black clothes of mourning for her mother.

Peter instantly noticed the change in Melissa's wardrobe and, interrupting the conversation that he had been having with Selby about the workers' corn crop, he said to Melissa, 'Hey. It really looks good seeing you like that again, Melly.'

Picking up the skirt of her dress between her fingertips, Melissa twirled in front of the table.

'And a bright mood to go with it.' Selby said, adding a spoonful of honey to his coffee. 'That's what I like to see.'

'Your father and I were just talking about growing more corn for Niggertown,' Peter said.

Melissa made a face, wrinkling her small nose.

'What's the matter?' Selby asked.

Shaking her head, Melissa answered, 'Do we really have to go on calling it that?'

Selby looked up from his cup. 'Calling what *what*?'

'That name,' she said. 'Niggertown.'

Selby answered, matter-of-factly, 'That's what it is, ain't it?'

'But, Papa! Niggertown sounds so . . . terrible!'

'How about Negroville, then? Does that suit your taste any better?'

She frowned at him. 'Really, Papa!'

Leaning forward, Peter said, 'I think I know what Melly means. By calling it Niggertown, well, it just—'

Selby was waiting. 'Yes?'

Peter blurted. 'Disrespectful to those people there.'

'Exactly!' Melissa chimed.

'So what do you two want me to do? Take down a barrel of flour, sprinkle it over their heads and—snap!—things are all white!'

'Papa, you're side-stepping the question.'

'I'm not side-stepping anything,' Selby drawled, stirring the sweetness into his coffee more thoroughly. 'I'm just waiting for you two to give me a good explanation. Maybe if you could tell me why "Niggertown" is not good enough for Niggertown, maybe we can do something about it. Come on. Come on. Give me some reasons!'

Melissa looked at Peter. 'Can you tell him?'

Peter shook his head. 'I'm having a hard enough time talking about planting a few more rows of corn, letting them have more time to hoe their own gardens.'

Raising his eyebrows, Selby asked, 'Who's going to do our work then?'

Melissa pleaded, 'But their work is our work, too, Papa! We're all here together!'

Selby sat back on his chair, saying with a twinkle in his eyes, 'What do I have now, two abolitionists?'

'Oh, Papa, you're jumping the gun again,' Melissa said.

'You two do seem to be siding against me this morning. First, saying Niggertown is not good enough. And then that they should have more time to work for themselves.'

Peter and Melissa looked at one another again, shaking their heads in amusement. They knew that Selby was not angry. They realized his ideas were planted deep in this earth, conditioned by the old times when he had first come here.

After gulping down his coffee, Selby lifted his straw hat from the table and rose to his feet. Walking slowly from the table, Selby centred his hat on his head, and said, 'The simplest thing to do, I suppose—you two not approving of how I run things here—is for you to get hitched and then you can do what you want together. The place would be all yours then.' Selby nodded his head as if the idea had only come to him now—had not been his secret plan these last weeks, even months—and said, 'Yes. Maybe you two should get hitched. Marry up with each other.'

'Papa!' Melissa called.

Standing in the archway between the dining-room and the entry hall, Selby asked, 'What's so wrong with that? Making a respectful man out of me? People are starting to talk about me, you know!'

Then, shaking his head again, Selby shuffled across the hall toward the double doors and called, 'Don't worry if I'm not home early. I've got to ride over to see Judge Antrobus.'

He left them.


The silence which Selby had left in the dining-room was an embarrassment to both Melissa and Peter.

Melissa wanted to run and hide.

Peter felt stupid and childlike, as if he were only a boy.

But he was a grown man. And reminding himself of that fact, and remembering a few thoughts that he himself had been thinking lately, he began by saying to Melissa, 'I didn't know your Father thought like that.'

Fumbling with her white damask napkin, Melissa kept her eyes to her lap. 'Oh! He's such a dear, isn't he? But he does set himself up for these disappointments!'

Peter made himself say, 'Do you think you'd ever be dis-appointed with *me*, Melly?'

The question shocked her and, raising her head with a jolt, she stared at Peter. ' "Disappointed"?'

'As a—' He shrugged. 'Being your husband.' He did not care if she laughed at him. He had been mocked before.

Melissa suddenly blurted, 'I'm four years older than you!'

Peter could not hold back his smile. 'All you have to say is that you're four years older than me?'

Realizing her blunder, she lowered her head again, hiding a deep blush.

In a serious voice now, Peter said, 'You won't have to—I mean, I wouldn't make demands on you, Melly. You could live here, you can be like you always have.' He was proud of him-self for finally having the courage to talk to her this way. 'See, us maybe being . . . like that, I could stay here, too!'

She quickly exclaimed, 'Oh, Peter, I want you always to stay here!'

Their eyes met a second time and no embarrassment exchanged between them at this moment, no feeling of awkwardness. Like butterflies suddenly sprung from their larvae, Melissa and Peter had their own kind of wings. They were no longer make-believe sister and brother. They were a woman and a man.

Peter asked, 'Would you maybe like to think about it,' he added for propriety, 'Melissa?'

She nodded in short jerks. 'Yes, Peter.'

'Then after you've had a few days to think about it—take a few weeks, even months . . .'

But she interrupted him. It was her turn to be bold. 'No, Peter, you've misunderstood me. I didn't mean to "think" about it. I said yes because I already think it's a—' her voice softened. 'I think it's a good idea. For both of us. Yes, Peter, I will marry you.'

Their eyes stayed fixed on one another for a moment, a new understanding between them, until Melissa slowly rose from her chair. Smiling faintly, she said, 'Let me gather these dishes. Storky is out looking for Biddy again. Really! Since Posey's come into Biddy's life, she's not done a lick of work here!'

'I've got to go up to the ridge, anyway. We're limbing some trees today.' Peter rose from his chair as Melissa was moving toward the kitchen door. But, pausing in front of the door, she turned and called, 'Peter?'

'Yes?' He waited.

'I hope I don't disappoint you either, Peter.' Then Melissa disappeared into the kitchen.


Melissa shared everything with Storky but she did not have a chance to tell her the news until later. When she had gone into the kitchen, Storky still had not returned to the house with the stray Biddy. And Melissa was glad for that fact, too, because this was the first time she had to herself, to sit by the worktable and ponder the possibility of being married to Peter Abdee, the boy whom she had grown up calling her brother, Peter Selby.

Selby had told Melissa about Peter's discovery of his true

identity. He had gone directly to Melissa from the study after Peter had left in such an angry mood. Selby had asked Melissa if Peter had ever said anything to her.

But Melissa knew nothing, nor had she suspected anything about Peter's past. She thought of him only as a permanent fixture at The Star, remembering how glad that she had been as a little girl to have a companion for playing. Brother Roland had never been close to her and, because the houses in the South were so far apart, it was difficult to find playmates.

There was also a difficulty in Louisiana for girls to find husbands. The most likely possibility was for a young lady to marry a neighbour or a second or third cousin. In Melissa's case, such an arrangement was either impossible or repulsive. The Witcherleys were the closest neighbours, the Breslins and the Nortons had no sons who were anywhere near Melissa's age, and her cousins were all freckled-faced, mealey-mouthed, money-hungry Rolands. Melissa would rather die an old maid than to be married to Hiram Roland, Joe Billy Roland, Louis Peregrine Roland, or any Roland at all.

But Peter. Peter Abdee. Melissa sat by the kitchen worktable in a trance now, wondering why she had so hastily agreed to be his wife? Was she really that anxious to get married? Did the future of spinsterhood frighten her so much that she would risk shocking the entire neighbourhood by marrying the boy who had been raised as her brother? (And Melissa was keenly aware that some people—especially the Rolands—would be scandalized by the match.) Or, Melissa wondered, was she really doing this to please her father? She knew her father well enough to suspect that he would like nothing better than to see her marry Peter. Like herself, he had grown very fond of him. Melissa laughed now as she thought of how Selby had even baited the trap for them this morning.

Melissa suddenly felt a cold shiver run through her body when she thought about what her mother's reaction would be to this decision. Her mother would try to do everything in her power to stop it.

But what man would Mama want me to marry? Melissa

231

asked herself. Mama hated all her relatives. She thought the neighbours were nothing but white trash. And she would rather die than let me go to New Orleans looking for a husband!

Nobody. Melissa realized that her mother would want her to marry nobody. To live a virginal life of a lonely, old spinstress.

Virginity. Melissa's heart quickened when she thought of certain marital obligations. To marry Peter would not only mean that they would not be able to continue living together as brother and sister. Peter would have the privileges of a husband. Every last privilege.

Melissa remembered an exchange that she had had years ago with her mother, an experience which still stuck in Melissa's mind, that horrible time when Rachel had gone berserk, screaming about raping and black men. On that same morning, Rachel had asked her daughter if Peter had 'touched' her yet. Melissa remembered the question clearly. And, throwing her chin into the air now, she said as if the question were only being asked this moment, 'No, Mama! Peter has not touched me. He is waiting till we're married. And then it is his right, Mama. That is the husband's right.'

Hearing Storky coming up the back steps then, and also hearing Biddy's screams, Melissa jumped up from the chair, thinking that she had been daydreaming for long enough.

But it was no daydream. She was really going to marry Peter. She was going to be Mrs. Abdee—Mrs. *Peter* Abdee.


It was on the night of that same day that Monk arranged a meeting with Lilly. They had been meeting secretly now for three weeks.

Lilly worked in the building called The Barn. She was one of the six girls who carded the wool sheared from the sheep on The Star. The raw wool was stored in wooden barrels until it was needed.

As it was spring, though, Lilly had little work to do carding. She spent most of these days sewing light clothes for the summer.

This evening, work finished in The Barn at seven o'clock. But not going back to Niggertown to eat supper in the shack which she shared with nine other black people, she went to meet Monk.

Monk was waiting for her at their usual spot—the place by the stream where he had seen her lying with Peter.

When Lilly arrived, Monk was sitting soberly on the ground, pulling clumps of moss from the earth.

Falling down on the coolness beside him, Lilly put her hand through his arm. She did not speak.

The evening breeze creaked the tops of the pine trees around them and they sat together listening to its restful sound and the light trickle of the stream.

Finally Monk spoke. Without raising his eyes from the ground, he asked, 'Girl, you wants to run away from The Star with me?'

Lilly's finger stopped tracing his arm.

He asked, 'You ain't heard about niggers who run?'

Lilly was surprised. 'We ain't runners.' She thought and then added, 'are we runners, Monk? You and me?'

'We can be if we get money!'

Pulling her hand from Monk's arm, Lilly lay back on the ground and laughed.

'What's so funny?' Monk asked.

Controlling herself, Lilly lay on the ground and raised one long arm above her head. She said, 'Where niggers like us getting money?'

Monk mumbled. 'I know where there's lots of money. A whole sack of money.'

She sat up. 'Where?'

'In the ground.'

She narrowed her eyes. 'In the ground?'

Monk nodded. 'Buried in the ground. Somebody buried a sackful of money in the ground and I know where.'

Grabbing his arm again, she asked eagerly, 'Where? Who buried it? How much money is there?'

Ignoring her question, Monk pulled another hunk of moss

233

from the earth. He asked again, 'Girl, you willing to run with me?'

Kneeling beside him now, Lilly said, 'You tell me about that money first.'

Monk crumbled the moss into his hands. Studying the mixture of dirt and green mixed in his palm, he did not answer.

Reaching forward now, Lilly ran her long finger down the back of Monk's neck and whispered into his ear, 'The money? Where is the money?'

Monk still did not answer.

She now put her other hand on Monk's shoulder and began to rub her breasts against his bare arm. She repeated, 'Where is the money?'

He sifted his palmful of dirt to the ground, saying, 'Down here. Down in my pants.'

Quickly pushing Monk onto the ground, Lilly lifted her leg over him. Then straddling Monk, she looked down at him and smirked. 'You talking shit to me about money?'

Monk answered Lilly by shoving his groin up between her spread legs. Lilly excited him like no other girl on The Star.

Smiling down at him, she said, 'You ain't going to do no good with those pants on.'

'Screw you through them.'

Lilly crossed her arms to lift the shift from her body.

As she was pulling it over her head, Monk quickly moved and toppled her off him. Pinning her down to the ground, he said, 'What you going to do next? Take off my clothes like you do to that white man?' Monk was not teasing now. His almond-shaped eyes were fierce.

Lilly looked up in terror at Monk's face. She knew what he could become like when he got angry. She pleaded, 'Monk, you promised me we ain't going to talk no more about him pestering me.'

Monk coldly surveyed her lying on the ground beneath him. He looked at how her arms lay stretched above her head. He saw her breasts spread like two firm mounds. He realized then that he could never get enough of Lilly, no matter what she had done with Peter.

234

Shifting his weight to one knee, he pulled down his baggy pants and then freed his other leg. Tossing the pants behind him on the ground, he lay down on Lilly's warm body and, grabbing her in his arms, he began to kiss her neck, kneading her breasts, pressing the thickness of his groin against her slimness.

Accepting Monk with equal passion, Lilly tore at his hard-muscled shoulders and scraped her fingers down his strong back. When he continued to drive his groin against her, she opened her legs and scissored him between them.

Monk now was accepting the kissing from Lilly. He let her suck at his lips, chew his cleft chin, run her tongue around the inside of his mouth. He held her tightly to his chest as he slowly inched his erect penis in between her legs.

Lilly's kisses became more passionate as Monk came closer to easing himself fully inside her.

It was not until he began to pull himself out, and push himself back inside her with a definite rhythm, that Lilly threw back her head and began to moan.

Keeping his tempo, but deepening the plunges, Monk reached toward her breasts and began to fondle them, to prod them, working them into full excitement, too.

No time could register the passage of sensations, only emotions could. Monk felt power and love and closeness. Lilly sensed thrills and—when she began to feel herself giving away inside—she thought that she was achieving something powerful.

Lilly and Monk reached their orgasm together, Monk arched above her clinging body, and they did not fall back down to the ground until a few moments after their final jerk of completion.

Then, lying curled together on the mossy earth, Monk rested his head on Lilly's arm as she traced her finger around his ears again and petted his shaved head.

She was waiting for a few more seconds to pass before asking Monk to explain about the money that he had mentioned earlier.

Monk knew it, too.

But he was not ready to tell Lilly the full details about the money which he had seen the Tuckers bury in the ground. He wanted to make certain that Lilly would run with him from The Star.

## Chapter Fourteen

# WEDDING PLANS

Melissa and Peter both agreed that they wanted to keep their wedding and the reception as small as possible. They did not want to turn it into a real Southern 'crush'.

It was not until they were discussing the plans for a minister, trying to decide who should marry them, that Storky solved the problem of the whole ceremony.

Abandoning her usual *panache*, the personal code which Storky had perfected when butting into other people's affairs, she blurted straightforward, 'Why be married here at The Star at all? Why have a reception? Why not ride over to Carterville? Sure, it's a long trek but, now that the preacher from Troy is gone, somebody's got to come from Carterville to marry you anyhow! So, why not go to him?'

Albert Selby, Melissa and Peter all looked up in astonishment at Storky. They had been sitting in their usual cluster of three chairs in front of the fireplace in the downstairs parlour, talking amongst themselves, and not aware that Storky was lurking behind them in the evening shadows.

As Storky now lit a green glass lamp with a taper, setting the hand-painted dome back down onto its brass-mounted base, she continued, 'White folks will see reasoning in that plan. White folks ain't as greedy for wedding cake as you might think. It's planting time soon and they're going to have plenty of work keeping them busy at home.'

Peter looked in astonishment at Melissa sitting in the chair next to him. Together, they turned to look at Selby.

Still staring at Storky's rustling, starched-white figure moving in the darkness behind the bright burst of light from the table lamp, Selby asked, 'You mean to tell me that you would forsake cooking and cleaning and making fancy cakes all that easily, Storky? Just like that?' He snapped his fingers.

Busying herself by closing the plum-coloured draperies, Storky answered, 'Work! Pshaw, Master Selby, you knows niggers likes to get out of work when they can!'

'Storky!' Selby reprimanded.

Stopping, keeping her bent head to them, Storky said, 'Going to Carterville would solve problems for all you. Admit it, Master Selby, Sir.'

Selby, Melissa, and Peter all looked again at one another. They knew that Storky was indeed right. But they still could not understand why she of all people—the high priestess of proper conduct on The Star—should suggest such a breach of tradition.

Melissa and Selby both began to speak at the same moment. Shaking her head, Melissa politely demurred from what she was going to say, motioning for her father to continue.

Selby proceeded. 'Convenient or not, Storky, just going to Carterville is not fair to Melly. It's cheating her out of a big doings!'

Laughing, Melissa said, 'I was just going to say the same thing about you, Papa! I don't want *you* to feel cheated.'

'Me? Why would *I* want a party?'

'For The Star, Papa,' Melissa explained. 'For you.'

Selby blurted. 'For The Star? For me! The doings here would be for you and Sonny. The place is going to be yours.'

Peter interrupted, saying, 'No, Father. What I think Melly is trying to say is that this house, your home, the house of your children, should see a great big wedding with everybody invited from miles around.'

Taking a deep breath, a sigh of dread about such a festivity and everything that it entailed, Melissa nodded. 'Yes, Papa. Peter is right.'

Storky came out the shadows now. 'I just can't understand it. No, I just can't understand it one bit. The fact is as plain as

238

the noses on each of your faces that none of you want folks all piling in here. I heard you dreading the fact myself. All of you. Each by yourself to me. But, now, none of you will admit it to each other and I just can't understand it. No, I just can't make heads nor tails out of it.'

'Storky!' Selby called from his Dorset chair. 'Storky, why are you being so firm about Melly and Sonny going to Carterville? Why don't *you* want the wedding to be here?'

'Who said I didn't?' she flared, then, remembering, she added, 'Master Selby, Sir.'

Selby persisted, 'You don't want a big party here or you wouldn't be speaking out like this. I know you, too! So, come on, finish!'

Standing behind Peter's chair, Storky planted her hands on her hips, saying, 'Fine, Master Selby, Sir, you asked me to talk so I will. You asked me why I don't think no big party should be here and I tells you. No big party should be in this house, no fancy wedding ceremony and dancing and music for Miss Melly and Master Peter because it might makes them feel funny. That's what I thinks. Folks hereabouts are being mighty happy and sending wishes and good luck but I know Miss Melly and Master Peter about as well as anybody know thems, Master Selby, Sir, excepting yourself, of course, and I knows when they don't want to make something big out of themselves. And that's what this wedding here would be doing. Getting people to look at them when they don't wants it. And one more thing, too, Master Selby, Sir, I don't wants you thinking that I'm going to likes not fixing no party because fixing a party for me is like being there myself, it is. I love party-fixing. But I have been fixing parties for Miss Melly and Master Peter ever since they both little sprouts. Everyday-cooking for them is like party-fixing for me. I plan on fixing for them all the time. But fixing a wedding here means nothing to me. Nothing. I gets just as much party for myself by frying up a pan of old fritters for Master Peter when he comes in hungry from the field. Or making Miss Melly her little white-and-gold pot of tea in the noontime. That's my party, Master Selby, Sir. And I don't know if your Good Lord God says so in his book but my Gods sees them married from a long time ago and no party is going to make any difference up there! A buggy trip to Carterville is one good way to keep those big-eyed Rolands from grabbing this land but a lot bigger man that Preacher Grogan in The Peace Of Mind Chapel in Carterville has brought Miss Melly and Master Peter together a long, long time ago, Master Selby, Sir. That's what I think. You asks me for what I think Master Selby, Sir, and that's what I think.' She threw up her nose, turned and strode from the room.

Melissa and Peter exchanged glances, then looked at Selby. They all knew that Storky was right yet again.

There would be no wedding at The Star.


Storky's primitive interpretation of Melissa and Peter's relationship, an everyday pattern of life being their true celebration, was beyond rebuke. And, so, the future events at The Star—as well as the past—proved that no public acknowledgement of the nuptials, beyond a simple ceremony in Carterville, was necessary for their union. Continuing in the work schedule to which they had been accustomed, Melissa and Peter proceeded with their normal activities in the big house, the stables, the fields, until the morning came when they climbed into the wagon with Selby and travelled twenty miles to Carterville. Melissa wore the white cotton dress with lace bib and cuffs which Storky had made for her as a present.

Back again at home by early evening, Selby departed yet again, saying that he wanted to visit Judge Antrobus, leaving Melissa and Peter to have supper alone. Storky had prepared them roast chicken, butter-fried yams, fresh greens and two kinds of desserts—vanilla cake, being Melissa's favourite sweet, and chocolate blancmange, always the first choice for Peter. And, then, saying that she had to take a basketful of kitchen knives down to Samson to be sharpened, Storky left by the back door.

Finding themselves alone in a totally quiet house, Peter took the lamp from the sideboard and led Melissa slowly up the circular staircase. Silently, they entered what used to be the guestroom, now converted into their marriage chamber. Peter set the lamp on a birdseye maple bureau covered by a long lace shawl which Melissa had made when she was fifteen.

The burning wick flickered in the clear glass chimney of the lamp, throwing a moving light on the green-and-red leafed wallpaper in the newly decorated bedroom. The evening grew dimmer on the other side of the lace curtains while, inside the room, Melissa and Peter sat fully clothed on the tall-backed bed, talking in hushed voices. The conversation sounded like the exchange between an old married couple at the end of another long day.

Later, long after the evening turned into night outside the window, and the voices had faded in the bedroom, the light continued to flicker on top of the birdseye maple bureau. But, now on the large bed, Peter and Melissa lay together, unclothed, under the snowy white counterpane. Melissa's head rested on Peter's shoulder, her long, sandy-coloured hair spreading across the brown skin of his chest. Peter's arms held Melissa as if she were a sleeping child, his head comfortably propped by two pillows. They were now, in all respects, happily husband and wife.

Ta-Ta waited in the dark outside the door of Peter and Melissa's room until they were asleep. She then slowly rose from the floor and, gathering the long skirt of her Mother Hubbard with one hand, and lifting her tankard of rum from the floor with the other, she tip-toed back upstairs to her attic room.

Gently closing the door to her room, Ta-Ta set the tankard down on a chair.

The attic room was dark and Ta-Ta stood now facing the spot on the wall illuminated by a shaft of moonlight. She whispered to the spot on the wall, 'They's asleep now, Mistress Honore. Master Peter and his wife is gone to sleep married.'

Moving across the dark room, trying not to hit the furniture in her drunken state, Ta-Ta said, 'Miss Melissa is a good girl, Mistress Honore. She ain't got much culture but her heart's good. You don't have to worry about her hurting your baby, Mistress Honore.'

Ta-Ta picked up a hairbrush from her bureau and she weaved toward the picture of Honore which she had chalked long-ago on the wall—the image of Honore sitting at her vanity table.

Beginning to brush Honore's imaginary hair, Ta-Ta continued to speak to her, describing the wedding and the dancing and the rich clothes of the guests. Ta-Ta was telling her mistress what she thought she would like to hear about her son's wedding.

*Chapter Fifteen*

# MASTERDOM

Chad Tucker's hatred of Peter reached a pitch when word spread around The Star that Melissa—Mrs. Abdee—was expecting a baby, an heir to The Star.

'An heir!' Chad Tucker roared at his wife and Monk as he sat at the table waiting for his supper of clabber and hog's belly. 'How can a bastard, an illegitimate bastard have an heir?'

Tucker looked at Claudia for support. But she continued to work busily at the stove. Monk sat quietly at the table. Although Monk was in disfavour with the Tuckers he was still allowed to sit at their table.

Continuing, Tucker said, 'That's what your "Master Peter Abdee" is, too. A bastard. I remember when he first came here. Selby found him in a ditch, he did. Found him at the side of the road in a ditch. But when they couldn't find a man stupid enough to marry that girl of his, they give that bastard kid a name and makes up a fancy background for him. "Master Peter Abdee". Master Peter Abdee from the West Indies! Now, what kind of name is that? Abdee? Who but a bastard would let himself be called that? Abdee? Back in England, where my pappy's from, Abdee is like a nigger's name.'

Looking at Monk now, Tucker said, 'Hell, Abdee is so common that Monk here even remembers a whole tribe of Abdees from where he's from those long days back. You said those Abdees were running all over the place like gophers, didn't you, boy?'

Monk did not remember what he had told Tucker when he was younger. He could remember nothing about his childhood.

He just nodded to everything that Tucker said now. He was planning to get out of the Tuckers' cabin—and take their money from the ground.

Coming to the table to dish the clabber onto the plates, Claudia wiggled her rotund hips and said in an imitation of Melissa—or an imitation of how she thought that a grand lady would speak—'Mrs. Peter Abdee. From the West Indies. La-dee-da!'

Chad Tucker ranted, 'The West Indies, yeah! That's where they should send him back to. Him and his stuck-up wife. The West Indies. Send him there and let *me* run this place.'

Seated at the table now, Claudia calmly poured coffee into Chad's earthen cup, then her own, and handed the pot to Monk to serve himself. She said, 'He's got a big pecker, I hears.'

Tucker asked, 'Abdee? Peter Abdee? He's got a big pecker? How in the hell you know that?'

Spooning the first mouthful of food toward her open lips, Claudia answered nonchalantly, 'That's what the wenches been saying. Pecker as big as a fence post.' Her moist lips surrounded the wooden spoon.

'You talking to niggers?' Tucker demanded. 'You talking to nigger wenches about white men's peckers?'

Chewing, Claudia nodded toward Monk and said with her mouth half-full, 'You talk to him, don't you? He's nigger.' She took a drink of coffee.

Tucker protested, 'We don't talk about peckers.'

Sinking her spoon again into the plate, she answered coolly, 'Oh, yes, you do. You used to when I had my woman's ague. You used to sit out here side-by-side talking about peckers. Both of you had yours out comparing them and saying what you'd have your slaves do. Oh, yes, I heard it all when I had my ague. You might not think I did, but I heard it all lying on my sick bed.'

Tucker said, 'That was *our* peckers we were talking about. What were you looking at another white man's pecker for? You're my wife.'

'I ain't looking at another man's pecker. I just been hearing stories about it.'

Tucker pounded the table with his fist. 'Here's a white bastard threatening to take over The Star and you sit there gabbing about his prick. Repeating stories you heard from wenches. Well, if you're so God-damned interested in his pecker, do you want me to bring it down here for you to pester with?'

'You know I ain't interested in pestering,' Claudia said, sniffing. 'Not since my woman's ague.'

'Well, you're talking about peckers, ain't you?'

'I was just repeating facts.'

'Facts about peckers,' Tucker shouted.

Losing her own temper now, Claudia shouted back at him, 'I don't want to hear no more pecker talk now, understand? I don't want to hear no more pestering talk, neither, or talk about mastering and slaving. I'm just eating my supper. I'm eating my supper and trying to make some supper talk about what I hears today. Master Peter Abdee has got him a big pecker and—' She paused to give her husband a cool look of disdain.

Tucker waited. He asked, 'And what?'

Raising one of her pencil-thin eyebrows, she said, 'And his wife is getting a baby from it.'

'So what?'

Throwing her spoon down to the table, Claudia shouted at him, 'So what? Well, big shot, do you see any babies sitting around *my* table? Keeping me company?'

Tucker's face whitened. 'Why you bitch. You dirty mean bitch.'

Closing her eyes, Claudia haughtily said, 'And don't try to push me into bed with Porkchop so he can do *your* work. Don't try on me what you tried on Tommy Joe Crandall's wife because I ain't that dumb.'

Tucker roared, 'That was your idea.'

'It was my idea to make some God-damned money for us,' she shouted at him.

Narrowing his eyes at her, Tucker said, 'Good. Good then. You wanting a baby means you're good and over your "woman's ague".' He said it with contempt.

'I ain't saying I want a baby—now.' She was beginning to squirm.

'No, no. You cussed me, woman, and so I'm going to fix you.' He pointed his finger at her. 'I'm going to make you eat your words.'

Throwing up her chin, Claudia said, 'I ain't afraid of you.'


Selby offered to send for a doctor from New Orleans to stay in the big house until Melissa's child was born. But Melissa laughed at the idea. She considered it a waste of money and a doctor's precious time. Melissa insisted that Storky should be the person to deliver her baby.

Storky and Mama Gomarrah had both mid-wifed most of the black babies born on The Star. But neither of the negresses had ever attended the birthing of a white child.

Such an honour first filled Storky with pride, then consternation, and during the last weeks of Melissa's pregnancy, Storky transformed into a completely different person. She broke bowls and pitchers in the kitchen. She forgot to salt the greens and she let the milk spoil in the sun. She could think about nothing but helping Melissa in her hour of mothering.

True to form, though, Storky rose to the occasion when she was needed.

It came on an afternoon when Melissa and Storky were working side by side at the kitchen table shelling peas.

Peter was digging a well with two workers near The Shed and Albert Selby was sitting in his study with Judge Antrobus. Although the Judge had taken to visiting The Star now that Rachel was gone, Selby still had many reasons to ride off and visit him. Melissa was thankful that her father had a good friend, as well as a legal advisor, in Judge Antrobus. She urged him to take his afternoon rides from The Star to meet with Judge Antrobus.

Storky was in the middle of berating Biddy for spending too much time with Posey and and shirking her kitchen duties when Melissa calmly set her pan down on the table. She told Storky that she thought her moment had come.

Biddy instantly began to scream and run toward the back door.

Storky grabbed Biddy by her mass of pigtails and set her to work boiling water, cutting linen, finding the shears.

Next, she shouted to Ruben's successor as kitchen-boy, Cajun, and dispatched him to bring Peter to the house. And during all this, Storky was leading Melissa from the kitchen, through the dining-room, out across the entry hall.

As Storky and Melissa made their way to the stairs, she also managed to shout to Selby and Judge Antrobus. They had both rushed out of the study at the sound of the noise but Storky told them that she did not need two old men under her feet at a moment like this.

Stoically, Storky led Melissa up, up, up the winding staircase, stopping to ask her if she could still walk.

Melissa bravely nodded her head, her pale face beaded with drops of perspiration. And Storky continued to lead her up, up, up the stairs again, beginning now to unbutton the front of Melissa's Mother Hubbard as they slowly moved together.

For the next three hours, the circular staircase was the centre of traffic and nerves in the big house. Peter arrived breathlessly at the front door with Cajun and ran toward the stairs. He met Biddy coming down the stairs. She airily informed him that Miss Storky had given her strict instructions to keep everyone away from the bedroom. Everyone. Biddy's fear of childbearing had been replaced by her new appointment as the-carrier-of-the-news.

Next, Selby and Judge Antrobus emerged again from the

study, wondering if they could go upstairs now, asking Peter if he had heard any news about the developments.

Peter shook his head, his brown face looking haggard with worry, a long fringe of black hair hanging in shanks of perspiration over his eyes. Still wearing workclothes, Peter's open nankeen shirt showed grime on his bare chest and his breeches clung to his long legs with a soiled dampness.

Nero had come through the back door and appeared at the bottom of the stairs. He asked Peter if he was a father yet.

With increasing nervousness, Peter locked his fingers together and sank down on the bottom step. Lowering his head to his hands, he told Nero—everybody—to go away for the moment.

Biddy rushed up the stairs again, followed this time by Posey, both barrelling past Peter as if they did not notice him sitting there.

Selby and Judge Antrobus emerged from the study for a third time. They invited Peter to come in and join them for a whiskey and listen to a plan that the Judge had suggested to Selby—now that Peter was giving Selby a grandchild, Selby should give him something.

Peter begged them to wait, to hold any plans for him and Melissa and a grandchild until—

A noise suddenly filled the stairwell. It was the first cry of a newly born baby.

All three men—Peter, Selby, the Judge—rushed up the stairs.

Biddy met them at the top and, folding her skinny arms in front of her flat chest, she said, 'Miss Storky says you ain't to come in yet. None of you. But Miss Storky says to tell you—'

'What is it?' Selby shouted.

'How's Melly?' asked Peter.

Judge Antrobus blared, 'Blast it, you nigger brat, say what you're meant to say.'

Closing her eyes and throwing back her headful of pigtails, Biddy announced, 'Miss Melissa is just fine and dandy after birthing a sweet, little baby girl but Miss Storky says—'

Then Biddy raised her finger to her pink lips and whispered, 'Shhh!'

At the news, Selby and Peter threw their arms around one another, shouting and crying and shouting even louder.

Looking at this happy scene of a father-in-law and son-in-law, a new father and a proud grandfather—'Father' and 'Sonny'—Judge Antrobus thought of the plan which he had been discussing with Selby in the study.

Albert Selby was deeding the plantation over to Peter Abdee and his family.

At the top of the house—after Biddy's announcement that Melissa had given birth to a baby girl—the door suddenly closed to Ta-Ta's attic room.

Standing breathlessly in front of the closed door, Ta-Ta whispered, 'It's a girl, Mistress Honore. It's a girl. Young Master Peter just fathered a girl.'

Tears of happiness began streaming down Ta-Ta's sallow cheeks and, sniffing, she lifted the tankard of rum to her lips.

As the rum warmed her chest, Ta-Ta began to think about what Honore Jubiot would have wished to give to her son on this occasion. Madame Honore would want her son to be happy, Ta-Ta thought, and—secure!

Security meant money. Money came from treasures. And then Ta-Ta thought about the riches that her mistress had taken from Dragonard. The trunks that Ta-Ta herself had buried in East Florida. The treasures of Dragonard. She remembered where—by what trees—she had buried them in the forest.

Looking around the attic room, Ta-Ta studied the drawings on the walls for an empty space where she could begin drawing a map for finding the trunks.

She would begin the map now. Those trunksful of necklaces and gold would make a fine present someday for Master Peter and his children.

Taking another drink of rum, Ta-Ta moved for her wax crayons.



Word soon spread around the plantation that there was a baby girl in the big house. This news was received warmly in Niggertown.

The black people in Niggertown loved Melissa, even if they seldom saw her. Melissa was like a queen to them, an aloof but kind-hearted ruler.

The slaves had already heard that Mistress Melissa had wanted to give a beautiful new name to Niggertown. This story had come from Melissa's most ardent admirer—Storky.

Although the people saw no practical advantages for changing the name of the slave quarters, they loved Melissa even more for wanting to give them something beautiful. They had so little of it in their drab lives.

But there was one negress in Niggertown who calmly considered what Melissa and her new child meant precisely to her own life.

It was Lilly. She had heard many stories about white people. The topic of white people's lives intrigued the negroes. They whiled away their nights gossiping about the white people's private affairs.

According to one story that Lilly had heard, when a white woman has a child, she no longer likes to make love with her husband. That white women do not make love for pleasure.

Lilly was wondering thesedays if Peter would want to lay again with her. She knew by her womanly instincts that he had enjoyed their one time together. She wondered if Master Peter would want her again now.

Opinions in Niggertown also held that if a white man chose a black girl for his regular wench, the black girl often receives many favours on the plantation.

There were histories, too, of black wenches often moving to the big house to be closer to their white lover.

So, Lilly thought now of which way her life could go.

Monk had spoken to her about buried money. He had asked her to run away with him from The Star.

But did Lilly want to risk that? Even if Monk did have money, did she want to live a life running?

Or did she want to hold out for a comfortable existence in the big house?

Lilly knew one thing. She knew that she wanted to get out of Niggertown. She wanted to move away from the one-room shack which she shared with nine other people.

Peter had not spoken to her since their one night together almost a year ago now.

But, in the same token, Monk had not yet shown her any of the buried money about which he had bragged. Monk stood above the ordinary black slaves on The Star by living with the Tuckers. But Lilly saw how he was controlled by Chad and Claudia Tucker. They often treated him with more disdain than a fieldhand.

Master Peter was free. And he already had money.

Lilly thought seriously about Peter and Monk. With which man were her chances best? The black one or the white one? The master or the pushed-around slave?

*Chapter Sixteen*

# CAUGHT IN GOMORRAH

The prospect of Albert Selby relinquishing his hold on The Star shocked Melissa. She could not understand why he would want to deed the plantation to her and Peter.

But the matter of changing its name to something other than 'The Star' totally escaped her comprehension. Selby was insisting on doing that, too, and Melissa could not understand his reasoning at all.

Names. Melissa and Peter had had a difficult time trying to find a name for their daughter. Melissa did not want a name from the Roland family and Peter did not with to use the sole name—Honore—that he knew from his family. They both wanted a fresh start.

Imogen Abdee was six-months-old when her Grandfather Selby pressed Melissa and Peter to listen to his plans for The Star.

Selby explained to Melissa and Peter, 'The Star is the name of a Roland place. I married into it.'

Selby, Melissa and Peter were all sitting in the dining-room eating breakfast. They were back to their schedule of early mornings and long days of work.

Seated at his usual position of honour at the head of the long table, Selby continued to Melissa and Peter, 'You say you want a fresh start. So let me help you do that. Call your home by your own new name.'

Melissa still protested at the idea. She asked, 'But what's the matter with "The Star"?'

Resting his liver-spotted hand on top of Melissa's small

hand, Selby tried to explain in a softer voice, 'Melly, for years, I heard nothing but "The Star! The Star! The Star! The Peregrine Rolands and The Star!" Your mother—God rest her soul—hated, would rather burst a blood vessel in anger than to admit that the days of the Rolands were over. But they were! And—well—if your Mother had not married a man who had a nose for the soil, this place might not be here right now. Oh, I was a worker when I was young. You might wonder now, seeing me turning a blind eye to things—'

Melissa protested. 'You don't turn a blind eye, Papa!'

Peter sat silently, impressed with the old man for admitting his faults. He did believe that Selby had toiled hard in his prime. The Star was a testament, a relic but a testament all the same to Selby's former ardour and ambition.

Selby continued, 'So, any work that went into the place, I want it to be for *my* people. Not for the ghosts of some old Roland geezers who your mother went cock-a-hoop over, but for the young ones I seen grown up here. I want this place to be for you, Melly, for Sonny here, for little Imogen, and who ever else you've got coming.'

Melissa and Peter looked quickly at one another, a glimmer of pride in their eyes. Melissa was pregnant again. She and Peter wanted to have a big family.

In an empty voice, both its tone and the words surprising Melissa and Peter, Selby said, 'Ro—your brother, Roland, left The Star by his own free choice. He left with not even a so-long or a hoot. He just left us. The Star's not going to be sitting around waiting for him to come back to, not with *his* family.' Selby's green eyes blazed with anger, thinking of his son eloping with a Witcherley.

Peter's question rescued Selby from his hatred. 'Did you have any particular name in mind, Father? What would you like to see The Star called?'

Selby took a deep breath, beginning, 'That depends on what you and Melly agree. But Judge Antrobus and me—'

As Selby paused, staring at his empty breakfast plate, Melissa and Peter exchanged another quick look, a glance of merriment at the fact that Selby and his crony had undoubtedly settled that point between themselves.

'The Judge and me talked all this over, seeing the legal sides of the matter and what not—' Selby said, slowing his words as if he were merely passing time until he got to the important detail, '—and we both agree that *you* should be taken into consideration, Sonny.'

Peter protested. 'I think you've done that already.'

Selby shook his head. 'No. I mean with the name.' Then, looking quickly at Melissa, he asked, 'You know how we've always liked our hills here, Melly? Especially that big one north of the top pasture?'

Melissa nodded, wondering why her father had mentioned that.

He continued, 'Yes, this place has always been known around these parts for its hills and rises. Alot of grumbling about plowing on slopes. But, for me, I like it better this way than looking out over two thousand acres of flat land. That gets a little tedious for a man over the years, I think. Flatness for miles and miles.'

Melissa could stand it no longer. 'Papa! What are you getting at?'

'Hold on! Hold on, Melly! There's not just you now. There's Sonny to consider, too. See how patient he's sitting there. And that's not surprising to me, neither. Sonny's always been good and patient. I'm proud of you, Sonny,' Selby said, speaking to Peter, but not looking at him. 'Lots of times you didn't know where you were standing. You didn't know which end was up. Where you were going. Where you had come from. And that's why I thought—'

Peter and Melissa both waited eagerly for his next words.

Fumbling with a bone-handled knife, Selby said, 'You know, though, that if you don't like this idea, Sonny, you don't have to agree!'

Peter nodded.

Raising his head, finally looking into Peter's face, Selby

said, 'I see no reason you shouldn't call it—' He paused. '—Dragonard Hill.'

Peter's face went ashen. Again, Selby had completely taken him by surprise. Looking across the table at Melissa, he still did not speak.

Reaching toward her father, but looking at Peter's dumbstruck face, Melissa said, 'I think that's wonderful, Papa! Wonderful!' She understood the gesture. Dragonard. Dragonard Hill.

Selby fidgeted, still not knowing Peter's feelings. 'We do have all these hills here. And in no time at all, those hills are going to be the real plantation. That's where the green cotton is growing and that's your big future, Sonny. Cotton.'

Peter interrupted, 'Before I say anything, Father . . . Melly. Before I say what I think, can I ask you one thing?'

Selby nodded.

Peter asked soberly, 'You do know what that name means, don't you? What it stood for in the West Indies?'

Selby tossed his hand in the air. 'Pshaw. What it stood for? Who gives a damn what it stood for. It's here that it counts, Sonny. *Here*.' He banged on the table with his fist.

Shaking his head in amazement, Peter said, 'I never thought I'd have this much of a home. Have these kind of ties to anything.'

'Exactly. "Ties",' Selby shouted. 'That's just what old Judge Antrobus said. The Judge might strike a lot of men as a windy old cuss but he's got some sense to him. As well as feelings. And the Judge said the same thing to me—"ties". "Name it something that'll give Peter some ties." '

Peter slowly began to smile appreciatively. And combing his fingers through his silky black hair, he said, 'Dragonard Hill. It gives me—'

Peter looked across the table at Melissa and corrected himself, 'It gives us our own real start.'

Melissa nodded in agreement, a flush to her cheeks, biting her lower lip with excitement.

Peter's tone then became serious. He turned to Selby and said, 'But only on one condition.'

'What's that?' Selby asked.

Peter said, 'On the condition that while you're still—' He hesitated.

Selby ordered, 'Say it. You mean till I croak.'

Peter nodded. 'Until then, Father, I insist we still call it "The Star".'

It was the second time for Selby to bang the table this morning. He said, 'By God, then, Sonny, we've got us a deal. We're The Star until I decide to croak. But, when that happens—not before and not after—you take down that old wooden star hanging over the gate out front and this place is called "Dragonard Hill". And you'll be the full master of it.'

Melissa and Peter looked across the table at one another and, then, quickly jumping from her chair, Melissa leant over her father and hugged him, embracing the goodness and kindness inside his gruff facade.

And holding her father, Melissa remembered the wish that she herself had made long, long ago on the eve of the year 1800.

Melissa had wished then that she would never see the day that her father died.


Nero knew that one of his prayers had been answered, the prayer for Peter's peace of soul. Melissa and Peter Abdee were happily married; they had one daughter and were expecting their second child. Their home was The Star.

Seeing them living happily on The Star, Nero wondered if he had been wrong by praying long-ago for Dragonard. Had Dragonard really been that good? Would the black people have had as good a home on Dragonard as Nero felt that Peter would give to the people of The Star?

Nero's recollections of Dragonard were still painful. The trouble there had started when Manroot had hanged himself. Manroot's wife, Seena, soon after had become the lover of Calabar and—together—they had made trouble in the slave quarters. Calabar and Seena had held secret meetings at night for the rebellious blacks on Dragonard.

Calabar and Seena began to meet secretly with slaves from nearby plantations to preach their gospel of destruction.

The troubles grew as the slaves on neighbouring plantations talked to one another with drums. Those drums echoed only at night, a steady rhythm which came from beyond the rolling hills of sugar *plats* when the moon was high in a sky streaked with clouds.

Then, one night the rattan flap of a windmill was set afire. A week later, a torch was put to the second windmill and the breeze softly twirled the blazing flaps like a carnival pinwheel.

Naomi became frantic. She screamed that she was going to lose everything. Nero had never seen his mistress in such an uncontrollable state.

Richard Abdee told Naomi to flee to Basseterre. But she did not want to leave Abdee alone on Dragonard. She knew that the black people—even the Fantis—wanted to kill Abdee. Calabar had preached well.

Nero now saw the great house at Dragonard as a red strip of fire gashed against the sky, the roof bursting with flames, and he still heard the mutinous cries from the slave quarters.

Nero remembered the sudden burst of black faces as the slaves rushed up the hill with the machetes in their hands.

That night, Nero found the cook, Sugar Loaf, lying dead on the kitchen floor. Her black throat had been slit for remaining loyal to her white master.

From the kitchen, Nero ran to the centre garden of the greathouse. The ceiling there was afire and Nero saw Calabar going toward Naomi with two knives.

As Nero rushed to stop Calabar, there was a loud cracking sound over his head and the tenting started to fall from the ceiling. The last thing that Nero saw was Naomi tugging lengths of burning brocade from her face and Calabar lying on the floor under a blazing cross-beam.

When Nero regained consciousness, he asked where his mistress was.

No one would tell Nero about Naomi. The only story that Nero heard was about Seena. She had been found in the tackroom. She had been found dead but still clutching Richard Abdee's splayed-tip whip. He then was believed to be dead because no one used the Dragonard's whip but Abdee.

The slaves who had not run from Dragonard were seized by the British soldiers. The soldiers shackled them and chained them together. Then they took them away from Dragonard in wagons.

Nero was among those captured slaves. And on his ride to Basseterre that night, he saw the country road lined with the slaves who had escaped from Dragonard. But they were dead now. Hanged along the road by their necks. Nailed to stakes. Pegged to the ground. Decapitated. Nero saw innocent black people lying slaughtered among the troublemakers. It was a carnage of both good and bad.

It was then that Nero thought that there was no god who could answer his prayers. His home had become 'Trouble Island' and he felt that all Africans had lost their only hope for freedom.

But now on The Star, Peter Abdee was revitalizing Nero's hopes again. Perhaps Peter would give the black people a safer place in this world of white men than his father had done.

The only similarity that Peter Abdee bore to his father was the cornflower-blue eyes. And the hereditary equipment which had originally angered Peter now had become the means to sow a second child in the womb of his wife.

Nero just hoped now that Peter was not taking Melissa's recent illness too gravely. Her second pregnancy was being more difficult than the last. Melissa was not well.

Chad and Claudia Tucker took Monk beyond their cabin to the woods tonight. Claudia Tucker was carrying a flour sack filled with rocks. She wanted Monk to think that she was carrying the money. It was her plan to keep Monk from believing that she and her husband had *not* buried their money.

Monk went soberly along with the Tuckers. He knew that there was no money in the flour sack because he had seen them bury it under the chinaberry tree. This ploy only made Monk have more hatred for the Tuckers. He hated them for thinking that he was so stupid.

But Monk suspected that Chad Tucker had a plan of his own tonight. Tucker had seen Monk with Lilly and he had told Monk to have Lilly meet them in the woods near the cabin tonight. Tucker had said that he wanted Lilly to be part of their group, to make it sex for four. But Monk knew that Claudia did not like sex now and he suspected that Tucker wanted to do something else tonight.

Claudia Tucker now sat on a log and, holding the flour sack of rocks in her lap, she said, 'I don't think that black wench of Monk's is going to turn up for you, Chad. I think the next time you see her, you should touch her up with that hornet.'

'Any wench not turning up when she's told to will get more than the hornet,' Tucker muttered. 'She'll get the whip.'

Stifling her boredom, Claudia said, 'Just the same, I'm glad we didn't ask her to come to the house. Don't fancy no nigger wench stinking up my house with her juices.'

Tucker was still angry with Claudia for saying that he had not given her a child. He ignored her now and said to Monk, 'You sure you told that Lilly wench where to meet us?'

Monk nodded vigorously. 'Just like you says, Master Tucker, Sir.' He was thinking about the right time to steal the money from under the chinaberry tree.

Siddling up to Monk, Tucker asked, 'Is that Lilly as hot as she looks, boy?'

Monk nodded. He knew that Lilly was not going to come here tonight. He had told her to stay in Niggertown.

Chad insisted, 'How hot is she?'

Monk did not like to talk about Lilly this way. She slept with other men in Niggertown but Monk still wanted her for himself. He wanted to run with her from The Star.

To keep Tucker quiet now, Monk said, 'My Lilly is really

259

something, Master Tucker, Sir. She's really something special.'

'Tell me.'

'Rather shows you, Master Tucker,' Monk answered, wanting to hit Tucker now.

But Tucker would not let the subject drop. He reached to Claudia and, putting his arm around her, he said, 'Supposing Claudia here was just—' He smiled. '—a nigger wench.'

'Chad!' Claudia protested.

Still ignoring her, Tucker continued, 'Just say that Claudie here was a common nigger slut, Monk. You show me how you'd get started pestering her. How you would start feeling and petting and touching her up and laying her right down here on the dirt. Show me, boy.'

Monk hesitated. Claudia plainly did not want sex. But Monk realized that Tucker might want to humiliate her for revenge.

He was right.

Tucker turned to his wife now and ordered, 'Claudie! Hoist up that dress of yours and lay down here on the ground. Play you're a nigger. A nigger wench who talks all the time about peckers.'

Claudia gasped.

Tucker grabbed the sack of rocks from her arms and dropped it to the ground. Next, he seized one of her pendulous breasts and threatened, 'I twists this tit right off you, bitch, if you don't obey me. Get down . . . *nigger!*'

'But the—' Claudia looked at the sack. '—what about the money?'

'Money? Forget about your money.' He laughed at her.

'What about my ague then? You ain't telling me you're forgetting about my woman's ague?'

'Screw your ague, bitch.'

Seeing the rage in her husband's eyes, Claudia quickly lifted her flimsy dress over her head and leaned hesitantly back on the ground. She whimpered, 'This cold might bring back my ague and then you'll see.'

'I said, screw your ague!' Tucker then told Monk to drop his pants, take off his shirt and climb onto Claudia.

Monk asked, 'Don't you want pleasuring, too, Master Tucker?' This was the first time that Tucker had ever let Monk have first mounting.

Tucker said, 'I wants to see you screwing that nigger whore down there on the dirt. I want to see you screwing the tar out of her. I want you to get her screaming and shouting for that big hot pecker of yours. I want to hear her saying how beautiful that meat of yours feels inside her stinking pretty. And, then, when I hears her screaming for more of that thick prick of yours, boy, then, I comes in. I comes inside her, too. But I ain't coming in her pussy tonight. I ain't giving her pussy the privilege of holding my white pecker. I'm driving up her bung hole. And with no goose fat neither. I'm going to cornhole this nigger bitch *dry*!'

'Chad! Why you doing this to me?' Claudia tried to raise herself from the ground.

Kicking her elbows out from under her, Tucker said, 'You wanted a baby, didn't you?'

'Chad!' She wailed.

'You said you're too good for Porkchop. And you being so God-damned much smarter than poor Mary Crandall, I'm giving you Monk here for free.'

'I ain't wanting Monk's baby.'

'Well, you being so God-damned smart, why don't you grow one up your shithole. Because that's where I'm going to plug you . . . nigger wench!'

Turning to Monk, Chad Tucker ordered, 'Go on now, boy.'

Monk obediently directed himself toward Claudia. His phallus was already bobbing up and down in the perverse excitement of this arrangement.

Watching Monk climb onto his wife, Tucker hissed at her, 'Nigger. Nigger wench.' Then, fumbling with the buttons on his fly, he coaxed Monk, 'Call her a nigger, boy. Call her your nigger bitch.'

Monk stared down at Claudia's pudgey face and said, 'Sure, she's a nigger bitch. This is a nigger bitch-whore, ain't you . . . bitch?'

Strangely, the words had a strengthening effect on Monk. He liked this idea of debasing the white woman, especially this white woman who had ruined so many years of his life. She had threatened and trapped him and now he could bring her down not only to being his equal but to put her beneath him. And compared to Claudia Tucker, every black woman in the world was a goddess.

Driving into her, Monk continued to taunt, 'Sure, she's a nigger whore. She's the blackest one I ever seen. The biggest, hottest wench I ever screw. A big, hot, stinking nigger wench, ain't you, whore? Oooh, feel her pumping crazy for my cock. Feel her getting excited. Feel her getting all excited in that stinking pussy of hers. This nigger wench is getting crazier and crazier excited, ain't you? Ain't you a nigger wench?'

Curiously, Claudia Tucker, too, was being worked up to an excitement by acting the role of a black woman and she soon began to repeat the words with which Monk was taunting her. She repeated, 'Yes. Yes, boy. Yes, I'm nothing but your wench. I'm nothing but your black slave wench. I'm your nigger bitch, Monk, I'm your nigger bitch.' She had forgotten about her sickness and her months of abstinence.

'What kind of wench are you?' Monk demanded, staring down at her, his hips driving against her.

'I'm your nigger wench,' Claudia panted, 'I'm nothing but your no-good nigger wench.'

Standing above them, Tucker shouted, 'Flip the bitch over on her side. Flip her over on her side.' Kneeling to the ground then, he grabbed one of Claudia's fleshy buttocks and began to finger her anus. And, with a grunt—and no goose fat—he rammed himself into her.

Claudia screamed, both with excitement and pain, excitement for having Monk controlling her and pain from her husband's blunt jab.

But a second scream shrilled from the trees.

There was a loud screeching behind them and, suddenly, a white vision burst out from the dark as the long, greasy coil of a bullwhip curled sharply around Tucker, Claudia and Monk.

It was Mama Gomorrah.

Bringing the whip back over her shoulder, Mama Gomorrah let it fly at them again as she shrieked, 'The sin! The sin!'

But when Mama Gomorrah brought back the whip for a third lash, carrying out a duty commissioned to her by an angel, she realized what she had really discovered.

Mama Gomorrah was a negro. She could not whip white people. Especially not The Star's overseer and his wife.

Staring at Chad and Claudia Tucker lying on the ground, Mama Gomorrah gasped, 'The white trash ones!'

She turned, and ran through the woods calling, 'Master Selby, Sir! Master Selby!'

When Albert Selby had heard Mama Gomorrah's story last night and, also, when repeating it this next morning to Peter by the stables after breakfast, he confessed, 'I always wondered what those folks did in Gomorrah and now I know. Same as in Sodom. But with a little extra happening up front.'

Unlike with his blood son, Roland, Albert Selby could speak freely and openly to Peter about such things, however distasteful they might be. As they stood in the sunshine in the stable-yard, Selby asked, 'Sonny, I know of men buggering one another, too, and I know that that's also called Sodomy, like with a man and a woman. But what do you think is Gom—' Selby paused, scratching his goatee, thinking of what the descriptive word might be. 'What do you think just the men sinners of Gomorrah did? Do you think one got buggered while another gobbled at his pecker? Things like that do happen, you know,' he said, thinking quickly of some of the men about whom he had heard rumours at the Dewitt Place.

Peter preferred to be more practical, less theoretical, about the report. He asked, 'Do you think we can take Mama Gomorrah's word about what she found the Tuckers doing in the bushes?'

Selby answered point blank. 'What does it matter?'

Peter looked at Selby. Was he in for a surprise from his father-in-law?

Selby said, 'This gives us the chance we've been waiting for, Sonny. I've been lenient with that son-of-a-bitch, Tucker, for long enough. We need him around here like we need a cattle disease. Now's my chance to get rid of him.'

Peter asked, 'What do we do about Monk?'

'I think he might pull himself together after Tucker gets out. The man's been a bad influence on that boy ever since he was first sent there. I should've done something about that before now, too.'

Peter insisted on being practical. 'Who's going to be overseer?'

'Offhand, I'd say we don't need one. You do most of the work around here. But, at milling time, we need somebody in the fields. We need a go-between, too, riding from here to the mill in Troy when harvesting really gets hopping. And that's usually the overseer.' He shook his head, thinking. 'Yes, that puzzles me. Who are we going to get to take Tucker's place?'

'Have you ever thought about a black man?'

'Monk?'

'No. And to be honest, I didn't even give Monk a thought. Funny, too, us being brothers.'

Selby did not want to hear Peter say any more on that subject. He asked, 'Who were you thinking about then, Sonny?'

Nodding toward the stables behind them, Peter answered, 'Nero.'

Selby pulled at his goatee, pondering the suggestion. 'Not a bad idea, Sonny. It might raise a few eyebrows around here in the neighbourhood, having a nigger overseer on the place but who cares about that? Do you?'

Peter shook his head. 'But don't mention anything about this to Nero. First, let me go down to the Tuckers.'

Selby wrinkled his shaggy eyebrows. 'Are *you* going to break the bad news to Tucker?'

'Why not?' Peter asked honestly, 'If you wanted to do it, you'd done it a long time ago.'

264

Selby nodded. 'I hate causing an upset.'

'Well, I don't. Not when it's to men like Tucker. In fact, I'm looking forward to this visit to Tucker.'

'Good. Then I can get on my way over to Troy to meet Doc Riesen's coach.'

Peter's face suddenly dropped. He had completely forgotten that today was the day that the doctor was coming from New Orleans.

Albert Selby had convinced Melissa that he should bring a doctor to The Star for her second pregnancy. In fact, Melissa had been too frail to argue with her father. Every day saw her weakening.

Sensing Peter's concern, Selby said, 'Nothing to worry about, Sonny. Just think it's time we start acting like quality folk around here. Can't have niggers bringing all your kids into the world.'

'Don't you say anything about Storky!' Peter was trying to pick-up Selby's attempt for cheerfulness. They both were worried about Melissa.

Forcing a laugh, Selby said, 'Oh, that Storky! I'd rather have a wrestle with a polecat than get tangled with her!' Then, turning, he called over his shoulder to Peter, 'Take that whip with you from inside the door of the stable. You might have to use it on Tucker, to finish up the job from last night.'

Both men waved good-bye.

The stable was empty, and, as Peter saddled and mounted his horse, he tried to put Melissa out of his mind for the moment. He had to complete this job of finally getting rid of Tucker. It would be one more step forward for The Star—Dragonard Hill and his own family.


Peter had never had any formal confrontations with Tucker but he always had been able to tell by the brawny man's smirking attitude that he thought Peter was incompetent, not experienced enough to run a plantation; in fact, a sissy. Peter had seen, too, that Tucker's bullying ideas had influenced what Monk had come to think of him over the years. Peter had no intentions of telling Monk that they had the same father. He thought such an action should wait.

Peter tied his mare to the chinaberry in front of the Tucker's cabin and rapped lightly on the plank door. Inside, he heard Claudia call, 'Chad! *Chad!* Think you better come here quick!'

Next, Peter hear the sluffing of boots across the dirt floor and, then, the plank door opened. Tucker towered in the doorway, unshaven, wearing no shirt, only his soiled breeches and boots. Peter could see no lash welts on Tucker's shoulders or chest but, then, his body was covered with a dense growth of black hair.

Peter began, 'I would like to have a word with you, Mister Tucker.' He realized now talking to Tucker that he was not really that much bigger than himself. Tucker's stockiness and brutish attitude only made him seem bigger than Peter.

Looking at Peter with narrow eyes, Tucker said, 'Thought it might be Selby . . . I thought it might be Mister Selby coming down. I thought he would be the one to notice I ain't been seeing to those hoemen this morning.'

'Mister Selby has other business this morning,' Peter said.

Tucker snapped, 'And so do Claudie and me! We've got us a sick nigger on our hands! We got us a nigger pretty well whipped up last night. We found him laying in front of the house and we dragged him outback to tend him. That crazy old coot, Mama Whats-her-name, she turned crazy last night, the nigger tells us, and she really lets this particular nigger have a taste of her snake. I don't understand why that old wench is even allowed to have a whip in the first place! Especially when the overseer himself can only use—' He spat. '—the hornet.'

Claudia grunted her agreement from the darkness of the shack behind Tucker.

Peter answered, 'Yes, I heard about that little commotion last night.' Then, looking past Tucker, trying to see in the dark cabin, he asked, 'Is your patient better now?'

'Not much,' Tucker grunted. 'But my missus here, *Mrs.*

Tucker, she being so handy with medicines and ointments and such, she was able to see to a few of those nasty welts on that poor critter's back.'

Behind him, Claudia said, 'During my ague, I learned myself doctoring.'

Peter said politely, 'You're better now, Mrs. Tucker, I hope.'

She sniffed, 'Not much.'

Peter said, 'Well, it's best the sick man isn't here right now. I want to talk to you alone, Mister Tucker.'

'About what?'

Peter held Tucker's gaze, saying, 'You see, Mister Selby and myself have both agreed that we can't afford your services anymore at The Star.'

'What do you mean?' Tucker asked.

'That we have to ask you to leave.'

'Leave? You're kicking me out?'

'You can't kick us out!' Claudia said behind him.

'Shut up, you,' Tucker shouted to his wife, then turning back to Peter, he continued, 'What you kicking me out for? My work? That's what not pleasing you?'

'I said that we agreed that we can't "afford" you. Please, Mister Tucker, I know you're a gentleman. Let's leave it at that.'

Tucker swelled with anger.

'Course, I'm a gentleman. I'm white, ain't I? White as you are. And I ain't going to have no crazy old nigger wench going around the place accusing me of wrong-doing, neither!'

'Sinning!' Claudia shrieked behind him. 'Accusing good decent folks like us of sinning. It's shocking the things what that crazy, old nigger woman calls us! Shocking! She should be whipped herself!'

'I thought I told you to keep out of this,' Tucker shouted at his wife.

Then, facing Peter, he continued, 'And affording me is not good enough reason to tell me to go. There's something else to this, so say it!'

Peter held his ground. 'I'm afraid that you're going to have to accept that as the reason, Mister Tucker. Whether you're willing to recognize it or not, I do know this place, if not as well as you, then nearly as well, and I say that we—cannot—afford—you!'

'You're going to take my place, aren't you?' Tucker laughed so loud and so near Peter's face that Peter could feel his hot breath blowing on him. 'You're going to try to be overseer! Well, if that ain't a rich one! Har, har, har!'

When Tucker had finished laughing, Peter said, 'No, Mister Tucker, I'm not taking your place. Mister Selby and I are giving your job to Nero.'

Tucker quickly sobered. 'To Nero? To that black groom of yours? A nigger?'

'A nigger?' Claudia yelped. 'A nigger taking my man's job?'

Tucker was too horrified by the prospect to reprimand his wife for speaking this time. He repeated her words, 'A nigger? A nigger taking . . . my job?'

Peter nodded his head, saying, 'Yes, Nero is being made overseer. But Mister Selby and I realize that it will take you some time to settle into a new home. So, we're allowing you one week to move all your belongings from here. To leave The Star.'

'One week?'

'Leave our little home?' Claudia cried.

Peter continued calmly, 'Your wages will be up at the big house, Mister Tucker, when you care to collect them.' Then, nodding politely at both of them, he turned away, walking towards his horse.

When the sound of Peter's horse thundered away from the Tucker's dirt yard, Monk rushed from the lean-to, shouting at Tucker, 'A nigger? A nigger is taking your place? A nigger who's not even *me*?'

Tucker was still too dazed by the idea to listen to Monk. He muttered to himself, 'A nigger. Taking away my job from me and putting a nigger in it.'

Holding onto her breasts, Claudia wailed, 'And we have to be out of here in a week! In just nine days!'

Tucker turned on her. 'I wouldn't stay in this dump a day longer, neither. This dump is not fit for a dog to live in. Just look at the dump they made us live in all these years. Made us live like niggers so no wonder they're getting themselves a nigger to do their work . . . A nigger. I've never heard the likes of it. A nigger. Getting my job?'

Holding her breasts, Claudia said, 'Thank God. Thank God for the money I saved away.'

Tucker glared at her, then nodded in Monk's direction.

Looking at Monk, Claudia shook her head. She did not think that he had heard her slip of tongue.

But Monk had heard what Claudia had said as well as seeing Tucker nod at him. But Monk was not worried about the money now. He knew where that was. He was more concerned about Nero—another black man—becoming the overseer of the whole plantation.

This jolt had even made Monk forget about running away from The Star.

*Chapter Seventeen*

# TORCH

Monk worked quickly but quietly the next night. The pile of soft earth grew behind him as he dug deeper and deeper under the Tucker's chinaberry tree. Monk was digging for their money.

The Tuckers had left their shack early this morning. They had decided not to take their money with them when they went to look for a new place to live.

Monk had heard the Tuckers whispering into the late hours the night before. They were planning to drive in their wagon to a farmer called Jack Grouse. He had bought two slaves from Tucker twenty years ago. Grouse was a prosperous man now. He planted green cotton and owned nearly a hundred black people. Chad Tucker was hoping that he could get a job there.

Today had cooled Monk's mind. With the Tuckers away from The Star, Monk had been able to sit and carefully lay out his plans.

The white people in the big house were having their own problems, Monk knew. A doctor had arrived to see Mistress Melissa. Monk had heard in Niggertown that she was very sick.

Monk had spent most of today in Niggertown. He would go back there tonight after he had found the money and reburied it in his own secret place.

The tip of Monk's shovel now struck a soft bulk in the earth. Dropping the shovel, Monk fell to his knees and clawed at the earth with his crooked fingers.

Uncovering a folded worsted quilt, Monk pulled it from the ground. He quickly opened the quilt and saw the white flour sack. Untying the top of the sack, he looked to see that the money was still there and then he lay the sack on the ground behind him.

Putting the quilt back into the hole, Monk reached behind him again for the large black book that he had found in the Tuckers' cabin. He had known for a long time what this book was. It was the slave ledger for The Star. Monk would bury this book in the hole where the money had been.

Quickly filling in the hole with dirt, Monk thought of what Chad and Claudia Tucker would say when they came back to The Star for their belongings and the money but found the slave ledger where the money had been hidden.

But Monk had no time now to gloat over his plan. He still had more trouble to do tonight. He had to go back to Nigger town now and start the big fire.

Storky was too nervous to sleep that night.

Samson had come from the blacksmith shop to visit Storky in the kitchen of the big house. But, seeing that she was not feeling amorous, Samson sat by the kitchen worktable and he talked to Storky.

Samson was telling Storky about Monk. He said, 'That boy is running crazy, Miss Storky. Running crazy mad because Nero has has been named overseer.'

Storky never had much curiosity about Monk. She yawned now and, securing the knot on the white handkerchief tied around her head, she asked disinterestedly, 'Monk thinks what?'

Samson repeated, 'Monk thinks Master Peter should have named him overseer.'

Storky snorted. 'For what reason? That he learned overseeing from Tucker?'

'Yes, that's it, Miss Storky! That's what that Monk boy believes. And he's causing trouble on account of it!'

'What kind of trouble?' Storky's face had hardened. She was listening now.

'Setting niggers against Master Peter and Old Master Selby.'

'Well, why didn't you thump that boy a good one and tell him to shut his big mouth! You're big enough, ain't you, you big ox?' Storky glared at the candle flickering in front of her on the table, grumbling, 'Monk. Don't know why we still calls him "boy". He's old enough now to know better. You should've landed him a good one right on his head. Shamed of you, Samson. Shamed of you for not thumping him.'

Samson leaned eagerly toward Storky, explaining, 'But I don't hears this myself. I hears abouts it!'

Storky sat upright in her chair. 'Then, first thing tomorrow morning, I plans to go out and thumps him myself. Where exactly that no-good nigger trash hanging out these days?'

'Niggertown.'

Thinking of Niggertown, and all the changes that Peter was planning for down there, Storky said, 'I'll go ask Posey tomorrow morning, that's what I'll do. I'll ask Posey where Monk is. That sissy nigger boy knows more news about Niggertown than even I do. Hmmph. Never thought I'd see the day when I'd have to go looking for no sissy boys just so I'd hear what's happening around this place!' She shook her head, bewildered by the changes of customs and rank on The Star. Then, concentrating on the more serious aspect of Samson's story, Storky turned to him and said, 'That's all poor Master Peter needs now, trouble from some trash niggers. The plain truth of the matter is that some niggers will not listen to sense. As much as you do for some niggers, they always want more.'

Samson asked, 'Ain't some white people same way, Miss Storky?'

She scoffed. 'Sure! The trashy ones. Niggers and white folks can be trashy alike. Whites can be worse because they had the chances.'

Then, stopping, thinking that she heard a commotion overhead, Storky bent her head and listened more closely. She whispered to Samson, 'You hears something, honey?'

He listened, too, saying, 'Sounds like lots of feet running around upstairs to me.'

Storky's hand flew to the white handkerchief tied around her head and cried, 'I knows it! I knows it!'

'What do you knows, Miss Storky?' Samson asked.

But, before she could answer, they both heard feet running down the stairs and, soon, the door to the kitchen flew open.

Peter stood in the doorway. He was dressed in only his shirt and underwear. His hair was tousled. He was too alarmed with his news to say anything about seeing Samson in the kitchen. Breathlessly, Peter told Storky, 'Doc Riesen wants hot water. More quilts. Make that lots of boiling hot water. It's happening, Storky. But it's happening too quick. It's happening too fast'. He turned and ran from the kitchen, his footsteps racing upstairs.

Without a question, Storky had sprung from her chair. She pulled open the fire door on the cookstove with one hand and grabbed toward the kindling box with the other. She wanted to catch the embers before they went down for the night.

Soon, three separate kettles were singing on the stove and the kitchen worktable was a mountain of linens and quilts for the doctor.

When Storky now propped open the kitchen door with the long gun always kept next to it, preparing an free exit for herself to move upstairs with the boiling hot kettles, there was a loud pounding on the door behind her. Spinning around, she called to Samson, 'Open that door and tell who ever it is to stay out of my way.'

Samson obeyed Storky, opening the door, but before he could warn the late caller, Nero burst into the kitchen.

'Samson. Storky. One of you must get Master Peter. A fire's broke out in Niggertown.'

'A fire?' Storky stood dumbstruck.

Nero nodded. 'I know Monk's behind this but Master Peter must get down to Niggertown right now.'

Samson said, 'That fire is just going to have to burn! There's a baby's being birthed upstairs.'

Seeing the stoveful of boiling kettles and the table of linen, Nero cried, 'Oh, God. *God!*'

Storky's mind was working fast again. She turned away from the door and said, 'Well, it ain't Master Peter who's birthing that baby upstairs. And if what I fear is happening up there, it's best to get Master Peter out of the way. Samson, you stay here with Nero. I'll be right back.'

Storky disappeared from the kitchen.

A few minutes later, Storky returned to the kitchen with Peter. He was fully dressed but his face looked worried. He spoke soberly to Nero, 'Storky here said there was trouble and I should come quick. What is it?'

Nero excitedly began, 'It's Niggertown. That damned Monk got some niggers to set fire to their cabins.'

'Monk?' Peter asked. 'Fire?'

Nero nodded. 'He's still down in Niggertown shouting bad things about you.'

'Me?'

'He's gone plumb crazy, Master Peter,' Nero said. 'Plumb crazy that you gives me the job of being overseer.'

Peter looked from Nero to Samson and, finally, to Storky.

Storky shook her head and said, 'Nothing you can do here for Miss Melly, Master Peter. The Doc's doing all he can.'

Looking back to Nero, Peter ordered, 'Nero, take Samson here with you. Load shovels and axes in the wagon. I'll ride ahead.'

Then, looking fleetingly at Storky, Peter moved quickly toward the back door.

'Ride the gelding,' Nero shouted as Peter rushed down the back steps. 'The gelding's already saddled.'

Pausing at the foot of the steps, Peter looked in the direction of Niggertown and saw that the dark sky was coloured red and yellow. The arc of fire painted the night like a smudged rainbow.

Peter could hear the wild shouting of voices, and smelled the smoke, before he galloped around the last blind of trees. Then, coming within sight of Niggertown, he saw the licking flames.

He felt a small sense of relief when he saw that it was only the first cabin of one row that was burning. But realizing that the surrounding houses were made of old lumber—one spark could set the dry timber ablaze—he galloped directly toward the crowd of black people surrounding the fire.

Peter then heard a voice call to him.

The voice shouted, 'Go back to your big house, white man.'

Peter could not see which of the black faces had shouted to him but he suspected that it was Monk. Sitting on his horse, Peter faced the crowd and looked for faces that he recognized.

The man's voice called again, 'We're all nigger overseers here now.'

Peter ignored the jibe. He knew now for certain that it was Monk. He shouted to the black people he instantly recognized, 'Bluebody. Felix. Zeb. Get these people back from the fire. Crow. Zeke. And, you there, Bramble. Divide the men into groups.'

'It's no good trying to get us to help you no more,' Monk called at Peter.

Standing on his stirrups, Peter called to the people, 'I've got shovels coming to dig with. We need dirt to put out the fire. Lots of dirt and lots of men to throw it.'

Monk emerged from the shadows of the blaze. He was shirtless, wearing only his baggy white pants. He held a pine-knot torch in one hand.

Sidling his horse toward Monk, Peter shouted, 'Monk, you've already made enough trouble. Go back to the Tucker's shack.'

'The Tuckers!' Monk laughed at Peter. 'The Tuckers have been stealing slaves from The Star for years. And none of you white men ever guessed it. That's how dumb you white people are.'

Peter did not know what Monk was talking about; he only wanted to clear away this crowd and get the men working.

Monk stood in front of Peter. He held the torch high above his bare shoulder and the light from the fire made his brown skin shine as if it were polished. His muscles were hard and tight.

Peter's horse shied at the fire. But steadying it—and ignoring Monk—Peter called to the people, 'All you. All you who want to sleep outside in the cold, step back. You listen to Monk. But those who want to save your houses, you work with me.'

There was a rumble of voices from the crowd. The men and women of Niggertown milled together, their half-naked bodies streaming with perspiration.

Still struggling to control his horse, Peter called again to the black people, 'Those who don't want to help, get out of the way. Let the rest of us work.'

At that moment behind Peter, there was a clatter on the hill.

Turning on his saddle, Peter saw Nero and Samson rushing down the slope in the wagon. They were bringing shovels and axes.

Peter turned back to the crowd and called, 'Come on. Let's get to work.'

'Don't listen to that white man,' Monk shouted. 'His nigger there in the wagon is Nero. He's the nigger who's going to be your new overseer.'

Peter took up the jibe. 'Yeah. That's Nero. He's coming here to help you. He wants to save your homes.'

There was a pause suddenly in the crowd.

Waiting, Peter looked anxiously to see which side they were going to take.

Then, like a bursting dam, the black people of Niggertown rushed for the wagon. They collected axes and shovels while others turned to run to their houses to grab quilts and rugs to beat out the fire.

Peter did not remember how long, or how hard, that he had stayed with his people that night. But the fire had been stopped before it had been able to spread far.

That night—very early in the morning hours after the fire

276

was under control—Peter made a promise to the black men and women. He promised that they would all work together. Peter promised that he and Nero and all the black people would work side-by-side to rebuild the cabins. They would start the next day, as soon as daylight broke. And he also promised that there would be no other work to do on The Star until the houses were restored, plus repairs done on the others.

A cheer welcomed Peter's tired speech.

But the black people's gratefulness fell on deaf ears because Peter turned and saw his father-in-law.

Albert Selby was sitting on his horse at the top of the slope.

The fire had left Peter exhausted and coated with soot. But he ran all the way up the slope to Selby and shouted, 'Melly? How's Melly doing?'

Albert Selby sat on his horse and stared blankly at the grey smoke rising from the charred cabins below him.

Tugging at Selby's leg, Peter cried, 'God-damn it. How's Melly?'

Without looking down at Peter, Selby smiled and said, 'Twins. Melly had twins. Two little girls. The sweetest little pair of sisters you ever did see.'

'But Melly?' Peter insisted, 'how's Melly?'

Without a tear in his eye, Selby kept staring blankly at the smouldering remains of the fire and said softly, 'She's dead, Sonny. Our Melly left us.' He shook his head. 'Melly's gone.'

*Chapter Eighteen*

# THE BASTON ROOT

As Peter had promised, he and Nero both had begun rebuilding the burnt cabins of Niggertown at dawn, and restoring the ones that had been touched not by the fire, but only many years of neglect.

Peter helped the black workers shave pegs, prepare caulking, sharpen axes, split cedar into shakes. The negroes worked happily alongside Peter. And they readily accepted Nero as their superior, even seeming proud to have one of their own people—a black man—taking charge of rebuilding their homes.

Monk did not make one appearance in Niggertown during this entire day. And neither did anyone make a reference to him.

Nor did any of the black people mention Melissa. Peter was grateful to them for not giving him their condolences.

Evening came and the black men and women retired to eat their cornmeal, greens, possum, and dried beef.

Peter did not feel hungry. He had swallowed a few mouthfuls of the cornbread and cold ham that Storky had sent down to him during the day. But he ate nothing more.

At sunset, Nero asked Peter to ride up to the stables with him in the wagon.

Peter declined. He wanted to walk.

The evening was light blue. The air was filled with the cry of the katydids and the faraway call of a mockingbird. Peter followed their noises.

He stood now in the spot of the woods where he and five men

278

had felled trees this afternoon. The ground was still littered with chips. He walked slowly across the patch of brittle whiteness, his boots crunching on top of them.

The pregnancy had killed Melissa.

Walking alone in the evening, Peter thought how the pregnancy had come too soon. Although Melissa had looked like a healthy person, she was frail. She had not been ready to bear another child.

Peter blamed himself. He could not blame Melissa for wanting to share love with him but he felt now that he should have been the wise partner.

Peter blamed himself now for having pressed the physical side of love onto Melissa. She had never rejected him. She had been as eager to make love as Peter. The love-making had been beautiful.

Love-making.

Was that why the white men had black wenches? Peter wondered. He had heard the stories about the frailties of white women. Melissa had never seemed frail to him. She had never showed any prudery. She was a 'lady' but she understood physical love. A family had been her life.

But she was dead and, as he walked aimlessly in the evening, Peter blamed himself. He should have had black wenches for sex and then Melissa might still be alive.


A small creek tinkled near Peter. The night was all dark above him now. He was lying back on a bed of damp moss, his hands behind his head, staring up at the lacework of stars in the sky.

Somebody's hand unsuspectingly rested on his thigh. He was not startled.

Peter soon saw a black wench kneeling next to him. He thought that he was dreaming—that he made love to black wenches on The Star and Melissa was still alive.

He felt his pants lower to his boot tops. But he refused to lift

279

his legs for the boots to be removed.

Eventually, the black wench began to fondle his maleness. Letting her proceed, Peter slowly felt a hardness, a crude passion beginning to build inside what had been only a bulk of limpness.

Peter watched the wench as she stood now and lifted her dress above her head. He looked at her shapely brown body with no repugnance—nor interest.

Silently, the black girl stepped over him and squatted down to ease him in between her straddled legs. But when she leant forward to let her breasts drag on Peter's chest, he pushed her away. He wanted no contact with her except the pull and contraction against his hardness.

The wench silently obeyed.

Finally, feeling the sensation spreading from the core of his penis, encouraging a stronger passion, Peter moved to roll the girl on her side. But, with the hindrance of his tall boots, and the restriction of the breeches around his knees, he had to move slowly, changing to long and slow drives, as he turned her around.

Peter achieved this position and, with his arms now firmly planted on the ground, he arched his back in the moonlight and deepened his slick rhythms into her.

Tingling with the first hint of an explosion, Peter drove his hips harder into the wench, prodding for the heat and the grip. And when he knew that his orgasm was approaching, his eyes lowered to the body below him.

Peter focused on the wench.

But it was not just an anonymous black female. It was a person. It was somebody with a name. It was the negress called Lilly.

Peter immediately pulled himself out of her and, as he did, a thick flood of whiteness jutted up across her brown stomach, streaking over her full breasts and hitting her cheek.

Laughing, Lilly raised herself by her elbows and said, 'I see you ain't changed, Master Peter. I sees you still wastes all that spunk.'

Then, like the last time, Lilly reached for a handful of leaves to wipe the thick sperm from her body. She said, 'I thought maybes you outgrows that, Master Peter.'

Peter knelt back. His anger was growing. He said, 'You slut. What do you think we are? Animals?'

She blinked at him.

Peter said, 'Don't you care what happens?'

Lilly shrugged. 'Happens, Master Peter? I think it's might already happens. But I think the sucker inside me is a black one.'

'You're pregnant?' he asked.

Nodding, she admitted, 'I missed my bleeding. But after I has it—and you still likes me—you can moves me to the big house with you.'

Peter gasped, 'To the big house?'

'To be your special wench. Now that your wife is dead, Master Peter, I thought for sure—'

'Stop,' Peter said, rising to his feet.

Lilly blinked at him again.

Hurriedly, Peter dressed himself. He wanted to leave here.


Peter was gone and Lilly sat alone on the moss. She was confused. She did not know what she had said wrong to Master Peter.

Reaching for a piece of grass, Lilly idly began to chew its sweetness and she wondered if Peter really wanted her for his mistress. He had started to make love to her again, hadn't he?

But why had he stopped?

Lilly wondered if she was wasting her time thinking that she could move into the big house.

Suddenly, she was knocked to the ground. Her head reeled from an unexpected blow.

Next, Lilly felt somebody kicking her thigh. And then she felt a pounding fist.

Struggling, Lilly managed to see that it was Monk assaulting her.

Kicking her again, Monk shouted, 'I watched you. I watched you screwing that white man.'

'Stop,' Lilly pleaded, trying to protect herself. 'Stop, Monk.'

Standing over her now with clenched fists, Monk said, 'I hears you lays black men. But you knows, you knows damned well I hate that white bastard. I hate you love-making with him.'

Monk pulled back his arm to slug her again.

Rolling quickly over on her side, Lilly screamed, 'Stop, Monk, *stop*!'

'Not 'til I kills you, slut.'

'Monk,' she wailed. 'Stop. You can't hit me no more. I'm carrying your baby.'

The words surprised Monk. He stood staring down at Lilly lying on the moss.

Pulling herself up to her knees, Lilly said, 'I'm carrying your sucker, Monk.'

His face hardened. 'You lies.'

'Ask Mama Gomorrah.'

'How do I know it's my sucker?'

'You the last buck to screw me, Monk. Ask around Niggertown, too. No nigger screws me but you now, Monk.'

He raised both fists at Lilly. 'How do I know it ain't him? How do I know your sucker ain't going to be half-white?'

'But you see that he don't stays inside me, Monk.'

Monk thought about what Lilly said. She was right. He had seen that Peter did not stay inside her. Peter had exploded his come all over her body.

Lowering his fists, Monk asked, 'You telling me the truth, bitch?'

Holding her arms out to him, Lilly said, 'I promises you, Monk. I promises I'm carrying your baby.'

'My baby,' Monk repeated. The idea made him feel good.

His anger disappeared.

Soon, Monk and Lilly were lying together on the moss. He was smiling while Lilly covered his face with kisses, telling him that she was having his baby.

She whispered now into his ear, 'And we runs, Monk. Just like you asks me. You digs up the buried money and we runs together.'

Pulling Lilly closer to him, Monk said, 'You got my baby inside you.'

'Ain't we going to run, Monk?' she asked. 'Ain't you got the money yet?'

But he did not want to make any plans for the moment. He was too happy with the news that he had planted a child.


Albert Selby arrived at The Shed around midnight on that same night. He knew that Mama Gomorrah would still be awake.

Letting Selby into The Shed, Mama Gomorrah asked, 'Not more trouble with them Tuckers, Master Selby, Sir?'

Selby kept his voice low. 'They've gone looking for a new place.'

'I hopes they ain't stepping foot back on The Star,' Mama Gomorrah said as she led Selby across the board flooring to the hearth.

Explaining to Mama Gomorrah that the Tuckers must come back to The Star to collect their personal belongings, Selby looked around the large room.

The black children were all asleep on the roosts built along the walls. There were thirty-seven children living in The Shed this year.

Standing in the small glow of light from the small fire on the hearth, Selby said softly to Mama Gomorrah, 'I come for some special root you keep here.'

She wrinkled her nose at Selby. 'Root? What root you needing, Master Selby, Sir?' He had never before asked for any of her voodoo potions and powders.

Selby looked away from Mama Gomorrah when he said, 'The baston root.'

'The baston?'

Selby pulled nervously at his goatee as he nodded. 'You got any left?'

'Master Selby, that's poison. The baston's for killing.'

'Yes.'

Mama Gomorrah explained, 'The baston ain't even real voodoo, Master Selby. Good voodoo is for spirits. But the baston's just killing.'

'Did you ever use it?' he asked.

'Not on folks,' she said. 'But I thinks once of using the last of it on the Tuckers.'

Then Mama Gomorrah stopped and looked suspiciously at Selby. She asked, 'You say the Tuckers come back here?'

Selby said firmly, 'Give me the root.'

Mama Gomorrah studied Selby's face. He looked grave. She knew that he had troubles at the big house. But she knew that the Tuckers could still probably cause more trouble at The Star.

Leaving Selby alone in front of the hearth for a few moments, Mama Gomorrah returned with a small pouch. It was made from a small squirrel skin and tied with a red rag.

Handing the squirrel pouch to Selby, she murmured, 'There's no baston after this.'

Taking the pouch, Selby asked, 'This is the last?'

'Remember. We salted the ground where it growed on The Star.'

Selby stood studying the small furry pouch in his hand.

'There's the powder of the baston in there,' Mama Gomorrah whispered to Selby. 'And there's one trouble with it.'

'What?'

'The baston ain't painful enough for the Tuckers. Your heart starts beating faster and faster and then—' She looked at the pouch. '—then you sleeps.'

Selby asked, 'You don't need no prayers? No secret mumbo-jumbo?'

Mama Gomorrah shook her head. 'If you want real

284

voodoo, if you want bad pain for them, I can fix the witch's ladder.' Her eyes danced with the idea of torturing the Tuckers.

'This will do,' Selby said.

Then he turned and walked to the door of The Shed.

*Chapter Nineteen*

# A DUEL WITH SNAKES

Peter woke early the next morning and looked around him to see where he had spent the night. He was in the stables of the big house. He had crawled up into the loft and slept here last night.

Looking down over the edge of the loft, he saw Selby and Nero standing in a flood of bright morning sunlight pouring through the open doors of the stables.

Peter had not seen Selby since the night-before-last, not since Selby had come down to Niggertown to tell him that Melissa had died.

Peter called to him, 'Looking for me?'

Selby and Nero both turned.

Selby said, 'I was just giving Nero a message for you, Sonny.'

'Wait,' Peter called, clammering toward the ladder.

Selby wore fresh linen this morning. His long white hair had been immaculately brushed. His boots were polished like black glass. He had even combed some fresh henna into his goatee. Glancing down at Peter's shabby appearance—but not mentioning it—Selby began, 'I've been thinking, Sonny—'

'Yes,' Peter said, brushing the straw from his breeches. They were still dirty from working yesterday in Niggertown and soiled with char from the fire.

Selby continued, 'My mother's name was Victoria. And her mother, my grandmother, was called Veronica.'

Peter's mind was sluggish this morning but he immediately grasped what Selby was saying. Victoria and Veronica. Two names for his new daughters. He had not even given it any consideration.

Tilting his head, Selby mused, 'Victoria and Veronica. It has a nice ring.' He looked at Nero, asking, 'Don't you think so?'

Nero quickly agreed. 'Real nice, Master Selby, Sir.'

Selby turned to Peter. 'What do you think, Sonny?'

Peter nodded. 'I like it.'

Selby asked, 'You haven't seen them yet, have you?' It was not a rebuke.

Looking down at his scuffed boots, Peter shook his head. He felt ashamed of himself. He had been wallowing in pity.

'No worry,' Selby answered, patting him on the shoulder. 'Storky has everything under control. She had a wench sent up from Niggertown to nurse them.'

'Father—' Peter began.

But Selby had not finished. He said, 'Now about the burying, Sonny. What do you think—' He stopped.

Peter waited. That was exactly the point he wanted to raise.

Turning to look outside the stables at a smart little buggy already hitched to a dappled mare, Selby said, 'Storky has got Melly laid out in the upstairs parlour. The parlour where Melly used to meet her Mama's lady-friends in when she was—'

Selby was choking now, trying to hold back his tears. 'Sonny, don't make plans about burying Melly till you next hear from me, okay?'

Peter agreed with a quick nod. He dreaded making plans for the funeral and was only too glad to agree.

Wiping his nose on the back of his hand, Selby added more brightly, 'I've got to drive Doc Riesen to catch the coach in Troy now. He didn't want to accept no payment' Selby patted a pouch of money in the left pocket of his white jacket—saying nothing about the bulge in the other pocket—adding, 'but, I'm insisting he takes a hundred.'

Peter nodded in agreement.

Resquaring his straw hat on his head, Selby said, 'On the way home from Troy, I'll be stopping to see Judge Antrobus.'

Again, Peter nodded. There was nothing unusual about that.

Walking to the doorway of the stables, Selby squinted at the sunny morning and drawled, 'One more thing, Sonny.'

'Yes?'

'Nero just told me the Tuckers have come back to fetch their belongings. Do you think you could go down to see they leave?'

'Sure.'

'I'd appreciate that, Sonny,' Selby said.

'I'll wash and go right away.' This prospect was another relief for Peter. It was something to do, a reason to keep out of the oppressing big house.

Waving again, Selby walked to the buggy and climbed up on its one wooden step.

Before riding away, he called to Peter, 'Now you won't forget about Niggertown, will you, Sonny?'

Peter had his shirt half-off, getting ready to wash and shave in the horse trough. He called to Selby, 'Work's already started on the houses.'

Selby shouted, 'No. I mean about giving it that new name. Remember? Melly never did like it being called Niggertown.' Then, cracking a small whip over the dappled mare's head, Selby called to Peter, 'Think of something good to call it, Sonny. Think of something pretty for Melly.'

Albert Selby bounced away in the buggy toward the front of the house to collect Doctor Riesen and take him to Troy.


The Tuckers had come back to The Star for their belongings. Claudia Tucker was rummaging through the small cabin this morning. And, as she lifted and appraised every item in the cabin to find something approaching value, she smiled smugly as she listened to her husband telling Monk the news they had heard yesterday.

Tucker was saying to Monk, 'Boy, do niggers named "Tim" and "Perky" mean something to you?'

Monk shook his head. He was wondering why Tucker had not shown any interest in his own story, how he had aroused some of the black men in Niggertown to burn their shacks.

But Tucker was insisting on telling his own tale.

'A few hours' drive from here,' Tucker explained, 'is a place belonging to a man called Jack Grouse. I've known Grouse when he didn't have a pot to piss in. Fact is, I sold him a couple niggers from here on the cheap a good twenty years ago.'

Claudia interrupted, 'That's why he's so glad to see us. Chad sold him a buck called Cal. Grouse says Cal turned out to be the best buck he ever owned.'

Chad Tucker continued, 'Since those days, though, Grouse has come up in the world. He had him a few hundred acres of green cotton and now he's owning near a hundred niggers. He picked up a lot of them cheap after the West Indian troubles.'

'He wants to breed niggers now,' Claudia interrupted again.

'That's what he wants me for,' Tucker bragged. 'He wants me to oversee the breeding side of his place.'

Behind him, Claudia added, 'And my hubby will be called "master" again, won't you, sweetie?'

All grievances between the Tuckers had disappeared. They were friends, even flirting with one another this morning.

Tucker proceeded to tell Monk what he had heard yesterday. 'Well, anyhows, two of Grouse's niggers are from an island called "St. Kitts".' His eyes twinkled.

Monk had heard that name before. He began to listen with more interest.

Expanding his chest, Tucker said, 'And not only are those niggers from St. Kitts, but they were owned there by a fellow named "Abdee".'

Monk was not impressed by that fact. As Tucker had told him before, Abdee was a common name. The world, according to Chad Tucker, was full of Abdees, like Smiths. It was a common white-trash name.

Tucker continued enthusiastically, 'And that Abdee fellow, he was married to a white French woman.'

'Those niggers tell you this?' Monk asked.

Claudia turned again, saying, 'They tells us all of it, boy.

Everybody treated us like visiting royalness at the Grouse place. Now you just shut up and listen to what Mister Tucker has to say to you.' She waved a wooden spoon at Monk. And then, studying the spoon, she dropped it into the hopping sack resting at her feet and looked for more things to take.

Tucker said gleefully, 'But that French woman Abdee was married to left him. He was a right mean bastard and she left him high and dry. But she left with a kid in her belly.' Tucker could see that Monk was slowly getting his point. 'And she took her maid with her, too. And that maid was called—'

'Ta-Ta,' Claudia shouted to Monk, holding an iron skillet now, its bottom caked with cold grease. 'And she had a git of her own called—'

Tucker said, 'Monkey!'

'The same as you were called when you first comes here to me,' Claudia said excitedly.

Then, lowering her head to examine the greasey skillet, she dropped it into the sack, too.

Monk stood still. He was becoming confused.

'But the best part of the story,' Tucker roared, 'the best part of this story is that Ta-Ta's git—you, boy—is that you are Abdee's son, too. That's who your Daddy is, boy. Didn't I tell you once you might have a Daddy someplace in the world?'

Monk blinked at Tucker. He did not know if he was supposed to thank him for telling him this or what. The story still was not clear to him.

'Don't you see, boy,' Tucker explained. 'That whitie up at the big house is the son of that West Indian Abdee. And you and him is near enough brothers!'

Monk scratched at his cheek.

Tucker simplified the matter for him. He asked, 'Why can that so-called 'Master Peter' be the God-damned big shot here and you're not even good enough to have that job he gives to Nero.'

Monk started, 'You mean—'

Tucker shouted, 'I mean that Peter Abdee is a big shot. And that crazy old Ta-Ta wench who lives in the attic at the big house gets all the whiskey she can drink because she was that Peter's ma's maid. But you, you God-damned nigger, you're nothing but shit to any of them. You are nothing. You get nothing.'

Monk finally understood. His face was hardening. He was feeling now—more than ever—that he had a right to be the overseer.

Tucker goaded, 'Brothers. You're brothers with that fine "Master Peter" yet he keeps you under his feet like a dog.'

' "Master Peter",' Monk repeated slowly.

Tucker reached to the table beside him. He grabbed his whip and said, 'And all the training I gives you, boy, it all goes wasted because some other nigger gets your place. The job I've been training you for all these years. Some other nigger is getting it.'

Monk glanced at the whip in Tucker's hand. He asked, 'You really been training me to be overseer?'

Tucker lied, 'Why in hell you think I've been wasting time on you, boy? Cause I love you?'

Monk kept staring at the whip.

Holding it to Monk in a glistening curl, Tucker said, 'I thought I was training a nigger to be a man. A master. I always knows it's hard to keep down a smart nigger. Sure, dumb niggers are slaves. They're just animals. But not you, boy. You're smart. And you smart niggers go out and get what you want.' Tucker's eyes glistened. 'Don't you, boy? Don't you go out and get what you want?'

Monk grabbed the whip.

'Yeah! That's the kid I know. Go on. Let them see who you really are. Let them see what you know about mastering and whipping and overseeing. Go up to that big house right now, boy. Go up to that big house and show your white brother. You ain't scared of your brother cause he's white, is you?'

'Scared?' Monk bellowed. 'Scare of my white—' He laughed— 'brother? Hell no I ain't scared of him.'

Claudia snatched a butcher knife from a pine drawer and shrilled at Monk, 'Take this along with you, Monk. Take along this knife and drive in a few holes for us.'

Monk gripped the coiled whip in one hand and the butcher knife in the other. He said, 'I'll go right now.'

'And it's about time, too,' Tucker said, following him to the door.

Chad and Claudia Tucker stood in the doorway of the shack and watched Monk make his way up the hill.

Claudia said to her husband, 'What if they finds out we put him up to this?'

'Who the shit cares?' Tucker said and, turning back into the shack, he added, 'We'll be gone by the time he even gets there.'

Claudia said, 'Why don't you start digging up the money? I'll just finish in here.'

'Right,' Chad said, quickly going for the shovel.

He and Claudia were both anxious to get started on their way to Jack Grouse's.

The mid-morning sun was hot and, as Monk hurried along on the path to the big house, he ripped off his shirt, tossing it to a clump of ferns alongside the path.

Near The Shed, Lilly called out to him, 'Mama Gomorrah touches me again, Monk. She says I got a sucker inside me.' Lilly was happy and excited this morning.

Not stopping to talk to her, Monk called, 'Tell me later.'

'What you so mad about now,' Lilly asked, running along beside Monk on the path.

'Nothing to do with you,' he mumbled.

'Didn't you get the money? Did you forget about digging up the money, Monk?'

He suddenly stopped. He realized that the Tuckers had not known that their money had been stolen when they told him about Peter and the West Indies. The Tuckers had been in a good mood.

Starting to walk again, Monk said, 'We'll talk about the money later.' He knew it was safe where he had moved it.

Still running alongside him, Lilly asked, 'Why you got that knife and that bullwhip, Monk? What's you doing with them? And why you taking this path to the big house?'

'None of your business,' he muttered.

'You're going to do trouble at the big house, ain't you? You're going to fight there.'

'I'll tell you when it's over.'

'Monk? What if you lose?'

'I ain't going to lose.'

'But you're a nigger, Monk. They don't let niggers win at the big house.'

He repeated, 'I ain't going to lose.'

'But if they kill you, Monk, who'll know where the money is?'

'I AIN'T GOING TO LOSE!'

Still running alongside him, Lilly said, 'Maybe I can help you, Monk. Can I help you?'

'Maybe,' he said, thinking now of how he would approach his white brother, Peter.

Then, seeing the roof of the big house, he slowed and heard voices in the stables.

Stopping, Monk told Lilly where to wait.

Monk stood alone in front of the stables.

He called, 'White boy? White boy, you hiding in there?'

Nero appeared in the doorway.

Monk shouted, 'Not you, pet nigger. I've got no troubles with you. It's my white brother I come for.'

Peter emerged from the shadows behind Nero. He saw Monk standing in the sun. Monk was half-naked and holding a whip in one hand, a long knife in the other.

'Who you been talking to, Monk?' Peter called.

Monk answered, 'I ain't been talking. I been listening. I been listening to stories Tucker brings back about you and me

293

having the same daddy, white boy.'

Stepping in front of Nero, Peter asked, 'Who told Tucker that?'

'Never minds who told him that,' Monk called back. 'Why don't you tell me why you ain't making me overseer here.'

Peter answered, 'Because I think Nero will do a better job that you, that's why.'

Monk unfurled his whip in the air with a loud crack. And, as he held up the knife in his other hand, he called, 'Then you come outside here, brother, and we sees who does a better job of this.'

Moving alongside Peter, Nero held a pitchfork.

Seeing Nero, Monk called, 'Let the white man fight his own fights, pet nigger.' He snapped the whip again and dust rose around him in the yard.

As Monk was speaking, Peter quickly reached toward the whip hanging inside the door of the stable. But his anger did not match Monk's. He did not want to fight him.

Nero pulled a knife from the wall above the rainbarrel. And holding the knife in his hand, Nero said to Peter, 'He means it. That crazy guy means it. Give me that whip. I·wants to fight him.' Nero grabbed for the whip coiled in Peter's hand.

But Peter would not release the whip.

Standing in the sun, Monk called to Peter, 'What's the matter? You tired from pestering black wenches last night? Tired from shooting spunk all over my Lilly?'

Peter shouted, 'I didn't know Lilly was your woman, Monk.'

'She's having my baby, white boy.'

'Then why do you want to fight me?'

Monk's upper lip curled. 'Cause I hate you. And I want you to leave my woman alone.'

'I will. I don't want your woman.' Peter did not want to fight anyone for Lilly.

Monk repeated, 'I want you to leave my Lilly alone.'

'I said I will.'

'Go find another white bitch to take your dead woman's place.'

Peter snatched the knife from Nero's hand and rushed out into the sun toward Monk.

That was all that Monk had to say—to talk about Melissa.

Monk's bullwhip cracked at Peter as he came hurling out of the stables. Although Peter was quick to jump aside, the tip of Monk's whip caught his shirt, half-shredding it from his chest.

Peter waited, coldly studying Monk.

Crouching, Monk moved toward Peter like a crab. He wagged the whip in one hand and made jabbing movements with his knife. He then made one, two, three moves to strike out at Peter with his whip. Suddenly, he brought it back behind his back and it sang through the air.

Peter jumped to his left, casting his own whip at Monk as he moved.

He missed Monk. And, as he curled the whip over his shoulder, Monk's whip snapped again at him.

Peter was hit on his side. He felt his flesh burn. But he moved quickly, keeping Monk on guard, watching him dash back and forth in mock attacks.

Monk was fast on his feet.

Peter whipped at him now as he moved.

He hit Monk; blood appeared in a red line across Monk's bare chest.

Then, Monk and Peter stood staring at one another, waiting for a next move. A crowd of anxious black faces was gathering in front of the stables.

A black man called, 'Help Master Peter.' A woman shouted, 'That nigger's going to kill Master Peter.' Some black people were even moving to grab Monk, but moving cautiously in fear of Monk's whip.

Peter ignored the black people's loyalty to him, their dislike of Monk. He called to them, 'Keep back.' He glared coldly at Monk, calling to the black people, 'This is *my* fight—'

Monk was crouching forward to strike again as Peter called to the people.

More cries rose against Monk.

Watching Monk move, Peter said, 'Monk burned your houses. Now he—'

Peter's words were broken by the crack of Monk's whip. Peter had foreseen it and he moved in time.

Soon, though, he and Monk were charging one another again like two angry stallions—one black, one white. The air was filled with the cracks of their whips, followed by the softer sound of feet dancing on the dirt as they attacked and recoiled, rushed forward and withdrew.

Now the tips of Monk's whip hit Peter's back. There was a sharp digging sound. When the whip snapped in the air, the crack echoed and the whip quickly recoiled, thudding onto the ground.

Peter's back was bleeding—and he was cut on his thigh—but he avoided the next snap of Monk's whip. He was learning the rhythms of Monk's tactics.

Monk was still the aggressor, bluffing a snap of his whip and then following it with a quick movement that dug into Peter's flesh.

Peter scored a deep strike, ripping the skin from Monk's shoulder.

But then the heel of Peter's boot slipped on a rock. He fell to the ground.

Monk ran toward him with his knife.

Lifting both legs, Peter caught Monk's stomach on the soles of his boots and threw him to the ground behind him.

Peter sprung to his feet and flailed his whip at Monk's rolling body. The third snap caught him on the calf of his leg.

But Monk was standing again. His half-naked body was covered with dirt and blood. He was gasping now for air. But his brown face was set with hatred.

He moved toward Peter again, toying the whip at him, jabbing the knife as he moved. And, suddenly, he curled the whip sideways in a strong throw.

296

He struck Peter's face.

A line of blood gushed across Peter's forehead.

Trying to keep the blood from dripping into his eyes with the perspiration, Peter made his first lunge at Monk.

Monk jumped aside.

Peter steadied himself long enough to mop the blood away from his eyes. Then he lunged the second time at Monk, snapping his whip this time as he moved.

He struck.

Monk staggered.

But as Peter hurled himself toward him, Monk quickly grabbed his whip near the butt and swung that end of the whip at Peter's face, catching him on the jaw.

Losing his balance, Peter stumbled backwards.

Monk came barrelling toward Peter now, holding the butt of his whip between his two hands and he went for Peter's throat.

Rolling quickly out from Monk's flying body, Peter raised himself to his knees, and saw Monk lying on his stomach in the dirt.

A voice screamed out at them from the side.

Peter impulsively turned. He saw Lilly.

But before he saw anything else, he felt a hot sting across his back. Monk had hit him. And, next, Peter was tumbling to the ground.

Monk was on top of him now.

Peter's whip was lying away from his hand. His knife was gone. And he saw the long blade of Monk's butcher knife gleaming over his face. His mind flashed with the realization that Lilly had been waiting for that chance to help Monk.

Staring down at him, Monk gasped 'White boy.' He lowered his knife toward Peter's throat. His perspiration was falling onto Peter's face. His chest was heaving for air. He repeated, 'White boy. White boy. White—' The knife was pressed against Peter's throat.

A loud boom exploded behind them.

Looking up, Peter watched Monk's face suddenly become gnarled with pain. He saw a patch of redness spread on Monk's chest.

Then, as blood spurted from Monk's chest, he slumped forward onto Peter. He finally rolled over onto the ground.

With his eyes swimming in blood and perspiration, Peter struggled to his elbows. Beyond him, he saw the vague figure of a negress dressed in a long white gown. In one hand, the negress was holding a long gun. But its barrel now rested in the dirt.

Peter saw she was Ta-Ta.

There was a hush now in the stableyard.

He heard Ta-Ta slur, 'That nigger going to kill Madame's boy. I has to do something. That nigger was going to kill Madam Honore's boy.'

Dropping the long gun to the ground, Ta-Ta turned and dragged her bare feet toward the big house.

Peter then fell back onto the ground in unconsciousness.


The black spectators immediately began to swarm around Peter's and Monk's bodies, seeing for certain that Monk was dead and Peter was alive.

But Nero pushed his way through the negroes.

Behind him, Storky screamed to the curious people, 'Get away! Get away! Maybe Master Peter is dying!' She made a path with her sharp elbows.

The slaves soon gave way, letting Nero and Storky pass to the two bodies in the dirt.

Kneeling beside Peter now, Nero nodded that he was still alive. He was only unconscious.

Storky clasped her hands and looked toward the sky.

Then, behind them, they heard a woman sobbing. It was Lilly. She was kneeling among the bare feet of the black people and cradling Monk's blood-stained body on her knees.

She cried to him, 'Monk? Speak to me, Monk.'

He lay limp and covered with the blood from the raw hole in his chest.

Lilly begged, 'Monk? Where is the money? The money? Where did you bury the money, Monk?'

Looking up at Storky, Lilly said, 'I'm having his sucker. And he was saving us money.'

'Money!' Storky laughed bitterly. 'This ain't no time to be putting on airs, slut.'

Lilly screamed at Storky, 'Monk knew about money!'

Storky looked down at Lilly with disdain. 'You gone crazy in the head over all this, wench.'

'But he did!' Lilly insisted. 'He did know about money!'

'You lies,' Storky said, adding as she turned back to Nero, 'and even if he did buries money, wench, you ain't going to find out about it now. So get your black ass off that ground and let somebody haul his body out of here.'


Albert Selby had dropped Doctor Riesen at Troy and reached the Dewitt Place by midday. He knew it was the Dewitt sisters day to go shopping in Carterville—no one would be here, not even Judge Antrobus.

George answered the door and offered Selby his respects for the loss of Melissa.

Selby thanked him then asked boldly, 'Remember that Fay Willows, George. That hussy from a few years back? Who in the house do you have up to that snuff?'

George thought. 'There's that Miss Sue Ellen from Gettysburg. She's pretty sprightly. Got her a real neat little waist and titties—' George held up his black hands, cupping them.

'She sounds just what I need today.'

'You sure that's all right, Master Selby, Sir?' George asked, eyeing him. He knew the stories about Selby's heart.

For the first time that Selby could remember, he became stern with George. He said, 'Are you questioning me, boy?'

George shook his head. He mumbled, 'I go tell Miss

Sue Ellen to gets ready.' He turned and climbed slowly up the stairs.

While Selby was waiting, he took a small stub of a graphite pencil and a piece of paper from the pocket of his jacket. He quickly scribbled, 'MISS SUE ELLEN NOT GUILTY OF NOTHING'. He signed it, 'YOUR FRIEND ALWAYS ALBERT SELBY'. He quickly drew the usual rough star under his signature and, folding the piece of paper, he propped it up by a milkglass vase setting on the hall table.

George finally called from the top of the stairs, 'Master Selby, Sir, Miss Sue Ellen is waiting to see you.' George added, 'She's in the Rose Room, Master Selby, Sir.'

Selby paused at the foot of the stairs. The Rose Room. That was his and Charlotte's usual room. Did he have to go in there? Selby lifted his head to protest but, then, realizing that he was already making too much of a fuss of this, he slowly proceeded up the stairs.

Keeping his head lowered as he passed George, Selby murmurred, 'Leave my horse and buggy out front where it is, George,'

'Yes, Master Selby, Sir.'

Selby continued down the carpeted hallway and opened the door at the end.

Inside the Rose Room—on the bed where he and Charlotte Dewitt had shared so many afternoons and evenings—Selby saw a young lady with long brown hair, widely spaced eyes, and a small pointed chin. She sat on the edge of the bed, dressed in a turquoise robe. Her feet were bare, the counterpane of the bed already turned back for herself and Selby.

First seeing the girl, Selby thought about Melissa. She did not look at all like Melissa. But Selby could not get Melissa out of his mind. That was why he had come to the Dewitt Place today. To do that.

He forced himself to continue with his plan.

Gently closing the door behind him, Selby nodded ·at

the girl and removed his straw hat. Setting it on a small rattan-seated chair, he reached into his jacket pocket and removed a small brown pouch. He said calmly to the girl, 'There's five hundred dollars in here for you, Miss Sue Ellen.' He set the pouch on the bureau.

Her eyes widened. 'Five hundred dollars?'

Selby nodded. 'And outside is a horse and buggy. That's for you, too. I'm in a generous mood today.'

Then, proceeding to slip off his jacket, Selby said, 'Don't be frightened, young lady. I ain't come here to hurt you. Miss Charlotte knows all about this. You just take the money and my buggy and leave here.' Selby did not consider this to be a lie. He had left the note by the milkglass vase.

'Leave?' the girl asked, nervously fingering her brunette hair.

'Why not? Go wherever you want. As I said, I feel generous today.' Selby sat now on the edge of the bed and said, 'Now, if you'll be so kind as to help me off with these boots, I'll manage the rest for myself.'

'The rest?' She was suspicious.

'Just my undressing,' Selby assured her. 'You help me with my boots and then you lay back on that bed there so I can see how pretty you are. When I'm all undressed, I'll join you. But it probably won't be for long. I'm not that young. Oh,' he added, 'one more thing, Miss Sue Ellen.'

She nodded, waiting anxiously.

Selby explained, 'It's my habit to fall asleep when I finish with a young lady. Take no notice of that. Don't worry about me. You just concern yourself with leaving.'

'You mean I can leave today?' She was already on the floor helping Selby with his boots. 'Take the five hundred dollars and go?'

'Why not? Miss Charlotte expects you to be gone when she gets back from Carterville. I told her all about it.' The inventiveness of the situation was making it less difficult for Selby. He enjoyed seeing the excitement in the girl's eyes.

All his life, Albert Selby had liked seeing people getting what they wanted.

The young prostitute was lying obediently on the bed now, her eyes shut.

Standing beside the bed, Selby looked at her soft skin. He enjoyed the way that she was gently fondling her breasts to arouse him, letting her hands move down over her stomach to the small patch of hair between her smooth legs.

Losing himself in this visual delight, Selby's penis reached a firmness with his hand more quickly than usual.

The girl still had her eyes closed. But before Selby moved toward the bed, he reached behind him to the pocket of his jacket.

Selby withdrew a small squirrel skin pouch from the pocket. He pulled the red rag from the pouch and—keeping his hand moving on his firm penis—he held the squirrel pouch to his mouth and swallowed its contents, the powder from the baston root.

Quickly stuffing the pouch back into his pocket, he turned and faced the girl.

His heart was already quickening. The blood was rushing into his penis. He moved toward the girl now.

The entry into her was easy and, soon, he closed his eyes and began to see flickering colours. But, then, they turned into blinding white flashes. And, finally—it was over.

Albert Selby's body was still.

The girl, thinking that he had finished with her—and had fallen asleep as he had said that he would—quickly crawled out from under him. She was careful to leave the counterpane over his body.

Slipping quickly into her turquoise robe, she grabbed the pouch of money from the bureau and tip-toed hurriedly across the floor in her bare feet.

Before opening the door, though, the girl stopped and blew Albert Selby a kiss for being so generous to her.

She did not know that she was blowing a kiss to a dead man.

## Chapter Twenty

# LAST CALL AT THE STAR

When Peter had regained his consciousness, he was lying on the couch in Selby's study. Beginning to look around him, he saw from the light that it was late day—almost evening—but he did not see Selby. Next to him, Storky was kneeling with a pan of cool water, strips of linen, and medicines. Trying to raise himself, Peter asked, 'Father? Is he back yet?'

'Master Selby ain't back from Troy yet. Now you just lie still, Master Peter,' Storky soothed, trying to push him gently down onto the couch.

Beginning to remember the incidents of this morning, he thought of Monk, the blood, and, recalling the last sight that he had seen, he asked, 'Where's Ta-Ta?'

Storky answered calmly, 'If you wants, Master Peter, you can talks to Ta-Ta later.'

'I can't just lie here.' He tried to move again.

But Storky would not let him budge from the couch. She said, 'You got that Nero to do things for you. He's herded all those gawking niggers away from the stables. He's got them all back working already. So, rest now. You had enough excitement for one day.'

Looking up at Storky, Peter asked, 'Why did she do it?'

Dabbing at a welt on his shoulder, Storky said, 'Ta-Ta? Well, Master Peter, I figure she does it the same reason any decent nigger would do it. Protecting you. You've had a big sadness, Master Peter. But that ain't all the reason. You didn't let that sadness get you down, get you to moping. You went out and helped those poor niggers get their houses back. Helped them get those houses that that trash Monk nigger only burned. That Ta-Ta, she was mumbling about you being somebody's boy and I suspects—well, Master Peter, I suspects that's just between her and what's happening in her mind. But one thing I do thinks, Master Peter, I wouldn't mention anything about this to that Ta-Ta wench right now. I would just let her be. A wench like that don't expect no thanks. Even old niggers like her have duties to be done.'

Storky stopped wiping, confiding now, 'I don't know if you knows this or not, Master Peter, but no reason you shouldn't knows now. That Master Selby, he gives that Ta-Ta wench a bottle of brandy three times a week now. He leaves it outside her door up there in the attic. He's been doing that ever since she comes here. But knowing what things have been here this week, I don't think that Master Selby has had much time to leave Ta-Ta her brandy. So, if you wants to do something, I thinks leaving her brandy is the best idea.'

Clenching Storky's forearm, Peter asked, 'Will you do it for me? Right now?'

'Not this minute, Master Peter. I got you to look after. But I sures will do it. And I tells Master Selby about it when he comes home so that Ta-Ta don't get herself more bottles of that powerful stuff this week than she's needing.'

Peter tried to laugh but it hurt. 'Hell, Storky; give her all the brandy she wants.'

Storky scowled. 'And have her falling out that upstairs window of hers, Master Peter?'

He nodded. She was right. Then, looking around the study, he asked, 'You said Father's not home yet?'

'At the judge's, I reckons.'

Peter sighed, wondering what Selby would say about what happened here this morning. The fight with Monk. Ta-Ta shooting him, her own son, just to save Peter. And, also, Selby still had not recovered from the shock of losing Melissa.

But Storky had other things for Peter to think about, more specific details. Rolling him over on his stomach to bathe the welts on his back, she said, 'Just in case you likes to know,

Master Peter, while you were passed out in here, Nero had that Monk's carcass carted away from the yard out back. Mama Gomorrah said that the best place to stick trash like that was in the ground. She wants him buried near The Shed in case any spooks try to get out of him. She said that she could whip any bad spooks right back into the ground. So Monk's being buried over there. Probably already in the ground.'

Did Storky know about his relationship with Monk? Peter wondered. Did she really know why Ta-Ta had shot him? Because of Storky's particular way of storing facts until she could use them, Peter never could tell exactly what Storky knew. But he did have to say now, 'Monk never had a chance, Storky. Any spooks in him were the Tuckers!'

'And they're gone,' Storky said, 'and that's good riddance!'

Ponderously, Peter said, 'They're gone but poor Monk's being buried. It's sad, Storky. It's not really fair, is it?'

'How can you say that? Sometimes your heart is too big, Master Peter! That trash nigger tried to kill you.'

Peter began to explain his feeling about Monk to Storky but, then, he stopped. There was no use.

Storky had more of her own to say, though. Washing Peter's shoulder with damp clothes, she said, 'But there's one thing worse that can happen to a trash nigger. One thing worse than burying him. And that's setting him free. Oh, buries me any-day!'

Medicine now stung into Peter's welt.

Storky continued, 'Especially a no account nigger who's just nothing but trouble-makers. Sets them free or sells them to poor white trash. Course, with poor white trash niggers gets to lord it over them, bragging about the quality folks that used to own them. Poor white trash don't stand a chance with a head-proud nigger. Never has. Never will.'

Peter's mind was still swimming. 'What are you talking about, Storky?'

'Niggers, Master Peter. Niggers. If there's one thing I knows about it's niggers. Especially if she has a pup in her belly.'

'You're talking about Lilly!' Peter remembered her now, too, how she had shouted to get Peter's attention so Monk could attack him.

Storky grunted. 'I even hate to say that trashy slut's name. After Ta-Ta shot that Monk, all that Lilly could say was he knew about buried money. Buried money! Ha! She's crazy in the head as well as being a slut.'

Peter thought now. He said. 'Lilly does give us a problem. Monk did say she was pregnant.'

'Pregnant? With Monk's sucker? Then I say gets her off this place for sure.'

'Yes, Storky. I think you're right. Setting Lilly free would be the best thing to do. But I just can't send her out into the world. I have to give her something. Some papers. Some notes to go working. I'll have to give her some money, too.'

Storky laughed at his generosity. 'Give her papers to go to work and she rips them up! Gives her a hundred dollars at breakfast and she has nothing by dinner. That wench is trash through and through!'

'But I just can't send her away from The Star without anything, can I, Storky?'

'You can't rightly asks me, Master Peter. I just a nigger myself. But whatever you do decides, I sees that it's done. In fact, I can sees to it right now. I knows I got fifty dollars in the kitchen from dairy money from that Turpin bunch for the last seven years. I can gives that to Lilly quick as a flash, and a slap in the face to go with it! And if you wants work for her, how about that place called Treetop House? They got jobs there for freed niggers to do. And there's a wagon travelling from Troy to Treetop House once a week. That Lilly can hop on that wagon from Troy and be gone from these parts in no time, Master Peter. Plus, on tops of all that, Master Peter, I know where the deeds of 'manumission' are kept. Right in this room. I knows that since the last big Witcherley fight. So, whatever you decides to do, Master Peter, you tells me and I tries to helps you.'

Despite Storky's prostestation, Peter sat up on the couch and hugged her. She squirmed, trying to free herself, warning Peter that he should rest.

Holding her hands in his, he said, 'But I can't keep lying down.'

Invigorated by the tonic of Storky's control of life, he said, 'I got to clean myself up to go pay a call.'

Storky stared at him, repeating, 'Pay a call?'

'I've got two new little girls, Storky. Two new little baby girls.' He stood up from the couch, feeling a bit shakey at first. Also, the thought of Melissa returned to him now, that her body was lying upstairs in the small parlour. But he would try to think of her in some happier place. He had to concentrate his life now on what he was going to do for his three daughters—Imogen, Veronica, and Victoria.

The sky was darkening as the Tuckers approached Jack Grouse's farm. They sat side-by-side on the wooden seat of their wagon. A mountain of furniture, barrels, and bundles rested in a heap behind them in the wagon.

The Tuckers' reconciliation had not been long-lived. They had begun arguing when they discovered the slave ledger in the hole under the chinaberry tree instead of their money. The flour sack had disappeared. And Claudia Tucker accused her husband of stealing the money. But he said that she had buried it in another place.

Claudia next said that Monk had taken the money.

But Chad Tucker disagreed. He said that black people were not that intelligent. The Tuckers' only other suspects were white people—Peter Abdee, Albert Selby, or both. And if either Abdee or Selby had taken the money—and left the slave ledger in its place—the Tuckers both agreed that they should leave The Star as quickly as possible. They did not even collect Tucker's wages from the big house.

Having taken the road to Carterville, the Tuckers turned right at the forks and were now travelling on a trace which passed through a thick of willows.

The horse was beginning to balk and nicker.

'A rattlesnake nearabouts,' Tucker grunted, using a rope to beat the old horse. He had given his bullwhip to Monk.

Claudia muttered, 'It ain't going to help by you strapping the hide off the animal.'

'You want to drive?' Tucker shouted at her.

She snapped, 'I'd probably do a damned sight better than you.'

Before Tucker had time to answer, the figure of a man stepped onto the trace in front of them.

The man held up both hands for Tucker to stop.

'What the hell?' Tucker said, reining the horse.

'Fool!' Claudia whispered. 'What you stopping for? Run him over. He might be a thief.'

'What we got to rob?' Tucker said, and then stood in the wagon to see who the man was.

As the man walked toward the wagon, Chad Tucker saw that it was Jack Grouse.

But Jack Grouse was not smiling as Tucker remembered last seeing him smile. His lean face was set in contempt.

'What's the trouble?' Tucker called.

Looking at the willows on the right, Grouse nodded. Then he nodded to the left of the trace.

More men emerged from both sides of the wagon. They surrounded the Tuckers. Three of the men carried guns.

Grouse ordered, 'Get down, Tucker.'

'What is this?' Tucker asked, looking around him. 'Who are these men?'

But then he began to recognize their faces. One was Marvin O'Shea. One was George Gresham. Another was Johnny Tolmer. Bob Colborn and Zebedee Flannery were there, too. They were all men who had bought slaves from Tucker—sick slaves, old slaves, slaves stolen from The Star and sold to these men at night. Billy Joe Crandall was among the wronged men.

Claudia Tucker pulled her shawl around her shoulders and gasped, 'My God, my God, my God.'

Jack Grouse repeated, 'Get down, Tucker. We don't want to hurt your missus. We got no bone to pick with her.'

'Claudie—' Chad Tucker whispered from the side of his mouth, '—Claudia, say something to stop them.'

She remained motionless on the wagon seat.

Grouse repeated, 'Get down, Tucker, unless you want us to shoot your wife by accident.'

Pulling away from her husband, Claudia hissed at him, 'Get down, you yellow coward. You want me to get hurt, too?'

The other men were beginning to close in now around the Tuckers' wagon. Their mouths were slowly sneering under the shadowy brims of their greasy hats.

'What is this?' Tucker asked nervously. 'What you all doing here? Grouse, you said you'd give me a job.'

'I'll give you something all right. But it ain't going to be no job.' He beckoned again to the trees.

A black man now emerged from behind a willow. He dragged an iron machine behind him.

Tucker did not recognize the negro nor the piece of iron. He asked, 'What's that?'

'You must remember seeing that on The Star,' Grouse said, walking toward the negro and the machine. 'It's called 'the Scavenger's Daughter.' And look who's pulling it here. You should remember him, too, Tucker. It's Cal.'

Tucker squinted at the negro. 'Cal? I'll be damned. It *is* Cal.'

Grouse said, 'Cal was dying when you sold him to me, Tucker. He almost died but he finally came through.'

'That's good. That's real good,' Tucker said, trying hard now to think of a way to escape. 'That's what I understood you to say yesterday.'

Grouse continued in his dry voice. 'Surprised you don't recognize "The Scavenger's Daughter", though. It's been around The Star for years. I bought it off your boss, Albert Selby.'

Tucker said, 'Selby?'

'Well, indirectly,' Grouse said, looking at the iron bars connecting a head clasp to the hand and feet irons. 'It's an old time torture instrument. And we're going to lock you up in it,

'Tucker. We're going to lock you up in it and see if you can help nurse Cal better.'

'Lock me up? Nurse Cal better? I thought you said Cal was—' Tucker was beginning to shake.

Grouse wryly explained, 'Oh, Cal is over his old sickness. But lately he's been eating too many green apples and peaches. Cal's got himself the shits real bad.'

'Oh, yeah?' Tucker said nervously.

Grouse continued, 'Cal's got himself the green apple shits. And being we folks over here keep our places so clean, we ain't got no hole for Cal to dump all that shit rearing to explode from his ass. So me and my friends here thought we'd lock you up in 'The Scavenger's Daughter' and let Cal shits in your mouth. Shits all he wants and you eats it, Tucker.'

Tugger gagged.

'Tucker, you're the only man in this country we thinks has a right to eat nigger shit.'

Tucker began to shake his head.

'Now, let me explain how this iron contraption works.' Grouse beckoned to one of the men. 'Tommy Joe, you come here and help me open this.'

Tommy Joe Crandall emerged from the crowd of waiting men.

Grouse called to Tucker, 'You remember Tommy Joe, don't you, Tucker? It was Tommy Joe's wife who turned pecker-crazy and ran off North with a nigger. According to Tommy Joe, she got her taste for black meat at your place, Tucker. Seems that it was you who turned poor Mary Crandall into a bitch on heat for black men.'

Tucker shouted, 'Listen to me. Wait a minute. Let me explain about Mary Crandall. That wasn't my idea. That was her idea.' He pointed at his wife.

Claudia gasped on the wagon seat beside him. Pulling the shawl tighter around her throat, she shouted, 'Get me out of here! Get me away from this monster!'

Tucker lunged for her.

A gun exploded behind him in the night.

310

Tucker stopped.

Moving around the wagon, Jack Grouse said, 'We'd hate to kill you just yet, Tucker. But you harm that lady there and we'll do it.' He reached to help Claudia Tucker from the wagon.

Clammering down to the ground, Claudia gasped, 'My saviour. My saviour. I've been praying for years. For years I've been praying some kind soul would see through him.' She was sobbing into Grouse's shoulder.

Tucker stood on the wagon. 'You bitch. You lying, conniving bitch.'

Sniffing, Claudia Tucker raised her head. But without facing her husband, she said, 'I tried to help you, Chad Tucker. I tried. You never told me where you got that extra money. But I suspected all along you were up to no good. Oh, why didn't you talk to me? We could've talked and maybe I could've told you you were wrong. Wrong!'

'You lying bitch.'

Grouse motioned for the men to pull Tucker from the wagon. And then, wrapping his arm around Claudia Tucker, he said, 'Ain't nothing you can do now, Mam. I suggest you go down the road apiece to my house. The missus is there. You rest there.'

Gulping back her tears, Claudia nodded. She did not turn to look at her husband. She said to Grouse, 'He ain't been easy to live with, Mister Grouse. But what's a poor woman like me to do? I ain't been well. I ain't well at all.'

Patting her on the shoulder, Grouse assured her that she was safe now. He repeated, 'Go to my house. You'll be safe with my missus.'

Thanking him profusely, kissing his hands, Claudia Tucker hurried then down the dark trace toward the safety of the Grouse home.

By the side of the wagon, two men were holding Chad Tucker by the arms. Two men were opening The Scavenger's Daughter. A fifth man held a mallet, waiting to drive the pins into the iron clamps. And a sixth man threw a rope over a tree, preparing to lynch Tucker at the climax of his punishments.

The negro, Cal, waited at the side of the road. He called to Grouse, 'Tell me when you're ready, Master Sir.'

Grouse answered, 'You can start dumping pretty soon. First of all, we got to fix up your privy.'

Then, turning back to the other white men, Grouse ordered, 'Be careful you don't screw it too tight when you get him in that contraption. We don't want the blood popping from his fingers and toes like they say this machine can do. We just want to play with him till we lynch him.'

Tucker's boots had been pulled off and his ankles were already secured into the clamps at the base of the torture instrument.

Two men next forced Tucker down onto the ground on his back, making him clasp his hands together so that they could lock his wrists.

Grouse interrupted again. 'You got to get that top-end clamp around his neck at the same time you hook his hands together. It all comes fit with the same screw.'

Tucker's body was weak now with nerves; he pleaded for mercy.

But the white men ignored the cries, continuing to clamp him into The Scavenger's Daughter, locking him with his knees pressed up to his stomach and his hands held in front of his chest.

Grouse now stood next to Tucker and studied the way in which the neck band held his head forward. He said, 'Cal, come over here now.'

The negro slowly walked toward the group of men surrounding Tucker's doubled-up body.

Grouse said, 'Cal, you're going to have to crouch with your feet on each side of his shoulders. And you're going to have to face outwards, I reckon. Hold your rump to his body because—' Grouse turned Cal around, saying, '—the way this contraption holds his head forward, you've got to be damned near on top of him to hit his mouth.'

Tucker gave a loud cry.

'Good,' Grouse said, looking at Tucker's anguished face. 'You just keep on shouting big and wide like that, Tucker, and Cal here can have himself a real good target.'

Then Grouse nodded to Cal to step out of his trousers.


Peter sat alone on a porch swing, gently rocking in the dimming light of the evening. He had seen his new daughters and gone in to say good-night to little Imogen. Now, he had come to wait here on the porch for Selby to come home from visiting Judge Antrobus.

The air outside the big house was cool, the world seemed at peace. Peter's body still ached from the welts, though, and his bones felt stiff.

Peter thought about telling Selby the events that had occurred here today, the fight that had started soon after Selby had left with Doctor Riesen and had culminated with Monk being buried near The Shed and Lilly being sent away from The Star.

Then, Peter realized how lucky he had been that Ta-Ta had seen the fight from her attic window. And, as he thought how closely his own life was knitted with the lives of the black people here, he remembered Niggertown.

Peter recalled Selby's last words to him this morning—to think of a name for Niggertown that would have pleased Melissa.

As Peter sat on the porch considering possibilities to name Niggertown—New Start, Hopetown, Homestead—he suddenly saw a small light bobbing at the far end of the drive way. The light was coming toward the big house.

It could not be Selby, Peter thought. Selby had gone to Troy in the buggy. The person who was carrying the light up the driveway was on foot.

Rising from the swing, Peter stood to see who was coming to The Star.

A woman's voice called to him. 'Is that you, Mister Abdee?'

Peter recognized it as a white woman's voice but, still, he did not know who she was. He answered, 'Yes, Mam. I'm Peter Abdee. And who do I have the pleasure of talking to?'

As the light grew closer to the house, Peter could see that she was an elderly woman. Her hair was white and crowning her head in a neat plait. She had a sweet face—but a face that he did not recognize—and she wore a long plum-coloured cloak.

Stopping in front of the porch, she set her lamp down on the ground and announced, 'I'm Charlotte Dewitt. Miss Charlotte Dewitt.'

The name did mean something to Peter. The Dewitts had a place to the west of here. But he did not know much about them. They kept to themselves. Moving toward the top of the steps, he offered, 'Please, Miss Dewitt, come in. Let me get you some coffee.'

Holding up both of her mitted hands in polite refusal, Charlotte Dewitt answered, 'No, please, Mister Abdee. I've come here on a rather queer mission. It's not social at all. It's . . .'

Peter looked quizzically at her. 'Yes?'

Standing in front of the porch, looking up at Peter, Charlotte Dewitt folded her hands and said, 'First, let me offer my condolences about your late wife, Mister Abdee.'

Nodding, Peter said, 'Thank you, Miss Dewitt.'

She continued in a firmer voice, 'Judge Antrobus was going to come and see you but then he didn't feel up to visiting The Star. Not now.'

'That's strange,' Peter said, remembering the Judge's recent visits now that Rachel was gone. 'Perhaps it's good that he stayed at home, though. My father—Mister Selby is visiting the Judge now.'

Charlotte Dewitt smiled forlornly, shaking her head.

Her gesture confused Peter. He said, 'But he most certainly *is*, Miss Dewitt.'

She began, 'Mister Abdee?'

Peter knew now that something had happened.

'Mister Abdee, your father-in-law passed onto his rewards at my house about noontime today.'

'At your house? But he went to Troy and then to see Judge Antrobus!'

Charlotte Dewitt said with kind assurance, 'Albert Selby often saw Judge Antrobus at my house, Mister Abdee. Many people do. Gentlemen in the neighbourhood. That is one of the customs here. It has been that way for many years. You look like a sensible, level-headed young man who will understand what I mean when I say that my house serves as a meeting place. An oasis of discreet hospitality for gentlemen in the neighbourhood. My sister, Roxanne, and I have kept our house open to gentlemen friends for twenty-five years now, Mister Abdee. Some people might call the Dewitt Place by another name. Or slander the young ladies who come to help us. But we like to think that we are giving gentlemen such as your father-in-law a second home.'

Peter grasped onto a pillar, realizing this other side of Selby. But more important was what else Miss Dewitt had said. 'Are you really saying that Father is dead?'

'Yes, Mister Abdee, I am. He apparently had a heart attack. But to save any complications for you and your family, I've come to you tonight to make arrangements for his body to be brought here. To create the appearance that he passed away on The Star.'

'Dead? I can't believe it?'

Charlotte Dewitt momentarily looked forlorn. She confessed, 'Neither could I.' But, raising her head, she said proudly, 'He was always a gentleman, though. A true, kind-hearted gentleman! Thinking of others to the end.'

But Peter was not listening to Charlotte Dewitt's last words. He was remembering Selby's advice to him this morning, his words in the stables about not making any arrangements for Melissa's funeral, not to make any burial plans until he heard from him. Selby had known then that he was going to die. He wanted to be buried with Melissa.

Peter asked, 'How did he die, Miss Dewitt?'

'His heart.' Charlotte Dewitt did not elaborate.

Nor did Peter want to hear any more than that.

There was a lull of silence then between them until, nervously, Peter said, 'I do wish you would come in, Miss Dewitt.'

Bending to lift her lamp, she said, 'No, my sister is waiting for me with our coachman on the road.'

Rushing down the front steps as quickly as his sore limbs allowed him, Peter said, 'At least, let me walk you to your carriage.' He reached to take her lamp.

'That's very kind, Mister Abdee,' she said, demurely wrapping her cloak around her.

'Nothing kind at all! You're the kind person, Miss Dewitt.'

'And your late father-in-law,' she said, wishing that she could tell Peter the whole story of Albert Selby's demise this afternoon at the Dewitt Place, his carefully laid plans which she had readily recognized as complete thoughtfulness when George had told her the story. But Charlotte Dewitt would not divulge that now. Perhaps she could tell Peter later. Much later, if he ever had reason to visit the Dewitt Place. Already, she knew she could trust his discretion.

As they slowly strolled on the driveway, Peter discussed with her when the best hour would be to bring Selby's body back to the house. They decided that the early morning was best. Charlotte Dewitt offered to provide the transportation. Peter warmly accepted this token of friendship.

Nearing the public road, Peter saw two figures sitting side-by-side on the front seat of the open carriage. The two figures quickly moved apart when Peter and Charlotte Dewitt approached them. Peter could see that the coachman was a broad-shouldered black man. But, because of the woman's hooded cape, he could not see her face.

Helping Charlotte Dewitt into the carriage, Peter handed her the lamp and said, 'I know Father would want you at the funeral, Miss Dewitt.'

Settling herself in the front-facing seat of the carriage, she answered, 'No, Mister Abdee. Albert Selby had another world at my house, another life at the Dewitt Place.'

Looking up at her, Peter said, 'You are a remarkable

woman, Miss Dewitt.'

'Only because I have remarkable friends, Mister Abdee,' she answered. Then as Charlotte Dewitt tapped on the seat in front of her, the carriage began to move.

Peter stood alone on the public road. Albert Selby was dead . . . *Albert Selby was dead*.

When the clatter of the Dewitt carriage and the pound of the horse hooves disappeared in the dark distance, Peter turned and looked at the gates.

Raising his eyes, he saw the wobbly wooden star hanging from the crossbeams of the gates. He knew that the hour had come to take down Albert Selby's favourite symbol. The Star was finished. Albert Selby had gone. And he, Peter Abdee, had emerged from pain and misery and losses—but with three fine daughters—and was now officially 'the Master of Dragonard Hill'.